NEAR MISS

NEAR MISS

Quotes

favourite scenes

haley warren

This book is a work of fiction. Any references to historical events, real people, or real places are used fictitiously. Other names, characters, places, and events are products of the author's imagination, and any resemblance to actual events or places or persons, living or dead, is entirely coincidental.

Copyright © 2025 by Haley Warren

Cover Illustration and Design: Summer Grove

Editing: Briana Ozor

All rights reserved, including the right to reproduce this book or portions thereof in any form whatsoever.

First paperback edition January 2025

ISBN 978-1-7782483-9-9 (Paperback)

To you, the girl who gave away pieces of herself so others could be whole. And to you, the girl who became who other people needed her to be, instead of who she wanted to be.

Author's Note

Dear Reader,

Thank you so much for picking up Near Miss. Despite it's beautiful, bright cover (thank you endlessly to the talented and magical mind of Summer Grove), there are some things in this book that might not feel beautiful or bright when you're reading them.

I've described Near Miss as a *Grey's Anatomy* meets football romance, and in many ways, it is. It's funny. It's hot. It's giggle and kick-your-feet worthy. But it's also a love letter to parentified children, adult children of alcoholics, and children who had to grow up a bit too soon because maybe, their parents needed to have other priorities.

Beckett and Greer both have pieces of me in them. Greer's intrusive thoughts work like mine, her panic attacks are like mine, and her feelings about addiction and sobriety are things I've felt over the years at different times. Beckett's feelings about his struggle to achieve and his experience of growing up too soon are based in mine. Because their characters were shaped by my experiences, they might not be the same as others with similar family history, but I hope they make someone out there feel seen.

HALEY WARREN

At its heart, Near Miss really is a book about healing. I do think each time I write these deeply personally things, little bits of me heal, and I hope something in these pages heals you, too.

Content Warnings:

- Discussions of grief, trauma, and loss

- Substance use, abuse, addiction & sobriety (Neither of the main characters, and all instances of abuse and addiction are past and off-page)

- Parental abandonment (Past, off-page)

- Mentions of childhood cancer, specifically Leukemia (Neither of the main characters, past, and off-page)

- Mentions of IVF and infertility (Neither of the main characters, off-page)

- Panic attacks, anxiety, and intrusive thoughts (Described, and on-page)

- Therapy (On-page)

- Car accidents involving water (Past, off-page, but loosely described)

- Medical content including procedures such as transplantation and organ donation (on-page, but not described in detail)

All my love,
Haley

NEAR MISS

Beckett

Being paid a few million dollars to kick a football a few times a game is arguably the best job in the world.

It's a stupid thing to be a generational talent at. But up until recently, it's made my life pretty easy.

No one usually cares much about the kicker. You're not the quarterback, the wide receiver, a tight end—no one important on a minute-by-minute basis.

You show up, you go to practice. Train on special teams, stay flexible, keep the strength in your legs, and kick.

If you're me, and you get to be stupidly good at something irrelevant to most people, you focus on breaking records for yourself. You kick well for your team, and sometimes you get to win them games.

You rarely do press, you're rarely in the media. But if you're also me, your agent and team really capitalize on the fact that you've made a career not only on power and accuracy but also on being likeable. Then, you get shoved everywhere. You're doing more post-game press than any kicker ever has because you're nice. You're the face of fan and charity events because you smile more than anyone else. You're on advertisements all over because people think you're photogenic.

But you're not important until you are.

And no one hates you until they really, really do.

And people really, really hate me.

I can't say I blame them. Who likes someone who misses the most important kick of the year and costs the first and only Canadian team in the league their first championship in franchise history?

I would have preferred to spend my summer the way I usually do: in relative solitude at my cottage, only showing up for events when I'm asked, but otherwise just doing the things I can't do during the season.

But now, one week leading up to preseason, my agent has me trailing behind my brother while he does rounds in the hospital.

Nathaniel looks at home here—white coat, stethoscope hanging around his neck. He's even got what I'm pretty sure is a Pokémon clipped to it because we're in possibly the most depressing place here—a children's oncology unit.

I'm definitely not at home—I fucking hate hospitals. Rolling my shoulders back for the millionth time, I take my hat off and tug at the ends of my hair. I'm trying to relax, but I don't like it here.

Even though the hallways are bright, paintings hang everywhere, nurses and doctors skate by on wheeled shoes, and I've heard more children's laughter than I would have thought could possibly exist here—those bright colours and paintings and games and nurses and kids just remind me of everything I try to forget.

I clear my throat. "Are we almost done? I'm only supposed to be here so people see me. I didn't agree to visits, so no one will know—"

I can't see him, but I can practically hear the eye roll in his voice when he speaks. "Wouldn't dream of dragging the great Beck Davis anywhere he might not be photographed at an opportune time. I just have to run these labs by my attending, and we'll be out of here. You can make your big show in the parking lot."

"Ouch. That was rough." I force a grin when he turns around.

I'm always grinning, even when I don't feel like it.

My agent calls it "the grin." It puts people at ease, makes people like me, and that, plus whatever work the muscle fibres of my legs somehow manage to do, gets me endorsements, and has my team shoving me in front of cameras at every opportunity.

Until I failed one time. And everyone forgot that knees allegedly go weak when the dimple in my cheek pops, that I always show up for practice even when my contracts are being negotiated, that I rarely, rarely miss, or that I'm generally nice and affable and I've never once mouthed off to a reporter.

My brother looks over his shoulder at me, eyes narrowed. "Was I wrong? You've not set foot here once since I started my residency, even when I've asked."

There's a reason for that, and it's probably something he should know, but I'm not really sure he knows me, at the end of the day—so I keep grinning and I shrug. "I'm here now, aren't I?"

"Convenient timing." Nathaniel rolls his eyes and I see it this time, but he holds up a hand when he stops in front of a paned window with pictures of cartoon ducks dotting the edges.

He waves, and a doctor a few years older than him pokes his head around the door. "Are those the labs?"

"They look great." Nathaniel raises a manilla folder before holding it out. He turns to look at me and I widen my eyes expectantly.

This is what I'm supposed to be here for. My agent, Yara, wanted to socialize people to my presence, test the waters and see if people might be receptive to me doing some volunteer work here or showing my face at a fundraiser every once in a while.

Everywhere else seems hesitant to commit to making me the face of anything now, but here was my brother, a pediatric oncologist at one of the largest hospitals in the city, an opportunity ready-made.

Nathaniel gestures to me. "Dr. Ladak, this is my brother, Beckett Davis. Beck, this is my attending, Dr. Ladak."

Dr. Ladak's finger moves at rapid speed down the stack of papers, but he pauses and does a double take when he hears my name.

One eyebrow rises on his forehead. "Quite the kick to miss last season."

"No shit. Wouldn't mind a do-over for that one." I hold out my hand to him and grin again, like we aren't talking about one of the worst moments of my life and the source of my never-ending public embarrassment.

He leans forward and shakes my hand, lips twitching upwards. He turns to my brother and taps the stack of papers. "Call Dr. Roberts for a consult. I want her eyes on the labs and her lead."

Nathaniel pales, his nostrils flare and his lips part. He opens and closes his mouth for what seems like the world's longest minute before he speaks. "Can't we just email her? She's so mean."

A laugh catches in my throat, and the million-dollar grin I've grown to hate shifts into a real smile.

My brother cringes when Dr. Ladak narrows his eyes at him. "She's not mean, Dr. Davis. She doesn't tolerate mistakes or lazy surgical work, and it's not her fault some of your colleagues can't perform to her standards. I mean it, she signs off before we move forward."

He hands the folder back to Nathaniel and nods at me, like maybe he's warming up to me and the Beckett Davis charm hasn't lost all its shine, before disappearing back through the doorway.

"Who the hell are you so afraid of?" I ask, crossing my arms and leaning against the wall, obscuring what I consider to be a fairly terrifying photo of a clown and a donkey.

Nathaniel pulls his phone from the pocket of his jacket, thumbing out a text before dropping it back. "She's a transplant surgeon. She's a fellow and she terrifies me."

"Why?" I prod, still smiling. My cheeks start to ache, and I forget I'm in one of my least favourite places. It feels like I'm just a regular person, teasing his younger brother for something inconsequential.

"You wouldn't understand." Nathaniel's eyes are still wide, and he starts to look around like whoever this Dr. Roberts is, she might also possess supersonic hearing and be able to detect her name being uttered from anywhere in the hospital.

My brother doesn't look like a twenty-eight-year-old pediatric oncologist who saves children's lives every day. He looks a bit like he used to when I gave him shit for not finishing his chores, because our mother and father certainly weren't around to do it.

"Enlighten me." I shrug one shoulder.

He shakes his head, voice dropping to a whisper. "She's—"

"You paged?"

Nathaniel's nostrils flare, and he takes a measured swallow before scrubbing the five-o'clock shadow on his jaw and turning around.

I tilt my head so I can peer over his shoulder and get a look at whoever has him so terrified.

A dark eyebrow rises on her forehead, arms cross over teal scrubs, and the fingers on her right hand tap impatiently against her bicep. Eyes that sort of remind me of mine—and Nathaniel's and our sister, Sarah's—widen like she's trying to encourage speech. Green, and even under the shitty fluorescent lighting embedded in the panels above us, amber flecks shine.

Her nostrils flare with exasperation, full lips purse as she stares at my brother. Even her hair—impossibly shiny and this deep brown, pulled back in one of those bubble braids—looks annoyed at Nathaniel where it swings slightly behind her.

Beautiful, but thoroughly unimpressed.

"Well?" she asks again. She has one of those raspy voices—I sort of hope she keeps talking, because even when she's mad, it sounds nice.

Nathaniel clears his throat and holds up the manilla folder in a pathetic display. "Consult. Dr. Ladak and I have a patient, fifteen years old, in remission, but her kidneys are shot. Everything's in there. She's not high on the donor list, but her cousin is a perfect match, and she's willing to donate."

"I'll be the judge of that." She uncrosses her arms and takes the folder from my brother. She tips her head from side to side, her features soften, lips moving ever so slightly as her eyes track the words on the page.

My brother looks nervous, and I feel a bit like an asshole for making him take me around because my agent told me to—this is obviously important to him.

So I do what I do best—I try to get her to like me. I push off the wall, my smile changes, and I stick out my hand to her. "Great to meet you, Dr. Roberts. I'm Beckett—my brother speaks very highly of you."

"He's the one who plays football," Nathaniel blurts, and I cut him a look, lips pulling back and eyes sharpening on him before I look back to her and that stupid smile slides back into place.

My hand stays outstretched, her eyes flick up to me, finger pausing halfway down the page. She blinks. Once. Twice.

And I wait for the inevitable, but it never comes.

"I don't watch football," she mutters before looking back down at the stack of papers and closing the folder.

She hands it back to my brother, his hand shaking when he takes it. She notices, and one eyebrow arches up again. "You're right. I couldn't have found a better match. Run it all again tomorrow so we can be sure. I'll do the transplant as soon as we have OR time, and I'll ask Dr. Godoy to do the harvest. You can scrub in and observe, if you'd like. I'd say you could even hold a retractor, but we both know it was wise you didn't pursue surgery when your hand shakes like that."

Nathaniel's mouth opens and closes again uselessly. He looks a bit like a fish—gasping for air like she had him on her hook and dangled him above the water for too long. He doesn't say anything until she's gone, halfway down the hall. "Thank you!"

"Page me when you have the latest labs." She doesn't turn back, but she raises a hand in acknowledgment.

"Dude, that was so fucking rough. 'We both know it's wise you didn't pursue surgery'?" I crack a smile. He still looks a bit dumbstruck standing in the middle of the hallway: a Pokémon clipped to his stethoscope and the folder gripped loosely in his hands.

Nathaniel finally comes to and gives me a flat look. "Shut up, she wouldn't even shake your hand."

I look down and realize my hand is still there, fluttering by my side, waiting for hers.

"Huh," I mutter, stretching out my fingers and examining them like there might be something all over me. I glance back up at my brother and offer him a shrug. "At least she didn't throw a drink at me."

He winces, and it's exaggerated for a moment before he remembers to feel sorry for me. "People don't actually throw things at you. Do they?"

"You'd be surprised," I tell him. But I'm grinning when I say it, and that puts him at ease. "Come on, let's get out of here."

I toss my arm around my brother's neck like I'm going to try to shove him the way I did when we were kids, even though we're much closer in height now, but I glance back over my shoulder before pushing him down the hallway.

She's gone.

Nathaniel might think she's mean, but I think she was probably nicer to me than most people are on a day-to-day basis.

Greer

It really is a beautiful kidney.

Dr. Davis and Dr. Ladak wouldn't have known just how wonderful it is from labs alone—sometimes labs lie. You get in there and the organ just doesn't look as healthy as it should.

But this one—this organ that belonged to a seventeen-year-old who turned out to be kind, thoughtful, and maybe a bit too wise beyond their years so that now it belongs to their fifteen-year-old cousin they so desperately wanted to give a new lease on life to—this one is perfect.

A small smile tugs at my lips behind my mask. I stare at the kidney for a few seconds longer, eyes tracking where I just sutured off the reconnected blood vessels. The stitches stay taut.

My shoulders relax, and I roll them out as I step out from under the glare of the overhead OR lighting and off the platform. "Dr. Ihnat, you can close up."

She beams at me in thanks, stepping up to take my place, one hand extending for the forceps.

I usually like closing on my own work, but my neck was getting sore. I don't sleep well the night before I operate on someone young. I have a harder time detaching from those donors, whether they're living or dead.

Dr. Ihnat starts murmuring and making conversation, leaning forward as her hands start to move.

My fingers twitch in my gloves, the ghosts of all the movements I've spent the last seven years perfecting.

Movements I'm not so sure about anymore.

I notice Dr. Davis when I turn around to push back into the scrub room. He did end up scrubbing in to observe, and he's standing at the back of the operating theatre with most of the surgical oncology and general surgery residents.

He raises his eyebrows at me, and I don't realize he's followed me until the door doesn't swing shut—it catches on the toe of his pristine white Hoka.

A terrible shoe for the operating room. You're just asking for blood splatter.

He clears his throat, and my eyes cut to him as I stand by the biohazard disposal and start to doff my gloves and gown.

"Thank you." His voice is hesitant, almost like he's nervous.

I don't like that I make the residents nervous. I don't mean to. It's just that I take my job seriously. All surgery is serious. All medicine is.

But there's this tagline one of the donor networks uses about giving the gift of life.

The whole thing just feels significantly more fragile to me. If you're a living donor, you're trusting me with a part of yourself that you've given up—you've given me or someone like me permission to excise from your body—so that someone else might live a little easier. Get to make mistakes and fix them and love and laugh and see sunsets and sunrises.

And if you're a deceased donor, you're going to live on with this beautiful, insurmountable legacy and someone is going to hear your heart in the chest of someone they love and they're going to love you, too.

I can't think of anything more serious or more beautiful than that.

Even if sometimes, it hurts me.

Dr. Davis clears his throat again; his voice low, tentative, and hopeful—I know he understands—that he thinks it was a serious, beautiful thing we just did in there, too. He repeats himself. "Thank you."

I hit the tap with my elbow, and water splashes into the basin, droplets peppering my scrubs. "I was just doing my job."

He nods, considering, when he starts doffing his gloves and gown.

It wasn't the answer he was expecting—maybe he wanted the whole soliloquy about the gift of life. How I'm not really mean. I'm only hard on residents because this is just so important. And it is—but I'm just me.

The water hits my hands, and I can see my reflection in the window looking into the operating theatre when I start scrubbing.

I think of my sister, Stella. She tells me I need to be friendlier, so I clear my throat and try again. "And I'm happy to do it."

He glances at me before lathering his hands and arms. "You really didn't know who my brother was?"

"Your brother?" I ask, moving the soap up my forearms, but when I look at him, I remember. "Oh, the other day. Beckett. You two look alike."

He drops the scrub brush, and it clatters loudly against the bottom of the basin.

I wince, but I squeeze my eyes shut, and the feeling passes.

"We look alike? I look like him? The man with the endorsements who once modelled for Saxx and regularly gets named one of the sexiest athletes of the year by every magazine in North America?"

They do look alike. Same eyes—bright and green. Dr. Davis has lighter hair. Golden to the messy mop of chocolate hair his brother hid under a hat. The same straight nose. Sharp cheekbones and defined jawbone covered in stubble. But as far as I can tell, the brother is the only one with a singular dimple.

I nod, looking back at my hands and flexing my fingers. "Very all-American."

"We live in Canada."

"Figure of speech." I attack my nails with the bristles of the scrub brush.

"Well, thank you . . . for that, too."

"For not knowing who your brother was?" I ask, inspecting my nail beds.

Dr. Davis snorts, and I see him take the brush from the basin, throw it out, grab a new one, and start the process over. "He's had a rough few months. He probably appreciated the anonymity. He uh . . . missed a record-breaking kick that would have won us the championship last season. First one in franchise history."

"Us," I repeat, moving the bristles over to my left hand. "That's the thing about sports. Fans think they have all this entitlement to people who're just out there trying to do their jobs. I'm sure your brother feels worse than anyone else."

Dr. Davis nods, a smile tugging at the corners of his lips. "You're probably right about that."

We finish scrubbing in silence, and I peer up when I hear muffled clapping. Dr. Ihnat just stepped back from the table—it's the first time she's closed solo.

I smile—and it's big and bright and wonderful. My cheeks hurt. I remember what that felt like for the first time.

"Do you always let residents close?"

I glance at Dr. Davis. "I let anyone who deserves it practice."

"And you let people who've been suffering from public humiliation for months, like my brother, off the mat." He grins at me, backing up to hold the door open for me. "I'm not sure why I was so scared of you."

"It's hardly letting your brother off the mat if I had no idea." I give him a pointed look as I walk past. "Now, if your brother starts showing up and improperly rounding on my patients or giving unsound medical advice, I'm sure I'll hop on the bandwagon. I'll be by to check on your patient before I leave tonight."

He offers me a smile, softer this time. "Thank you, again. I've been with her since I started my residency and she's a good kid. She deserved it."

I wrinkle my nose. He doesn't realize what he's said, that in this world, there's a hierarchy and all sorts of rules and judgements that sometimes take the place of compassion. "They all do."

"And thank you for giving my brother a break, even though you didn't know it."

"Like I said"—I turn and walk backwards for a moment, shrugging—"it doesn't seem like the type of thing to get upset over. You can tell your brother there's one person in this city who doesn't care, if you think it'll help him sleep at night." Raising one hand, I offer him a small smile.

I do hope he tells him, and even though I don't know him, I hope Beckett Davis sleeps better tonight.

The house I grew up in isn't far from where my dad lives now. It's only a few blocks away.

It was a house, not exactly what I'd call a home—an innocuous bungalow nestled on a side street in the Danforth, long before it fell victim to gentrification.

It looked nice from the outside, and sometimes, it was nice on the inside.

But not all the time.

August in Toronto can be sweltering. At some point, it'll convince you it's fall, and you'll start getting excited to say goodbye to the way the heat quite literally radiates off the pavement and all the concrete.

But that's not today. My scrubs stick to my skin the second I shut my car door behind me, even though we're moving firmly into the twilight hours. I clamp down on the paper bag from the pharmacy between my teeth, trying to shove my keys, my phone, and my pager into my purse.

Overgrown hosta and flowers spill onto the cracked cement of the walkway leading up to my dad's front door, their leaves turning inwards, tired from the humidity.

Someone needs to trim them and it's not going to be me. Lawn maintenance is firmly in my sister's department.

She's better at that sort of thing. I stick to medication delivery and obsessively checking our father's blood pressure.

In a bizarre twist of fate, or just a sign of the architectural times, my dad moved into a house that was practically a mirror image of the one I grew up in. I've never lived in this house—but it's done a significantly better job at feeling like a home.

The porch creaks under my feet when I kick my shoes off beside the mat. They were the ones I wore at the hospital all day and god knows what they're covered in.

Another wilted plant sits to my right, and my lip curls back at the sight. Maybe I should try to water it before I leave.

I knock, but I don't wait for an answer before unlocking the door.

"Dad?" My voice comes out muffled. I drop my bag at the side of an end table adorned with another plant, which looks to be doing better than the ones outside, and a neatly stacked pile of mail.

"Greer? You're early."

I hear him as he rounds the corner from the living room.

He looks older than he should—shoulders curved inwards and skinnier than they used to be under a worn flannel. It's too hot for that, but he's cold more often than not. His brown hair was always thin, but now, it's become nothing more than feathers dusting his scalp. Eyes just like mine protrude a bit too much from a too-prominent brow bone, but he still smiles at me.

In some people, all those things might be a sign of a life well lived—of too many nights staying up too late and singing too loudly and living too much.

But on him, they're signs of how he lived and what that cost him.

"No, I'm late." I shake my head, finally taking the paper bag from between my teeth. "You can't leave your prescription refills to the last minute like that. What if I got stuck in surgery? Or Stella was away? Try to fill them at least a week in advance next time."

He takes the bag, frustration, and maybe kindness and caring, etched in the lines of his face. "I could say the same thing to you."

"I'm not the one on immunosuppressants for the rest of my life." I pinch the bridge of my nose. I've tried several times to get my father and sister to understand the difference between a lifesaving, required, daily medication that keeps the part of his liver that didn't belong to him from being eaten alive by his body and my occasional need for a sedative because my nervous system forged some connections a long time ago I can't seem to shake.

He looks troubled, nostrils flaring, and he wrings his hands. His fingers are too thin. "I mean it. You've been feeling okay, right?"

"Dad, I just got here." I press my fingers to my temples and squeeze my eyes shut. My eyes burn, and I can't tell if it's tears or they're too dry because I've been awake for too long. "I'm exhausted. I was on call last night and I did three kidney transplants today. I'm waiting on a call for a patient that desperately, desperately needs a liver I can't guarantee is ever going to come. Can we just—not?"

It probably seems rude, and if Stella was here—she'd elbow me in the rib cage and tell me it was before taking our father by the arm, leaning in conspiratorially, whispering to him about the latest drama on the set of any TV series they watch together.

But I'm trying to be better about setting boundaries and drawing lines in the sand instead of giving pieces of myself I can't afford to give, and sometimes it comes out wrong.

He cocks his head to the side, and I think he's chewing on the inside of his cheeks, like he's mulling over something, before he gestures for me to follow him into the kitchen.

"How was your meeting?" I ask, trying to throw out a peace offering, even though I don't have to.

At least my psychiatrist says I don't have to. He tells me it's okay to create a boundary people are uncomfortable with. It doesn't mean we have to appease them afterwards.

I follow my father into the kitchen, light from the setting sun spilling across the hardwood floor through ancient wartime windows he won't replace.

It's a normal kitchen. More modern than the rest of the house because someone saw fit to update it before my father landed himself here. But with more pill bottles dotting the counter and more reminders for upcoming appointments than your average household.

"Good. I presented someone with their one-year medallion."

I hear the pride in his words when he drops the bag from the pharmacy alongside the empty bottles and makes his way to the fridge. He pulls it open and grabs me one of those boxed waters I'm particularly fond of that he keeps here even though he can't afford them.

"Cool." I smile at him because I can't really think of anything else to say.

I'm happy for him, and I'm happy for this stranger.

We say we've come so far in understanding mental health, and I do think we're leaps and bounds ahead of where we used to be. But addiction remains this elusive thing people can't really seem to understand.

Sobriety is rare and difficult and wonderful and challenging and beautiful.

And I'm always proud and overjoyed and thrilled for anyone who finds it.

But my father's sobriety came at a cost I'm not sure either of us should have had to pay.

"Is your sister coming over tonight?" he asks, handing me the box.

We stand there in the kitchen, staring at one another awkwardly for a moment before I clear my throat. "No, she's got a group."

Stella and I somehow became the most stereotypical children of addicts you'd ever find—she spends her days trying to help people get sober and I put organs back in people whose disease ruined theirs.

It was all we knew, and I don't think we ever left.

"Oh." He looks troubled for a moment before he tips his too-pointed chin towards the living room. "Did you want to watch a movie then?"

They say addiction is a cycle you can't escape. I think of all those cirrhotic livers I've removed and replaced with new ones. I think of all the people my sister listens to so intently, night after night, day after day, trying to help them find their own version of peace. I think of my father, soon to be practically housebound because flu season is coming up and he's forever immunocompromised because he has an organ that didn't always belong to him.

I think of my mother—gone before Stella and I were even old enough to really know her.

I think of all the things that landed us here, in these worn chairs in this bungalow on another random side street in the east end of the city. I think of my father's too-frail fingers on the remote control. And mine, too-tightly gripping the twist top of my box of water because I wince when the opening credits started too loudly.

And I think they might be right.

Beckett

Pilates is fucking hard. And anyone who tells you otherwise either hasn't tried it or is a liar.

Beads of sweat drip from underneath my hat, hitting the carriage of the reformer.

Back when I could do my job effectively and score points when the team needed me, the training staff thought it was a great idea to put the proper equipment in one of the workout rooms, so I had a place to do it after meetings on days I didn't have practice.

It's a popular workout with kickers. It builds length in your muscles, strengthens them, and opens up your flexibility, and I don't have the typical body of a kicker so I need it—I'm on the taller end at six two, broader than most, because once upon a time, this wasn't what I thought I was made for.

I've been doing it since college when my time as a just-fine wide receiver came to an end when I fell ass-backwards into kicking. Both our kicker and punter got injured, and in a moment of game-time desperation, our coaching staff asked the team if anyone played soccer growing up, and they picked me because I played competitively year-round until I was sixteen.

I became stupidly good at something most people think is useless. I broke college records. People talked about me on ESPN. I got drafted when I was twenty-three even though kickers rarely do, and I got traded here when the expansion opened the first Canadian franchise team.

I was happy to do it. I grew up outside of Toronto. It's where I'm from. It's where my family lives. Canada has some of the best sports fans in the world. But something the general world seems to not understand about Canadians—we don't forget.

I went from someone everyone loved and wanted to put on their billboards and to sign their jerseys and to kiss their babies because I was going to keep smashing records and keep smiling, to someone who literally had a fucking Timbit thrown at them from a moving car last week.

"Davis, you're done. Coach wants you upstairs."

I glance over at the open doorway. Darren stands there, clipboard under his arm and his hat folded between his hands.

"Sure, thanks." I nod, sitting back on my heels and grabbing my towel to scrub some of the sweat off my face.

"I'll see you Wednesday. Hit the gym tomorrow, but don't kill your legs. I want range from your kicks."

"Got it," I answer, and he taps his clipboard like that might drive his point home more before turning and disappearing down the hallway. I spend more time with Darren than anyone. His whole job as the special teams coordinator is to develop people like me.

I rarely talk to Coach Taylor one-to-one during the week.

NEAR MISS

I've been avoiding talking to him as much as possible since training camp started, and I certainly haven't darkened the door to his office. It's my fault there isn't a shiny gold championship trophy sitting behind him on the empty mantle.

The sight of my name, spelled out in block lettering along with the number nineteen, stretching across the side of my bag, feels like something I wish I could avoid, too. Like it's something to be proud of—that I'm so special and so important and so full of generational talent, people should know who I am just by a stupid gym bag I carry around. It has the opposite effect. I hate myself, and I'm really not proud at all when I pick it up on the way out of the studio.

There's a photo of me in the main concourse that stretches the entire wall I'm also pretty intent on ignoring, so I duck down a set of stairs at the end of the hallway instead and head to the executive offices.

It means taking the stairs instead of the elevator when my legs are already dead, but the stadium is well and truly alive now that preseason is about to start. The stores are putting out the new stock, the restaurants are opening, the staff are all back to work.

I've generally made it a point to be nice to everyone who works here, at least before the stadium is crawling with fans. I stop by and get coffee before or after practice instead of making my own because I think they deserve to be recognized, too. There're all sorts of things that keep a franchise going that have nothing to do with the players on the field.

But I doubt they want to see me, and I don't want to see them.

My footsteps echo on the concrete stairs against the empty stairwell, and sunlight beats in through the glass windows. The whole stadium has this crazy view of the city—there isn't a single part of the building that doesn't give you an angle of the Toronto skyline.

It was strategic construction when the expansion was just a whisper floating around in the ether. There wasn't a place that could house enough seats, and the league had concerns about the proximity to Buffalo impacting another fanbase.

And some architect came up with this idea to go higher with the seats instead of stretching them out. It's probably a feat of engineering, because it hardly looks taller than other teams' stadiums, and it's great at blocking the wind.

It made me more effective, until it didn't.

I stop when I get to the sixth floor—the painted white lettering on the polished cherry door seems more threatening than it should. Taking my hat off, I try to smooth down my hair, but it's useless because it gets even curlier when it's sweaty.

The hallway is empty, and most office doors are closed—a small mercy. The sound of my footsteps dies on the padded carpet, and I stop when I reach the only open door.

The shiny, gold plate that reads "Coach Taylor" still looks brand-new, and from this angle, I can see the mostly empty mahogany shelves that line his office. We're a new team, so maybe it's unfair for me and the rest of the general population to put the responsibility for that on my shoulders, but winning a championship in the first decade of a franchise when we're the only one in the country is something everyone really, really wanted.

I raise my fist and knock, letting that stupid fucking grin fall into place so it looks like I'm still being a team player. "You wanted to see me?"

He doesn't look away from the screen mounted to the wall, but I can see his eyes flit to me in between tracking the routes he's watching. He gestures to the chair across from him, and I say nothing when I drop down in it.

"You're out there practicing field goals with your headphones in." His voice is clipped, and he tips his head, watching a successful pass before scribbling on his clipboard.

"I'm trying to concentrate."

Apparently, I can't even do that right.

He finally looks away and takes a measured exhale before leaning back in his chair. "One of the things that made you the best wasn't the fact that there's usually more accuracy in your kicks than a nuclear homing beacon. It wasn't the power behind them. It was the fact that you worked with the other guys. You were friends. It didn't matter that you had separate practices. Worked on separate drills. You ran routes with anyone who wanted to try something out or practice in off-hours even though you shouldn't have risked your legs like that. You've let every backup quarterback we've ever had pass to you until their fingers bled. Christ, you had half of them in there on the reformers with you every week."

And I let them down so colossally some of them didn't speak to me the entire offseason.

I don't say it out loud, but the words hang between us.

Coach Taylor appraises me, and it's sort of like being looked at by your grandfather, like he's got generations of wisdom on me, not just the seven years older he is. "You could have made that kick. I've seen you make that kick in practice."

He's not wrong. I've broken the record more than once. Two separate practice kicks: 67 yards and 69 yards, respectively. But there was nothing at stake then. I palm my jaw. "I know."

"I want to switch up your long field goals and points-after-touchdown practice. Wednesday afternoon so I can be there. I planned on using you a lot this season, and I don't like when my plans change." He looks back at the screen, the game tape still rolling, and I take that to mean I'm dismissed. "Darren let me know you're doing some press at the hospital. That ends when regular season starts, got it?"

I nod, pushing up from the armchair and I get halfway across the office before I turn back to him. It's a childish question, but I'm not exactly sure what the future holds for me here. Or anywhere, really. "What if people still hate me by the time regular season rolls around?"

He doesn't bother looking at me when he says it. "Then you better start making fucking kicks and scoring points or you'll be out on your ass with only that stupid grin to keep you warm."

We both know it's not that simple, but it feels like it might be.

I've only ever really been two things my entire life: reliable and likeable.

And now I'm neither.

Hospitals don't look any better in the daytime.

At least not to me.

They're busier, and I think that just gives the illusion that they're a bright place where good things happen.

And good things do happen in them. But whenever I step through the doors, I can only ever think of the bad.

The volunteer badge hanging around my neck feels more like a noose than anything. I could pretend that's what's weighing me down when I cross the lobby towards the elevator, eyes firmly glued to the floor and my face half hidden under a nondescript black hat. I ditched the one with my last name and number—all the information identifying me as someone people hate—and left it on the console of my truck when I got here.

I've been dreading this little positive press exercise since Yara came up with the idea. My least favourite place and a sea of people who are already unhappy.

The elevator is mercifully empty, and I press the button repeatedly, like that's going to make the doors close any quicker. My sister, Sarah, told me when we were kids that the close button is just for show, and it was one of those glass-shattering moments for me.

I really wish it wasn't true, because I see someone coming towards the elevator, her head down, completely oblivious—and even though I want nothing more than to be alone, I can't help myself from reaching out a hand to stop the doors from shutting.

She slides in, one hand lifting in thanks, dark hair swinging in a slicked-back ponytail, and her eyes stay glued firmly to her phone.

She's in a different colour of scrubs today, but I don't forget anyone. It's part of the reason people like me so much.

But I don't think it's very hard to remember someone. At least not someone like her.

"Dr. Roberts. Nice to see you again." I grin and hold out my hand—I can't help myself from doing that either—but I'm a bit hopeful she might shake it this time.

She startles, looking away from her phone, fingers tensing against her coffee cup. Green eyes narrow on my hand before they flick up to my face. She cocks her head, and her ponytail swings across her shoulders. One eyebrow kicks up, she drops the phone in the pocket of her navy scrubs, and she reaches out to meet my hand with hers. "Oh. Dr. Davis's brother. The one who doesn't sleep well at night because everyone hates him."

I pull my head back and my grin fades, but it's replaced with the real one. "How do you know I don't sleep well?"

"Your brother has a big mouth when he's nervous." The corners of her lips twitch, and her cheeks soften. It's the closest thing I've seen to an actual smile on her. The flecks in her eyes come alive and I think a part of me does, too.

She drops my hand and I wish she hadn't. She tips her head, eyes assessing, before continuing. "I don't know if that big mouth happened to pass on my message, but I don't hate you."

He didn't pass on the message. But I nod, wishing he did. "Seems like there's a thinly veiled insult in there somewhere."

"There isn't," she answers, turning away from me and pulling her phone out again. She's not looking at me, but she points to the illuminated elevator panel, leaning forward and finally pressing a button. The number eight lights up. "Your brother's probably on six. You pressed four."

"I'm not here to see Nathaniel. I'm uh—" I pick up the volunteer badge hanging around my neck and shake it. "I'm here for some positive press. I'm not sure if you heard, but the whole city, and most of the country, hates me. No real plan on how I'm supposed to achieve that, but I thought I'd go to pediatrics for visiting hours. I've been told I do a great impression of Chase from *Paw Patrol*. Maybe I'll do story time."

Her eyes cut to me. "And what are the kids supposed to do about that? They don't control the news cycle."

I grin, crossing my arms and leaning back against the mirrored panels lining the elevator. "Maybe they'll be so taken with the impression, they'll put in a positive word with their football-loving parents."

She snorts. "How do you know they love football?"

"Everyone loves football."

One of her eyebrows rises, followed by the shrug of one shoulder. "I don't."

"Maybe that's because you've never seen me kick."

A laugh—it's really more a cackle—tumbles from her lips. Her eyes are wide, and she looks amused. "Well, if the general populous is to be believed, I'll consider myself lucky for that."

"Ouch." I say it, but I don't feel it. I think I feel lighter than I have in months.

She cocks her head, eyes flitting back and forth between mine and the volunteer badge. "I'm going up to inpatient recovery. There are a few post-ops I want to follow up on. All adults. It's visiting hours. If you want to talk to people who might actually care and don't want to spend all afternoon straining your vocal chords to sound like a cartoon dog, you're welcome to come with me. You just can't come into the room until they say it's okay."

I scrub my jaw when really I feel like pressing a fist to my chest, so it stops my heart from hammering against my rib cage. My resting heart rate is usually a lot lower than this, but it's only the second time she's met me, and it's the second time she's been nicer to me than almost anyone else on the planet. "You haven't told me your name."

"You never asked." She shrugs again. The doors to the elevator open on four, but neither of us gets out. "Greer."

"Greer," I repeat. "Do you think the adults like story time?"

"Depends on how good your Chase impression is." Her voice is deadpan. Raspy. I feel it in my chest—strolling across my rib cage and planting itself there, kicking its little feet right alongside the still-too-fast beating of my heart.

I forget I ever wanted to be alone.

Greer

I think there's bile in my hair.

I'm not really sure. I got paged to look at a liver during a trauma to see if it was salvageable, and when I leaned in—everything went wrong.

Trauma isn't my thing, fortunately—I think I've had enough of that for a lifetime.

But that didn't change the fact that organs perforated, blood sprayed, and things ended up in my hair that didn't belong there because I hadn't bothered to tuck my ponytail under my scrub cap.

I had no one to blame but myself for that one. I'd spent approximately one hour in my own bed last night before getting a page that there was a match for one of my patients who desperately, desperately needed a new pancreas and kidneys.

That took about seven hours, and I was overtired and somewhat delusional, if the low-hanging ponytail and the fact I invited a football player I've only met once to do rounds with me were any indication.

He was good with the patients—I'll give him that. I imagine he's probably good with people in general. A smile like that, eyes that are wholly focused on you, so you know he's listening.

Only one of my patients, Jer, was a football fan, and it turned out he cheered for a team in Philadelphia, so it was sort of a moot point in terms of the grand reputation rebuild I proposed it to be when I was running off three hours of combined sleep. But Beckett sat with him, and they talked stats and rumours and all sorts of things I don't care about and don't plan to care about while I finished my rounds.

I left him there when I got the page about the lacerated liver.

I could have showered here, but I have an entire twenty-four hours off, pending no organs suddenly becoming available, and I wanted out of the hospital as soon as possible. My sister gave me one of those wax sticks for your hair to keep in my bag so I could "look good" during long hours here. It's come in handy a total of zero times, but today I wet a brush, slicked the whole thing back, and tried to pull off a bubble braid so maybe no one would notice.

I'm not entirely sure it had the desired effect, and I didn't drive today so someone somewhere is going to be subject to medical waste when they sit beside me on the subway, but the people of the Toronto Transit Commission have definitely seen worse.

The night air hits me when the revolving door finally opens, and I tip my head back, inhaling. I don't always mind when I get stuck here longer than I should, but tonight, I just need my own space and I really, really want to go home.

But Beckett Davis stands there just beyond the curb, one leg kicked up against a white truck, hat on backwards, hair curling against the nape of his neck, and one of the lampposts shining down on him like it's a fucking runway.

"Hey, I just wanted to say thank you for today." He's smiling at me and it's one of those stupid, moony smiles I bet people melt for: full lips framing lovely teeth, and one dimple popping in his cheek. His eyes—an otherworldly green—drop to my chest, but then he grins again. "Cool shirt."

"What?" I pluck the worn cotton between my fingertips and look down. I don't even remember what I'm wearing. An ancient, worn cotton shirt my sister gave me that says "Dorsia," the name of a fake restaurant from my favourite movie, in faded lettering. "Oh. Yeah. I'm sorry, were you waiting here for me?"

"No, I was hanging out with Jer. We were watching some old highlights. The nurses kicked me out about five minutes ago." He pushes off the truck and cocks his head. "Can I take you for dinner or for a drink? It's the polite thing to do."

Those are just words. Just something a sort of acquaintance might offer to another as thanks for helping them out. But they aren't, not really. At least not to me.

They're also things you do with someone you might be trying to date. My heart beats in my chest, but not really filling itself to its full potential or capacity because it exists in this little cage I've drawn around it.

I don't date. But I don't know Beckett Davis enough to tell him that. I cross my arms over my chest, protection and deflection all at once. "Maybe you shouldn't worry about being polite and do what you actually want to do."

He huffs a laugh, taking his hat off and running his hands through his hair like I'm an exasperating piece of work. I am, but he keeps grinning at me anyway. "I actually want to get some food. I'm starving. And I'd be happy to take you, too."

My nostrils flare. I just want to go home and go to sleep—but he's looking at me, and he reminds me a bit of a lost puppy. The heart that's constantly bleeding, according to my sister, twinges in my chest, and I roll my eyes. "Fine. Can we go somewhere dark so no one notices when I fall asleep at the table?"

Beckett's grin splits across his face, and that stupid dimple pops. He points his thumb over his shoulder towards the truck. "Perfect. It'll reduce my chances of getting a drink thrown at me."

I narrow my eyes. No one can possibly care about one missed kick that much. "People don't actually throw drinks at you?"

"Not yet, but last week someone did make contact with a Timbit." He raises his palms and smiles at me before turning and opening the passenger door.

"Oh, that's a shame. Not Canada's favourite donut hole. What flavour?"

"Birthday cake." He gives me a resigned nod I think he thinks is a joke, before jerking his chin towards the pristine leather seat.

One of my brows rises. I'm not sure it's entirely wise to be hopping in a stranger's truck, even if he is some sort of celebrity. But I tip my head to the side, and his eyes go from these shining emeralds to something that looks sort of muted and sad.

His brother and the other residents think I'm mean, but my sister says I actually feel too much.

"What a waste, that's the best kind." I offer him a rare, soft smile, moving past him to hop up into the truck.

"That's what I said." Beckett's smile widens and he holds out his hand for me, and against my better judgement, I take it. I don't know anything about football—but these seem more like the type of hands that should be catching footballs, not wasted fluttering at his sides while he lines up a kick.

Wide, calloused palms, with veins traipsing the back of them.

I always worry about my hands—they're dry, covered in chapped skin, and my nails are filed down to the quick. In the winter, they're red and practically raw from the bitter Toronto cold and the sheer amount of antiseptic they're exposed to.

But Beckett says nothing, offering me another grin, but this one seems soft—like he's thankful, quietly so, like I might be doing him a favour by spending time with him.

He closes the door on me, and I catch a glimpse of my slicked-back hair in the passenger's side mirror. I'm not sure how much of a favour it could possibly be when one of us may or may not be covered in medical waste.

The bar *is* dark—some hole in the wall pub on a side street close to the east end I'd never seen before. I wouldn't be able to fall asleep if I tried.

Not only is someone obnoxiously tuning a guitar on a poorly lit stage five feet to my left, but Beckett Davis talks. A lot.

It's not a bad thing, necessarily.

It's just a lot more conversation than I'm used to.

My father isn't a talkative person, at least not with me. My sister knows me enough to know that sometimes I prefer to sit in silence. My two best friends, Willa and Kate, don't live in town, and most of our conversations consist of text messages or voice notes that I can send when I do feel like replicating a conversation.

But Beckett really likes to chat. So much so that he didn't leave a ton of room for me to say a lot on the way over here.

He didn't seem to mind—happy to recount his afternoon sitting with Jer, watching old highlights and SportsCentre coverage, huddled over a small iPhone screen, telling me how surprised he was to have enjoyed his afternoon in an otherwise sterile, unforgiving place.

He tossed the occasional question my way, asking how far I lived from the hospital, how long a typical shift was, and whether I ever saw anything weird because sometimes I took the subway home in the middle of the night instead of driving.

The answer was yes, but he barely left me enough time to answer before he was asking me if I ever did reformer Pilates.

On anyone else, it might have seemed rude. But his fingers gripped the steering wheel, and he couldn't stop tapping his thumb against the leather. It seemed sort of like he was excited to have someone to talk to. It would have been cute, if it didn't seem so sad.

He hasn't said much since we got here, flipping his hat forward so the beak cast a shadow, eyes darting around like he was worried someone might pop out from behind a wall and tell him they hate him before proceeding to throw a drink in his face.

But he visibly relaxed when he slid into the cracked vinyl booth in the corner. And it looked like the weight of the world melted off his shoulders when the server came along with nothing but a kind smile on her face to take our drink orders.

He looks positively alight when she brings them back, practically ignoring us when she drops off the perspiring glasses of beer and peeling plastic menus.

"So how was your day?" Beckett asks, taking a sip of beer. Drops of condensation fall from the glass and splash across the worn wood table.

"Fine," I answer, scanning over the menu before I look back up at him. "I have bile in my hair."

He grins, dimple illuminating in his cheek. "Sexy."

It's a beautiful smile, and it's a beautiful dimple.

Most people don't know this—but a dimple is actually the result of a muscle in your cheek splitting in two.

It's not a failure of the muscle that makes it that way, just a random act of biology during development.

But it makes me feel a bit like I'm split in two—heart sitting neatly in its cage where it's safe, but perking up and watching Beckett from behind those bars, my cheeks burning with a flush I hope he can't see, and my brain screaming to life with warning.

And that makes me a bit of a failure, because I don't date.

"Good thing this isn't a date." I arch an eyebrow, dropping the menu in exchange for my own drink.

"Just one new friend, taking the other out for a thank-you drink." He holds his glass up in cheers before setting it down, green eyes tracking over the menu. He taps an index finger on something I can't see. "Do you think the steak is any good?"

"No."

A laugh catches in his throat, and his eyes light up. "I have my doubts, too. But I need the protein."

"For all your reformer Pilates?" I ask, voice dry.

"Yeah, for that." He studies me for a second before clearing his throat. "I meant what I said earlier. Thank you. I don't love hospitals. We spent a lot of time in them as kids. Our sister . . . she had childhood cancer. Leukemia. She was diagnosed when she was six and it went on for almost a decade."

I exhale, biting down on my lips. I hate stories like this. They're beautiful and inspiring, but there's something about a child being shaped in such a specific way that leads them down a path as an adult they might never have followed—but I don't say that. Instead, I whisper, "I'm sorry."

"It's okay. I mean, it's what made Nathaniel become a doctor. But you know that." Beckett shrugs, taking another sip of beer.

My lips pucker and my eyebrows knit. "Why? Why would I know that?"

He swallows, looking confused. "You're both doctors. You sort of work together. You guys don't . . . I don't know, share your reasons for pursuing such a noble occupation?"

I laugh now, incredulous. "Do you think that's what we do in the break room? Sit around in a circle and share our hopes and dreams and our inspirations?"

He pulls his head back. "Why not? It's what we do during training camp."

I give him a flat look. "Really?"

"Nah." He grins, dropping his head against the vinyl of the booth and propping one hand up under his head. He leaves the other on the table, his fingers drumming against the worn wood in time with the music. "Seriously. What made you want to be a surgeon?"

A path that I was shaped and moulded for, that I might never have followed otherwise.

But I don't tell him that either. I wrinkle my nose instead. "I was shockingly good at the game *Operation* as a child."

"Alright, Dr. Roberts, you can keep your secrets." Beckett appraises me for a minute, hand still cupping the back of his head. All that does is highlight the sharp edges of muscle in his arm, the curve of his bicep, the jut of a defined tricep, and all those cords and veins drawing a map to those hands.

He's looking at me, and he doesn't know me, but I feel a bit like he might—like we might have more in common than we ever would have dreamed.

"I'm sorry football fans weren't plentiful on the post-op recovery floor today," I deflect.

"It's okay. It was a pleasant surprise. I'm supposed to be going to pediatrics and oncology because of Nathaniel but . . ." He rubs his jaw before throwing me a rueful, sad sort of smile. "You probably have a higher IQ than everyone in this room combined, so I'm sure you can infer why that wouldn't be my favourite place to hang out."

"Is your sister okay?" I ask, tipping my head.

Beckett nods, smiling softly. He pulls his phone out of his pocket and flashes the screen at me. The photo illuminates, revealing Beckett and Dr. Davis, each with an arm slung around the shoulders of a beautiful brunette, smiling over a cake littered with burning candles. "Sarah's good. She turned twenty-six this year. She's been in remission for about a decade. Her immune system is a bit fucked, but for the most part, she's okay."

"You have the same eyes." I flick my gaze up to him, another tiny smile pulling at the corners of my mouth. It's ironic, my love for happy endings, seeing as I can't help but lament the path that led to the one my family got. But I hope that maybe, his was unencumbered. "I'm glad she's okay."

"Me too." He flips the phone towards him, and his lips twitch in the ghost of a smile as he stares at the picture before pocketing his phone.

He loves his sister, just like I love mine.

And mine might be right. I might feel things a bit too much. I know what it's like to be forced to live or exist somewhere that hurts you, and I might have made that choice willingly, but he didn't.

Even though I certainly don't have time to shepherd Beckett around the hospital, I offer anyway.

"You could come back, if you wanted." I drop my head against the vinyl booth, taking a sip of my beer. "Unfortunately, Jer will probably be discharged tomorrow, but I'll have a whole new cadre of patients for you to try and woo back over to your side later this week."

"Yeah?" Beckett's eyebrows come together, and he leans forward, dropping his palms to the table. "Alright. I might take you up on that. Law of averages, right? One of my fans is bound to end up on your table."

I tilt my head. "I'm not sure that's how that works, but sure. We'll go with that. Just give me until the end of the week, if you're going to keep coming back. I'll see if I can clear it with my chief."

He nods, grinning again. "Your chief. Is that like your coach?"

"No." I snort into my beer. I think I'm overtired. It's not even funny, but my cheeks start to burn with a smile.

"Ah, well." He shrugs. "My coach wants to supervise one of my regular practices Wednesday, so the time moved. Not something he usually shows up to, so later this week works for me."

I'm about to ask a question because it's not out of willful ignorance or an attempt to be so above something popular that I don't know anything about football, I just don't have a lot of time.

But our server comes back, smiling expectantly.

Beckett looks back down at the menu, drumming his fingers before tapping it. "Fuck it, I'm getting the steak."

He looks back up at me, and he winks, like he doesn't realize he's probably one of the most beautiful people someone has ever seen in real life.

The server looks to me, pen poised over her notebook.

I hadn't really looked at the menu. I press my head into the booth and wave my hand around. "I guess I'll have the steak, too."

Beckett holds up his palm. "Here's to protein."

I roll my eyes, but I meet his hand with mine. "To protein."

He smiles at me, and it feels real—like his muscles twitched upwards in spite of themselves. Like his brain sent all his neurons firing to tell him that this was a nice, safe, happy moment. That he could relax.

I smile back, and that feels real, too.

Beckett

The steak wasn't good, and the protein probably wasn't worth the risk.

Greer took two bites of hers before she wrinkled her nose, pushing the plate to the side.

But the company was nice.

It was refreshing to talk to someone about something other than last season, how I dealt with all the memes, TikToks, general national hatred, whether I was working with a mental performance consultant, and what my strategy was for this season.

She didn't ask me anything about football, she mostly just listened to me. And I definitely talked too much, but it sort of felt like I was a whole, real person again after a really, really long time.

Trees boughed down with leaves, lifting in the breeze, looking a bit like they're ready for fall, obscure most of the two-level bungalows lining her street.

"This is me." She points to one just ahead. It's almost identical to every other one, except for the wide, white wooden arches wrapping around the porch.

I nod, pulling up alongside the sidewalk. "Nice place."

"Oh, thanks." Greer glances at her porch, illuminated by one single light mounted in a brass sconce beside the door. "It's just a rental. But it's nice. Spacious. Lots of exposed brick, a great kitchen and bathroom. And there's a big balcony around the back that's got a ton of privacy."

"Spacious and private? What more can you ask for?" I toss her a wry grin and put the truck in park.

She gives me a flat look. "There's more of that in the east end. Where do you live? Yonge and Eglington?"

"Ouch." I grip my chest. "I'll have you know, I live in the west end."

A mocking sort of gasp comes from her, and she makes a surprised face. "Oh? Are you secretly a big, crunchy hipster? What with this massive gas-guzzling truck?"

I raise my eyebrows and give her a noncommittal jerk of my chin. "Nah, it's just close to the field."

"Well." Greer tips her head, studying me, before turning to the door. "Thank you for dinner. Even though I think we have legitimate cause to be concerned about E. coli."

"Good thing you're licensed to practice medicine." I bring my hands back to the steering wheel. I don't really want her to go. I'm not good at being alone anymore. "Wait—can I get your number?"

"You're asking for my number?" she turns and repeats, voice deadpan and eyes sharp.

I hold my hands up before pulling my phone out of my pocket. "Business only. I'll text you when I think I can come by the hospital, and we can try to coordinate?"

"Business only," she agrees, plucking my phone from my outstretched hand. Her fingers fly across the screen, and her eyebrows lift when she hands it back to me. "Here you go. I don't give unsolicited medical advice, and I don't write prescriptions for painkillers or sedatives, so don't bother."

"I've got a team doctor for that." I hold up the phone. "I'll text you."

Greer tips her head, and her ponytail falls across her shoulder. Her nose wrinkles, but it's not out of distaste this time. "But if you find yourself lying awake at night, crushed under the expectations of a city and its sports fans alike, and you want to talk to someone who doesn't care, who doesn't hate you—that counts as business, too."

A grin stretches across my face, and it's not the one I've grown to hate. It's the one I think I used to make all the time. "You want to tell me bedtime stories?"

"No, I'd be terrible at that." She looks at me for a minute longer, before finally opening the door and jumping out of the truck. "Good night, Beckett."

"Night, Dr. Roberts." I lean forward, about to grab the handle of the door, when she turns back, rolls her eyes at me, and slams it shut.

I wait and watch to make sure she gets in safely, even though a potential intruder should probably be afraid of her.

But I think I might actually wait to watch her a bit longer because she's not as mean as she thinks—she's actually quite thoughtful, and she's actually quite beautiful.

Bile in her hair and all.

NEAR MISS

"Again. Sixty yards this time."

Coach Taylor's voice cuts across the field, and one of the equipment managers runs out to set up another ball 3 yards back from the last one.

My quads are on fire. Kickers don't often break a sweat, but I've been sweating on this empty practice field under a particularly oppressive August sun for the last two hours. I lost count of how many kicks he's asked me to attempt, each getting progressively farther back, and I have a feeling he's making his way back to that record-breaking 67 yards I've hit before—just not when it mattered.

"I need him for kickoffs on Friday morning. Don't kill his fucking legs," Darren calls from the sidelines. His voice is sharper than it should be when he's talking to his boss, but technically, he manages me. Not Coach Taylor.

"Last one then, Davis." Coach Taylor's eyebrows rise, and he eyes the football, innocuous and propped up there on the stand. He holds up a hand to stop me before I can start to line up, and he whistles to get the attention of the equipment manager, beckoning him back across the field. "Move it to 67 yards."

"Is that really necessary?" Darren cuts in again. I can see the whites of his knuckles against the grip of his clipboard from here. "The last thing we need is him"—he punctuates his words by jerking a thumb at me—"losing confidence before preseason even fucking starts. He's broken the record, we've seen it. Leave it."

Coach Taylor's lips pull into a thin line, nostrils flaring. But before he can reprimand Darren the way he probably should, and before they can keep talking about me like I'm not even here, I follow the equipment manager down to the 67-yard line. "I can do it."

"See?" Coach Taylor raises his shoulders before clapping his hands in that weird, sharp way only coaches ever seem to. "Let's see it then, Davis."

I'm actually not sure I can do it. At least not this version of me. The other version of me—whoever that was, because I'm not sure he was a real person at the end of the day if he crumbled into nothing so fucking easily—he would have been pretty confident.

And he was pretty confident when he stepped up to kick during that game last year. But the second my foot connected, I knew it was wrong.

I've thought about it a lot, and I'm thinking about it now, while I swing my leg and pound my fist into my quad to try and delay the inevitable cramping that's going to have me in an ice bath for hours. I'm not sure where I went wrong in my approach, I did the same thing I always do.

But I don't think about it.

It feels okay when my foot connects. It goes far enough.

But it's just off. It hits the uprights before it goes in.

"Dead ball." Coach Taylor claps his hands again.

I know it's a fucking dead ball. I feel a bit like kicking another one at him, or at the very least telling him to fuck off—but the old Beckett Davis made a career on being nice and reliable, so I scrub my face instead.

I grin, lifting one shoulder. "Kick went far enough though."

His eyes sharpen on me, and Darren starts shouting again about how I'm done for the day because I'll be no good to anyone if I tear a muscle before preseason starts next week.

I'm already no good to anyone, but I don't say that.

"Jesus Christ, Darren, he's done. I need to talk to him for a few minutes. Is it alright with you if I talk to one of *my* players?"

I don't turn to watch Darren inevitably run away with his tail between his legs. I scrub my face again and walk towards Coach Taylor, my hand firmly clamped on my jaw to hide the wince I make with every step.

His eyes cut to my thighs, my quad muscle twitching away under the bright light of the sun.

I swallow, exhaling and ready to start making excuses. "I can make the kick, it's just because—"

"I know you can make the kick, Davis." He cuts me off with a sharp jerk of his head. "I want you to break records as much as you want to break records. But that's not what this is about. You played with Pat Perez in college?"

"Uh, yeah. He was my QB when I was a wide receiver. He transferred after I started kicking though." Back when I was perfectly content to be a wide receiver who was just good. Nothing more. Nothing less. No real potential there. No real pressure after a lifetime of too much.

Coach Taylor nods, rubbing his jaw. "We're going to trade Diggs for him. Love is going to retire soon enough and Diggs isn't a viable enough QB2."

"Oh." I shrug. I get along with Diggs—I get along with everyone even when I don't feel like it—but he's right. He can't hold a candle to Love's passing or leadership in a locker room. "That's smart. Pat's too talented to ride the bench. He's been unlucky since he was drafted. He's always stuck under a veteran, and he hasn't really had his chance to shine."

"I happen to agree. You're smarter than you give yourself credit for." Coach Taylor rests a hand on my shoulder, like he's going to give me a nice old clap for being such a team player, but he doesn't let go. His hand lingers there, like he's some sort of paternal figure to me, and he's about to impart some sage advice. "He's thrown to you before. It would be much appreciated by me, and everyone else, if you'd walk through some routes with him. But don't do anything stupid. You might be off right now—but those legs are worth twenty-five million over the next three years."

Running routes with someone who used to know me when I was nothing, when I was finally able to breathe, to do something and not really care about it and have it not really matter, doesn't appeal to me. It's not how I want to spend my time before the season starts. But Beckett Davis is a team player.

"Sure, happy to." My voice sounds fake even to me.

He does clap me on the shoulder this time and points at me before he starts walking backwards, leaving me alone on the practice field with another failure. "Don't kill your legs like this ever again."

He says it like I had a choice. But I'm not really sure I've ever had much of a choice about anything.

Greer

"Look at these fucking abs!" Stella whistles, fanning herself with her menu and dropping her phone onto the table with a loud clatter.

She's practically yelling—but that's her. She hasn't cared much about what people think, or how much space she's taken up, since she was a kid.

We grew up in one of those houses where you opened the door tentatively, peered around the corner, and hoped and prayed or crossed your fingers that it would all be okay.

She bloomed in that environment. Unfurled her petals and put down roots and said fuck it to everything else around her.

Stella grew. I shrunk.

My psychiatrist tells me that's common—kids act out, or they internalize. It wasn't that Stella acted out, necessarily. But she asserted herself and took up space and did all the things a kid should.

I turned inwards, couldn't set a boundary to save my life, and tried to be an adult before I was even a child.

"Who are you talking about?" My eyes flick up from my own menu to my sister. She's still fanning herself, and one heavily ringed finger reaches out and points at her phone.

Stella drops her menu before slumping backwards in her chair dramatically. "Your football star."

"Cash—*what* are you talking about?" I say her childhood nickname like that's going to somehow cut through the theatrics and reach forward, turning her phone to face me, tapping the screen so it lights up again.

It takes me a minute to recognize him—but it's a photo of Beckett. Shirtless, hat turned backwards, skin bronzed and practically glowing under the summer sun, standing behind the wheel of a boat.

She's not wrong. Stacks of abdominal and oblique muscles draw ridges and valleys along his torso.

But he's not my football star.

"He's not my football star." I shove the phone across the table and look back down at my menu.

I'm starving. I was too tired to eat after Beckett dropped me off last night, and I'd only suffered approximately two bites of subpar steak before calling it quits at the bar. I was serious about the E. coli.

"Oh, so you just happened to run into him in the hospital elevator, did him a favour, and he just so happened to be waiting to take you for dinner?" Stella slaps her hand down on the table, eyes wide and expectant.

I roll my eyes and take a slow sip of my coffee, looking at all the families crowded around tables, couples huddled close together in booths, and groups of girls indulging in the well-known bottomless mimosa deal boasted by the restaurant.

Stella taps her fingers impatiently.

I give her a flat look. "His brother works at the hospital. It's not that weird. He's doing some volunteering there. Something to do with whatever happened last season?"

She snaps her fingers, pausing to take a sip of her own coffee. Wisps of her hair curl around her face and across the nape of her neck, where they've escaped the haphazard bun she's tied it back in.

Siblings don't always look alike, but sometimes I think looking at Stella is like looking in the mirror, at the reflection of a freer version of me.

She's light where I'm dark—auburn hair to my deep brown, and jade eyes that reflect all the beautiful things in the world. Same pale complexion we inherited from both of our parents. But according to our father, she takes after our mother. I inherited the dark hair and forest eyes from him.

Stella drops her cup onto the table without a care in the world. It's on the precipice of tipping over—droplets of coffee fly up over the rim and escape, splattering over her already worn menu.

"Yes, he missed a very, very important kick." She snaps her fingers again before leaning forward conspiratorially. "I looked it up after you told me that's who you had dinner with. Do you want to see it on YouTube? TikTok? He's been the source of some very unfortunate memes and edits since."

My lips pull back. I can't imagine anything I want to see less. "No thank you, Stella. I'm not sure why you would want to watch that either—the source of someone's public humiliation and pain?"

"Doesn't that all come with the territory of being a public figure?"

I shake my head, taking a measured exhale and look back down at my menu. Maybe it's the fact that I've met Beckett—that I know he's a real, living person who breathes in oxygen and breathes out carbon dioxide and feels things. Not some pixelated stranger who doesn't really exist for me.

"Does that suddenly make it okay? He's not a ripe carcass on the side of the road for vultures to pick at. This is what I don't get about sports," I mumble, glancing back up at my sister. "It seems unfair to shoulder all your expectations, your hopes and dreams for a team to win a trophy, on one person. Who, at the end of the day, is a person just like you—fallible and capable of making mistakes and, you know, feeling?"

"Sports bring people together." Stella tips her chin up.

"Oh, I'm sorry. I must have missed the episode where you became a football savant."

She rolls her eyes, plucking my menu from my hands and stacking it on top of her own. "You know what I mean."

"I do, and bringing people together can be a beautiful thing. I'm just saying, I think it's unfair he has to suffer because people were disappointed." I grab my menu back. I wasn't done. "And speaking of people suffering, if you're at Dad's, please don't forget to check his medication. It can't run low like it did the other day. If he misses one dose—"

Stella tips her head back, an exaggerated, high-pitched groan escapes her. "It can lead to acute rejection, chronic transplant damage, and ultimately, failure, if the behaviour occurs. I know. It's almost like I've heard this speech before. I might not have a license to practice medicine, but I'm not stupid. I know he can't miss a dose."

I pull my head back, blinking at my sister. "I don't think you're stupid, Stella—I wasn't trying to—I just want to make sure it's the only one he ever needs."

She cocks her head to the side and chews on the inside of her cheek. Her voice is barely a whisper, and she's just a shadow of the life spilling from her minutes ago. "I know what it cost you."

I swallow, biting down on my lips. I hate it. I hate how deflated she looks. I hate that this thing that happened takes up so much space in our lives all these years later. I don't want to have this conversation—not again, not here. "Stella—"

"Ladies, I'm so sorry." Our server practically skids to a halt in front of our table, pressing a palm to her chest like she's out of breath, the other clutching a notepad. She waves it around the crowded restaurant. "As you can see, we're slammed. Can I get you started with something?"

Stella blinks rapidly, looking between the two of us and back down to her discarded menu. "Oh, sorry. I haven't even looked. Can you give us a few more minutes?"

The server's mouth opens and closes for a minute before she gives Stella a hurried nod, practically sprinting to the next table.

"I don't know what to get," I say, more to myself, but Stella claps excitedly.

I glance back up at her, and this upturned, sly grin spreads across her face. She looks like the Grinch.

"I think you should order Beckett Davis's dick for breakfast."

I narrow my eyes at her before shrugging one shoulder. "I don't think the nutrient profile in dick is quite enough for a balanced breakfast, but thank you for the suggestion."

Stella lights up, and her mouth drops open before she tips her head back. Her laugh is this larger-than-life, wonderful thing, and that big, ugly, horrible bit of baggage I can never seem to shake, loosens its knots, and it makes me remember what it was all for.

Beckett stays true to his word, and even though I said business included any time he was feeling particularly lost—Stella said that was my heart bleeding all over the place again—he doesn't text me until he has a free afternoon to come to the hospital.

He's punctual—I'll give him that. Foot resting against one of the pillars in the lobby, arms crossed over his chest, another nondescript hat—navy today—pointed forward on his head and pulled low, still-damp hair curling around his ears and at the nape of his neck.

He kicks off the pillar with a grin when he sees me coming down the stairs, holds out his hand to me. "Afternoon, Dr. Roberts."

I wrinkle my nose, reaching out to shake his hand. "Beckett. Hello. Is this a thing we do now?"

The grin stays put, and our hands move up and down in space, like we're strangers who've never met. His grip tightens on mine just for a moment before he lets go, shoving both hands into the pockets of his linen shorts. They pull up, revealing an extra inch of muscled thigh. "Just making up for lost handshake time."

My eyes snap back up to him. "Pardon?"

Beckett angles his head. "The first day we met—when I was with Nathaniel, I held out my hand for you and you just left it there."

"Oh." I blink. I hadn't really thought about it. "I'm sorry. I think I was in my own world that day. I'd just done a harvest on a child. They're never . . . pleasant."

"I was just joking. I can't imagine a world where that's ever enjoyable." He studies me, and his mouth pulls to the side before he grins again, changing tune, like he can see right through me, and he sees this thing that lives in my chest with my heart behind its bars I try so hard to hide. "How do you take your coffee?"

"Why?" I wrinkle my nose.

Beckett shrugs, and the cotton of his shirt buckles against the trapezius muscles straining there. "I hear doctors drink a lot of coffee. Thought I could bring you one next time I'm here."

"That's not necessary." I give him a tight smile and gesture towards the elevator bay lining the wall by the stairs. His eyebrows knit, and not for the first time he reminds me of a lost puppy. "Black, though. Just black coffee."

He nods, taking his hat off and quickly running a hand through his hair, keeping his head ducked the entire time.

I didn't know him before—but seeing someone who seems like they were almost effervescent, so full of life, reduced to someone who thinks they have to hide—seems impossibly sad to me.

His eyes press closed when he takes a step, otherwise full lips pull taut, and the lines of his jaw clench.

I reach my hand out on instinct, wrapping it around his arm. "Are you okay?"

Beckett shakes his head, and he smiles at me again, but it's strained. "Coach killed my quads earlier this week. And there's a new dynamic kickoff formation this season, so Darren, the special teams coordinator, had me for about an hour and a half longer than usual. Skipped the ice bath to get here on time."

"Why?"

He gives another shake of his head, a bit incredulous. "I didn't want to be late."

I widen my eyes at him, finally letting go of his arm. "We could have rescheduled. Your job comes first."

Beckett tips his head back, exposing the column of his throat, reverberating with his laughter. "How nice of you to call it a job. Nah. I only have a few weeks to please my agent and maybe the masses by showing face. I'm done with the public appearances once regular season starts."

His hands are still firmly in his pockets, and he tips an elbow towards the elevator bay.

I cross my arms, eyeing him as I follow. "There's a difference between self-deprecation and negativity. I only tolerate one from my residents, and I'll only tolerate one from you."

"Negativity?" He pauses dramatically, clapping a hand to his chest before hitting the button. "Beckett Davis isn't negative. Beckett Davis is an affable ray of sunshine."

"Does Beckett Davis always talk in third person? Because I don't tolerate that either."

"Nah. I just—" He shoots me a wry look before scrubbing his jaw. "Sometimes I wonder if I was ever a real person, you know? Something beyond all these cookie-cutter adjectives people have stuck to me my whole life."

"Are you always this philosophical?" I tip my head.

The elevator dings, but it's practically impossible to hear against the incessant buzzing and chatter of the lobby. This is one of my least favourite areas of the hospital—it's the loudest, and to me, it's the most unpredictable.

"No. Beckett Davis is not philosophical." He cracks another grin, and I can tell this one is real. Lines at the corners of his eyes wrinkle and he gestures for me to go first into the elevator. "Beckett Davis just really, really doesn't like hospitals."

I study him when the door slides shut, effectively sealing us in for the next eight floors. The mirrored surfaces of the elevator distort our reflections: Beckett, standing taller than me, but stretched almost impossibly as he angles his head back and stares at the ceiling, breathing in and out carefully.

He rolls his neck and gives me a tight smile. Even though it's not a physical pain like the one I saw in the lobby, it has me reaching forward and grabbing his wrist again all the same. "Do you really have to do this?"

His eyes cut down to my hand, and I go to take a step back, to let go, when his fingers wrap around my wrist briefly. He gives me another grin that doesn't meet his eyes. "Yeah, I really, really do."

"Okay then," I whisper, offering him a small smile. It's real, and I mean it, and even though nothing earth-shattering or beautiful and wonderful has happened, I think he could use it. "Then let's hope I have some football-happy patients for you."

"Well, that wasn't a total bust." Beckett holds his arms out, walking backwards through the lobby doors out onto the sidewalk.

The sun inches lower in the sky behind him, clouds tumbling across the horizon while they turn pink and orange. Dusk settles over everything like a blanket, and the haze of the city seems dull.

But it makes everything look beautiful. It even makes the concrete look pretty.

Beckett looks more alive than he has in hours, like someone plucked whatever weight and baggage he carries around from whatever happened to him and his family in a building not unlike this one from his shoulders and threw it away.

He turned his hat backwards before we came back down and he waited outside the staff locker room for me to grab my bag, and I think that was a good sign.

"No." I nod in agreement. "Not a total bust. But I think you made more of an impression with the staff than the patients. What did that one guy say?"

"That he'd never heard of me," Beckett answers, his whole face on display and lit up with a smile. "How fucking freeing was that?"

"I wouldn't know." I cross my arms. "But I think, maybe, you've chosen the wrong career if you find anonymity freeing. I've seen you in, like, four commercials since I met you."

Beckett flexes his fingers before he finally drops his hands, shoving them into the pockets of his linen shorts. "There you go, calling it a career again. If I didn't know better, I'd think you're starting to—wait. Which commercials? I hope Gatorade. I look great in that one."

"I really couldn't say." I lift one shoulder, pursing my lips. It was the Gatorade commercial. I didn't watch the whole thing, but Stella sent it to me and told me to fast-forward to the one-minute mark where he pours a bucket over himself shirtless.

His eyes go wide, and he shakes his head before tipping it back for a minute. He's smiling when he looks back at me, and he looks beautiful under the sky, too. "You'd remember if you saw the Gatorade commercial."

"I don't know, I see a lot of commercials," I lie again. I'm not big on TV, I prefer reading.

Beckett leans forward with an exasperated groan. He gives a jerk of his chin, fishing his phone from his pocket. "You'll never be the same after you see this." He pauses, pointing at me. "Don't say I didn't warn you."

It all happens at once, the way that most things do when they go horribly wrong.

A car backfires a few blocks over somewhere to my right. Sirens start somewhere to my left. And Beckett steps into my space, thumb hitting the volume button on his phone.

My blood pressure plummets, and the edges of my vision go fuzzy. I feel my heart pressing through my chest against my rib cage. I think it might break it—that organ that's supposed to keep me alive is going to find those weak, old striations from those old breaks and that other time my ribs were shattered and it's going to shatter them again and impale itself and I'm going to die outside this hospital.

I hear a lot of things very distinctly—none of them are real and none of them are here. But they're impossibly loud.

I blink, and I think I'm underwater.

I take a sharp exhale and plant my palm against my sternum. Maybe I can manually palpate my heart when it bursts through my chest.

"No." I take a step back and give a tiny jerk of my head. I flex my fingers in and out. "I need to catch my streetcar."

"What?" Beckett looks up, confused. "I'll drive you. My truck is—"

"No," I repeat, shaking my head more fervently now. I can't breathe.

"Greer, are you okay?" He steps forward, and I think he might look concerned, and I think that might look nice and beautiful. But I need to leave.

I shake my head again. "I'm fine. I just need to catch my streetcar. I have—I forgot about an appointment."

I don't wait for his answer, and I think he says he's going to text me, so I hold my hand up over my head in acknowledgement, and I keep walking down the sidewalk but it's impossibly hard because the water seeps through my scrubs and it feels cold against my skin.

"The water isn't real," I whisper, and I focus on the things that are.

The sunset. A bird perched on the streetlight in front of me. The feel of my hand against my scrubs where it presses against my chest. They're worn. I brought them from home.

I smell metal, but I know that's not real either.

This sidewalk is real, and it leads me around the side of the hospital, down into the open shipping bay where deliveries are made. I press my back against the concrete wall.

"Please . . . please be in here . . ." I rifle through my purse, fingers slipping on old receipts and the leather of my wallet. But then I feel it. Worn, creased paper smoothed down over a small plastic bottle.

My hand shakes, so I bring the bottle to my mouth and pull the cap off with my teeth.

NEAR MISS

Tiny pills, covered in dust and chalk from their time living in my purse, roll around the bottom. My fingers still shake, but I fish one out and place it under my tongue.

I drop my head against the wall and close my eyes while it dissolves. The sensation of water inching higher and higher on my legs fades away; I only feel the cotton of my scrubs.

My heart and my breathing slows, and I blink.

I'm here, and I'm not there.

I look back in the open pill bottle, clutched between my hands. There are only a few left, some broken off or chipped away because they're so old and I haven't bothered to keep on top of the prescription.

I always say my dad and my sister can't leave his refills until the last minute, and they're just tiny pills—1 mg of Lorazepam staring back up at me—but I think they tell me to extend the same courtesy to myself that I do for others.

Beckett

My parents have this beautiful suburban home. It's nothing crazy—no sprawling mansion with rolling hills and a pool or anything like that.

Twenty minutes north of Toronto in a suburb that started to blend into the city, it was built before every house became a replica of the one next to it, so it has a bit of character—two-car garage, wraparound porch, and beautiful bay windows.

I offered to buy them something bigger—something better. But they wanted this one. They mortgaged it twice, and I guess the sentimental value won out.

It was where Sarah got sick and where she got better, where Nathaniel practiced equations and conducted fake experiments with a chemistry set in the basement, and where my dad first threw me a ball in the backyard.

Picture-perfect and beautiful, if it weren't for all the memories of vomit, blood, hair fall, chemotherapy drugs being administered by IVs, and Nathaniel and me being left alone more often than not when we were both too young.

It's picture-perfect right now. You'd never know anything bad ever happened—my mother and sister wrapped up in big, fluffy blankets sitting on the patio while my dad stands vigil over steaks he's probably going to overcook anyway and my brother haphazardly tosses me a football in the backyard.

He can't throw for shit, but I don't catch for a living so it's fine.

"How's it going with the kids? I haven't seen you around during visiting hours. Thought maybe you bailed." Nathaniel pulls his arm back and releases the football. It wobbles horribly, and I lunge forward a few feet to catch it so it won't hit the ground.

I palm the football and cock my arm back a few times before tossing it to my brother. He lurches forward, arms splayed wide, hands flexed entirely, his palms slapping it with no purchase, and he fumbles it.

"Don't be so rigid. Your hands should be looser." I tip my chin at the ball where it lies in the grass.

"I'm not trying to go pro here. And last time I checked, you're not a wide receiver anymore." Nathaniel rolls his eyes, but he bends to retrieve the ball anyway, his hair flopping over his forehead. He pushes it back with his elbow, palming the ball again and winding his arm back unnecessarily. "But seriously, where've you been? Did you give up on the publicity stunt?"

"It's not a stunt," I mutter, raising one hand and snatching his wobbly throw from the air. "I didn't bail, I've been hanging out with the adults. Greer's been taking me on rounds with her."

"Greer?" Nathaniel blinks, before his face pales again. "You're not talking about Dr. Roberts?"

I nod, tossing the ball up in the air and catching it on the inside of my foot. "Yeah. I ran into her in the elevator on the first day. She said she didn't think children had any influence on public perception, so I went with her instead. We hung out a few nights ago after her shift."

I texted her after she left the other night, looking half like she wanted to run away from me at top speed, to ask if she was okay, and all I got was a thumbs up. We don't text—like she said, it's strictly business—and I haven't had a chance to go back to the hospital yet. Preseason starts tomorrow, and despite all the warnings, I don't think I've ever come closer to ripping a hamstring or quadricep from overuse than I have this week.

Maybe she just really didn't want to see my Gatorade commercial.

"Why?" Nathaniel practically hisses, leaning forward and dropping his voice to a whisper. "She's scary."

"She can't fucking hear you, man." I widen my eyes, kicking the ball up again and catching it. "And she's not scary. Or mean. She's prickly at best."

"Prickly? Prickly?!" His voice goes higher the second time. He shakes his head. "I can think of ten residents off the top of my head that she's made cry."

I lob the ball to my brother, who snatches it from the air with more finesse than he's been managing all evening. "That doesn't really sound like her."

Something that's half like a scoff, half like a snort comes from him, and he clutches the ball to his chest. "She's brilliant. She's an incredible surgeon, but she's fucking terrifying. You can ask anyone. I talked to her for, like, ten minutes last week when she was scrubbing after surgery, and it was the scariest ten minutes of my life."

"And was she mean to you?" I hold out my hand for the ball again, but he clutches it tighter to his chest. "Or prickly?"

Nathaniel narrows his eyes before passing me the ball. "No. She wasn't what I would call friendly, but she wasn't that bad. I don't know how to explain it, sometimes she's just short. And it comes out of nowhere. Or like, in the OR, apparently she won't let anyone change the song or touch her playlist. She prefers when people don't speak if she's concentrating. She's weird about shit like that."

"Huh." I shrug. She definitely left abruptly the other night. I'm about to cock my arm back to toss him the ball again when our dad calls us over. It's almost like a scene from an idyllic childhood—wholesome, endearing. Two brothers passing a football back and forth while their proud father watches on, their mother and sister huddled together whispering secrets.

Ours didn't look like that. Our parents were never here. Or if they were, it was just one of them and they were trading off shifts with Sarah at the hospital. Whoever was home, slept. I made all of Nathaniel's food, I picked up after him because my parents were on a hair trigger more often than not, and I practiced calculus equations with him even though I had no fucking idea what I was doing or saying.

On the rare nights both our parents were home, they were usually alone in their room because one of them was crying.

If Sarah was here—if we were all home—we certainly weren't sitting outside, because it was too cold for her and she got tired too easily.

I came out here sometimes after everyone went to bed, running routes by myself or lobbing a ball up as high as I could to practice catching it from different parts of the yard.

My dad smiles broadly at us, and he looks significantly happier than he did back when all those sad, lonely things happened during our childhood. A happier man, lines around the eyes but ones that tell stories of how much he has to smile about, not all the ways life started carving chunks out of him before his time. A fuller stomach from nights out here, acting like the dad he never really got to be.

I look at him, and I smile, because it is a nice sight—my father, healed and whole. My entire family, healed and whole.

But sometimes, when I look in the mirror, I see this person who's probably just a shell of someone he was expected to be, not actually who he was, and I wonder if it all came too late.

He reaches forward and messes up Nathaniel's hair, like he's still a child running around the house. I know what's coming before it happens—he's going to reach out and punch me in the shoulder.

He does that sometimes. Treats us like we're still children in these odd, affectionate ways.

It used to be my thigh, like a fatherly attempt at a charley horse, but he stopped doing that when my legs started making millions and solving years of family debt brought on by childhood cancer.

His fist connects with my shoulder, and I only have it in me to raise my eyebrows before I duck into the chair my sister pulled out for me.

Sarah smiles up at me, wide and big and beautiful. I can't help it, but I reach out and mess up her hair, too.

She likes it when I do that, I think, even though she's twenty-six; she's in love and trying to have a baby, like the fully-fledged adult she is.

But she never got to be a child whose older brother tugged on and cut her hair when she wasn't looking or stuck gum in it.

I spent a disproportionate amount of time making sure whatever hair she had, or her wigs, were in pristine condition.

Sarah blinks, leaning into my hand for a minute before she sits back, wrapping the blanket tighter around herself. "How's work going this week?"

"You're the second person within a few days to refer to it as a job." I say, voice dry.

She cocks her head to the side and studies me. Like she sees right through me, and I'm not always sure how that could be, when to me, for better or worse, she's stuck in time as this little girl who needs me to be something for her.

But she looks at me like she wants to be something for me, and I don't know what to do with that.

"It is your job," Sarah whispers softly, lips tugging up. She stares for a moment longer before she scrunches her nose and turns back to the table, eyeing our brother. "How's the hospital?"

Nathaniel raises one brow, leaning back in his chair and looking a bit to me like a kid trapped in time, too.

I wonder what I look like.

He shrugs, reaching forward and grabbing a beer from the perspiring bucket our father left on the table. "Good. I've got some really great kids I'm working with. And the other week—we found a new kidney for that girl I told you about. Actually, Beckett's special friend came through and operated on her."

Sarah furrows her brow, but before she can say anything, our mother leans forward, green eyes just like ours practically bugging out of her head when she drops her chin to her palm, propping her elbow up on the table. "Beckett's special friend?"

Nathaniel nods enthusiastically while he sips from his beer. He practically fucking chokes trying to hurry up and speak. "Dr. Roberts. She's a transplant fellow. She's taken Beck under her wing."

Our mother bats her eyes at him, her special little star who fixes daughters just like hers before her eyes swing to me. She's still looking at me like a mother looks at a child, like she loves me, but it's not the same.

My mother looks at Sarah like she can't believe she's real—like she's the most precious thing in the world to her. A shooting star she saw in the sky and chased to the ends of the earth.

As she should.

She looks at Nathaniel with this sort of understated reverence. Her smile softens and her eyes go watery, like she might prostrate herself at his feet and thank him for saving kids like Sarah for the rest of her life.

As she should.

She looks at me like I've done her a sort of favour. Held open a door for her, picked up something she dropped in the grocery aisle. She's thankful for me, but she doesn't really understand my value. What I did to change or shape her life. Like she can't see the future and she doesn't know that if I hadn't held that door open for her, the handles to all her bags would have broken, and everything she had worked so hard to be able to afford to buy would have shattered on the floor. That if she hadn't stopped to say thank you to that stranger who took a few minutes out of their day, she would have left the grocery store a few minutes earlier and she would have gotten hit by a car, and life as she knew it would have ended.

She looks at me like I'm something—not nothing—but she's not quite sure what.

As she should.

Because I think I look at myself like that—I'm something, not nothing—but I'm not quite sure what either.

She's looking at me right now like she's amused by the whole thing. She means well. But sometimes, her well hurts.

"Oh?" My mom smiles, scrunching her nose up, barely sparing my father a glance when he drops a glass of wine in front of her. "Who's this Dr. Roberts, Beck? When do we get to meet her?"

"I'm not sure you want to meet her, Mom." Nathaniel snorts, kicking one foot up on the table for a minute before Sarah reaches across and shoves it off. "She'd scare the shit out of you."

My dad pulls out a chair beside Nathaniel, pointing at me and the bucket of beer. I shake my head. "No. Preseason starts on Saturday. I need to be at the stadium early tomorrow. And she wouldn't scare the shit out of you. She's just a friend, helping me out." I narrow my eyes at Nathaniel, tempted to reach out under the table and kick him in the shins. "Quit saying shit like that. She's not mean. She's nicer to me than most people are lately."

Nathaniel pulls his head back, our mother deflates, our father looks awkward, taking a too-long sip of his beer, and Sarah blinks.

No one tells me they don't hate me. That it's okay. That it was a mistake, that humans are allowed to make them and that's the beauty of being alive—that it was just a kick, and it was just a record and it was just a stupid trophy and just a stupid game.

They're looking at me like they feel sorry for me in the face of my public humiliation.

I bite down on my lip and shrug, leaning back in my chair before throwing them a grin. "Gatorade commercial's still crushing though."

Everyone lightens at once, like whatever my feelings have done to weigh them down, gets picked up off their shoulders and put on mine.

I sink in the chair a bit, I think. But no one notices, because I've been smiling while I carried a mountain for them for years.

Our mother gives me a small smile, and then she turns to Sarah, reaching out to tuck her hair behind her ear again even though she doesn't have to. "How'd it go at the specialist?"

It's a weighted question. Sarah wants nothing more than to have a baby she can give the childhood she never had, but she's too nervous to try and get pregnant because she's scared of her own genetics—so I paid a dumb amount of money for something that should probably be fucking free for more than one round so her partner Lily could try to get pregnant through IVF.

I didn't mind. I'm glad I can do it. But I hate that every failed embryo makes her feel like this, and I hate that I feel like I'm failing her, too.

"We're out of embryos." My sister looks down, picking at a loose stitch in the blanket she's still wrapped up in.

"Oh." Our mother's voice falls, and her eyes start to go glassy. She reaches out, a hand finding Sarah's shoulder, fingers feathering there before she snatches it back. She pauses, thumbs digging in and picking at cuticles that already spent a lifetime raw before she looks at me. "But that's okay. There's always the chance to try again with another round."

She's not looking at me because she's a mother looking at her son, hope and desperation pouring off of her and out of her.

She's looking at me like she needs me to hold the door open for her. To pick up the box of cereal she dropped.

NEAR MISS

She's not looking at me like I'm her son, or a living, breathing person who had things taken from him, too—she's looking at me like she needs another favour.

I'm happy to do it. I am. I have this stupid life and this stupid job. But sometimes, I wish they'd just look at me like they loved me.

I wish they'd just ask.

I'd say yes.

But I glance at my sister, lips tugging up to the side before I reach out and ruffle her hair again. "As many tries as you want, Sarah."

Greer

"This is all very *Grey's Anatomy*, don't you think?" I dig my thumb into the seam of the worn leather couch, my other hand toying with the stethoscope hung haphazardly around my neck. "Me, sitting here on your therapy couch on my lunch break, a few floors up from where I perform lifesaving surgeries?"

Rav cocks his head and taps his pen against the edge of his oak clipboard. It's pretentious. I tell him that at least once a session, and I offer to trade him for one of the cracking plastic clipboards we keep downstairs.

He smiles at me, lines around his brown eyes crinkling, and sometimes, depending on how exuberant he is, a curl might flop down onto his forehead.

But he's not exuberant right now. His mouth pulls into a tight line, and he raises a brow knowingly. "Deflection, Greer."

I sit up straighter, tipping my chin. "This is my place of work; you should call me Dr. Roberts."

"Oh?" He grins, nodding. "Alright, let's go from Rav back to Dr. Mardhani then."

"Great. Very professional." I give him a thin smile and sink back on the couch.

He waits—he's great at waiting.

But today, I win, because his nostrils flare and he looks down at the watch on his wrist. We only have forty-five minutes. "Okay, Dr. Roberts. Tell me, did anything out of the ordinary happen this week? You called and moved your session up."

"Can't a girl just want to see her favourite psychiatrist slash colleague on a . . ." I pause, looking down and checking my watch. "Tuesday?"

He taps his pen again. "She can, but you don't. Out with it. I, too, would like to get to lunch."

I inhale, and I think of my sister. She sits across from people like me—like us—on couches like this all the time. She's endlessly patient, and she doesn't mind sitting with people who're just trying to understand or trying to unpack something. People who maybe don't even know why they're sitting where they are.

But I know why I'm here.

And I value Rav, his time, his expertise, his field of medicine. I really, really do. So I stop picking at the seam of his couch, I blink at him, and shrug one shoulder before I speak.

I don't want it to, but my voice cracks. "I took a kidney from a perfectly healthy teenager the other day. They gave me permission to take it. No coercion, as far as I could tell. They gave it up willingly. All so their cousin could live a better, easier life, after years and years of cancer treatments. What do you make of that?"

The tapping stops and his nostrils flare. Rav sets his clipboard beside him on the arm of his chair and leans forward, hands finding his knees.

"I think that people can be wonderful, generous, and kind in a very cruel world."

I nod, lower lip puckering, and I blink again. My eyes burn, and there's this phantom sort of twinge across the bottom of my right rib cage. "Do you think it's fair that we take organs from people who aren't even fully realized adults yet?"

"You tell me." Rav raises his hands, gesturing towards me. "You're the transplant fellow. What do you think?"

"You know what I think," I whisper.

He pinches the bridge of his nose, sighing. But he's not annoyed or angry, I know him enough to know that. He seems sad. "What's this really about, Greer? We've talked about this. We've established what you want to work on. Your boundaries."

"Boundaries," I repeat. But the word feels heavy on my tongue, like it might slip down my throat and choke me under the weight of its expectations. I gesture around the room, mimicking him. "Come on. How good am I at those? Look around. I dedicated my entire life and hundreds of thousands of dollars to the thing that practically destroyed whatever semblance of family I had?"

Rav has this air of maddening patience about him—he always does. He nods along before he speaks, his words quiet. "Boundaries can change, and they can be established long after they were needed. You save lives, Greer. That's what you do. Whether you want to rewrite history or not."

I wish someone would have saved mine.

I don't tell him that because I'm alive and breathing and whole, and that counts for something. Instead, I tell him about the other day. "I had a particularly bad panic attack a few days ago. Just outside, I'm sure security caught it on camera."

"Brought on by . . . ?"

"Noises. A few different ones. A car backfired. Sirens. A friend was showing me this commercial and he turned the volume up when he leaned in and—"

"A friend? Beckett Davis?"

My eyes pinch at Rav. "Yes. How do you know?"

He gives me a flat look before pushing his hands into his knees and leaning back in his chair. "People in this hospital talk, Dr. Roberts. It's not uncommon knowledge he's doing some sort of PR volunteer image-rescue campaign here, nor is it uncommon knowledge that he's been spotted with you doing your rounds."

I'm tempted to offer him a slow clap, but I feel more tired than mean. "Who needs a psychiatry degree when you have gossipy hospital staff?"

"Could have saved me a few hundred thousand dollars, too." He smirks, nodding along. "Are you reconsidering what we've been working on? The idea that you want to prioritize yourself? Live for you?"

"Reconsider? Why would I reconsider the very thing that made me come see you in the first place?" My fingers twitch against the arm of the couch.

"Maybe you're lonely." He shrugs, like it's a nothing statement and not something that someone might find insulting. "You ended your last relationship in pursuit of your goal to live for yourself, like you say."

I purse my lips, and my nostrils flare. "I'm not lonely. I have my sister. I have my dad. I have Kate and Willa."

Rav doesn't look impressed by the mention of my two family members and my two best friends who don't even live in Toronto, so I push against the couch and straighten my shoulders. "And I have Beckett. He's my friend."

"Oh?" Rav crosses his arms, looking amused, as he leans back in the chair. It doesn't feel like a terribly professional pose, and I feel a bit like taking his clipboard and smacking him with it. But he cocks his head and continues. "The Near Miss superstar is your friend?"

"Near Miss?"

"That's what they call him, in the media. Online." Rav studies me, like he's waiting for some sort of reaction, and I don't want to give him one—even though my nose wrinkles, my stomach knots and I think my heart hurts at hearing that. "Beckett 'Near Miss' Davis."

"That's rather cruel," I whisper.

Rav nods, fingers flexing and drumming against his bicep. "I agree. So, if he's your friend, have you talked to him since you had your panic attack in front of him? Or did you run away and avoid all contact since?"

I don't give him the satisfaction of answering, because we both know he's right.

The silence falls again, and Rav waits. Fingers occasionally tap against his arm. His eyes glance to the clock on his coffee table, until he finally exhales. "Well, you've bested me again in these last fifteen minutes, Greer. So I'll leave you with some parting words of wisdom I hoped you'd arrive at yourself: There's a difference between setting boundaries to protect yourself and being alone."

My mouth parts, indignant. I'm not sure what I'm about to say. I don't like the feel of those words either. They hit too close to home—they touch that phantom ache under my right rib cage and they crack the bones my body worked so hard to repair.

NEAR MISS

But my phone starts going off. I glance down. It's an emergency page. I hold it up, triumphant and vindicated, like the session wasn't ending anyway. "I have to go."

"That you do." Rav leans forward again and raises his eyebrows at me before picking up his abandoned clipboard. "Think about what that page means, Greer. It might just be an insignificant noise, something you're used to now, so it doesn't startle you or hurt you. But it means something. However you want to think about and categorize all the events in your life that made you, well, *you*. They all led here, and there's a real, living, breathing person on the other end of that phone who needs you to save them. Regardless of whether or not someone was there to save you."

Rav's psychoanalysis works.

Not for the first time, something he said worms its way into my brain, like some sort of unwanted parasite, and festers there until I can't think about anything else.

He was right—I practically sprinted away from Beckett, and I responded to his one check-in text with nothing more than a thumbs-up emoji.

It wasn't a very nice thing to do to a stranger, let alone one you promised to help, or a "friend" as I called him, in a sad attempt to provide something to Rav.

It wasn't just the idea that I'd somehow maybe done myself a disservice that permeated my brain and caused all my neurons to misfire in Beckett's direction—it was the idea that there were people out there cruel enough to craft some stupid nickname for him that was kind of a double negative and didn't really make a lot of sense.

I texted him last night and asked if he had time to come in this afternoon. I actually had a patient who was interested in meeting him. A teenage boy who hadn't shut up every time I came to round on him, asking whether Beckett Davis was coming in.

I think I lied when I said he was my friend—it wouldn't be the first time I lied to Rav. I lie to him on a semi-regular basis, at least when he opens up a door to a room I don't particularly feel like looking into.

He says I lie a lot, about a lot of things, to a lot of people.

My father. My sister. My friends.

Myself.

I justify this one as a white lie, though. A fib, maybe. Because we might not exactly be friends—but we were friendly, and even though I don't know Beckett Davis terribly well yet, I know he doesn't deserve that.

I never bothered to ask what kind of coffee he liked in return—so I'm standing in front of the hospital, squinting against the late-afternoon sun, clutching two perspiring iced lattes in either hand, staring at the pedestrian exit from the parking garage, waiting for him to appear.

And he does.

Beckett jogs up the steps—golden all over. Except for the mop of chocolate hidden under a backwards hat. Not a nondescript one today, but one with the number nineteen stitched there. Thigh muscles tense under linen shorts that fall a few inches above his knees, and those muscles in his forearms, finely dusted with hair, somehow look even more impressive today.

He grins when he sees me—and I think it's a real one. He lights up, and even though they're hidden behind sunglasses, I imagine those green eyes do, too.

Beckett raises a hand, like he's trying to make sure I see him. General good looks aside, I'm not sure how it would be possible to miss someone as effervescent as him.

"Dr. Roberts." He's still grinning, and he stretches out a hand for me to shake, but I raise the plastic cup. His eyes cut down to the latte that probably isn't a latte anymore because of how quickly the ice melted, and he glances back up, one eyebrow lifting behind his sunglasses. "For me?"

"For you," I confirm.

He flexes his fingers, and they brush against mine when he grabs the cup.

It's just a touch, but it lingers against my skin. Against me, against the lines around my heart, and it feels nice.

But then it brushes across the right side of my ribs, and it feels more like this nefarious thing that's going to take something from me.

Beckett cocks his head, dimple digging in. "To what do I owe this surprise? Did you see my triumphant return to preseason football? Now you're sucking up to me so you can say you knew me when I was downtrodden?"

I roll my eyes and watch as Beckett smiles—seemingly becoming this lighter version of himself, bringing the straw to those full lips like he doesn't have a care in the world, even though I'm starting to suspect he has too many.

A drop of perspiration rolls down the plastic straw, and I stare at it for a moment, the way it looks poised right below his lips, but I blink, and my eyes snap back up to his.

He looks at me expectantly.

"Sorry, I didn't even know you had a game." I shrug one shoulder, taking a sip of my own latte and clamping my teeth down on the straw. "Did you . . . kick well?"

Beckett snorts, shaking his head. "Sure, yeah. I kicked well. Three field goals. And a spectacular kickoff, if I do say so myself. SportsCentre even referred to it as a 'startling comeback.'"

I wave my hand around, like I could possibly gesture to the way he's carrying himself differently, how much happier he seems. "That's really important to you?"

"Playing well?" He pulls his sunglasses off, narrowing his eyes when he tips his elbow towards the revolving lobby door. "Of course it's important. It's what I'm paid to do."

I shake my head, glancing up at him as we step through the door together. "No. What other people think. You don't play for you?"

He pauses, a confused sort of look crossing his face—brows furrowed, jawline somehow softer, and lips almost in a pout with the straw still poised there. "Huh. No one's ever seen through me quite like that before."

Dropping into a brief curtsy, I raise my eyebrows at him. "I was the star of my psychiatry rotation."

"Were you really?" He looks amused, eyes all alight and even though his legs must be killing him—he's walking like he's all so much lighter.

I snort, reaching out my elbow to hit the button for the elevator. "No. That's my sister's department."

Beckett holds out a hand so I can walk in the elevator first. "Oh? Is she a doctor, too?"

Shaking my head, I chew on the straw again. I can practically hear her—telling me that sort of behaviour is indicative of a deeply anxious, unsettled soul. "No. Stella's a social worker. She loves people. She'd spend all day talking to anyone about anything."

"And do you . . . not love people?" Beckett kicks one foot against the wall of the elevator, tilting his head as he leans back against the mirrored wall.

The straw still sits there, right on the precipice of his lips.

I give him a flat look. "What do you think? Half the residents see me in the hallway and they turn the other way. They used to keep count of how many tears I'd caused. They said I drank them for breakfast."

"Oh, come on." Beckett laughs. "You're not serious."

"I'm too serious, some might say." I give him a rueful smile and a tiny shrug. "I don't do it on purpose. It's just . . . important. That's all."

My hand drops to my side, and my fingers press against the bottom of my rib cage. Beckett blinks, and when he does, I feel like maybe he's trying to peel off these layers to understand me, but I don't think I'm ready for that so I dig my fingers in and hold on to them for dear life.

The elevator stops, and the doors slide open.

Beckett gestures for me to walk out first, and I think it's all safe—that he doesn't know me, not really—that he doesn't see right through me. But he grabs the crook of my elbow, all of it fitting into the palm of his hand. And he does look right through me when he whispers, "It is important."

I glance down to his hand, the way his fingers feather against the sleeve of my scrubs, and I swallow, offering him a small nod before taking a measured step back.

If it bothers him, he doesn't say. The usual friendly mask slips back into place as we fall into step beside one another, winding through the halls peppered with carts and empty cots and abandoned IV poles. He keeps up easily, one stride equaling two of mine, a bit like a puppy, bounding along beside me. "Who are we here to see?"

"Theo." I glance down at my watch. "His parents told me yesterday he's a big football fan. They heard you were volunteering and asked if I could put in a good word."

Beckett falters, a furrow creases his brow, and a muscle in his cheek twitching. "He's a kid? And he wants to see me?"

"Oh—" I stop, pausing in the middle of the hallway. "I'm sorry, I should have asked. I know this is a weird place for you. I wasn't thinking about your sister. I was just excited that he wanted to see you. He's a bit shy, but he's almost eighteen, if it makes a difference."

He shakes his head, and those worry lines around the corners of his eyes disappear. "Nah, it's fine. I'm just happy I played well this week. The last thing I need is for someone to throw a subpar hospital meal in my face."

"I'll have you know the food here is actually pretty good. It's a point of pride." I gesture towards the door at the end of the hallway.

Beckett cuts me a look, his strides more purposeful again. "I'll be the judge of that. You can take me to the cafeteria sometime."

"So you can make fun of our cuisine?" I arch an eyebrow, raising a fist to knock on the open door. "I don't think so."

There's this tiny voice calling from the room, one that doesn't seem like it would belong to an almost-eighteen-year-old, but I think there's something about this place that reduces us all to nothing more than children. "Come in."

Theo sits propped up on his hospital bed, brown curls pushed off his face and hidden under a hat that's not unlike the one Beckett wears, eyes firmly glued to the iPad in his hands.

"Hey, Theo. How are you feeling today?" I smile softly at him, and I mean it. "Can I come in?"

Theo's eyes flick up. "Did you bring him?"

"I did." I nod in confirmation, hiking a thumb over my shoulder. "Theo, this is Beckett. Beckett, this is Theo."

I don't wait for Beckett—I know enough about him to know he's going to come right in and make himself at home.

He does. He strolls in, grinning and looking like he doesn't have a care in the world when I sit down at the computer and start to pull up Theo's labs.

"Theo." Beckett nods. "Great to meet you."

"Nice field goal Saturday. The one in the third." Theo looks at him for a minute before looking back down at his iPad.

Beckett's smile splits. "It was nice, wasn't it?"

He turns to look at me, giving me an obvious thumbs up before he grabs the chair beside Theo's bed and swings it around. Beckett drops his arms over the back of it, the picture of casual, and he leans forward, looking at something Theo points to.

They're in their own little world, I think. Neither seems to care that I'm supposed to be rounding and checking on Theo's vitals and his incision. Beckett's childlike in his exuberance, and Theo nods along, pointing at different things on his screen, eyes all wide.

But Beckett looks back up at me and my eyes find his instead of all the things I need to be looking at. His features soften, and the left corner of his lips kick up, that dimple in his cheek pops, and he mouths the words *thank you*.

I swallow, and I feel my heart beat in my chest—this irregular sort of pattern that would usually scare me. But it doesn't. I blink at him mouthing, *You're welcome*, and before I can glance back to the screen, Beckett gives me another exaggerated thumbs up.

I roll my eyes, like I'm bothered by him and his presence has been this great, big nuisance.

Theo starts talking loudly about the start of the season—and I remember what Beckett said. That he's only here until regular season starts.

I didn't think anything of it at the time, but now I think I might miss him when he leaves.

Beckett

Preseason goes like this: I practice. I play. I score. I hang out with Greer and whatever patients she digs up for me to talk to.

I think she must have more friends than she lets on, because we end up on more floors than just post-op, talking to patients that aren't hers. And I don't think people really look at her like they're afraid of her. Impressed with her. In awe of her, maybe.

She doesn't notice. She's too in her own little world—with her patients, watching her pager, running off to check on organs and save lives.

Maybe once upon a time they looked at her like they were afraid of her. I could see why—she doesn't have much to say, maybe because she's not as concerned with hearing herself talk as most people—and when she does speak, she says what she means.

She doesn't smile as often as, say, someone like me, who quite literally made a career off a stupid skill and a stupid dimple. But when she does—even those soft, tiny ones I've seen her give her patients when their labs are perfect and they can go home, or those big, brilliant ones she's shown me when an organ becomes available—it's radiant. They're all radiant.

She doesn't give them away for free. Certainly not to people who maybe, once upon a time, thought she was mean or scary.

But they look at her like they might see her a bit differently now. Maybe they've realized how rare and special she is. That a thoughtful, funny, entirely too brilliant, generous person lives just behind all the sharp edges of her.

People look at me a bit differently now, too.

Reporters and analysts have toned down on the use of the nickname Near Miss, I haven't missed a kick all preseason, and all the unfortunate prop bets people were making about how horribly I'd choke on the first kickoff of the season have dried up.

No one's thrown anything at me in a while—it's been a nice reprieve.

I'm sure it'll all come back around again when regular season starts in two weeks and everyone remembers we should be having a nice ceremony to open things up with new banners to christen the stadium.

But I tried to enjoy it while it lasted.

I enjoyed the visits to the hospital while they lasted, too.

But I think that largely had to do with the doctor waiting for me in front of the revolving door—brow furrowed and nose wrinkled in concentration while she texts at insane speeds with one thumb, balancing a tray with two iced coffees in her other hand.

The sunlight hits her and, not for the first time, I think about the fact that she's beautiful, but she has no idea.

And not like in the movies where the main character finally gets a glimpse of themselves or takes off their glasses and looks in a mirror and realizes they've been beautiful the entire time.

I just don't think she really thinks about herself much.

Greer looks up right when the sun shifts. It catches her eyes—and I'm sure she'd be horrified at the description, but they sparkle. Her mouth moves from this taut, little line of concentration to something softer, not quite a smile, but the corners of her lips twitch upwards and her cheeks go all pillowy.

She raises the tray of coffee instead of waving.

I jog the last few steps to the sidewalk, even though my legs are killing me. I ended up needing an IV for a foot cramp after the final preseason game last night. In both an attempt to make a point to anyone that doubted whether Beckett Davis was still the best and save any of his offense a stupid, last-minute injury—Coach Taylor had me kicking way more than usual.

I hold out a hand. "You should really let me grab those. You're doing me the favour, after all."

Greer raises her eyebrows, drops her phone into the pocket of her scrubs, and takes her coffee from the tray. "Well, your final day has come. You can get them the next time you make a public mistake and need me again."

I groan, clapping my hand above my heart before grabbing my coffee and tossing the tray in the garbage can by the door. "You wound me. You wouldn't be talking like that if you saw the game on Saturday. I'll have you know I was phenomenal. Six successful field goals. That's almost a record. You're telling me it's been, what"—I glance down at my watch to see the date—"almost three weeks of this, and you still haven't watched a game?"

"No." She cuts me a sideways look as she steps through the revolving door. She waits for me to follow, arms folded over her chest, one hand clutching the coffee, like I'm taking too long, before she answers. "I caught the end when I was finishing my shift. My dad and sister had the game on."

"Oh yeah?" I ask, grinning. "They big fans?"

Greer makes a noncommittal shrug of her shoulder, her braid swings across her back, and she starts walking towards the elevators. "My dad is more into fictional shows about dragons than he is into sports, but my sister knows you're sort of volunteering here with me, and she was a big fan of the Gatorade commercial."

A laugh catches in my throat, and I kiss my fist before raising it in the air. "Gatorade commercial coming through clutch, as always. I take it you've seen that, then?"

She shakes her head, practically ignoring me in favour of answering whatever page or text came through on her phone. "No."

"You're not the least bit curious?"

"No." She sticks out her elbow to touch the elevator button, and I drop against the wall with another exaggerated groan.

She's still looking at her phone, thumb flying across the screen and teeth chewing on the end of her straw.

"I would have thought you would be. What with the inquiring scientific mind and thirst for knowledge you have." I widen my eyes, teasing. "You ran away pretty quick to your appointment. You didn't even see the opening credits or the first slow-motion, up-close shot of my abs."

She flinches. Eyes pinched closed, her phone slips in her hand, but her reflexes probably rival mine and she catches it before it falls. Her nostrils flare and I see her take this deep, measured breath before she cuts me a sideways look. "Don't flirt with me."

I cock my head. "Hey, you okay?"

Greer blinks, before turning and giving me another flat look. "Yes. But talking about your Gatorade commercial incessantly really seems to compromise the whole 'just business' thing we've got going on. It's your last day, don't ruin it now."

I eye her for a minute before the elevator dings and I follow her in. I know what Nathaniel's talking about now—I've seen it a few times—where she just sort of shuts down. She flinches randomly or takes this big inhale and needs to steady herself for a minute. Sometimes she's short when she responds, but it always passes and she always looks apologetic after.

I ask her if she's okay each time, and she always says fine or breezes by the question like nothing happened to begin with. I go along with it, because Beckett Davis is affable and easy to get along with, even though the idea that something hurts her—that maybe I've done something to upset her—makes me feel a bit like someone hurt me.

I hold up my hands in surrender. "You're right. Who do you have for me today? My very last day of PR damage control, as Nathaniel calls it."

She hits the button for the fourth floor. Pediatrics. "Theo's still here."

"What?" I blink. I've seen Theo every week since preseason started, but he was supposed to be discharged. "Is everything okay?"

She shakes her head, biting down on the straw. "He's fine, but some of his levels just aren't steady enough for me to feel comfortable discharging him."

"Is he still not peeing enough? He was telling me last week his urine needs to be in the acceptable range before he goes home. We need that up to about 1.5 ccs, right?"

She tips her head back, laughing—this throaty, beautiful noise she doesn't make all that often either. "You're right. We do. You can come away from this exercise with more than an improved image—newfound knowledge to impress your teammates with."

"Sadly"—my lips tug to the side—"my teammates don't care much about urine output."

"It sounds as though they need to get their priorities in check." Greer's voice is dry, she gives me this sideways glance, and I think there's the ghost of a smile there.

It's another thing I don't think she's aware of—I don't think she'd say she's a particularly lighthearted person, but she's funny and I think she tries really hard to make me smile in this place that I used to hate.

She wrinkles her nose, eyes shimmering in this sort of sad way, and points with her almost-empty coffee cup when the elevator door slides open. "Your last day awaits."

I won't miss the hallways here—all the ducks and cartoon clowns and other weird things taped to the walls that probably scare the children more than help them.

But I'll miss these elevator rides. The anonymity of this elevator. The coffee that's much better than hospital coffee should be. This girl.

It feels a bit too much like I might be overstepping the business line to tell her that, so I grin and follow her down the hall for the last time.

Greer gets paged when I'm halfway through helping Theo with his fantasy draft. He doesn't even spare her a second glance, but I do.

Her eyebrows knit, eyes move across her phone at rapid speed, and she holds up her hand before practically sprinting out the door.

I thought she was gone—that it was the last time I'd see her in here like this, but she stopped, grabbing the doorframe. "I'm sorry. I need to go. Theo, your parents said they'd be by this afternoon. I'll be back to talk to them, I promise."

He grunts noncommittally, eyes focused on his draft.

Greer raises a hand to me. "Beckett. I'll see you around."

And then she's gone.

It was fairly anticlimactic as far as goodbyes are concerned. I'm not really sure what I was expecting, because this is the end of whatever this was—not even an arrangement really, but the steady presence of someone who just . . . seemed to maybe like me for me.

I only make it as far as my truck when I break the business-only texting rule.

> Beckett: I didn't get to properly thank you for letting me tag along the last few weeks. Can I take you for a real dinner to say thank you? Tonight? No questionable steaks from sketchy bars, I promise.

I have no idea where she ran off to—whether she's even going to answer. But my phone buzzes when I pull into my parking garage.

> Greer: Sorry. Can't tonight. I'm on call.

I hate that.

> Beckett: What about there? Been a whole three weeks and I haven't tried this allegedly palatable hospital food.

She types, those three dots popping up and disappearing a few times before her answer comes through.

> Greer: Fine. As friends. Come back around 7. I'll be done with evening rounds then.

> Beckett: A business dinner, if you will.

> Greer: Goodbye, Beckett. See you at 7.

I can hear her raspy voice, and I can even imagine what she would look like if she was standing in front of me: lips pursing into a thin line, right brow raised, gemstones for eyes, rolling them before she answers.

The way she'd emphasize the word *friends*.

I'm not entirely sure where her commitment to business-only dealings comes from, but I don't really remember the last time I had a real friend.

Especially not one like her.

Greer

He's holding fucking flowers.

Standing just past the elevator bay, looking like he stepped out of an ad in a magazine. Chocolate hair pushed off his face, curling around his ears and a few stray waves around the nape of his neck, green eyes practically golden in the setting sun, and a dusting of stubble that makes that dimple even more noticeable.

His clothes are casual enough. Just a charcoal long-sleeve sweater rolled up his forearms and nondescript khakis.

But the flowers—this gargantuan display of peonies, hydrangeas, and lilies.

I blink for a minute, not because I'm blinded by him, unlike everyone else in the lobby who not so subtly stops to stare. But because I'm not entirely sure what I'm looking at.

I narrow my eyes at him when I cross the floor. "You can't have those in here."

"What? Why?" Beckett's brow creases and he looks down at the flowers, before his eyes snap back up and he offers me a lazy grin. "Are you worried people will think I'm your boyfriend?"

"No." I reach forward and snatch them from his hand. "It's a scent-free environment."

"Do you not like them?"

"No—they're—you just can't—" I exhale, tempted to pinch the bridge of my nose but I shove the flowers back at him. "Fine, just go put them in your truck and I'll put them in my locker after dinner."

Beckett gives me a rueful shake of his head, before this crestfallen look takes over his face that makes me want to give him a hug or something. "I took the subway here."

My lips part and I'm about to apologize when he cracks a grin, all of him lighting up.

He shakes his head, fingers grazing mine when he takes the bouquet back. "I'm fucking with you, Greer. My truck's just around the corner. I'm sorry, I didn't realize the scent rules were so strict. The last thing I need is for my carefully restored image to get destroyed on my last day if someone goes into anaphylactic shock over my flowers. I'll leave them on the passenger seat, and you can get them later."

Beckett holds the flowers in the air before turning and jogging out the lobby door.

He's only gone for a few minutes—just enough for everyone lingering around to stop staring and then start again as soon as he walks back, raising his empty hands.

"Dinner?" he prompts, eyebrows lifting.

I point towards the opposite end of the lobby, and the long sunlit hallway that leads to the cafeteria. "What's with the flowers?"

Beckett shoves his hands in his pockets, falling into step beside me. "A friend can't bring another friend flowers?"

"Flowers aren't friendly." My voice is flatter than I mean for it to be, and I can hear my sister in my ear—hear Kate and Willa—telling me not to be so harsh. Just because I drew lines around myself like a child might in an attempt to make a self-portrait—scribbled and everywhere, jutting out around certain parts of my body because I can't seem to stop giving away pieces of me—it doesn't mean I can't be kind.

"What's with the commitment to business-only friendships?" He angles his head, tousled hair catching the sunlight streaming through the windows.

I glance sideways at him, and he looks curious, eyebrows furrowed and lips in this quizzical sort of line that makes him look cute instead of earth-shatteringly, Gatorade-commercial-level handsome—the kind of boy in another life I'd have run straight home each day to tell Kate and Willa all about.

I give him a small shrug. "I just don't date."

"Too committed to saving lives?"

Trying to save my own, I think.

But I don't tell him that, I just shrug again and say, "Something like that."

In addition to their commitment to ensuring high-quality food, the hospital redesigned their cafeteria to be warm, welcoming—a place families could come and not be forced to sit in uncomfortable cracking plastic chairs. It's quite nice now. Cushy leather chairs with polished wooden arms spread out around trendy concrete tables. Waxy, impossibly green palms tower over everything in wooden planters, and the buffet line looks like something you'd find in a first-class airport lounge.

Beckett stops abruptly as soon as we round the corner. "What's with the Michelin-Star restaurant? This is a hospital. Shouldn't we be eating shitty egg salad sandwiches?"

I give him a pointed look and walk towards the tray line. "You know that's not very good for recovery. There've been studies. Patients and their families score higher on different indexes when they're fed well."

"Huh." A muscle in his cheek ticks, but he lines up behind me, hands practically dwarfing the grey plastic tray. "Well, the world is your oyster, Dr. Roberts. Don't let cost stop you. Dinner is on me, so you can have whatever you want."

I glance back at him. "Sorry to break it to you, but food is free for staff here."

Beckett slowly turns away from the array of salad options to look at me with wide eyes. "What? Since when?"

"Recently, actually." I reach forward and grab a bowl, piling it high with different leaves and greens. "It's part of a resident wellness initiative, but we bargained to have it extended to all staff."

He scoffs, helping himself to two separate bowls of salad. "You're a cheap date."

"Not a date." I cut him a sideways look, and he holds up his hands in defeat before following me down the line, picking up a seemingly endless, and random, array of food. "Your tastes are . . . varied."

Beckett picks up his tray, barely sparing it a glance as he follows me towards the register. "As are my dietary requirements."

"I didn't realize a kicker would need to eat so much. Don't you practice significantly less?" I ask, parroting back one of the endless tidbits of information my sister keeps inundating me with.

"It's not necessarily the practice." Beckett shakes his head, like he can't believe me, picking up an apple from a bowl, tossing it in the air a few times before leaving it beside one of his seventeen plates. "I practice different types of kicks three times a week, at least. But it's the workouts. I'm in the gym or stretching about double that amount."

"Where does the reformer Pilates fit in?"

"You remembered." Beckett smiles at me before he drops his tray and taps an index finger to his temple. "I do it a few times a week. Great for flexibility and strength. Really extends a kick."

It makes sense, but the idea of impossibly tall—too tall for a kicker, according to Stella—Beckett strapping his muscled legs into reformer straps seems impossible.

I raise my badge and smile politely at the woman sitting behind the register. She glances at my tray before waving me on. She throws a bored look towards Beckett before blinking rapidly, a blush rising on her cheeks, and she quickly looks down, fingers slipping over the keys on her register as she rings all his food through.

Beckett reaches into his back pocket, fishing out his wallet with a grin, and I swear to god she looks like she might need to fan herself. My eyes narrow, flicking back and forth between the two of them. He pulls a nondescript black card from his wallet and holds it out to her between two fingers.

He grins when she takes it, his voice dropping an octave when she hands it back. "Thank you."

Her voice is nothing more than a squeak. "You're welcome."

Practically ripping my tray off the metal rungs, I roll my eyes and tip my elbow towards an empty table in the corner of the cafeteria, pushed up against one of the giant paned windows.

Glancing back over my shoulder, I notice she's moved from staring to texting frantically on her phone. "Are you always such a flirt?"

"I wasn't flirting." Beckett shakes his head, lips pulling down in confusion. "I was just being nice. Likeable."

"You were being likeable?" I ask, incredulous. "Who tries to be so likeable they're actively aware of it?"

He shrugs, stopping in front of the table to pull out my chair for me. "Lots of people."

"I'm not so sure about that." I eye him as I sit. He makes his way around the table and folds into a chair, long legs stretching out underneath.

"What can I say?" Beckett unrolls his cloth napkin and holds up his fork before stabbing at one of his two salads. "It's how I grew up. Sarah healed, Nathaniel studied, and I became likeable. Reliable."

"That's . . ." I pause, pulling my head back. "Kind of a depressing sentiment."

"Is it?" he asks vaguely, but he glances up at me and by the way the corners of his eyes crinkle, the way his cheek twitches—I think he knows it is.

I feel a bit like reaching across the table and telling him I understand. Maybe it's not quite the same—but it's close enough. He became someone else, because other people needed him to be, and I gave away pieces of myself so other people could be whole.

But I tip my head to the side, make a show of unfolding my own napkin, and start to chase the salad around my bowl like him. "I imagine it was difficult, to grow up while your sister was sick so young. We see it a lot. You know, we talk a lot about what it does to the parents, to their marriage. But no one ever talks about what happens to the other children in the home."

Beckett makes a noncommittal noise, but I notice his fork hits the bottom of his bowl harder.

I feel like asking a bit more. Because I'm not so sure anyone ever cared enough to ask before.

But I think of all the things I don't like to talk about and I blink at him, this man who pretends to be so carefree, who's really, maybe, too wonderful to be so sad, before changing the subject. "How'd you become a kicker, then?"

"Do you always ask such hard-hitting questions?" He's grinning again, but his eyes don't seem quite as bright.

I point my fork at him. "You were the one who wanted to have dinner."

"I was actually a wide receiver in college. Went to school in New York on a partial athletic scholarship. But I was probably never going pro. I was okay, but nothing special. The kicking thing was kind of serendipitous. I played soccer too, and one day both our kicker and punter were injured, and I stepped in. Turned out to be really, really fucking good at it." Beckett sets his fork down and leans back in his chair, crossing his arms over his chest. The material of his sweater pulls taut over his biceps. "Kind of a stupid thing to be good at."

"Talents aren't stupid."

He points to my hands. "Yours aren't."

"Maybe I'm bad at my job." I shrug one shoulder, stabbing at a particularly tricky piece of lettuce. "What did you study in college?" I ask another question before he can. I can already hear the inevitable follow-up on the tip of his tongue—why did I really become a surgeon, why did I choose my specialty?

I hear the questions and I don't want to answer them.

Beckett stays there, leaning back in his seat when he answers. "History."

Looking up, I widen my eyes at him. "Oh no, you're one of those."

His lips turn down. "One of what?"

"One of those white boys who loves history a little too much."

Beckett blinks before tipping his head back—this deep, reverberating laugh shakes the column of his throat.

It's a picturesque sight—all of him relaxed, leaning back in this chair, laughing in this beautiful and real way with the last rays of sunlight streaming through the window.

He finally sits up, grinning at me, and the lines around his eyes crinkling, but in happiness this time. He picks his fork up and points it at me before moving onto another plate. "I will give you that one, Dr. Roberts."

I smile at him, and it's real.

But he asks another question before I have a chance.

"My brother said you were a fellow. What does that mean?"

"Oh." I pause, setting down my fork carefully and flexing out my fingers. "Essentially, I'm a board-certified general surgeon. But I'm finishing up additional training in transplant surgery. I'm a second-year transplant and hepatopancreatobiliary surgery fellow. It just means I'll specialize in abdominal organ transplants, basically. Livers, kidneys, and pancreases."

Full lips curve into a smile, and he nods. I think he's about to ask another question, but someone shouts his name.

"Beck!"

He glances over and he's still smiling—it's full of affection, but something, somewhere, seems like it's hurting him just a bit. He raises a hand and beckons them over.

I shift in my seat just as his brother and another two oncology residents I've only seen in passing come to stand beside the table, coffee cups and charts in hand.

"What are you doing here?" His brother looks confused, but when his eyes land on me, his face pales. "Hi, Dr. Roberts."

Beckett tips his chin to me, dimple popping in his cheek, and winks. "Just trying to take Dr. Roberts to a thank-you dinner. Low and behold, she invites me to a place where her meals are free. What do you guys make of that?"

"Sounds like she didn't want to have dinner with you." Dr. Davis grins at Beckett with a shrug, and the other two glance back and forth between us with wide eyes.

"I'm on call. I can't leave," I blurt, and it comes out harsher than I mean it to. All three of them pale now, and I wish I could take it back.

"So she says." Beckett's brows quirk up, and he throws them a good-natured smile.

The one standing on the other side of Dr. Davis peeks her head around, blonde ponytail swinging wildly—Dr. Lowe stitched into the chest of her scrubs. "Congratulations on the fellowship award, Dr. Roberts. You deserved it."

"Oh." I blink. "Thank you, that's very kind."

Beckett cocks his head, and he's looking at me with this faint appraising smile that has his brother glancing back and forth between us, and I think there's a false sort of understanding dawning in his eyes.

Dr. Davis takes a measured step back—he looks infinitely softer and significantly less afraid when he glances back at me. "Well, we should go." He practically drags them away by their elbows.

Beckett watches them before his eyes swing back to me. His voice is low, teasing. "Award?"

He looks at me like, maybe, I've been keeping some sort of secret from him. When really, I just forgot. It was nice when I got the email saying I was being recognized. And then it didn't feel much like anything worth celebrating at all.

I shake my head, looking back at my salad. "It's just a stupid, made-up award. They give them away at this gala the health network hosts each year. One fellow gets one for 'dedication to clinical and surgical excellence.'"

"You're a big deal, eh?" His eyes glint, and all of him looks amused.

"I'm really not."

"You are to me." His voice softens, and my eyes cut up to him. He clears his throat. "I meant it when I said thank you. Thank you for helping me, when you didn't have to. These last few weeks were a lot easier because of you. I'm glad we met."

For some reason, I think of Beckett as a child—Beckett growing up when maybe he shouldn't have had to. Beckett smiling and laughing and grinning when maybe he didn't feel like it. Beckett becoming this person—likeable and reliable—because he didn't have another choice.

And I think of little me. The path carved for her that maybe she didn't want to follow but she had to because other people needed to be whole, so she gave and gave and gave until they were.

Not quite the same, but I wonder if there's a world out there where we grew up as next-door neighbours—where we tied cans together with string and dangled out our windows each night so we could whisper to each other and keep each other safe—little him and little me.

Not the same, but not really all that different.

I set my fork down and flex my fingers again. "I don't date so I don't... I don't have a date. You could come with me. To the gala. If you wanted. One more kick at the PR can."

"As friends?" He tilts his head, all of him suddenly serious and the lines of his jaw looking sharper now that the last rays of the sun are gone.

"Friends. Business acquaintances." I shrug.

He nods once, thoughtful, before grinning. "Yeah, alright. I look incredible in a tux."

I wrinkle my nose, roll my eyes like he's insufferable instead of funny and maybe sort of wonderful. But I'm laughing a bit when I speak. "Shut up."

He smiles at me, entirely different and entirely radiant, before he points at my tray of practically untouched food. "Eat your food. I paid a lot for that."

Greer

Events like this—stupid, made-up, fictional, entirely derived so the health network can pat themselves on the back for producing such fantastic practitioners of medicine, when really we're all miserable and exhausted and disillusioned with the whole thing—really bother me.

I tend to avoid places like this, and not because I'm so mean and miserable like all the PGY1s seem to think because they saw me snap at someone for dropping a retractor.

They're noisy and unpredictable. And even though I wish it was different—that *I* was a different, healed, whole person—unpredictable, loud, jarring noise still bothers me.

I debate not going for a long time—it's quite the debate, actually. I wage it in front of this ornate, golden floor-to-ceiling mirror in my room that's draped with eucalyptus. Stella gave me the plant because she said it's calming. It hasn't worked.

I think I had a temporary blackout in the cafeteria last week—imagining the childhood of someone that, for all intents and purposes, I don't really know—inviting him to come with me when I should have declined the invitation myself. There are all sorts of names for these things—and depending what field of medicine you practice, you might diagnose it differently.

And seeing as I'm very confident I didn't have a cerebrovascular accident, this probably falls firmly under Rav's jurisdiction.

Our brains are funny. Wonderful, magical, endlessly fascinating, and capable of hurting us horribly—but funny.

The leaves of the eucalyptus rustle when the air conditioner kicks on, and I narrow my eyes at it. I'm tempted to jump up and rip it down, but the eucalyptus queen herself kicks open my bedroom door.

Stella smiles brightly at me in the reflection of the mirror. Auburn hair piled high on her head, jade eyes wide with delight. She holds up the seemingly endless pile of garment bags weighing down her arms.

I point up at the eucalyptus. "This stuff doesn't work."

One eyebrow rises and she widens her eyes. "I don't think the eucalyptus is the issue."

In a futile attempt, I reach my arm towards the leaves, but my fingers only skim them before I give up. I watch in the mirror as Stella tosses all the bags on my bed and starts undoing all the zippers, revealing swathes of colour, silk, and to my horror—taffeta.

My lip curls up. "What are all these for? I have dresses that are perfectly fine."

She barely spares me a glance, smoothing out an emerald silk dress. "The plain black ones you've worn to every other event you've had to go to?"

"Yes." I tip my chin up. "And they're *perfectly fine*."

My sister turns to me and snaps her fingers. "Well, it's not every day your sister is being honoured at a banquet with such a prestigious award."

"I've gotten lots of awards, actually." I point to my bookcase, and it's not like it's covered in trophies, but I was chief resident, and stacks of conference awards or high-impact research papers sit askew on the shelves.

Stella rolls her eyes before tipping her head back. "Okay, well her first award she was so humble about."

It's because I don't want it, I think.

Not that I've ever sought out awards, and I was never really one of those highly competitive students or residents when it came to accolades and achievements. I just wanted to study and to do well.

But there's something about this one that feels nefarious, somehow.

An award for clinical and surgical excellence in fellowship.

It makes that spot under my right rib twinge and all I can think about is what I gave up, and what I take from people.

I don't tell my sister those things—I don't want to hurt her. Thoughts like that, how I wonder if maybe I'm doing something wrong when I take an organ from a healthy body and put it into someone else because I have no way of knowing what path these people were set upon without their choice—those are thoughts reserved for Rav.

Stella huffs—loud and significantly deeper than the actual cadence of her voice—before she tips her head back again in exasperation.

She stops rifling through the gowns and pulls out her phone.

"Who are you calling?" I purse my lips.

"Bringing in the expert opinions." Stella snaps her fingers before pointing to the flowers, sitting in an old, chipped vase beside a stack of books on the shelf. "Where did these flowers come from?"

"Oh." I glance over at the flowers; the edges of the lilies starting to brown and wilt. "Beckett gave me those when he finished at the hospital."

Stella isn't listening to me anymore; she's waving excitedly into the phone and spinning around the room. I catch a glimpse of two different screens, slicked-back ebony hair, high cheekbones as sharp as the girl expertly highlighted against olive skin—Willa—and a red bun stacked on top of a head, a small upturned nose smattered with freckles—Kate.

She called my two best friends, which seems a bit absurd, seeing as I'm perfectly capable of dressing myself. They both compliment my style all the time, actually—modern grunge, according to Willa, and comfort in one's own skin, according to Kate.

My sister stops twirling abruptly, pointing at me, and the corners of her lips turning up. "Oh my fucking GOD, Kate—Willa—did you hear that? Beckett Davis—Gatorade-commercial abdominal Adonis—gave Greer those flowers!"

They speak at the same time, and it's a fairly accurate representation of their personalities. Willa speaks with disdain, her voice flat and dripping with poorly veiled displeasure when she says, "Don't you mean Beckett 'Near Miss' Davis?" at the same time Kate gasps and tells me they're beautiful.

"Don't call him that." This weird, innate need to defend him—to defend little Beckett who grew up shouldering expectations he never should have had to bear—rises and makes me want to reach through the phone and pinch my best friend's arm like a child.

Her mouth pops open, expertly lined lips filled by a plastic surgeon who probably charges too much but probably has better work-life balance and brain chemistry than any of his counterparts because he's existing outside of a surgical system meant to break you. "Do you know what he did?"

"What did he do?" Kate peers closer to the camera of her phone, chin propped up on a hand.

Willa speaks before I can, sitting taller in the high-backed leather chair in her office. She's still at work. "He missed not what would have been a record-breaking kick, but a championship-game-winning, first-in-franchise-history kick."

Kate nods, drumming her fingers along her chin. "How unfortunate. Canadian sports fans are so mean, too."

"Greer told me someone threw a Timbit at him." Stella nods sympathetically.

I pinch the bridge of my nose. "I told you that in confidence, Cash."

Stella swings the phone around. "And it remains, in confidence. Inner circle shit. Not to worry."

I see a flash of Willa's palm, followed by her voice. "Wait. How do you even know him? Why is he giving you flowers?"

Before I can answer, another grin splits across Stella's face. "He's volunteering at the hospital. Dr. Roberts generously took him under her wing. But I think it's more than that. She invited him to this gala tonight where she's getting an award for clinical excellence!"

It's not more than that, but I don't know how to explain to my sister that looking at Beckett is a bit like looking in a mirror. A different life, a different path laid out, but it's a reflection all the same.

Kate says congratulations at the same time Willa says it sounds like a date. My sister darts over to me and pushes her face against mine so we're both in the shot and starts singing. "Greer and Beckett sitting in a tree, k-i-s-s-i-n-g!"

I close my eyes briefly and shake my head. "I don't—"

Willa rolls her eyes and bangs her head against the back of her leather desk chair. "We know. You don't date. You're choosing you; you're picking yourself against a job that leaves nothing for anyone else. All pieces of your heart belong to you. We've heard the whole soliloquy."

"I don't think that's fair." My voice drops and cracks a bit, even though I don't want it to. "You're reducing it to some pedantic diatribe when it's not like I got this idea on some self-help infomercial."

My hand finds my rib cage, and I press down. All eyes flick to me, and they watch me make this innocuous, nothing gesture.

But it's not nothing and everything gets heavy. Kate frowns, golden eyes misting over. My sister presses her head to mine, softly—a gesture of love and comfort and not one of mocking. Willa blinks an apology.

"How's your dad?" Kate breaks the silence, and her voice lightens in this way that I know means permission to change the subject.

And I do. Happily.

"Fine. But flu season is coming up, so, Stella, don't forget to get your shot." I take a step back from her and give a pointed look towards the phone. "You two either."

There's a unanimous sort of groan, and a resigned mumble of "Yes, Dr. Roberts," even though I know they mean it fondly.

"Stella—" Willa cuts in, glancing away from her phone. "Can you show us these dresses? I have a meeting soon."

Stella snaps her fingers again, a wide grin stretching across her face when she starts fanning out the dresses on my bed.

The air conditioner kicks on again, and there's this twinge in my chest, but I think I hear the eucalyptus leaves rustle.

Beckett

The last time I stood outside a door like this, in a tux, raising a fist to knock on it, I was eighteen and half drunk, going to my senior prom.

I didn't bring flowers tonight. I'm sure her house isn't a scent-free environment, but in hindsight, the whole bouquet might have been a bit much.

It was a decision made out of exuberance. I'm not sure she really understands, or that words could really convey, what it meant for her to save me twice—once from having to suffer in a pediatric unit where all I'd be able to see was my sister hooked up to tubes, hair fall everywhere, and my parents clinging to nothing, and the second time from having to endure someone else's disappointment.

It was refreshing to be around someone who didn't care about me.

Even though I think it made me wish she did.

I'm finally about to knock when the door gets thrown open. It's not Greer standing there.

Someone who looks enough like her to tell me it's her sister. Hair that could be red under the sun, eyes just a shade lighter than Greer's—but everything else is the same. The nose, the jawline, the high cheekbones.

Even her voice is similar.

"Good evening, Beckett." She grins, eyes flashing, and holds up a phone. It looks like there's an active FaceTime call there, a girl with hair darker than Greer's and a redhead both peering at me.

"You must be Stella." I grin, holding out my hand.

Her face shines, brows rising and eyes wide, delight etched in all her features.

"Great handshake." Her gaze cuts to the side, and she gives a firm nod towards the phone.

Stella drops my hand, pointing to herself. "Sister." She taps the phone. "Best friends."

I nod, repeating with a tip of my chin to her and then the phone, "I'm here to pick up your sister, and your best friend."

She looks triumphant, like I've just revealed something, a bit like she's about to say something more when Greer appears in the doorway behind her.

I flex my hands, lips parting with nothing on them before the corners tug upwards. I take a sharp inhale when I remember to breathe. I've only ever seen her in scrubs and a ratty T-shirt with the name of a fictional restaurant from a movie.

She was beautiful then—but now, I'm not sure.

I think she's something else entirely.

Dark hair slicked back into a high ponytail. Cheeks flushed and lips painted with something that makes them look almost iridescent. Green eyes, looking like gemstones, brighter than probably anything I've ever seen—and this emerald silk sheath dress that ties around her neck, shoulders straight and exposed.

"Enough, Cash." Her eyes flick to her sister, and her cheekbones look like they could cut glass for a second before all of her softens. She raises a hand to her mouth when she walks out, placing her fingers there in some semblance of a kiss I sort of wish was mine, then she waves at her sister and her two best friends, slamming the door behind her.

"You look"—I palm my jaw—"really, really fucking beautiful."

Greer looks up at me and blinks, her cheeks pink, and she smooths the front of her dress unnecessarily. "Thank you. But please don't tell my sister. It's her dress and I don't need the I told you so."

"Were you planning on wearing a pantsuit? Maybe something that screams 'strictly business'?" I grin, trying to pretend like I can't feel my heart in my chest and hold out my elbow.

She tosses me a flat look, eyes sharp and lips pursed, but her hand finds my arm and she gathers her dress in the other. "You'll never know."

"Happy to be your business partner for this venture, Dr. Roberts." I take her porch steps one at a time, slowly, so her heels don't catch, and she rolls her eyes, tugging me along and marching determinedly down the sidewalk towards my truck.

Greer drops her dress, and points at me. "Don't even think about opening my door. Friends don't open friends' car doors."

I hold up my hands, walking backwards around the front cab. "I don't know, I'm starting to think you've got some shitty friends."

She jerks her head back towards her house. "I'm not sure I'd call them shitty, but I'm certain they're probably watching through the phone while my sister peers out the window."

We both turn and look, and there's a distinct swish of the white linen curtain falling back into place.

Greer lifts her eyes skyward with a tiny shake of her head, ponytail dancing behind her before yanking open the door of the truck. "Fucking Cash."

I debate waiting to make sure she gets in okay and doesn't catch her dress on anything or close the door on it, but I doubt that's going to play well, so I walk the rest of the way around the truck and hop in just as she's slamming the door shut.

I glance at her as I start the truck. She shifts in her seat, smoothing out her dress again and fidgeting with her ponytail before taking the small purse from the crook of her elbow and setting it in her lap.

She blinks rapidly and her brow furrows. She looks nervous.

Palming the steering wheel, I glance in the rearview and pull away from the curb. "Why do you call your sister Cash?"

"Childhood nickname. Our dad called her Cashew, and it transitioned into adulthood with her," she answers, but she stares out the window, watching the neighbourhood lights blur into the lower lights of the east end.

"Cashew." I nod, taking another glance at her in the mirror. "What did he call you?"

Greer cuts me a sideways look, tipping her chin up. "Nothing that journeyed with me into adulthood."

I tsk, smiling, and give a jerk of my head. "Secrets don't make friends, Dr. Roberts."

Her chin tips up further. "It's a good thing we're business acquaintances then."

I raise my eyebrows and nod, drumming my fingers on the steering wheel. "Alright, business acquaintance. At least tell me what I'm walking into here. What should I expect at a health network gala where my acquaintance is being honoured?"

She laughs, and it's raspy like her voice. I like the sound. But she doesn't do it nearly enough.

I think I can count on one hand how many times I've heard it, or seen her smile, and I feel a bit like collecting them—keeping them safe in my back pocket.

Greer rolls her shoulders back, like she's trying to relax. "You can expect several burnt-out doctors, self-important surgeons who should have retired years ago, and philanthropists with too much time and too much money that they've run out of worthy causes to spend it on so they make up awards for people like me who are really just nothing but by-products at the end of the day."

Her lips tug down to one side, and her thumb taps against the console of the truck. By-product seems like an off sort of way to refer to herself—to what most people would consider a worthy way to spend your time—but she blinks again, and I think she's keeping more secrets.

I wish she'd give me one of those—I'd put it beside the smiles and the laughter, and I'd make sure it was safe, too.

But she doesn't waver, she's resolute. Greer sits up straighter in her seat just as we pass under a streetlamp, and it catches her eyes and her dress at the same time. She reminds me a bit of a brand-new flower, not quite ready to open, but maybe one day soon.

So, I lean back in the seat, one arm slung over the steering wheel lazily, rap my knuckles on the console beside her hand, and throw her a grin. "You think they like football?"

It is a lot of people with too much time and too much money, too many inflated egos, and too many doctors that look seconds from falling asleep standing up.

But it's a beautiful venue—floor-to-ceiling glass windows on the top floor of a building that belongs to a newspaper right downtown. A giant stage, illuminated with tiny lights, and a small ornate table with three crystal awards practically sparkling. Passed trays of champagne, freshly uncorked and poured, bubbles splashing over the crystal. Low lights and pretentious, small bites of food floating around on silver platters.

More than that—it's a beautiful girl.

For someone who didn't seem like she wanted to be here, she blends in well. She isn't exuberant—but she smiles quietly, politely, at everyone and shakes their hands before introducing me as her friend, Beckett Davis.

I grinned the first time, mouthing the words *business acquaintance* before she gave me a flat look and moved on.

"It looks a bit like a wedding in here," I mutter, glancing sideways at Greer.

"It does." She nods, tapping her champagne flute to her lips, before pointing it at a large acrylic sign hanging suspended before the doorway. "The seating chart is a bit much."

I cringe. It is a bit much. Shoving one hand in the pocket of my suit pants, I drain the rest of my champagne and set it on the table behind me. "Are we sitting with anyone good?"

She snorts, tipping her chin towards a table across the hall. Three men in suits crowd the table, leaning around the towering taper candles that serve as a centrepiece. They all clink what look to be ridiculously expensive glasses before slapping the table and throwing their heads back in what's probably grating laughter.

"They look—"

"Self-important?" Greer widens her eyes at me.

I hold my hands up, giving her a lazy grin. "I was going to say fun. Beckett Davis gets along with all kinds."

Her full lips draw a flat line, still pouted, shining, and made even more beautiful by whatever she painted them with, and she points towards the table before gathering her dress in her hand. "Right. Remind me not to strike up any future business deals with people who speak in third person."

"You know I don't actually speak in third person, right?" I scrub my jaw and extend my elbow to her.

Greer levels me with a look and ignores my offer of escort. "I know, Beckett. It's a joke. Some might call it self-deprecation at its finest. Because who is Beckett Davis, really?"

I smile, exhaling softly, shoving my hands in my pockets, and trail after her—this emerald blur that's really a beautiful woman who says we aren't even friends, but sees right through me all the same.

She raises her hand in greeting when we get to the table, stopping at the only two empty chairs. Two formal place settings wait for us, with two pieces of cardstock propped up in front of smaller, floating candles, our names etched in gold.

Dr. Greer Roberts

Distinguished Laureate: Clinical and Surgical Excellence

Beckett Davis

Guest

I turn to grin at her, about to tell her it's not the worst thing I've ever been called, when someone shouts the worst thing I ever have.

"Near Miss! Heard you were here with one of the honourees." A man sitting directly across from us grins widely, brown cheeks flushed and eyes a little too dazed, like he's had more than one of those nice glasses of scotch. "You're going to come through for us this season, right? You lost me a lot of money last year."

Raising my eyebrows, I pull out Greer's chair even though she wouldn't want me to, and I wait until she folds herself down and straightens her dress before dropping in the seat beside her. I open my mouth, the signature, affable Beckett Davis grin sliding into place. "Hey, if I could place a bet, I'd have lost a lot of money, too. Wasn't banking on missing that kick."

But Greer stills, her voice cool when she speaks. "And how many balls have you kicked professionally, Samir?"

It's the first time she's ever referred to one of her colleagues by their first name.

He blinks slowly, stunned, but then an overlarge smile falls into place that doesn't quite meet his eyes. "I'm a bit busy saving lives for that, but someone has to do it."

It's nothing I haven't heard before, and it's nothing I haven't told myself. Reliable until I wasn't. Not really worth much because I'm not saving lives like my brother or living like my sister, but worth enough to pay everyone's bills when they need me.

I offer him a shrug, irreverent, and toss an arm over the back of the gilded chair. I'm about to tell him how it's the best job in the world because nothing I do really matters when Greer drops her hand to the crook of my elbow.

"Hmm." Greer's lips pull into a thin line and one eyebrow rises. She tilts her head, her eyes flash under the low light, and she looks almost predatory. "That's right. Plenty of emergencies in"—she glances down to the cursive place setting in front of him, angled towards her, before looking back up and giving him a flat smile—"dermatology."

I don't know enough about dermatology or skin in general to really know whether there are a lot of emergencies, or how accurate the sentiment that he spends his days saving lives really is, but I don't really give a shit.

My eyes cut down to where her hand rests, still in the crook of my elbow, fingers taut against my suit jacket. I think it's a protective gesture. I'm not entirely sure—because I don't think anyone has ever actually stood up for me.

Not that I've ever really bothered to set a good precedent and stand up for myself.

But I do know I like the way it feels—like maybe I'm someone. Something more than that random man in the grocery aisle who helped my mother out one time or a person that's nothing more than the sum of a bunch of nondescript adjectives you throw together that mean the same thing.

That maybe Beckett Davis really is real.

The corners of my lips twitch, and Greer presses her fingers down before folding her hands across one another in front of her plate.

"Well." Samir leans forward, smiling tightly, raising his sweating glass of scotch to each of us in succession. "I suppose not everyone can kick, and I suppose not everyone can receive a prestigious award for clinical excellence."

Something dims behind her eyes, her fingers tense against the table, but she just smiles politely.

"Not everyone can be clinically excellent." I shrug, raising my fingers off the back of the chair in a lackadaisical gesture, before glancing sideways at Greer and winking.

She rolls her eyes, but the corner of her mouth kicks upwards.

Samir leans forward, and I get a good look at how glassy his eyes are. I'm probably the least qualified person at the table to be giving any sort of medical advice, but it looks like he shouldn't have another scotch.

He swirls what's left in his glass and gives me a grin that feels a bit more like a leer. "And what makes a kicker excellent? Surely there's some level of precision required there? Or is it as simple as pulling your leg back and taking a swing?"

It's not. It's significantly more complicated than anyone gives it credit for. But I grin, sit up, and point to Greer's almost-empty champagne flute. "Dr. Roberts is definitely going to need another drink before I start boring you all with visualization techniques and the importance of wind speed."

Beckett

Samir has three more glasses of scotch during dinner. He places two unfortunate prop bets on kicks I'm going to miss against certain teams once regular season starts, flashing his phone at me like it's a joke I'm in on.

Greer's hand tightened around the stem of her wineglass, and I think he might have been afraid she was going to smash it and carve him up to take one of his organs, so he put a disproportionately large bet on me breaking the 66-yard field-goal kick record this season.

I haven't given much thought to trying to break another record—I've mostly been concerned about choking and failing everyone miserably. But the idea that he might benefit if I do makes me think I'll make up a lie about the wind not being right if Coach gets me to try.

Greer doesn't say much, offering the occasional comment about research when it's mentioned, and answering questions when she's asked.

But her shoulders relax as the night goes on, and there's this small part of me that hopes I have something to do with that, because more than once, her hand finds my thigh, eyes widening and nostrils flaring, but her forced smile still there when someone says something horribly pretentious.

It became a little game—which of us could grab the other's hand or thigh under the table quicker, who could keep their face straight.

She sits forward in her chair, chin propped up on her hand, the other dangling a third glass of champagne that's almost empty, and this really fucking beautiful pink flush on her cheeks from the alcohol. She's nodding along, listening intently to one of the other doctors at the table talking about regenerative medicine, the first time she's seemed truly interested all night, when the microphone kicks on.

Another man who looks like he's probably had one too many glasses of something, too, steps up to the podium on the illuminated stage at the centre of the room, and I already know it's going to be a cringeworthy speech when he leans forward, tapping the microphone unnecessarily in what might be his version of asking, *Is this thing on?* He doesn't wait for laughter that's never going to come, and starts into a horrifying rehearsed opening line. "Good evening, everyone! What a dinner, am I right? The steak could have put me into cardiac arrest, but I think I spotted a heart surgeon or two holding a sharp knife out in the crowd tonight. Guess I'm in the right place."

"Oh my god," Greer mutters under her breath, cutting me a sideways look.

Smiling, I lean in, dropping my hand to her thigh. "This is the best gala I've ever been to. Truly. Who knew doctors were more self-important than athletes?"

Her eyes sharpen. She plucks my hand off her thigh and makes a show of dropping it back in my lap. Her lips purse, and she's about to say something when the announcer cuts in again.

He calls her name and she starts; glancing towards the stage. There's a small smattering of applause, and she pushes back from her chair.

"You have your speech ready?" I whisper, arching a brow.

"I'll be back in five minutes, and we can get the hell out of here." She cuts me a look, finishes her champagne, gathers her dress in her hand, and walks across the room to the stage.

The clapping gets a bit louder, the presenter does some big rigamarole, jogging around her and gesturing to her, and I know she fucking hates it because she smiles and fakes a laugh when they stop at the podium and he makes a big show of handing her an ugly glass plaque.

Even though she doesn't want to be there, the bright light shining down on her, drawing all this attention to her—it does wonders. She looks beautiful. Hair impossibly shiny, ponytail swinging ever so slightly. Every jut of her collarbones and shoulders defined and on display.

She smiles softly at the presenter before turning and leaning towards the microphone. "Thank you for this. I don't take for granted what it means to have patients who—"

The sound of glass smashing cuts across the relative silence of the room.

I glance over my shoulder. The waiter scrambles to mop up the wine seeping from a tray of broken glasses across the wooden floor and raises their hand in apology to the table nearest them.

But when I turn back, Greer's taken a step back from the podium. Her grip on the plaque slackens. She blinks. Once. Gives a tiny jerk of her head. Blinks twice again in quick succession.

She takes a step forward, and the way her dress pulls, I can see her calf wobble. She pushes her hand against her chest and squeezes her eyes shut again. But when she opens them, she blinks again before forcing this smile and stepping back towards the podium. "Uhm—sorry. What was I saying? I'll just—let's just keep it brief."

Greer presses her hand harder to her chest, the skin of her fingers whitening. Her nostrils flare and she tries to smile but it looks like nothing more than a mechanical movement of some muscles. "Thank you. It's an honour and a privilege."

And then she turns and practically sprints off the side of the stage.

I think the announcer makes a stupid joke about keeping it short and sweet, but I push back to stand just as she throws open a door at the side of the room and actually does sprint through it this time.

My chair makes a scraping noise against the wood, but no one's looking at me, and no one's looking for her. Samir and his friends have their heads down, laughing over something on one of their phones, and everyone else's attention is back on the stage, waiting on bated breath for whatever terrible joke is coming next.

I'm faster than her—the one time in recent memory I'm thankful for these stupid legs and the stupid muscles in them.

I'm across the room and into the hall before she pulls open another door at the end.

I catch up just as she ducks inside.

It's a closet full of random shit, and one sad, dusty light hanging from the ceiling.

"Greer," I say, voice low, reaching forward to grab her shoulder, but she whips around, the stupid glass plaque raised in one hand, her other finding her chest.

"I didn't mean to scare you." I hold my hands up, before reaching behind me and gently closing the door so it's just us in here. "What's wrong?"

"Tachycardia. Dyspnea. Paresthesia."

"Greer"—I palm my jaw—"I don't know what that means."

She pushes her shoulders back against the concrete wall of the closet. "Accelerated heart rate. Shortness of breath. Pins and needles in your hands and fingers."

"What—"

She exhales, nostrils flaring, before taking in a gulp of air. "Panic attack."

I reach for her, but this sob catches in her throat, and my hand flexes uselessly in midair instead. I don't know how to help her. I take the plaque from her hand and set it on the ground before standing back up and leaning my head down so we're eye level. Her eyes—usually effervescent, cunning, beautiful—they're wide and she looks like a startled deer. "What happened? I need you to tell me what happened so I can try to fix it."

"The glass shattering." She closes her eyes and shakes her head. "It sounded like the window—when the window shattered."

"No window shattered," I tell her, leaning forward and grabbing her chin. She looks like she's going to dislocate her fucking neck.

Greer opens her eyes, nodding up at me with flared nostrils and tears streaming down her face. "It did. In the car accident."

"Car accident," I repeat, letting go of her chin and grabbing her shoulders. "You might have been in a car accident before, but it wasn't tonight, okay?"

Her voice cracks. "But I heard it. And now I can feel it."

She presses her hand to her chest, shifts back and forth on her feet, like she's trying to shake something off and she can't because it won't let her go no matter how hard she tries.

I drop my forehead to hers. "How can I help you? Tell me what you need."

"My Lorazepam. I don't have my meds. I don't—"

I pull back. "Are they in your purse? I'll go get it."

She shakes her head again, a tiny jerk of a movement. "No. No. I didn't—I didn't bring them. I didn't think—"

I hate how she looks right now. I fucking hate seeing her like this. "Okay, what can I do? What do you need?"

"I need you to tell me what you see. What you feel in the room." She gasps and pushes her hand against her chest. The other grips my arm through my suit. "The water. I can feel the water on my legs."

I shake my head, dropping down to my knees and grabbing her calves through her dress. "There's no water, Greer. Do you feel my hands?"

She's still shaking her head, hand finding my shoulder and her nails digging in. "I can—"

"Breathe."

She inhales and her shoulders shudder.

"Breathe. There's no water. It's just me touching you." I move my hands just under the hem of her dress, wrapping each one around her calves and pressing my palms into her skin. "Do you feel my hands?"

She squeezes her eyes shut again, but she nods.

"Eyes on me." I press my thumb into her calf and start moving it in small circles. "Greer, open your eyes. Look at me."

Her eyelashes flutter, but her eyes do open. They're too bright, lined with tears.

I look around. It's just a closet, filled with forgotten shit that no one would miss. But she's looking at everything like it's hurting her impossibly. "Tell me what you see, and I'll tell you what's real, okay?"

She nods and takes another inhale. Her hand presses against her chest, and her fingers dig into my shoulder. "Coats."

"Real," I answer.

"Broken umbrellas," she whispers.

"Real." I nod.

She blinks. "A stack of boxes."

"Real." I smile softly, pressing my fingers into her calves.

"You. I see you."

I swallow. "Real."

Beckett Davis. A real, whole person after all. Who knew.

Greer blinks, her grip loosens against my shoulder, fingers feathering softly, and the knuckles on her hand pressed against her chest go from white to pink. Her voice is impossibly small, but it cracks when she speaks. "I don't feel the water anymore."

"It was never here. It was never real, okay?"

"It was." The corners of her lips tug up in a sad smile I hope I never see her make again, and she gives me a tiny shrug. "Once upon a time."

I nod, and I press my forehead against her thigh before looking back up at her. "But not this time. Okay?"

"Okay," she repeats.

We stay there, silent, staring at each other—two real people surrounded by real things that aren't here to hurt us, just to collect dust.

I watch her take another deep breath, and I don't mean to do it, but I breathe in and out with her. Like we're in this together, we're going to take in the same amount of oxygen, be on an even playing field until she can breathe as well as she deserves and needs to feel better.

She looks at me like she's relying on me, and for once, the idea of it—reliable, dependable, Beckett Davis—doesn't feel like this burden that's going to weigh me down so much it sends me crashing through the floor into the sub-basement of whatever hell our expectations go to die.

My shoulders straighten. It feels easy, to carry something when she needs me to.

My thumbs still move in these small, tiny circles against the muscles of her calves.

My eyes stay on hers until she takes this little, even, low, regular breath that somehow looks beautiful.

"You feel better?" My voice is rough.

Greer nods a bit, giving me another sad smile. "Steady. My heart feels close to normal again. Lungs feel full and no more pins and needles."

"And the water?" I ask, drumming my fingers against her calves.

"Still gone."

"Good." I try to give her a reassuring smile. "What else can I do for you?"

"Nothing." She shakes her head, finally dropping her hand from her chest to my other shoulder. "Unless you can give me an injection of fast-acting serotonin or dopamine."

I give a jerk of my chin. "Sadly, fresh out of syringes with readied injectable brain chemicals in my suit jacket. What else gives that?"

"Some foods. Things that help you relax. Yoga. Massage. A cute animal video." Greer shrugs, her shoulders curving inwards a bit, skin somehow illuminated under the dim light. "An orgasm."

She says it through this tiny raspy laugh and it's meant to be a joke—but it doesn't feel like one.

My fingers tense against her calves. My suit jacket suddenly feels too tight, and I swallow, eyes on her.

Greer blinks, lips parting and her cheeks going pink. "A joke."

"A joke," I repeat. I don't find it funny—my cock doesn't find it funny. I like the idea of it. Making her feel good—being someone who takes care of her when I think she spends most of her time taking care of everyone else.

My thumb starts in slow circles against her skin again, and I grin up at her. "I don't mean to brag. But I've been told I'm pretty good. I can get you there."

Her teeth come down on her bottom lip, and another small rasp of laughter catches in her throat.

But she swallows, blinking at me, and her fingers still against my shoulders.

I slide my hand up her calf, over the arch of her knee. The silk of her dress shifts, and I pause, fingers hovering over the skin of her thigh. My lips part and I don't look away from her, waiting for any sign of permission that she wants me to reach up just a bit higher.

Her eyes flick down to her dress, the silk resting above my hand and when she looks back up at me, she inhales, moving her head in a tiny nod.

Grinning at her, I move my hand up past her knee, a shiver whispering over her when I trace the inside of her thigh.

We stare at each other as my hand climbs higher, fingers finding the edges of lace covering her. I graze where it meets her skin, and she gives me another small nod of permission.

My thumb scores up the centre of her, stopping right between her thighs. Her pupils widen, and she inhales.

I wish we were under the brightest sun in the world—so I could see everything about her, nothing shadowed under the dim light, but I know she looks beautiful: impossibly dark hair and bright eyes, full lips parting and a blush on the apple of her cheeks.

"Do you like this?" I ask, voice rough.

Greer nods. "It feels—" Her head tips back and her lips part when I move my thumb in a circle, before dragging it slowly down the centre of the lace. "It feels—I do, like it."

"Lift your dress up."

My hand stays where it is, moving in slow circles, tracing her, in reverence for this otherworldly girl who trusted me with something so much more than just her body. I can feel the lace get wetter when the silk of her dress slides up her thighs, until she holds it in one hand, revealing the underwear covering her.

I pull my hand back, and I don't think she means to, but she makes a small whimper and I grin up at her, grabbing either side of her underwear, slowly pulling it down her legs until it pools around her heels.

I lift one foot up, sliding the lace off, gently setting it back down and doing the same with her other foot, before I grab her leg and hoist it over my shoulder.

Her heel digs into my back, and I don't think I've ever been more turned on by someone in my entire life.

My eyes cut to her, bared to me, before I glance back up.

Her teeth come down on her lip again.

I swallow. "May I?"

Greer gives me one small final nod of permission, and I watch her teeth dig into that full bottom lip again.

I lean forward, inhaling, before sliding my tongue up and stopping at her centre.

"Fuck—you taste—" I groan, hoisting her thigh up higher and burying my face deeper. "I could fucking live here."

Another rasp of laughter, followed by a sharp intake of breath, and she moans my name. "Beckett."

I don't think I've ever wanted to be me more than I do right now—on my knees for her, head between her legs, tongue soaked with her, this girl who keeps too many secrets, with those beautiful eyes that hide someone who's nicer than she pretends to be, and a mouth that breathed life back into a person who wasn't even real.

"Say my name again," I ask against her, one hand gripping the muscles of her thigh so hard I think I'm going to leave a bruise on her skin, and I hope I do. I bring my other hand up, two fingers sliding inside her, moving slowly with the circles of my tongue.

She says it again, softer this time, one hand raking through my hair, and I'm real, I know I am, because how could I be anything else when she says my name like that—a tiny whisper, a tiny moan, with the tiny shift of her hips, bringing all of her closer to me.

Beckett.

I move my tongue in another circle. My hand grips her thigh, and my fingers move into her and out of her slowly.

Beckett.

I keep doing it—slowing down when she tells me to and moving faster when her fingers tug on the hair at the crown of my head.

Beckett.

My cock strains in my pants. I keep moving my tongue the way she seems to like, these deep circles, slower and faster, and I feel her clench against my fingers.

I flick my eyes up just as her back arches, her head tips back, and her eyes close—but her mouth opens, this fucking moan I want to hear for the rest of my life, and I keep going until her shoulders soften, those green eyes open and she blinks, looking down at me, cheeks flushed and everything about her radiant.

Pulling back even though I don't want to, I slide my fingers out of her—I meant it, I could live between her legs. I press my lips gently to her thigh and set her leg down.

I lean back, rolling my shoulders, my hands finding my thighs. I feel a bit like bringing my fingers to my mouth instead, so she can watch and see how fucking good she tastes, but this wasn't about me.

"That—uhm—" Greer breathes, eyes wide and bright and beautiful, before she drops her dress. "Thank you. That was—you did, get me there. Your endorsements were accurate. We should—we should get back to the party."

"You'll have to give me a minute." I grin, undoing my zipper and untucking my shirt so I can adjust the hard-on that's probably never going away for the rest of my life.

Her eyes flick down to my hands, watching, until I tuck my shirt back in and do my pants back up. I grab her underwear from the floor before shoving them in my pocket and pushing to stand. "You can put these in your purse later."

She laughs, and it echoes in the space that seems significantly smaller than it did before.

We're just on this side of touching, and if I moved not even an inch, I'd be pressing her against the wall.

Greer tips her chin up, offering me a small smile before she whispers softly, "Thank you."

I swallow. "Anytime."

I angle my head down, and her chin tips up just a tiny bit more.

Only a breath between us, and I lean in.

My lips brush hers, and hers brush mine, too. Just for a brief moment in time, forever to be locked in this closet with the dust-covered coats, umbrellas, boxes, and real her and real me—before she reaches down, grabs her plaque, opens the door, and I follow her back into the hallway.

Beckett

Apparently, surgeons don't get flustered. They're all masters of control and staying calm, cool, and collected.

Greer got back to our table and dropped into her seat like nothing happened, all polite smiles and thank-yous to anyone who stopped by to congratulate her.

But I could still taste her, feel her on my tongue, and had a distinctly hard time concentrating on anything else.

At one point, she dropped her purse into her lap and opened her hand to me.

"You weren't going to let me keep them?" I leaned forward, pulling the still-wet lace from my suit pants, and holding it out to her between two fingers. My voice was still rough, and all she'd have to do was look down and see me straining against my suit pants to know how turned on I still was, and probably would be forever.

She gave me a flat look and stuffed them in her purse, going back to the conversation like nothing happened.

Something did happen—and I don't think I'll forget it for the rest of my life.

The girl. The way she tasted. The way she felt against my tongue and fingers when she came.

What it was like for her to trust me.

Not because she thought I was dependable and reliable.

But because she saw the real me and still thought I was worthy.

It's probably dramatic, but everything feels different now. Like that girl altered my brain chemistry in that empty closet. Reached down with her hands that save lives, curled her fingers around my heart, and whispered that it should come back to life.

She looks different—shoulders straight, all that exposed skin alight under the moon.

We're just walking down the street to where I parked the truck, but she's got this pensive look on her face, silk of her dress fluttering around her legs, and she looks a bit like she should be wading into the water of a moonlit beach somewhere, thinking about burning the world down. I palm my jaw, glancing sideways at Greer. "Are you okay, to be in the truck? To drive home?"

She wraps her arms around herself against the night air. I'd take my suit jacket off and put it around her, but I doubt that would play well.

She tips her chin up, seemingly eyeing the stars in the sky before she stops in front of the truck. Her eyes cut to me, and she nods. "It was a long time ago. I get in cars and drive all the time. They don't scare me."

I don't say anything until we're both in the truck, and I'm driving down the street. "What happened?"

"Just your run-of-the-mill car accident on a bridge that ended with us in the water. I was with my dad and my sister."

She says it like it's nothing, and I take my eyes off the road to look at her. She's turned away from me, plaque discarded on the floor in front of her, purse in her lap and arms still crossed over her chest. "How old were you?"

"I was seventeen. Stella was fifteen."

My fingers tighten on the steering wheel. "Was everyone okay?"

"Eventually," she says softly, and I glance away from the empty city streets again. Her forehead rests against the window, eyes tracking all the buildings we pass, and the streetlights casting shadows across the sharp edges of her face.

"But it still bothers you?"

I see her shrug one shoulder from the corner of my eye. "Sometimes."

"Is that what happened the day outside the hospital? With the Gatorade commercial?" I ask, and I think she nods.

"Yes. There were sirens and a car backfired..." Her voice trails off, and I think that's all she's going to say, but she keeps talking. "It's a lot better than it used to be. But sometimes, when I'm not expecting it, my nervous system reacts before my mind can tell it to stop. That it's just a noise. That I'm not in a car. That I'm not sinking."

I see her shift in her seat, and I think, maybe I'm starting to understand her a bit more. "The car accident—is that why you became a surgeon?"

Greer turns, cocking her head and studying me. "Something like that."

I nod, even though I know it's just another half-truth, offering her a small smile that she returns before she looks back out the window.

We don't say anything for the rest of the drive. I'd usually try to fill the silence, to distract her, and if she was someone else who gave her smiles and laughter away more freely, maybe I'd grin at her and try for one of those.

But I don't think she needs me to, and I think I like being quiet with her.

Her street is empty, fewer houses with lights shining than the last time I dropped her off. But her porch light is on.

The curtain doesn't move when I park the truck out front, so I can't imagine her sister is in there. She seems like the type to wait all night, watching with another FaceTime call at the ready.

I think about Greer—nothing under that dress—and if I was a worse person, I think I'd ask if I could come inside.

But even though she says she's fine, her cheeks are softer than usual, lips parted at the Cupid's bow I'd love nothing more than to kiss, and all of her tired.

She unbuckles her seat belt, slides her purse back onto the crook of her elbow, and turns to me. "Well, thank you for coming. I'm sorry you spent more time in a closet with me than you did clearing your good name, but Samir stands to make some money if you perform this season."

I glance down at her mouth. "I'm really not complaining." She snaps her fingers and gives me a flat look, but she seems amused, a tiny lift at the corner of her lips. I grin at her and shrug. "Thank you, for all your help. Regular season starts next week so I guess this is it, for now."

Greer studies me for a second before her eyebrows rise. "Call me, if you ever have another business proposal."

If it was anyone else saying that to me, I'd think it was an invitation to ask her out. But she's not anyone else. I drum my fingers against the steering wheel. "Hey, it's a long season. I'm sure I'll miss something important at some point and come crawling back to you, tail between my legs."

She tilts her head, lips tugging to the side as she shrugs, turning and opening the door. One hand grabs her dress as she hops down from the bed of the truck. She turns back to me. "Maybe. But I doubt it. You don't strike me as the type to miss more than once. Good night, Beckett."

She doesn't wait for me to respond, shutting the door. I don't think I have anything to say, so I watch her walk away, but I notice the plaque still on the floor in front of the passenger seat.

Rolling down the window, I lean forward and call after her. "You forgot your award."

Greer looks over her shoulder, sharp features appraising before she wrinkles her nose. "Keep it. You deserve it after your performance. Great legs, great tongue. Who knew?"

She smiles softly, raising a hand before gathering her dress again and starting down the walkway towards her apartment.

I watch, waging an internal war and seriously considering sprinting after her, pinning her to a nearby tree and fucking her brains out. I shift in my seat, pulling at the thigh of my suit pants. They've been too tight ever since we left the closet, my cock permanently hard all night because of her.

My hand reaches for my seat belt, like it's got a mind of its own, but she pauses right before the bottom stair, turning back around. She tips her head, ponytail dancing over her shoulder, and she blinks those eyes at me before she says, "Peanut."

My brow furrows. "What?"

"Cashew and Peanut." She shrugs one shoulder. "Our nicknames as kids. My dad called me Peanut."

"Huh." I nod, the corner of my lip kicking up. It might not seem like much, but I know she just gave me something, cracked open the door of hers she keeps closed and shared a secret with me. Whispered it to me like a child might.

I tuck it in my back pocket with her smile and her laugh.

Greer raises her hand again and she goes to turn, but I lean forward so I'm closer to the open window. I want her to hear me, and I hope she knows I mean it. "You've listened to me for the last few weeks. If you ever want to talk to someone, I'd be happy to listen to you."

Her smile turns rueful, and her hand stays up in farewell this time. "Good night, Beckett."

"Night, Dr. Roberts."

I wait until she's inside, and when the door shuts, I see the curtain pull to the side. A flash of auburn hair and the shadow of someone hopping off the couch and sprinting across the room.

I kind of wish it was me in there with her, but I'm glad she's not alone.

Greer

I see Rav the third Tuesday of every month. Unless I have an emergency surgery, or my dad needs something, I'm punctual and I don't reschedule.

I thought about rescheduling this session—mostly because I can still feel Beckett's hands and eyes—his tongue—on me.

We haven't spoken since, other than a simple thank-you text I sent, that he followed up with a simple *anytime*.

Just a simple word, but I can imagine the way he'd say it—the lazy grin he'd toss my way, the shadow of the dimple.

It's not a simple thing, whatever happened between us, and I think that scares me.

I've been sitting silently on Rav's couch for ten minutes. I'm not trying to lie this time—he says most of the lies I tell are things I don't even realize, because it's not as if I set out to keep things from him. When I do feel like speaking, he says I'm honest to a fault. But there are these other things, and I think they must exist outside the confines of my lines—my cage—and that's usually where the lies start.

He usually waits for me to start, but today, he speaks first. "Congratulations on the honour. I'm sorry I wasn't able to attend."

I offer a tight smile. "You didn't miss much."

Amusement flashes behind his eyes when he taps his pen three times against his clipboard. "No? Nothing?"

I narrow my eyes. Rav stares back at me like he knows something I don't, or like he's waiting for me to spill some big proverbial secret about the night. I roll my shoulders back and tip my chin up, even though my skin heats and my heart stumbles the way it's started to whenever I think about the closet.

Beckett on his knees.

But there's no way he knows I let Beckett Davis go down on me in a hallway closet. He's a psychiatrist, he's not clairvoyant.

"Nothing noteworthy." I shrug.

His hand stills, and he pockets the pen, leans forward, and looks at me with this air of maddening patience.

I can tell he's going to wait today—that I won't win—so I roll my eyes and say, "I'm sure word has reached your ears that Beckett accompanied me."

Triumph flashes in his eyes. He leans back, folding his arms over his chest. "Does this mean you've changed your mind?"

"A girl can have friends." I tip my chin up, hoping he can't see the blush rising on my cheeks, or somehow detect the way my stomach tightens.

"There would be nothing wrong if you told me you were interested in someone. It doesn't mean you aren't putting yourself first. It wouldn't make you a failure," Rav says slowly, like he's explaining something to an infant.

"I'm not interested in him," I answer firmly, resolutely, but the way my heart dips and my thighs clench at the thought of Beckett probably say something else.

He pinches the bridge of his nose. "And I doubt you would tell me even if you were. But maybe you can tell me how the gala went? How did you feel about the award?"

I push back against the worn leather of the couch, setting my shoulders in a haughty line. "You know as well as I do, it's a made-up award."

"You might be right about that. But you still received the award for your work." He smiles encouragingly, but I say nothing, and in an uncharacteristic display, he drops back against the couch, raising his hands. "It seems like you're feeling particularly difficult today, Dr. Roberts, and we both know the more I push, the more you push back. So, why don't you just tell me about your evening?"

He's right—I am being particularly difficult, and I'm not entirely sure why.

I pucker my lips and give a tiny shake of my head. "It was fine. Until someone dropped a tray of champagne when I was accepting the award, and it sounded so much like a car window shattering, I sprinted off the stage and had a panic attack in a closet."

He cocks his head. "Did you take your meds?"

"I didn't bring them. I didn't think—it was stupid. I should have had them." I look away, like he's a parent and I've disappointed him.

"And what did you do without them?"

"Beckett—we breathed together. He told me about everything that was real in the room. Umbrellas. Coats. Boxes. Him. That there was no water." I can feel his hands—wide and splayed across my calves, thumbs rubbing these small, soothing circles. And I can see him, on his knees in front of me—chocolate hair mussed, green eyes staring up at me in the dim light, and the stretch of his shoulders under his suit. Unwavering.

I don't particularly like the way it makes me feel—like maybe I could waver, that there's a version of me who would drop to her knees, too, and cut out whatever piece of her he asked for, so I blink up at Rav, smiling blandly before continuing. "And then he went down on me and gave me an orgasm so I could relax."

Rav doesn't blink. He just nods. "Quick thinking. That's certainly one way to produce dopamine and serotonin. Surefire relaxation."

"Maybe you can change your prescribing habits."

He doesn't bite.

"And did you tell him about the car accident? All of it?"

I arch an eyebrow. Rav stares back at me, like it was a legitimate question. It's not. It's not the type of thing I tell people. "Did I tell him our father was so inebriated when he got behind the wheel with his two teenage daughters that he drove us off a bridge and the car flipped over and over and over until it landed upside down in the water? That it shattered my ribs and fractured my sister's skull and practically destroyed her pancreas? No. I didn't tell him that."

He opens his palm. "And why not?"

"It's not exactly friendly dinner conversation."

"You weren't having dinner," Rav states, matter-of-fact.

I tip my head. "Oh? And what was I supposed to say? Yes, right there—keep doing that with your tongue. By the way, did you know my father almost killed me?"

"I can see this is a useless avenue for us to pursue today." He raises his hands again, and I feel triumphant until he continues. "Have you thought about what you want to do after your fellowship?"

"I imagine I'll keep stealing organs." I want my words to come out dry, irreverent even, but my voice cracks horribly. The edges of my vision blur, and I slap at my cheeks, trying to stop the tears before they escape out into the world.

I think Rav shakes his head softly, that the blurred version of him might lean forward, rest his elbows on his knees, and sound impossibly sad when he speaks. "Greer . . ."

"What?" I sniff.

"After all this time—all this work we've done—is that really what you think? That it's stealing?"

"Sometimes." I put my hands under my legs so I don't tear up the seams of his leather couch. "But other times, I think it's wonderful and lovely and the best thing I could ever do with my life."

His eyes cut to the clock, propped up on a stack of psychiatry texts on the table, angled towards him. "I know we don't do homework. But between now and our next session, I want you to think about both of those things—the sometimes and the other times—and we can spend ten minutes on each at the start of our time together."

I say nothing, and he continues. "You might feel like someone stole from you, you might feel this innate need to protect what's left, but sometimes the best thing we can do is open ourselves up. All those spaces that you think are empty could be full again."

I smile, like I'm thinking about it. But I don't have the heart to tell him that even though there's nothing empty inside me, because your liver is actually this beautiful organ that can heal and regrow, I'm not sure when it was going about the business of healing itself, it ever bothered to heal me, too.

Beckett

The kicking net in the spare bedroom of my apartment takes up most of the back wall.

It was the one requirement I had of my real estate agent—find me a place with a spare room big enough for the net.

It would have been more practical if I'd bought a place with a yard or moved into a suburb like my parents.

But I wanted to be in the city. I had the money, and my real estate agent had the time.

He came through in the end, with a converted two-story loft in the west end with insanely high vaulted ceilings.

It's stupid—but I've always felt like I can breathe easier in here. No expectations, no burdens to bear. Just me.

My family always joke that it's harder to get a hold of me when I'm home, like it's some funny thing, the exact opposite of what it should be. I grin when they say it, offering them a shrug—like it's just me, Beckett Davis, who, despite being reliable and dependable, doesn't take things too seriously.

But it's on purpose. I keep my phone on do not disturb, and to the chagrin of my agent, I go hours without checking it.

Today, though, two things are taunting me, warring for my attention. The kicking net, probably going to fray or wear through soon if I keep sending footballs into the top corners and the middle.

And my phone, set to vibrate, sitting on an end table against the opposite wall, in between an empty protein shake and exercise bands I threw there after my workout.

It was a bit aspirational to turn on my notifications—the only person I want to disturb me probably won't.

Even if she's thinking about me the way I'm thinking about her—on a constant fucking loop—she's not that kind of girl.

I glance away from the phone, swinging my arm up in line with the middle of the net before hinging my leg a few times.

It's a visualization thing most kickers do. When I emerged as an accidental phenomenon with the stupidest skill set ever, my college coach sent me straight to a kicking camp and hired a kicking coordinator, which is something you rarely even see at the professional level.

But he believed in me, and I'm not sure anyone ever had before, so I bought into the whole thing. Visualization, mindfulness, stillness, yoga. You name it, I did it all.

It worked until it didn't.

It's not working today—every time I line up a kick, my knee comes into my periphery and all I think about is what the concrete floor of that closet felt like underneath it.

What it felt like to be on my knees for her. The point of her heel digging into my back. The sounds she made. How she tasted. How she felt around my fingers and how she might feel around something else.

What it was like for someone to trust me. The real me.

I swing my leg, my foot makes contact with the football, propped up on a stand instead of held in front of me by a punter, and it goes careening into the top left-hand corner.

If this were a game, it would probably be fair, but it might hit the uprights.

My quad twinges uncomfortably, and I pound a fist into it before palming my jaw. "This is fucking pointless."

"What's pointless?"

My brother leans against the doorway, arms crossed over his chest, looking at me expectantly.

I shake my head, not bothering to retrieve the football from where it sits in the corner of the net, then cross the room and check my phone again before conceding defeat for another ten minutes. "What are you doing here? You didn't call or text."

Nathaniel gives a shake of his head, nostrils flaring with an exhale. "Beck, you don't answer. It's always easier just to show up."

"Oh." I don't tell him that I would have answered today, probably sprinted across the room to grab my phone in time in case it was someone else on the other end. "Sorry, I guess I didn't hear you come in. I've been up here for a while."

"Practicing?" Nathaniel asks, eyes sweeping over me and pausing on the exposed muscle of my thigh. I can feel it jumping—a sign it's too tired. "You ready for the season to start?"

No.

But I grin, grabbing my water and taking a swig before shrugging. "Ready as I'll ever be."

Historically, my family haven't been good at telling the difference between a fake smile and a real one—they went almost two decades without noticing.

Something flashes behind my brother's eyes, and he might notice today.

All it took was my public decimation before any of them started to realize that I was a real person.

Nathaniel nods. His jaw tenses, and he looks like he might say more, but his eyes go to my thigh right as the muscle gives another twitch. "Make sure you—"

I raise my eyebrows at him, pointing with my water bottle to the hallway behind him. "I know what to eat for muscle recovery, Nathaniel. I'm good."

He holds his hands up before pushing off the doorframe and disappearing down the hallway.

I pocket my phone, even though I know it's not going to go off, take one last look at the football nestled into the corner of the net, and follow my brother.

He's halfway down the wrought-iron spiral staircase, but he calls back, "I saw you guys traded for Pat Perez. Didn't you play together in college?"

"Yeah, for a bit. He came up last week. Should be good." I wince on the first step, a cramp starting in my right leg. I consider hobbling down the stairs after my brother, but I don't want to prove his point.

Fortunately, he's looking away when I step off the final stair, and a lazy grin slides into place just as he glances back at me.

Nathaniel stops at the kitchen island, drumming his fingers on the granite. "I saw your photos online, the spread Yara did about you volunteering at the hospital. Nice article about all the inner work you've been doing in the offseason. Visualization. Yoga. Time on the lake. Connecting to important causes."

His voice drips with irony when he says it. None of it was true, just a sad attempt at convincing everyone Beckett Davis won't fuck up again. I shake my head. "I didn't read it."

Yara told me it went live, and she seemed happy with the media pickup and response. But I wasn't interested. I stopped looking at the comments section of my social media when everyone started telling me how much they hated me.

Disbelief colours his face, and he folds his arms across the counter, leaning down. "You didn't read it? That's unlike media darling Beck Davis."

I know he doesn't mean for it to be rude. I know he sees all the media and press I've done—the endorsements and the commercials, everything the team's publicist and Yara trotted me out to do because I happened to be more likeable and photogenic than any other kicker alive—and he thinks it means I revel in the attention.

I don't, not really. I just did it because it was what was expected of me.

That's the thing about my family—they don't mean for any of it to hurt.

They love me, but they don't love me the same as they love each other.

I lift a shoulder, offering him another lazy grin, and change the subject. "What are you doing here? It's Sunday night. Shouldn't you be prepping for a week of saving lives?"

His eyes flash, like he wants to press, but he doesn't. "I was dropping off some stuff to Sarah and Lily. Lily just had another egg retrieval on Friday, and she's feeling pretty tired."

"Oh." I glance at the calendar hanging beside the fridge. It's littered with my messy penmanship, marking different workouts, daily caloric intake, and anything else I need to remember. But it's not the type of thing I would have forgotten. "Sarah didn't tell me. I guess I just write the cheques."

Nathaniel cocks his head. That same muscle in his jaw jumps, but his voice is uncharacteristically soft. "I think she just didn't want to stress you out this close to the start of the season."

He pauses, and when I don't say anything, he clears his throat and continues. "She worries about you, you know. We all do. I think you put an astronomical amount of pressure on yourself, Beckett."

I open my mouth to tell him it doesn't feel like that—that it's never felt like that—but I blink, and I see my brother the way I used to: small shoulders curved inwards over his textbooks, scribbling away to make sure his homework was done before our parents got home from the hospital. All while I studied game tape and memorized routes in between making sure everything was clean, neat, and tidy for our parents, because their minds and their hearts certainly weren't, and tried not to burn his dinner.

I blink again, and he's the adult version of himself now—and logically, I know he's fine on his own. That he's big enough and old enough and mature enough to navigate a difficult conversation with his brother—that maybe they all are—but I think a part of me got stuck back there and the idea of adding another brick, another weight, to those small shoulders of my brother makes me want to vomit.

"Thought you were an oncologist, not a psychiatrist." I raise my hands and start walking backwards towards the fridge.

Nathaniel narrows his eyes at me, like he isn't going to let this go and it's a hill he's happy to die on today, but his gaze cuts to the middle of the island. Greer's award's still there, right where I left it when I got home the other night. "Why do you have this?"

He reaches across to grab the plaque; the setting sun streaming through the windows hits it just so, illuminating her name.

Bright and impossible to miss, kind of like the girl.

"Oh." I swallow, palming my jaw, before offering him a noncommittal shrug. "She forgot it in my truck the other night after the gala."

I don't bother telling my brother she said I could keep it, or why.

Great legs, great tongue. Who knew?

He eyes the award before looking back up at me. "Are you with her or something?"

"No." I turn around, pulling open the fridge and rolling my shoulders back. "She doesn't date."

I'm making a show of pulling open all the crispers, like I'm on the hunt for the perfect fucking bell pepper instead of thinking about my head between Greer's legs, when my brother asks, "If she did—would you . . . want to?"

"Just friends." I grab the first thing I notice—an apple that looks like it's seen better days. I turn back to Nathaniel, grin, and toss the apple in the air a few times. "Hardly even friends, actually. Business acquaintances is probably a better term."

His lips pull down. Nathaniel appraises me, and I raise my eyebrows at him, tossing the apple to catch again before taking a bite.

"You know she really didn't know who you were when you stopped by the hospital that first day, right? That must be nice for you . . . someone with no preconceived notions. No expectations. No interest in your yearly salary." He shakes his head, setting the award down. "What are you doing for the rest of the night? I know you're probably back at the stadium for meetings and practice this week, but we could go grab some food? Catch a movie?"

I glance down at the award, the sun's rays barely touching it now as they slowly slink back across the granite.

No expectations. No preconceived notions. Just her saying my name.

Beckett.

Real her and real me.

"You know what?" My eyes cut from the award to my brother. "I actually have something I need to do. Make yourself comfortable, stay if you want. But, uh, I have to go."

I toss the apple into the garbage and grab my keys off the counter before I can change my mind.

Greer

I fiddle with the edge of the Band-Aid on my shoulder before ripping it off.

There's no blood, and I can hardly see the injection site.

I glance at my shoulder in the bathroom mirror, rotating it twice before tossing the Band-Aid. It's a bit stiff, but nothing out of the ordinary.

I dragged my father and sister to the clinic at the hospital this morning so he could get the high-dose flu shot he needed, and I took the opportunity to force my sister to sit still for three seconds so she could get one, too.

A nice, wholesome family outing.

Or it would have been if maybe they seemed to care and I didn't have to drag them.

It hurt me, when I had to remind them that he needed to take care—that we all needed to.

Stella had looked back at me with an exasperated sigh before slamming my car door and parroting my earlier words, "We know, livers don't grow on trees. We need to take care of them."

They don't grow on trees.

But one grew in me, and I gave it away, and sometimes I think I didn't want to.

I blink in the mirror, and my eyes travel down to the right side of my rib cage, the scar that sits there just under my T-shirt, slightly raised and pink, even after all these years.

I look back up, tipping up my chin, and I notice the things in me I see in my sister and my father: the cheekbones, the eyes, even though they're different shades of green, and all the things that sit just below the surface.

And I try to remember what it was all for.

The leaves of Stella's eucalyptus, draped over the golden edges of the mirror, rustle in the cool night air drifting through the open window in my bedroom.

When I leave the bathroom, I debate going in, inhaling, seeing if those leaves will finally do something—but I notice the gown from the gala, draped over the arm of a chair in the corner of my room.

And then I think of Beckett.

I think of his eyes when I round the corner from the hallway into my living room.

I think of his hands, firmly gripping my legs and keeping me afloat, rooted to the real ground and not helplessly suspended in a body of water, when I grab my book where I left it on the shelf.

I think of him breathing, in and out with me, when I light the candle in the middle of my coffee table.

I think of his hands moving higher, stopping at my knees, the way his eyes flicked up to mine for permission, when I sit down on the couch.

NEAR MISS

I try not to think of him anymore when I pull out my bookmark from where I left off. But I can't really see the words in front of me—they blur, my brain skips over them, and I have to double back.

I'm not really seeing anything. Only him, I think.

I see him: this effervescent person who tries to pretend that maybe he doesn't take things seriously. But he took me seriously.

I see him staring at me intently, nodding ever so slightly, before a gentle smile turns into a grin, and those hands slide higher.

But I don't see what comes next because my doorbell rings.

I drop my book, and I'm not really thinking when I walk down the hallway and open the door.

Beckett leans against the wooden railing, arms crossed over his broad chest, the curves of his biceps visible under the grey sweater pushed up his forearms, exposing all those cords of muscles and veins. One foot kicked up against the railing, laces of his shoes tied haphazardly, and thigh muscles on display where his shorts ride up his legs.

There's no grin on his face, and he looks all too serious. Even his voice sounds rougher than usual. "Evening, Dr. Roberts."

"What are you doing here? How'd you know I was off?" I haven't seen him since the gala—since his head was between my legs for an extended period of time—only that texted *thank you* between us. It wasn't for the orgasms—but for staying with me. For seeing me when no one else did and making sure I was okay.

"Took a lucky guess that a big, important fellow such as yourself wouldn't be working on a Sunday night." His eyes trail over me, and I notice they're barely green. Dilated pupils, jaw tense with a muscle popping in his cheek. He looks back up and raises his eyebrows. "I have a bit of a problem I was hoping you could help me with."

"Oh?"

"Yeah. I can't stop thinking about my head between your legs." Beckett shrugs, his voice gravelly and rough and wholly inappropriate. "Season starts this week, and I can't think about anything but you. Can't visualize. Can't aim for shit. Drove right by the turn to my street last night. Spending a disproportionate amount of time in the shower thinking about it. Thinking about a lot of things, actually. How I would very much like to fuck you."

"Oh," I repeat. I blink, and I feel my heart rate pick up. But it's not the increased rhythm that usually warns me of bad things to come. This is something else entirely. My skin pebbles, I shiver, and I don't think it's from the night air. "You can come in, if you want."

He nods, kicking off the railing. "I would."

Neither of us say anything, but everything sounds impossibly loud. His footsteps across the porch. The creak of the door and the click of the lock when it shuts. His breath on the back of my neck as he walks behind me.

His heart. My heart.

The light is still low, the candle still flickers on the coffee table, and the book is where I left it, open on top of a throw blanket. Beckett glances around, but he doesn't really seem to focus on any one thing before he sits down on the couch.

His eyes are on me the entire time I fold myself down beside him, only one cushion and the book separating us.

"Do you like reading about . . ." Beckett trails off as he picks up the book, glancing at the cover before flipping it around to read the back. He glances back up at me, and there's a shade of the boyish charm there for just a moment, but then he's entirely rough again. "Romance and sexy faeries?"

"Who doesn't?" I bite down on my lip, leaning forward and taking the book back. My fingers graze his, and I go to sit back, but his hand wraps around my wrist.

"What's this one about?"

My lips part and my breath stalls—I don't think there's any air left in my lungs at all, actually. But the thought doesn't scare me like it usually would. I swallow, brushing my fingers along the back of his hand. "A human who gets transported to another realm and is held captive by a brooding, dark-haired, six-five male who sometimes has wings. You know, the usual."

Beckett nods, eyes never leaving me. His voice drops again, and it's rougher than before, traipsing across my exposed skin like the brush of one of those calloused palms of his. "Is that what you like?"

"Sure, why not?" I say, finally extracting my wrist from him and leaning back against the arm of the couch, putting distance between us even though I'm not sure I want to. "But what you did the other night was satisfactory, too."

His eyes move over my shoulders, my arms folded across my chest, before they come back up to find mine. "I can do a lot of things."

"I'll bet you can." My voice is just a rasp.

"Want me to show you?"

I blink, and there are a million things I should be thinking about—why it's a bad idea, why I should ask him to leave, why I shouldn't let him in any more than I already have—but those things feel small, fleeting, and somehow inconsequential when he's looking at me like that.

I think about the fact that the air in the room feels impossibly heavy—that it feels a bit like there's a string between us, and it pulled taut the second I opened that door and he was standing there.

My eyes cut down to his mouth, full lips parted slightly, and I wonder what they would feel like against mine again.

I look back at him, barely nodding. "Sure."

Beckett leans forward, every muscle in his body tight, plucking the book from my hands. His eyes never leave mine as he sets it on the coffee table.

They're still on me when his hands wrap around my wrists. He leans back against the couch and pulls me flush to his side. I'm only there for a moment before his hands find my waist.

Like I'm nothing, weightless, not someone heavy with all this baggage they carry, stuck, sinking below water in a car she left years ago. He hoists me onto his lap until our chests and foreheads are practically flush.

I inhale. He smells like something I can't quite place—but I think it's something I used to love a long time ago when I was young and free and safe.

My hands find his shoulders and I can feel the ridges and valleys of muscle beneath his sweater as his fingers slide under the hem of my T-shirt.

"I don't think business acquaintances sit like this," I whisper, and I feel his hands tighten around my waist.

Even though I can barely see them this close, those green striations in his eyes light up, and the corner of his mouth lifts, the shadow of a dimple popping under his stubble. "They also don't go down on each other in hallway closets. I'm pretty sure they don't taste each other for days afterwards. And I doubt they spend every waking moment with their cock hard thinking about it."

My lips part, my hips roll, and I glance down, where I can feel him straining against me.

But his thumb and finger grip my chin, lifting my face back to his. His voice drops, and I feel it all over me. "Dr. Roberts, look at me."

His grip tightens, just for a moment, and his hand slides along my jaw, reaching the back of my head and tangling in the hair at the nape of my neck. His eyes are on me, and I think I might be a bit lost in them. My hips move again because the way he feels between my legs is something I can't quite place either.

My fingers dig into his shoulders, my lips part in a tiny moan, and his grip tightens.

We're staring, waiting, and I think I should tell him to go.

But his lips find mine, and then there's nothing in my head at all but him.

I'm not sure it's a kiss. It is by the definition of the word—our lips touch, his tongue finds mine.

I think it might be something else entirely.

His hand cradles the back of my head, the other splaying across my back, pushing me into him. His hips move up to meet mine, and we stay like that for quite a while.

Teeth nipping at lips, hands gripping at clothes and skin, and tongues moving against one another. My hips rolling down to his.

"Bedroom?" His words are low, rough, and punctuated by a groan catching in his throat when I arch against him.

He breaks away, mouth finding my neck and teeth scraping my skin. I tip my head back, words practically a whimper. "Around the corner."

Beckett doesn't wait, one hand cradling the back of my head and the other wrapping around my back, gripping the side of my waist. He stands, and my legs wind around him, desperate to be closer, ridges of his abdomen and obliques pressing into my thighs.

Like he knows where he's going, like he's lived here forever, he carries me out of the living room and down the hall, mouth on me, tongue never leaving mine, and he kicks my bedroom door open further.

His lips still. "Great room. Great bed. Can't wait to fuck you in it."

I blink, pulling back with a rasp of laughter.

He grins, eyebrows lifting before he instructs, "Down."

"Are you always this domineering?" I place both hands on his shoulders, and Beckett leans forward so I can touch the floor.

I don't let go of him when he stands. I don't think I could.

Both of his hands grip my hips. He grins again. "I'm whatever you want me to be."

I'm not thinking when his hands find the hem of my T-shirt, lifting, and his lips and teeth and tongue only leaving me for a second while he pulls it off.

Beckett drops to his knees, his mouth presses to the centre of me, and I tip my head back, a small gasp, because even through my clothes, I think he might be the best thing I've ever felt.

His hands find the waist of my leggings, and he's about to pull them down when his eyes cut up to mine.

But they pass over my stomach first.

And they stop on the scar.

As far as transplant scars go, it could be worse. It's nothing more than a pink, raised line that tapers off under the right side of my rib cage.

But it's there. And he notices.

His hands tense at my waist before he lifts one, tentatively, and his eyes look up to mine in permission.

I nod softly, and his thumb skates over the raised skin.

He pauses at the bottom, and his eyes never leave mine. "Pretty."

I blink and I think I might have made it up—because his hands are back at my waist, stripping me of the Lycra covering my legs, and my underwear with it.

"Bra off."

"You aren't going to take it off for me?" I ask, but I'm already reaching around my back for the clasp.

Beckett shakes his head, hands finding my hips, and he pulls me closer to him. "No, I'm pretty busy down here."

His tongue is on me before I have the clasp undone.

"Fuck," Beckett groans against me, tongue moving in lazy circles. His eyes cut up to mine.

He doesn't say anything, but he watches me. My bra falls to the floor, and my lips part in a tiny moan.

I don't really have a sense of time with his mouth on me like that, so I can't be sure how long we stay there—him on his knees again, tongue moving across the centre of me and into me, his hands bruising my waist, and mine digging into his shoulders.

But he stands, breath ragged, and drops his forehead to mine, shaking his head. "I'll fucking die if I'm not inside you."

I think I whimper, but his lips find mine, and he starts walking us backwards until the back of my knees hit my bed.

"Lie down," he says against my mouth.

I like it, I think—that he's in control.

My mind is quiet, and I don't feel this weird pang that I always do, echoing in the places where I think I'm empty.

Beckett reaches behind his head, pulling his shirt off and tossing it on the floor. His hands find the waist of his shorts. He pulls them down, muscles in his thighs tensing, black Lycra left clinging to them and leaving nothing to the imagination.

Those are gone next. My mouth dries out a bit because he's impossibly hard and quite unlike anything I've ever seen. I blink when he tenses, gripping himself.

"Condom?" he asks, voice rough.

"Top drawer." I point to my dresser, and it's really something—a once-in-a-lifetime experience, probably—to watch someone like him, sculpted and honed from years and years of this thing I think he loves and hates, walk across your room naked, muscles tensing and tightening, for him to look only at you when he rolls a condom on.

He stares at me when he does it—and then he's hovering over me. His voice is just this groan, rough all over but making everything else about me, all my rigid lines and rules, feel soft. "You're sure?"

I blink up at him, nodding, and he inhales sharply, hand moving between us, scoring down my centre, pausing where I'm entirely soaked.

He flexes his hips, a strangled moan coming from him as he pushes inside me. I inhale sharply against the pressure, but it shifts to something that feels wonderful before I can give it much thought. He buries his head in my neck, teeth scraping skin, and my hands find his back.

We stay there for a moment, hearts beating through chests and sweat-slicked skin pressed together, before he lifts his head, dropping his forehead to mine.

We start to move at the same time—and maybe it shouldn't feel as natural as it does, but it's sort of like our bodies know each other.

He presses his lips to mine, tongue sweeping across the seam of my mouth. "Tell me what you like."

You, I think. Everywhere he touches me feels like it's on fire, like I might spontaneously combust and die, happily, because Beckett Davis and his tongue were my cause of death.

But I say something else.

"I like—slower." I arch into his chest, nails digging into the valleys of muscle spanning his back.

He pauses, hand fisting the pillow beside me, his other palm finding the headboard, flexing his hips upwards. "Like that?"

"Yes," I rasp, teeth coming down on my bottom lip. My hips rise to meet his. "What do you like?"

Beckett's lips part, the muscles in his neck and shoulders tense, voice nothing but a rough groan. "I think I'd like anything with you."

That—the idea that maybe it's me, me with this scar and this once-missing piece of her body, who gives too much away, that maybe I'm whole enough for him, to make his body feel the way he makes mine feel—has me arching even further, my fingers digging into his back and a moan tumbling from me.

It's too intimate, the whole thing, but I can't concentrate on that thought—it's fleeting, melting away into nothing when his hand leaves the headboard to travel across my chest, down my rib cage, stopping at my centre where his thumb starts to move in small circles.

I can feel every part of him touching every part of me, and it's too late because I think I will combust, I'll die right here.

It's his name on my lips, the low moan in the back of his throat, the pressure of him inside me, and the sweep of his thumb—it all turns me into nothing but kindling, and I go up in flames.

His hips roll up faster, and I feel it when he comes, see his eyes close, his lips parted with a groan in his throat before he stills. He breathes for a moment before he blinks slowly, and there they are—emerald eyes that have no business being that beautiful.

Beckett hovers above me for a moment longer, eyes dark and breath heavy, lowering his head so his lips can brush mine before he rolls his shoulders back and moves to lie beside me with a groan.

Hair matted to his forehead and eyes entirely alive, he holds a palm up with a lazy, contented grin. "Excellent business meeting. Got a lot of work done."

And for the second time, I smile, and I raise my hand to meet his.

Greer

"Great bathtub." Beckett grins at me, stepping back into my room, running a hand through messy hair.

I arch a brow. "Are you big into baths?"

"Fuck yeah. Love a bath. Ice or otherwise." He nods, stretching an arm across his chest, making all the muscles in his obliques and abdomen flex. He hasn't put a shirt back on, only his shorts found their way back to his body.

He's made no moves to leave at all, actually.

He laid in bed beside me, fingers toying with the ends of my hair, wandering over my shoulders and down my arms, while our breathing slowed and the stars winked to life in the sky through the window.

I don't think it was friendly to sit there like that, talking to one another, naked, and to carry on casual conversation while we stood and got dressed, for him to tell me I should put on the grey pajamas because he thinks the colour is nice. To smile at each other and laugh.

I'm not sure how much time passed. He has this tricky way about him—time slips through my fingers when he's around.

But it's not just the time. My mind quiets down and I don't realize I'm on the precipice of one of my boundaries until I'm right there—toes off the ledge and about to fall to what's probably an uncertain death.

I should probably ask him to go—the warning sounds start in my brain; the scar twinges and I remember I scribbled all these lines in some sad attempt at a preservation instinct.

You can't give anything else away, my brain whispers. *You'll give and give and give and then there will be nothing left.*

But then Beckett speaks. His voice, still rough in this sort of post-sex haze, rolls across the room, wraps around me, and my brain shuts up because other parts of me like the way he sounds. He points to the remote, sitting haphazard on my bookcase, and then to the TV mounted on the wall across from my bed. "Do you want to watch something?"

And I find myself nodding. I never use it, but Stella insisted on having it for nights she stayed over.

Beckett stays standing, rubbing the back of his neck with one hand, the other pressing aimlessly on the buttons of the remote until the TV flares to life.

I wrinkle my nose, glancing between him and the channel he picks. "I'm sorry, did you just turn on sports highlights? That would be like me coming home and watching *Botched*."

He tosses me a lazy grin before climbing back into bed beside me. "Of course, I have to see what they're saying about me."

I pluck at the thin strap of my tank top and narrow my eyes at him. He rubs the back of his neck again before scrubbing his jaw. A muscle ticks in his cheek. I don't think he wants to know at all, actually.

"You don't have to do that," I offer, taking the remote from his hand and changing the channel.

Beckett furrows his brow and raises a hand behind his head, leaning back against the headboard. "Do what?"

"Be someone else. Reliable. Likeable. Who people expect you to be." I shrug. "You can just be you."

He stares at me for a minute, slight lines of age starting to show, crinkling around his eyes, and he smiles, nodding slowly. "You sure you aren't a psychiatrist? Didn't major in psychology?"

I shake my head. "No. I majored in biology, and I only did one psychiatry rotation."

Beckett keeps one hand cupped behind his head, the pop of the bicep and triceps in his arm even more defined when he shifts, the other hand finding the hem of my tank top. He toys with it before smiling at me. "Biology. Do you ever think about all the other biological life forms on other planets?"

"I'm sorry, are you asking me about aliens?" I widen my eyes, but a small rasp of laughter sneaks out.

"Fuck yeah." Beckett nods enthusiastically. "The universe is vast, Dr. Roberts. How do we know what's out there?"

"Don't tell me you minored in astronomy."

"Nah. I didn't have a minor. Too busy running and then kicking. But I specialized in the French Revolution."

"That's . . . niche."

He sits up, eyes wide, like the French Revolution is a newborn hippo that takes the internet by storm, and everyone should be obsessed with it. "Come on, what's more interesting than a man rising up from outside nobility, becoming the greatest military mind of his time, naming himself emperor, and betraying the ideals of the very movement that facilitated his rise?"

My nose wrinkles, lips turning down. "A lot of things."

One of his fingers sweeps up under my top—this casual movement, like he touches me all the time and we weren't two barely friends, sort of business acquaintances, who fell into bed together—and it grazes the scar.

His finger stills, and he glances down.

"Is your scar"—he swallows, eyes flicking up to mine—"from the car accident?"

I blink. It's a simple question, but it's not exactly a simple answer.

I'm not sure why I tell him. It's one of the top two things I don't share with people. But Beckett leans back against the headboard, expression earnest, waves curling around the nape of his neck, thumb and forefinger playing with the hem of my tank top again.

I shake my head. "No. It's a transplant scar. I donated half my liver to my father when I was eighteen."

"Because of the accident?"

Because driving his two teenage daughters off a bridge was apparently the final straw for my father, and they don't give livers to people who can't stay sober. But I was a perfect match.

My brain whirs back to life, and it screams at me: *Back away from the ledge because you're going to fall. You've already fallen off once, and you might not survive again.* I give him a small smile. "Something like that."

The corner of his mouth kicks up, and his dimple pops. "That's the third time I've asked you a question like that and you've given me that same answer." I'm not sure what to say, but the sharp planes of his face soften, and he whispers, "That was brave of you."

I don't think it can be considered being brave when you think you might regret it. When you did it because the only thing you've ever known was giving away pieces of yourself.

"Coming to the hospital was brave of you," I offer quietly. I mean it.

His eyes flash with a wince. "Yeah, well, if you ask Nathaniel, I should have been running PR stints there and fundraising for kids with cancer since he set foot through the door."

I shrug one shoulder. "Grief is complicated."

Beckett starts to shake his head, brow creasing. "Grief?"

"Grief," I repeat. Those lines stay between his brows, and his lips turn down. He still looks confused. It looks cute on him, but I cock my head. "Have you ever grieved?"

"What do I have to grieve? Sarah lived." Beckett rolls out his neck, like he can shake it all off, like it's this nothing thing.

"Your childhood?" I ask. He doesn't answer, but his shoulders slump an almost undetectable amount, and I can tell he's hurting. I sit forward, stopping his hand where his fingers still toy with my shirt, interlacing them with mine. "Imagine a positive, healthy, but hypothetical childhood. What would that look like? Would it look like yours did?"

He glances down at our joined hands, thumb brushing over the back of mine. "Huh. There you go again. Seeing right through me."

When he looks back up, he stares at me a little too intently, so I push my shoulders back and let go of his hand.

If he's bothered, he doesn't let on. He pushes back, hand resting behind his head again, and he rolls his neck to look at me. "What was your childhood like? It's just you, your sister, and your dad, right? Do you—"

I spare him from trying to find a polite way to ask whether I ever had a mother. "I don't really remember my mom. She left when I was four and Stella was two."

"But you were her kids."

We were. But she was also my father's wife and I don't think she could live with him for a second longer. Her self-preservation instincts kicked in, and for some reason, they didn't include us. She's not around for me to ask her, but she got out. Stella says I have more grace for her than I do anyone else, and I think that might be true. Sometimes, I understand why she did it and I'm not sure it's entirely unlike all the lines I try to uphold. "It's okay. I hope she's happy, wherever she is."

I mean that, though.

Beckett looks at me, and it's another look that's a bit too much, but he raises his eyebrows before reaching forward and grabbing the remote again.

"You're quite something, Dr. Roberts." He's not looking at me when he says it, but his voice is low, and the line of his mouth looks like it might be curving upwards into a smile.

I don't answer, but I sit back against the headboard, my shoulder resting against his while he flicks through the channels. He stops on one, glancing sideways at me and grinning. "*American Psycho*? Seeing as you love the fictional restaurant so much you have a shirt with its logo."

"Sure." I nod, even though I know I should ask him to leave, and I should go to sleep and let those lines around me darken their ink so I can wake up tomorrow and remember that boundaries exist to keep people like me safe. "We can watch."

And we do.

We get about halfway through when my phone starts going off with a page. My eyes cut to where it sits on the windowsill, and I'm hardly paying attention when I pick it up.

But when I see the screen, I inhale, a small audible gasp of excitement, and I'm climbing out of bed and over Beckett.

I glance back at him, holding up the phone. "I'm so sorry, I have to go. But you can stay—finish the movie. Shower, sleep. Whatever. Just press the lock button on the keypad when you leave."

"I take it that page means good news?" He smiles faintly.

"Yes." I smile—it's wide, and my cheeks hurt—pressing my hand to my heart. I think the beats are telling me that this is what it was all for at the end of the day. For my sister, for my father. For every other person I get to give life to. "A liver. For someone who's been waiting a long time."

"Someone who deserves it?" Beckett asks quietly.

He looks at me, and I know the question is bigger, grander, than just those four words strung together. My hand presses harder into my chest, and I give him a smile I hope he knows is just for him. "Everyone deserves a second chance, Beckett."

Liver transplants can take anywhere from five to eight hours, depending on a lot of factors.

This one only took six from the time I opened to the time I closed. It was routine as far as a transplant goes, but this one was special.

It wasn't just the fact that it was for a patient I'd been with for years. Someone who wanted to live so much—to see another sunrise and sunset and breathe fresh air and love—it wasn't that I held his hand and cried with him when other organs fell through. That I promised I'd do everything in my power to make sure he lived.

It was the fact that my heart beat differently when I was performing the surgery. The fact that I smiled so wide behind my mask when the new one was placed in his abdominal cavity, my eyes started to water. It was exactly the right size—a better match probably didn't exist anywhere in the world.

I didn't feel so much like I was stealing or taking something someone might not really want to give. I don't get to ask donors if they're like me. I don't get to ask them if they're the only choice for someone who's hurt them immeasurably, and if at the end of the day, they're just a young girl who wants their family to stay whole, so they give up one more piece of themselves.

I remembered what it was all about today—that it was a special, important, magical gift given—and I made sure it was treated with care.

It might have had to do with the fact that hours earlier, someone traced my scar with reverence and told me I was brave.

Not broken and desperate. Not a little girl giving herself away piece by piece.

I found an empty on-call room afterwards, and I think I slept better after a surgery than I have in over a year.

When most surgeons say they don't sleep well, it's because they just don't sleep—resident schedules are cruel. It's not something to be glorified, and everyone is walking around sleep-deprived almost ninety percent of the time.

But I stopped sleeping well when I started my fellowship and realized I was dedicating my entire life to the very thing that hurt me immeasurably.

I didn't go into surgery with the intention of performing transplants. It wasn't some sort of calling that was stitched into me when the surgeon excised my liver and sewed me up all those years ago.

It just sort of happened.

The whole thing has felt a bit like I'm still stuck in the car. The water inching higher on my legs, the seat belt jammed and compressing all my air while my hands claw at the buckle, trying to get out.

This morning feels inexplicably bright—like maybe the way the water looked in the early morning after the crash. When the sun slowly blinks awake and its rays aren't quite down to earth yet, but it's starting to warm everything.

It feels peaceful and lovely when I leave the on-call room. It's seven a.m.—not a notably busy time, but it's nice that the lobby isn't crawling with people or medical staff in search of caffeine yet.

It was only four hours of sleep, but I feel like a new person.

Early-morning sunshine spills through the floor-to-ceiling windows lining the cafeteria, warming the back of my neck when I sit down in one of the chairs in the corner.

I don't have to round until nine, and usually I start reading charts and reports from the night before when I'm at home, but it feels nice to do it here. I don't agree with romanticizing surgical schedules or the residency system in general, but it feels like another quiet reminder—sitting here in the sunlight, with coffee that's better than most hospital coffee, reviewing patients' labs and charts—that even though I chose to do this thing that had already defined me, it can be beautiful.

I've barely opened the first one when my sister calls.

She doesn't say hello or good morning. "I stopped by your place last night."

"Oh. I got a call around—"

"I know," Stella cuts in, and even though she's not here, I can see her mouth curling up into a saccharine smile, the way she would prop her chin up on her fist and blink at me. "Beckett told me."

My mouth dries out and my heart, expanded beyond its borders, shrinks in my chest. "He—"

"Save it. I saw your claw marks." She cuts me off again, words dripping and smug when she keeps going. "Imagine my surprise, throwing the door open to my older sister's house, just to yell in and ask if she wants to come down to our father's for a Sunday night movie, and who walks out of her bedroom as he's pulling a sweater on? Red welts across those beautiful shoulders that could really only be from someone's nails. Sleeping with a professional athlete and you didn't tell me? I'm hurt, Greer."

"I'm not sleeping with him." I try to swallow. "It was a one-time thing."

Stella scoffs. "Don't pretend. You've spent weeks gallivanting around the hospital with him. You took him to that gala, and now this? What's next? Marriage? Did your boundaries and plans to focus on yourself disappear and evaporate when he took his shirt off? I think mine would, too. I mean I only saw a glimpse of the abs last night, but I've seen the commercials enough to know."

She thinks she's joking. She thinks she's being sisterly and fun. And maybe in another world, she would be. But in this world, my sister doesn't live in a body she can't help but give away. To know what it's like to be the kind of abhorrent person who gives her father part of her liver and sometimes wishes she hadn't. To be such a fucking hypocrite that she dedicated her entire life to the thing that hurt her.

"Stop," I whisper.

She inhales. "Nutty—"

"Don't call me that."

"Greer, I was joking." Stella's voice cracks, the line she crossed scoring through it. "I was kidding. Of course I don't think that. You can date or not date or sleep with or not sleep with anyone you want. It doesn't mean anything about who you are as a person."

"It's fine." I wipe at my eyes. "Stella, I have to go. I need to check on a patient."

I hang up before she can answer.

I blink away my tears, and I try to swallow away the ache in the back of my throat. She might have been kidding, but she was right—maybe I can't help myself.

The sun doesn't look serene anymore. I don't find the early-morning quiet peaceful. I might be staring at a still lake. There might be birds chirping, a beautiful breeze and rays of sun inching across the body of water to touch the shore. But all it does is remind me there was a crash, that a car did go through the water, and maybe it still sits at the very bottom of the lake, sinking into the silt, and maybe I'm going along with it.

Beckett

She doesn't look happy to see me.

Her brow sharpens, braid in those cute little bubbles swinging behind her when she crosses her arms.

I toss her a grin and hold the cup of coffee up. "Definitely not the warmest welcome I've received after sex."

She widens her eyes, giving a pointed look around the hospital lobby, which feels a bit rich seeing as she let me go down on her in a hallway closet that didn't lock.

I deflate a bit, palming my jaw with my free hand, while my post-sex coffee dangles uselessly in my fingers. "Did you not—was it not good for you?"

"Of course it was good." Greer reaches forward, snatching the coffee from me.

"Then what's the problem?" I lower my voice and lean down.

Her eyes narrow on me. She tips her head back in an exasperated sigh before grabbing my forearm and pulling me towards the hallway by the elevator bay.

She lets go of my arm—I wish she hadn't, I think I want her touching some part of me for the rest of my life—and drops against the wall, holding the coffee to her chest. "The problem, Beckett, is that this is not the behaviour of a business acquaintance. This is not even friendly behaviour."

"Bringing you a coffee?" I ask flatly.

"Precisely. Now that that's sorted—"

I cut her off, taking a step forward and dropping one hand to the wall just beside her head. Her nostrils flare and I hear a tiny intake of breath. "Not sorted, Dr. Roberts. This is friendly behaviour actually. You let me into your home. Into your bed. Into you."

Her shoulder blades hit the wall and she blinks up at me. "I don't date."

"I'm not interested in dating you. I'm interested in being kind to you."

I would be interested in dating her, actually, and I'm certainly interested in more than just being kind to her. I'd actually like to do things to her that would definitely not be considered nice.

But she looks a bit like a scared deer—eyes wide, shaking her head ever so slightly. "This isn't a joke or a game. This isn't like the movies—I'm not going to wake up one morning and realize I'm this whole, healed person who actually just needed love the entire time. I gave a man a piece of my liver because I couldn't set a fucking boundary. But I'm trying to set them now. I don't date."

I take a step back, holding my palms in the air. Her chin tips up, all of her resolute, but her fingers whiten against the cup of coffee and she's blinking a bit too much.

If she realizes she gave something away, showed me something about whatever goes on in that big, beautiful brain when she referred to him as a man instead of her dad—that in her mind, something as selfless as that is considered an inability to set a boundary—she doesn't let on.

"I don't think your boundaries are a joke. I'm sorry I crossed one." I angle my head down, lips tugging into a rueful smile. "It won't happen again."

She exhales, rolls her shoulders back, and takes a sip of coffee. She stands taller when she pushes off the wall, like the words lifted something weighing her down off her shoulders. "Great. Thank you."

I grin at her. "We can be friends who've seen each other naked. It'll be just like college."

Greer rolls her eyes.

"I mean that. I'm not trying to date you. Don't get me wrong, if you wanted to throw the occasional business meeting my way"—she gives me a flat look—"I wouldn't complain. I'd be pretty fucking thrilled, actually. But I don't want to stop being friends."

I don't tell her that the idea of her suddenly disappearing from my life—this person who sees me and doesn't really care about anything other than what I have to say, what I'm actually thinking, who makes all those expectations I wear around feel like nothing—seems like a pretty bleak fate.

I'd probably drop to my knees and beg her to keep hanging out with me if it came to it.

But it turns out I don't have to tell her. She cocks her head, tapping the lid of the coffee cup against her lips, hiding a quiet smile. "Would it help you sleep better at night? Staying friends with the one person in the city who doesn't hate you?"

"It would." I nod.

I don't bother telling her that last night was the first night I've slept through since preseason ended. That the weight of everyone else's expectations didn't feel so heavy because I felt enough for her.

"Fine." She rolls her eyes again like it's this big inconvenience, but they look bright. "We can be friends. But I have to tell you, friends don't bother friends at their place of work."

She turns and starts walking down the hallway without waiting for me.

"You could bother me at mine," I offer, giving her a sideways smile when I catch up to her. I like my legs when I'm around her. I don't mind relying on them, because I know they'll always get me to her. "First game of the season is on Sunday. It'd be nice to have a friendly face in the crowd. I could get you tickets, if you wanted. You could bring your friends. Or your dad and sister. Whatever."

Greer stops when she reaches the lobby. Her nose wrinkles and she chews on the inside of her cheek. "I'm sure your tickets are all accounted for."

"No." I say it a bit too quickly, and I try to give a noncommittal jerk of my chin. I don't want anyone else there. I've actively avoided the conversation with my parents, with Nathaniel and Sarah. But I like the idea of her there. "Unless you're working?"

"I'm not," she answers softly, and her voice cracks a bit. "I don't—I don't go to things like that. The noise is . . . unpredictable."

I swallow. Scrubbing my jaw, I start to shake my head. I fucking hate that—the fact that there's this thing that hurts her and gives her pause about living her life. And I hate that I was selfish and stupid enough to forget it. "I wasn't thinking. I don't want you to be uncomfortable. Forget it. I'm serious." I toss her a grin. "We can still be friends."

She starts to shake her head. "No—no, it's okay. Uhm. Let me ask if Stella wants to go. I make no promises, but I'll think about it."

"Only if you're sure. You can come, decide you hate the picture of me hanging in the concourse, and leave before you get to ticketing. You can leave whenever you want and I won't be hurt." I lower my voice. "Promise me you'll only do what's right for you?"

It's a stupid gesture, and I'm not sure why I do it, but I hold up my pinky finger. Her head pulls back a tiny bit, she blinks, and it's probably a trick of the light—but her eyes gloss over, the amber flecks come alive, and her smile splits my chest open when she raises her finger up to meet mine.

Coach Taylor hired a motivational speaker for our first team meeting of the regular season, and she's staring at me a bit too intently for my liking.

And I don't think it's because she liked the stupid Beckett Davis grin I gave her when I sat down.

She's been making thinly veiled references to there being no singular factor that goes into winning or losing—that it doesn't come down to the successes or mistakes of one person.

The words *you win as a team, you lose as a team*, actually came out of her mouth.

It didn't feel like that when you were, in fact, the person they all put their faith in to win for them. I'd smashed every other record in my way—what was a 67-yard field goal to win the first championship in franchise history for the only Canadian team?

I turned my hat forward at that point, crossed my arms and sunk down in my chair.

I would have waited there—silently—doing the exact opposite of what used to be expected of me. There was a not-so-distant past where I would have been socializing with everyone. The team's publicist would have had me down there shaking the speaker's hand, being Beckett Davis friendly. My teammates were—are—my friends. There isn't a single person I don't get along with in this room, people who I would have argued that, in another life, I was close with.

If it was last year, I would have spent a lot of my offseason hanging out with them. I only gave a cursory wave to Nowak, the team's punter who I spent the majority of my time with, and reliable, likable Beckett Davis would have said was one of his best friend's, and tipped my chin to Pat, who I definitely should have gone to say hello to, seeing as he just got here and didn't know anyone but me, before I slunk down in my chair.

I'm still there, eyes on my phone like I'm having some sort of life-altering conversation, when really I'm wondering if Greer liked her coffee and debating the merits of only leaving my house for practice the closer and closer it gets to the game.

The people of the internet might have been onto something when they suggested I see a sports psychologist.

But there's a knock on the table, and my eyes cut to the side.

"Beck. Hey, man." Evan tips his chin before running a hand through close-shaven black hair.

Evan Chase, wide receiver and another best friend of reliable, likeable Beckett Davis.

The grin slips into place. "Evan. How are you?"

Eyes flash momentarily, and he studies me like he doesn't quite recognize me. Maybe that stupid fucking smile finally looks like the mask it is.

"Alright. Looking forward to the start of the season?"

It takes me a minute to realize he's asking a question, not making a statement, because I was too busy thinking about the fact that this entire room is an example of what happens when I fail.

At one point in time, it would have meant my parents' perpetual disappointment before their shoulders caved in from the utter exhaustion of it all. That Nathaniel's big, brilliant brain wasn't nurtured enough. That if I wasn't smiling, maybe Sarah wouldn't be either.

In this case, it was the decimation of career aspirations and dreams and livelihoods.

"Beckett?" he prompts.

I blink, tossing him a lazy smile and taking my hat off to run my hands through my hair. "Sorry. Yeah. Definitely looking forward to the Beck Davis redemption arc of the season."

Evan smiles back, but it doesn't quite meet his eyes. I recoil a bit internally, but the longer I look, the more I realize the disappointment might not be for him.

He knocks on the table again and raises a hand in farewell.

I raise mine, turn back to my phone, and think about the fact that previous me would have been looking forward to the season. Because despite being reliable and likeable, I was competitive and I wanted to win. I wanted to smash records and win championships. But there was never really anyone I wanted watching when I did.

I stand. "Does Brooke still design all those custom clothes?"

"Oh." He blinks, nodding. "Yeah—yeah, she does. Are you looking for something?"

"For a friend," I answer. I don't tell him that she's a friend I'll probably fantasize about for the rest of time. I roll my shoulders back and scrub my jaw, trying to think about anything but the way she makes me feel. "It's probably not something she usually makes, but I don't think it would take much time."

"Send her a text, and if she's got time, I'm sure she won't mind getting it done before Sunday."

"Thanks." I clap his shoulder, and I'm about to turn back and drop in my seat until everyone leaves, but he keeps talking.

"You have a good summer? We didn't talk much during preseason." There's that look in his eyes again.

I thought that was because no one wanted to talk to me, but I wonder how much of it has to do with the fact that I didn't talk to anyone.

My lip curls up before I can stop it. But I jerk my chin and laugh like it's something that just rolls off my back instead of locking manacles around all my limbs and keeping me chained to my failures. "Pretty hard being the most hated person in the city, man. But it could have been worse. What about you and Brooke? Were you back in Seattle?"

Evan nods. The lines around his eyes deepen, but he doesn't smile. "Yeah, we were. Just came back right before preseason."

"Glad you had a good summer." I'm still smiling.

I sound like an idiot. Like I'm not the person responsible for the fact that he wasn't celebrating all over the Amalfi Coast and was probably running routes in his backyard, watching game tape and chasing the one dream left outstanding.

"If you want to . . ." Evan rubs his chin. "If you want to grab dinner, have a drink, watch some tape, or even run around throwing shitty passes to each other before Sunday . . . just don't be a stranger."

I say nothing, but I nod and clap his shoulder again.

I'm about to drop back into my chair when I see my phone screen light up.

> Greer: Coffee was great.

> Greer: But I mean it. Coffee only. Don't go bringing me an iced latte.

> Greer: That's not friendly.

The corners of my lips tug up, and I don't realize I'm doing it, but I take a deep breath. It doesn't hurt, and my chest doesn't feel like it's going to crack open at any time, like it's so heavy it'll never feel right again.

It feels like maybe there are people out there who might like real Beckett, the way Greer sees him.

I pocket my phone and lope down the stairs to say hi to Pat and Nowak.

Greer

Promise me you'll only do what's right for you.

I wouldn't have guessed what was right for me would be standing here, in a line to get into the stadium, shoulder to shoulder with strangers draped in white, gold, and black, or in such proximity to so many people with air horns.

Stella cuts a look at the man standing in front of us, jade eyes tracking the horn as he waves it back and forth with a bit too much exuberance for my liking. Her hand finds the crook of my elbow. "Do you have your pills?"

"Yes, Mom." I hold up my bag, widening my eyes. "I don't think he's going to randomly turn around and blow that in my ear, Cash."

Her lips pull into a tight line and she tips her chin up, hooking her arm through mine. "He better not if he knows what's good for him. But you can't trust these people, Greer. Sports fans—Canadian sports fans—are a little too enthusiastic."

"I think I'll be okay. But you might be onto something. Remember Beckett told me someone threw a Timbit at him?"

Stella whips her head towards me. "What flavour was it again?"

"Birthday cake."

She purses her lips and shakes her head. "What a waste. I can think of so many other uses for a Timbit and Beckett Davis together."

"Ew." I wrinkle my nose, but my stomach twists uncomfortably. He's not mine. He's just my friend, but I think of Beckett on his knees for me, Beckett hovering over me, hand gripping the headboard, so he can find out what I like. What I don't like is the idea of him with someone else.

"What? You've seen it all up close. I know—" Stella snaps her fingers and fishes her phone out of her pocket. "Let's watch the Gatorade commercial while we wait."

I give her a flat look. "No."

She tips her head back, an exaggerated sigh towards the sky, and lets her phone fall back into her pocket. "Where are we sitting?"

"I didn't look at the tickets." I pull my phone out when we step towards the security guard at the door. "But he said he needed us to stop by the counter before we sit down."

"Why?" Stella asks, stepping back and dropping her bag into a bucket so it can go through the metal detector.

I shrug. "Who knows. But he was adamant."

Stella steps through the scanner after me, lips tipping up when she retrieves her bag. "Do you think he left a surprise for you? A sexy surprise? Like a signed shirtless photo?"

"How old are you?"

"Is one ever too old to tease their sister?" Stella laments. She looks like she's about to traipse right through the crowd towards the ticket counter, but she stops with a tiny gasp and points towards one of the giant pictures mounted to the walls along the concourse. "There he is—your lover. My god, he really is photogenic, isn't he?"

I grab her arm and I tug her towards the counter, but my eyes flick up to the poster. He's not wearing a helmet, unlike the rest of the players in similar photos spanning the concrete wall.

A smart decision by the photographer and whoever oversees marketing because Beckett really is beautiful.

He's smiling—one of those smiles that kicks the dimple up in his cheek—green eyes bright, and the lines of his jaw clean-shaven. Chocolate hair perfectly tousled with waves curling over his ears. He's in his equipment, white jersey with gold lettering, ridges of muscle in his arms taut and on display because he holds a football in his palms across the centre of his chest.

His name stretches across the bottom of the poster in block lettering, and underneath that, a list of titles.

Beckett Davis, #19
All-Time NCAA Division 1 FBS Field Goal Leader (Career)
All-Time NCAA Division 1 FBS Field Goal Leader (Single Season)
All-Time Rookie Longest Field Goal
Five-Times First Team All-Pro
Six-Times Pro-Bowl

I wonder what he thinks when he sees that—all these accomplishments spelled out for anyone to see, whether there was a time his chest would swell with pride, and he'd realize he's so much more than he gave himself credit for. Reliable and likeable, sure. But more gifted at something he might think is useless than most people could ever dream of being.

But a lot of the things that make up Beckett wouldn't be found on a banner.

They're found in the way his smile changes when he's comfortable in his own skin, the way he makes everyone feel seen and at ease. How when he speaks to you, his eyes are only on you—and he's always listening. The fact that he brings the most fragrant flowers to a scent-free environment. Loves obscure parts of history and spends too much time talking about reformer Pilates. That he gives away smiles willingly and I don't think he leaves much for himself.

The way he breathes with you when you can't do it on your own.

"Hello." Stella leans forward, crossing her arms on the ledge of the counter. "My sister is here to pick up a package from Beckett Davis."

A woman blinks at her from behind the glass, and I think a blush creeps across her cheeks. "Greer?"

"Yes?" I raise a hand and try to smile at her, but I don't think it's a terribly friendly thing—that he told this random woman my name.

She turns, producing a brown bag with my name scrawled across it in black marker.

"He did leave you a present!" Stella looks smug, eyes glinting as I take it.

I ignore her, peering in hesitantly before reaching in.

Earmuffs.

Giant, fluffy white sherpa earmuffs with the team's logo on either side, but just above, stitched in gold—the number nineteen.

Stella inhales, her fingers rolling down over my wrist.

I glance up at my sister, and everything about her is soft. The corners of her lips twitch, her nose wrinkles, and she blinks too quickly, like she's trying not to cry.

A note, on the same brown paper as the bag, sticks to the band.
I heard earmuffs were more friendly than a jersey. In case it gets too loud in there—Beckett

I tug the paper off. My fingers brush the material—it feels soft—but I think I can feel Beckett's pinky around mine, too.

I pull the earmuffs on, and everything around me dulls to a quiet, comforting, pleasant murmur.

I can't really hear anything except that pinky promise.

Promise me you'll only do what's right for you.

Nine words strung together and said by a friend with a simple enough meaning. But I think I hear him say something else—that maybe he could help me take care of myself, too.

Beckett

Three successful long field goals, a few extra points, and a win later—and everyone likes me again.

Reliable Beckett Davis is back. I've already seen a headline saying so.

But it doesn't really make me feel anything.

What does make me feel something is the text and accompanying photo from Greer on my phone.

> Greer: Earmuffs > Jersey. Very friendly.

I didn't feel particularly friendly towards her when I saw it after the game. And I still don't, now that I'm at home, staring at it like it's my own version of *The Starry Night*.

It's not because of the number nineteen I can see stitched in gold along the shearling. It doesn't really have anything to do with her wearing something that's supposed to represent my team or me. I asked Brooke to add my number more as a joke.

It has to do with the way she's looking at the camera. She's not even smiling. Impossibly dark hair tumbling around her shoulders, the earmuffs even starker because of it. But one hand presses against her chest, and the sunlight hits her just so—high cheekbones that for once don't look like they could cut a man, and full lips together but it's not a hard line. She looks content.

She looks beautiful.

I knew where she was sitting, and I tried not to look—but I did each time I stepped onto the field, even though she was lost somewhere in the blur of white and gold. I debated getting her seats right at the field, but then I would have been able to see her and that's probably not what Darren meant when he asked me if I had my visualization down.

It was an easy lie, slipping off my tongue while I pretended to be the me of last season. Said I'd been practicing all week. Old Beckett Davis, sure. He'd have visualized until all he could see were the uprights.

This me, though, she's all over me and under my skin and I can't really see anything but her. I thought maybe it would go away after we slept together, but I think she's probably in my veins now and even if I bled myself dry—she'd be all that was left.

She's there right now, just under my chest. It's her hands on me and her nails digging into my shoulders.

My calf twitches and it's not the overexertion of the muscle.

It's her fingers painting down my back, moving me like a puppet on a string.

I swallow and drop back against my couch.

> Beckett: Glad you liked them. Hope they helped.

> Greer: It made everything very comfortable. Thank you.

My chest swells at that—the idea that anything I've ever done might have helped her out just a little.

> Greer: My sister's taken it upon herself to learn everything she can about football in general, and she tells me it was great kicking. So, good job, you.

You.

Me. Real.

> Beckett: Thanks for spending your Sunday watching a bunch of men chase a ball around a field.

> Greer: I usually spend it reading about fictional men with wings.

> Beckett: How do you usually spend your Sunday nights?

> Greer: Same as above.

My visualization kicks in pretty easily—I can picture her on her couch. Low lighting of her living room. A candle flickering. Hear the faint flip of a page while she reads. Her lips moving ever so slightly as her eyes track the words.

My thumbs start moving because it's her lips I feel against my ear, her hair brushing my skin.

> Beckett: If you're worried about strain from your eyes bugging out when you get to the particularly sexy parts, you could come over.

Three dots appear.

Disappear.

They reappear.

I start to type an apology—to tell her it was a joke, that I'm tired.

And I am tired—but her hand makes a fist, and she pulls taut on the strings of me she holds in her fingers when she answers.

> Greer: Text me your address.

"No earmuffs?" I grin, resting my head against the doorframe.

Greer gives me a flat look, crossing her arms over her chest. The hood of her black sweater bunches around her neck, and her left leg shifts, like she's considering tapping her foot. "Are they required for admission?"

I shake my head and push off the doorframe, tipping my chin towards the kitchen just beyond the open door. "Nah. Surprised you came, though."

"I had to," she says, full lips curving in this stubborn line that makes me want to drop to my knees, before she walks right by me and into my apartment. "For the sake of my eyes."

"Right. Your eyes." I close the door behind me, watching as she tips her head back, eyeing the vaulted ceilings and exposed brick. "Can't strain those before all the big important surgeries you have this week."

She makes a noncommittal noise, but I think her arms tighten, and she takes a tentative step with a socked foot—these mid-calf, slouchy white crew socks that look cuter on her than a sock should on a woman—towards one of the chairs pushed haphazardly into the granite island spanning the length of the kitchen.

Greer cocks her head before pulling out a chair and swinging herself into it. "Nice place."

"Thanks. High ceilings are great for practicing kicks." I point towards the fridge. "Drink?"

"Whatever you're having." She tips her head back again, looking up, and all that does is give me a view of her neck. The lines of it. Where it dips under her sweater and meets her shoulders. Most of her skin is hidden—but I'd like to run my tongue over it. "Can you really kick in here?"

Clearing my throat, I grip my jaw and turn towards the fridge. "Yeah. I have a practice net in the spare room."

She makes another noise, a smaller one this time.

"Beer okay? I usually have one if it's an afternoon home game."

"Only one?" Her voice is just a rasp, but I roll my neck anyway because I think I can feel it burrowing into me.

The bottles knock together when I grab them off the shelf, twisting the caps off and pitching them onto the counter before turning back to her. "Only one. I know I don't run but I take my program seriously during the season."

"Reliable, likeable, and dedicated." Her voice is barely a whisper, and her eyebrows lift in acknowledgement when I hand it to her.

All those beautiful lines stretch across the column of her neck when she raises the bottle to her lips.

Her eyes find mine, and she might smile against the cold glass. "Thank you."

"Thank you." I swallow, taking a longer sip than necessary. "For coming today. Were the earmuffs okay?"

She really does smile this time—the corners of her lips furling upwards from behind the bottle. "They were. That was very thoughtful of you. My sister was quite taken with them, actually."

"Noted. I'll be sure to ask for another pair next time."

Her smile quirks up when she talks about her sister. It's another little thing I've noticed, collected and coveted and placed in my back pocket along with all those other pieces of her.

But it never lasts long. There's always this initial flash of love, then a tiny twitch in her cheek and she looks like something about all that love hurts her.

I jerk my head towards the couch because I don't quite trust myself with words. She nods and pads across the living room.

She folds herself down at one end, and her eyes cut to the TV mounted to the wall, where the countdown to the night game plays. She studies the screen for a second before rolling her shoulders and leaning back against the arm of the couch.

Greer swings her legs up, stretching across the cushions like she's at ease, and I like the idea of that.

I'm tempted to sit right beside her, but I doubt that's something she would consider friendly, so I sit at the opposite end and wince when I stretch my legs along the sectional. "Can I ask you a question? Just one friend trying to get to know another friend better."

Tucking a strand of hair behind her ears, she takes another sip of her beer and nods softly.

"The noises—at the hospital. Is that why—"

"Why they think I'm mean?" Greer angles her head. She chews on the inside of her cheek for a second before raising one shoulder in a shrug. "Sometimes. I don't let anyone change my playlist in the OR because I know all of the songs and I know what to expect. I don't like when people are chaotic or they drop things. But mostly, it's because it's not just one life we're playing with."

"And I just kick a ball. What an unlikely pair of friends we make."

Her eyes narrow, like the self-deprecation doesn't land. She blinks at me, slowly, sits forward, and all it does is highlight the way the amber flecks in her eyes look alive under the low lighting of my living room. "So today was game day. What does tomorrow look like for you? The rest of the week?"

It's usually a six-days-a-week job, whether people think it's real or not. I take a sip of beer before swinging my legs so I'm facing her. Our feet almost touch, but she doesn't move. "Body work. I'll do a lower body massage tomorrow, mostly on my kicking leg. Focusing on my hamstrings, adductors. Cryotherapy. I'll do a light Pilates class, and then it's game tape. It looks more or less the same for everyone else on the team. Different workouts and different therapies but we're all there together every day."

"What kind of tape?" She drops back against the arm of the couch.

She's looking at me like she's actually interested, and even though it's this thing I hate half the time, I find myself smiling at her anyway. "We'll review tape from today. Good plays, bad plays. And then it's onto next week."

Greer nods, taking another small sip of beer before asking another question. "Where did you play before?"

I'm not used to this. No one wants to get to know me. My family wants me to fix things and pay for things. My teammates want me to score them points and my agent wants me to smile because it makes her money, too. "Uh, after college, I was drafted to Cincinnati. I played there until the expansion a few years ago."

She blinks, and even though it's a gesture that doesn't say anything, I think I can hear it anyway. *These questions, they're real, just like you are, Beckett.* "Is that normal?" she asks.

I run a hand through my hair. "For a kicker? Not necessarily. It's a pretty fickle business. I've seen guys get traded after one bad game and someone who hadn't played all season get picked up. There isn't necessarily a lot of longevity. Kickers are rarely drafted but I—"

A dark eyebrow lifts and she looks amused. "It's okay to say you're good at it."

"Kind of a stupid thing to be good at."

"Why?"

"Because it's not helping anyone. It's not surgery."

"I'm not sure that's always helpful, either." She takes another sip of her beer before setting it down beside her and leaning forward, elbows coming to her thighs. Greer props her chin up on her hands. "You know—I'm not going to pretend I'm some secret sports fanatic and that being at one game unlocked something in me I didn't even know existed. But you made people happy today, Beckett. And that counts for something."

I don't mean to do it. I meant what I said when I told her I wouldn't cross her boundaries or her lines. That I'd respect them. And I do respect her—probably more than anyone on the planet.

But I've never counted for anything.

I drain the rest of my beer, discard the bottle, grip her calves, and I've got her on my lap, my hands in the back of her hair and my mouth on hers before I can think better of it.

She kisses me back, for the record.

Immediately. Enthusiastically. In all the ways.

Her back arches, her chest pushes into mine, the tiny noises I've already fallen in love with rising in her throat when our tongues meet. Her hands find my hair, nails running reverently over my scalp and tugging on the ends.

My hands find the curve of her waist, sliding up under her sweater to meet her bare skin. One finger brushes the raised edge of the scar and I hope she knows I think it's one of the most beautiful things about her.

She presses her hips into mine when my hand slides higher, under her bra, and I roll my finger and thumb over her peaked nipple. Her lips leave mine, head tipping back with the most beautiful fucking moan I've ever heard echoing across my apartment.

I could watch her like this—on top of me, feeling the way I think I'm making her feel, the way she makes me feel—forever.

My cock strains in my pants, and she moves her hips faster, back arched, my hand moving across her chest.

"Take my sweater off," she rasps, before her voice gets smaller, a tiny plea. "Please, Beckett."

The way she says my name makes me want to die. Granted, it would be a better death than I ever would have imagined for myself. The most beautiful person in the entire world arching into me.

Trusting me with more than just her body, but a body I want to take care of all the same.

Her clothes come off and so do mine.

She makes me get up to go get a condom, but she tells me she doesn't want to leave the couch.

I don't know if she thinks that's against the rules, but I'd bleed her if she asked me to.

Her thigh muscles tense on either side of mine, and she peers down at me, dark hair framing her face, when I roll my shoulders against the cushions of the couch and rip open the stupid wrapper.

"Can you—will you go on top?" I breathe, voice rough. "I want to watch you."

She hesitates, head tilting to the side.

"If you're not comfortable—"

Greer glances down, the raised pink edge of the scar hardly visible in the light, and shakes her head. "It's not the physical presence part of the scar that bothers me. Scar tissue is just healed skin." Her nose wrinkles. "I'm just realizing that maybe it feels sort of . . . unfriendly, for me to ride you on a couch."

I groan. My cock twitches and I pause halfway through rolling the condom on. "Don't say ride."

She smiles, and it's not like anything I've ever seen. The corners of her lips curl up, eyes sparkling, and she rolls her hips forward. "Mount?"

"Stop."

"For me to take a little drive on—"

"Enough."

She must think so, too, because her hands find my shoulders, and she lowers herself down onto me inch by inch, pausing as she stretches around me, her head tipped back with these breathy moans.

Our eyes meet, her lips part with a sharp inhale, and we stay there, joined, just for a minute. My hand moves up the centre of her, thumb pressing down where I know she likes. My other hand finds the small of her back, and she rolls her hips forward.

It's just a small movement, but my head drops back against the couch, and I move with her.

Greer arches her back, nails digging into my skin, and when her chest brushes my face, I take my hand off her back, palming her and rolling her nipple between my fingers again before replacing it with my tongue.

It goes like this: wandering hands, hips rising to meet one another, mouths crashing together, and really no echo of the word *friends* until she clenches around me and I swallow the moan she makes into my mouth, and I combust, too.

Her forehead drops to mine, and we're too close to really stare at each other but I think I see all of her anyway before she moves her head to the side and drops it to the crook of my neck.

"We're still just friends," she whispers against my shoulder.

I turn, pressing my lips to the side of her head. "You're probably my best friend, actually."

That might be true. But she's also this unyielding, unbreaking, beautiful person who sculpted me from crumbled clay.

She loves her sister and I know she loves her father even though it hurts her. She's funny when she means to be and endlessly serious the rest of the time, even though she reads books about faeries and doesn't appreciate the intricacies of the French Revolution.

My heart tells me this is a stupid fucking idea, because she's only given me tiny pieces of herself. But I can't really hear it because it's whispering to me from where she is, one leg on either side of mine, hands still on my shoulders, but not really, because they've got that stupid organ of mine in their palms.

Greer

Habits form anywhere between eighteen and two hundred and fifty-four days of repeated behaviour.

Beckett Davis becomes one in significantly less time than that.

As far as habits go, it could be worse.

It's not a habit that would kill most people, but I do worry it might kill me.

Not the sex.

It's the way he smiles. How his laugh strolls across my spine before wrapping around me and clasping itself in the centre of my chest. How the dimple in his left cheek scores, and I think each time it does, it carves another scar on the left side of my ribs to match the one on the right.

Like it might take another organ from me—one that lives just above in my chest, right behind and slightly to the left of my sternum.

I left his house that night and didn't think I'd end up back there.

But I did.

And all it took was him sending me a few facts about the French Revolution he thought I'd find interesting.

Somehow, that had my brain shutting up, lulling it into a false sense of security. Because what was that, if not friendly? It's not like he's been waxing poetic about his undying love for me. His body likes mine and my body likes his. A mutually beneficial arrangement that keeps my heart in its cage but feels more than good for everyone involved. Just sex.

But he might need to work on his definition of interesting—I've heard about Napoleon's alleged intense dislike of cats, that he was apparently afraid of open doors, and about his unrivalled sense of smell.

Those things had me back at his house. On his couch. In his bed. Even sitting at his island in one of his sweaters while he made me what he swore was a nutritious, post-sex meal.

He wasn't wrong. It covered all the bases—lean protein, complex carbs, and vegetables.

But it turns out he's not as lackadaisical as he might have you believe. He's serious about what he puts into his body during the season, and there wasn't much in the way of seasoning.

Earlier, he told me about the temperature Napoleon liked his bath.

Beckett swears all this knowledge is going to be a hit with my patients.

I test it out on Rav first.

"Did you know that Napoleon loved a scalding-hot bath?"

One eyebrow kicks up and amusement glints in his eyes. It echoes in his voice, too. "No, I can't say I did. Where'd you learn that?"

I wave a hand in the air. "I happen to know an expert on the French Revolution. Fascinating stuff."

Rav leans back, resting his feet on the coffee table between us. "How's your anxiety been? Any recent panic attacks?"

"Fine." It's not a lie.

I haven't worn the earmuffs since the game, but sometimes, I feel like maybe I never took them off. Nothing sounds as sharp or as jarring.

I think a lot of things in my life have dulled to the same quiet, pleasant murmur.

If my life were one of the books I read, it would be explained by the presence of Beckett, this person made just for me by whatever benevolent gods ruled the sky.

But here, in this life, it's just science. I'm having more orgasms. That equals more endorphins. Serotonin, dopamine. All the things that calm my brain.

My heart beats a bit funny at the thought—and it whispers, *Liar*.

"I've noticed something." Rav props his head up on his hand, elbow digging into the arm of the leather couch. "The closer we've gotten to the end of your fellowship, the more closed off you've gotten. You were close to an open book when we started seeing one another."

"I'm not sure anyone in my life would have defined me as an open book, Rav," I answer truthfully.

I'm not an intentionally closed-off person. I don't always mean to lie.

I think there are things I would like to share. But there's this weird code we learned when we were kids. I'm not sure where we picked it up because our mother wasn't around to enforce it, but even as children, we kept our father's secrets.

You don't tell your friends on the playground your father drinks too much. That he's not violent, but he can be unpleasant and just not a real dad. That you tuck yourself in because he needs bourbon more than he needs you. You certainly don't tell anyone that he drives you around like that and one time, he drove you off a bridge and you had to give him a part of your liver as a result because his wasn't healing properly and it was going to kill him.

I'm not even sure why it was a secret, but it was. I don't remember being particularly scared someone was going to come take us away. Those were just the confines of the cage we lived in.

The irony is that it is sort of a tenet of sobriety. Sobriety isn't yours to share.

Somewhere along the way, Stella shed the shackles clamping her mouth closed, and I think maybe during the car accident—the water rusted mine shut.

It took me all of college and too many bottles of wine to finally tell Willa and Kate.

Rav nods thoughtfully, before conceding, "An open book with me, then. I didn't know you before, but I'd wager your feelings of resentment about your donation have grown as your fellowship has progressed. How do you think you ended up here?"

"We were in the car and then we weren't and then I was short part of my liver and then I was in college and then I was in med school. I blinked and it was residency, and I took one step and here I was. Taking from people."

"You don't take from people," Rav interjects. You'd think he'd be tired of it by now—Willa said my whole "live life for me" was a diatribe, but this is probably the only sermon I make.

"Someone took from me." My voice fractures when I say it; it cracks my scar open too, revealing all that empty space in me, and I think little me peeks around the corner from wherever it is she hides in there, and she wonders where all the pieces of her have gone.

With an air of maddening patience, he shifts forward. "You gave your consent, Greer."

"I was eighteen." A tear escapes, tracking a path down my cheek.

"Have you ever told your father or your sister this?"

"How would you suggest I do that?" I choke a laugh and raise my hands. "Hey, Stella, Dad, I know I gave you my liver so we could try to be a family, and I did it without knowing if you'd stay sober, so thanks for doing that. But I think I regret it?"

"He stopped drinking, Greer. Do you think maybe that had anything to do with what you gave?"

I inhale and narrow my eyes. "No. Addiction doesn't work that way, and you know it. No one will get sober for anyone but themselves. And I don't say that with judgement. It's one person versus a disease we still don't understand. He did it for himself, and I am thankful he did. It would have been rather unfortunate if he killed my liver, too."

Rav says nothing, but today, it all feels so heavy in my chest, my scar twinges, and he wins. The edges of my vision blur, and I don't bother to wipe at my eyes. "I thought that maybe—I don't know. That it would make me better at this. More understanding. Give me unique compassion in a system that's meant to beat it out of us."

"If you could pick a different specialty, a different residency, would you? What would you pick?"

Blinking, I open my mouth and I'm about to tell him I'm not sure. But I think, despite it all, I am sure. I think of Theo. I think of Jer. I think of the people who died and breathed life into someone else. I press down on my rib cage and remember that it is a beautiful thing. I just wish it looked different. "I'd invent a specialty where I grew livers and pancreases and kidneys on trees and plucked them off for my patients instead of cutting someone else open."

"There's always regenerative medicine." The corners of Rav's eyes crinkle with a smile. "You could do research."

"Maybe," I say softly, offering him a tentative smile, watered by the tears staining my cheeks.

He sits up, swinging his feet off the coffee table. "Are you still seeing the football player?"

I purse my lips, those lines and boundaries and the bars making up the cage of my heart darken. "It's just sex. Surely, I don't have to explain base physical needs to you?"

"Can I offer one more thought before we're done for the day?" He pauses, but he's not waiting for permission. "Your mother left, and though that had to do with your father, I'm sure there's a subconscious part of you that told yourself there was something you could have done differently. That if you just gave more, it would have been enough for her. And then you did give more. You gave a piece of yourself away, and instead of acknowledging that it was a very painful thing you shouldn't have had to do, you've spun this tale about never really living for yourself and being unable to draw lines and boundaries. That if you can just be enough for you—you'll be enough for everyone."

Rav pauses and he says this thing I sort of wish he did ask permission to tell me because I'm not sure I'm ready to hear it.

"You don't have to be alone to be enough."

Beckett

Lights hang from what seem to be carelessly strewn strings attached to poles cemented in planters, strategically placed in each corner of the rooftop. Tables litter the surface, with the occasional heat lamp standing over them, glowing a faint red against the smoggy night sky. It's only mid-September, but Toronto can start getting cold at night pretty early.

I tug on the beak of my hat, pulling it lower over my face as I trail behind Pat and Nowak, the one beer a week I have during the season cold in my hands.

It's pretty crowded for a random bar on a random rooftop—but Nowak swore up and down when we left the practice field that it was the best undiscovered gem in the city.

Seeing as it looks like it's mostly college-aged hipsters, and we're a group of twenty-nine-to-thirty-one-year-old men, I'm not sure I'd give it the same label.

But he might be onto something, because I doubt anyone cares that Beckett "Near Miss" Davis is here.

He stops abruptly at an empty table pushed up against the edge of the rooftop, swipes a hand through his messy brown hair, and pulls out a chair.

Pat looks around, eyebrow rising apprehensively before dropping into the chair beside Nowak. He clears his throat, tipping his beer towards us. "Thanks for staying late today."

"Don't tell Coach Taylor I was running." I finally did what he asked, stayed late when the stadium was empty, practiced routes with Pat, using another skill I have that turned out to be useless, while Nowak watched and stretched.

It was his idea to come out. And if it was two months ago, I would have made up an excuse.

But I think a nice part of being real would be having real friends.

Pat smiles, one corner of his mouth kicking up when he shakes his head. "You can still catch, man. You sure you want to spend the rest of your career shouldering the expectations of a team, barely getting credit for a win but taking all the responsibility for the blame?"

No.

I'm not sure what I want, and I'm about to toss out a typical Beckett Davis grin and deflection. That I always get the credit. That I'm going to win and I'm going to break the next record.

And then I hear it.

They're only a few tables away. She's louder than usual, and her voice seems raspier. I can feel it against my skin, rolling down my shoulders all the way to my fingertips that clench against the perspiring bottle.

Dark hair pulled back into a ponytail, lights illuminating the planes of her face, and pillowy cheeks pink against the night air.

Her sister sits beside her, holding up a phone that looks like it's in the middle of a FaceTime call, and a perspiring ice bucket with a bottle of wine sits between them.

Greer leans forward, this sort of wistful expression on her face. "I'd just love to grow a liver that could grow itself, you know."

"No," Stella answers.

"None of you are listening to me." Greer waves her hands in front of the phone before pointing at her sister. "I'm saying that there's an unexplored area of regenerative medicine that could eliminate the need for living donations. Only one percent—"

Stella groans, drowning out Greer, and I wish she hadn't. I could listen to her talk all night.

I take my hat off, running a hand through my hair, before flipping it backwards. I don't really care who sees me—as long as she does.

It's quickly become the highlight of my day when Greer sees me. Whether it's when she opens her door for me, eyes like that peering up at me from the low light of her hallway, full lips in a soft smile. Or when she gets to my place, eyes always wandering around the towering ceilings of the apartment, the worn exposed brick, until they land on me.

She'd never admit it, but she's always happy to see me. I can tell by the way her cheeks soften, how her nose wrinkles and she smiles more freely than she does anywhere else.

I feel a bit more worthy when she looks at me, because it's never just a look. Not with a girl like that.

A girl I wish was a lot more than just a friend. I'd consider bringing it up again, but I'd rather not scare away the best thing in my life, so I'll have to sit on that for a bit longer.

"What are you—" Nowak squints at me before following my gaze. "Who's that?"

I shrug, take a sip of beer, but I'm smiling. "Just a girl I know."

"Look at his fucking face!" He hits Pat in the shoulder of his throwing arm, only glancing sideways when Pat jerks it out of his reach. "Oh, sorry. But look at that little smirk. Just a girl, Davis, really?"

No. Not even close.

I tip my chin. "I volunteered with her at the hospital. She's a transplant surgeon."

Understanding dawns on his face, and he turns around in his chair, hanging off the back like a child.

"Willa, Kate." Greer's voice rises, and she shakes her head. "Neither of you are being helpful so Stella and I are going to hang up now."

"Hey!" Her sister jerks the phone further from her grasp. "I wasn't done talking to them."

Pat winces, grips his jaw, and shakes his head. He leans forward with a poor attempt at a stage whisper. "Bit like you're eavesdropping, man. Let's just go over there."

"She's with her sister." I shake my head.

But Stella glances over her shoulder, eyes going wide when they land on me. Her mouth pops open before it shifts into a delighted sort of grin. She smacks Greer's shoulder and turns back to the phone, now propped up against the ice bucket. "Sorry, you two, we do have to go. Greer's special friend is here."

Greer turns, ponytail swinging across the back of her jacket, and she angles her head, eyes impassive as she studies me.

But she says my name with the faintest hint of a smile. "Beckett."

I clear my throat and raise my bottle. "Dr. Roberts."

Her sister makes a big show of hanging up the phone and grabbing extra chairs while she waves us over.

I wait for permission, because I only really care about whether Greer wants me over there, and one shoulder lifts in a shrug, like it's nothing, and she turns back to her glass of wine.

It's not nothing to me—to be invited into this small sliver of her personal life—and I don't think it's nothing for her either.

Pat pointedly walks to the other end of their table, avoiding the empty seat beside her.

Stella swirls her wineglass against the table, liquid rising around the edges and trailing down, and smiles knowingly. "What are you doing here?"

"This is Grant's favourite place." Dropping into the seat beside Greer, I jerk my chin towards Nowak. I glance sideways at her and mouth, *Hi*.

One eyebrow rises and I think she smiles at me when she takes a sip of her wine.

"This is *my* favourite place." Stella places a hand to her chest, chin tipping up in the same way I've seen her sister's when she's feeling petulant, emphasis on the "my," like this shitty rooftop is something either of them could claim ownership of.

"Wanna arm wrestle for it?" Nowak grins, turning one of the chairs around and sitting backwards, resting his arm across the back.

Stella sits back in her chair, straightens her shoulders, and folds her arms across her chest like she's considering it. One ringed finger taps against her jacket.

"This is Grant." I point towards Nowak before he swipes everything off the table and does try to arm wrestle her, and I tip my head towards Pat. "This is Pat. We played together in college, actually."

Greer glances between us, lips parted ever so slightly, lines of her Cupid's bow defined in a way that makes me want to run my thumb along it, before she tips her chin up. "Did he bore you with facts about Napoleon, too?"

Pat shakes his head, confused. "No?"

I toss an arm around the back of her chair and tap her shoulder. "Those are just for you."

"Lucky me." She wrinkles her nose, eyes finding the sky.

But then she looks back at me, and I think it's just us here.

"Okay." Stella leans forward, snapping her fingers between us. "Obviously my sister has forgotten her manners in front of Mr. Gatorade, but I'm Stella, and this is Greer. Forgive her, she says she's had a weird day."

Greer inhales, eyes on me for a minute longer before she turns back to her sister.

She doesn't say anything, and she stays quiet most of the night.

Stella and Nowak don't shut up, so it's not like anyone could get a word in edgewise anyway, but I don't mind sitting in silence with her. With them.

Kind of like the me I used to be before—but I think I might prefer this version because he knows her.

At some point, they all get up with poorly veiled excuses about needing to request a song change, or in Stella's case, claiming she needs to talk the bartender through the proper way to mix a Hugo spritz.

It's just us here, and I'd have to glance sideways to see her, but I'm already looking because I've been staring all night.

I tap her shoulder again. "Why was your day weird?"

She turns to me, exhaling, like she's considering what to say, chewing over her words the way her teeth find the inside of her cheek. "I was with my psychiatrist today, and he keeps asking me what I want to do when my fellowship is over. A lot of questions I don't necessarily have the answers to."

A small line of worry etches between her brows, and the corners of her lips turn down.

All that does is remind me how full they are—how she looks too beautiful to be sad.

"What typically happens after a fellowship?"

She shrugs. "You become an attending somewhere. In my case, I'd find a position here or somewhere else and I'd just . . . keep taking from people."

I reach up, brush my thumb along her cheek and shrug. "I think you give more than you take."

She blinks up at me, eyes wide and bright under the hanging lights. She has a lot of secrets, and this seems like another one, so I let her keep it and press my thumb to her cheek before letting go. "I didn't know you see a psychiatrist."

Greer smiles ruefully. "There are a lot of things you don't know about me."

"You could tell me, you know. Friends tell friends things."

She tips her head and sets the wineglass on the table.

She doesn't kiss me hello or goodbye. She doesn't kiss me if we aren't having sex.

But she kisses me tonight.

She tips her chin up, like she's considering something, weighing the merits of her choice, but something in her face softens and some part of her wins, because she leans forward and brushes her lips against mine.

Lightly.

Like she doesn't want to add the weight of anything more.

She doesn't realize she's not a heavy thing.

Her fingers whisper across my shoulders, up the lines of my neck, until each one of her palms finds either side of my face.

Her mouth lingers against mine, and when she finally pulls back, her eyes are a bit hazy, lips slightly parted and cheeks flushed with alcohol.

"You're drunk, baby." I grin when I say it because I can start to see those wheels turning in her mind as she realizes she's overstepped whatever lines she's drawn for herself, and I think she needs something that's going to give her permission to step back from whatever ledge she's teetering on.

She narrows her eyes, something shutters behind them, and she points at me. "No *baby*."

"I call all my friends baby. Just ask when they get back." I tip my beer towards Nowak's empty seat.

They do come back—Stella sans Hugo spritz, and the same tracks playing over the speakers—and they look between us, a bit like teenagers waiting for some big reveal.

There isn't one.

If the girl beside me hadn't made me real, I'd say the whole kiss was a figment of my imagination.

And it might as well have been, because Greer points at me before turning to Nowak and Pat. "Does he call you baby?"

"What?" Nowak looks confused for a second before he sits back down and decides to play along. "Oh, yeah. He does. Here." He reaches into his pocket and tosses his phone onto the table. "You can check our texts. Baby this, baby that."

Her lips pucker, and she eyes the empty bottle of wine on the table. "Stella, we should go."

Stella glances back and forth between us, assessing, like she's trying to parse out what did or didn't happen, before she rolls her eyes and pushes to stand. "Fine. Nice to meet you both."

"It was nice to meet you." Greer echoes her sister as she stands, careful not to brush up against me at all. "Good luck this Sunday."

She offers Pat and Nowak a perfunctory smile before she turns to me.

"Night, Dr. Roberts," I whisper.

She blinks. "Good night, Beckett."

We look at each other for probably too long before she grabs her sister's hand and tugs her towards the door.

"Davis." Nowak sets a palm on the table and shakes his head, messy brown hair flopping down over his forehead like it's rueful, too. "You're so fucked."

I make a noncommittal noise and glance back over my shoulder.

She's holding her sister's hand, weaving through the tables, growing more and more crowded the later it gets. But she stops right before the door, and she looks back at me, too.

She doesn't say anything, but she raises a hand and wrinkles her nose before disappearing through the open door.

I watch her go, and I'm not really sure about much anymore, other than the fact that she might have made me a living, breathing person—but he's someone who wants something I'm not sure he can have.

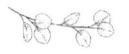

The league has all sorts of stupid distinctions and awards they give out each week. If you're someone like me, you've probably won a lot of them.

You've been to the Pro Bowl, and you've been named to the All-Pro Team.

My season is arguably off to a great start. And usually, I'd be all about celebrating that. I'd be chasing the stupid, meaningless awards each week because who am I if I'm not winning at this?

And it's not that I don't care. I do. But a few months ago, this would have been the only thing in the entire world I wanted, and I wouldn't have even had to chase after it.

They all would have belonged to me, week after week.

Old Beckett Davis was a certainty.

This me, though—I'm not sure he's certain about anything.

I don't know what I'm going to kick like on Sunday. I don't think I can trust these stupid legs anymore.

Maybe it's because that was the only thing I ever knew about myself.

But I think I'm learning other things about me.

I think real me, whoever he is, might actually be a good friend—and it's not because I pay for things for my family, or I deliver on the field. He's allowed to have bad days and complicated days and all the other days everyone else gets to have.

He can be who he is and still be worthy of a girl who isn't just a girl, a friend who isn't just a friend, brushing her lips against his on a crowded rooftop bar.

Still worthy of her time and attention and the three seconds she gifted me when she let her guard down, even though I had a bad practice that day and couldn't kick for shit.

Maybe whatever lives inside me behind the stupid grin and the stupid dimple might be worthy of a lot of things.

I wish I was with her now, not here in this stupid chair at the stadium.

Coach does this thing each week—when we're back to practice after a game, no matter the outcome, we don't open the week examining our mistakes. We sit in one of the conference rooms after the morning workout and we talk about everything that went well.

This week, he talks about me.

"Special Teams Player of the Week." Coach Taylor points the football towards me, and I feel myself sink lower in my chair. I'd turn my hat forward and pretend I couldn't see him if it wouldn't be so obvious.

"Four field goals. All over 50 yards. That's not counting the extra points. You haven't missed all season. Special teams secure wins, and you do what you need to do to make sure the offense and defense can do their jobs." He pauses again, like he's mulling something over, while everyone else claps or smacks the desks in front of them. "That record is yours, Davis. You're the best kicker in the league. We're going to be with you when you take it. It belongs to you, just like a championship belongs to this team."

He sits back against the desk, the knots in my shoulders loosen, and I think he's done. He'll move on to the next thing he deems necessary to laud and the next ego he thinks he needs to inflate, so we all go into this week feeling like we're unstoppable.

"That"—he punctuates the word with another point of the football that feels a bit like it's cutting me—"is the Beckett Davis we know and love. That's the Beckett Davis we need. Welcome back."

It's supposed to be motivational.

That's the Beckett Davis we know and love. That's the Beckett Davis we need.

Like that's the only version of me that ever mattered.

Welcome back.

Each letter in those two words lands on my shoulders at once, and I don't feel particularly worthy of anything anymore. And I bet if I looked down, I'd see the legs of my chair cracking through the concrete flooring.

Greer

In the way that Beckett becomes a habit, so does going to his house after particularly difficult shifts, usually when I've spent hours stealing organs from teenagers who didn't ask to die and putting them in teenagers who desperately just want to live.

A safe space, if you will.

A place where I can avoid things, and I've been avoiding a lot of things, including the fact that alcohol short-circuited my brain and I brushed my mouth across his in a too-intimate gesture in a too-public space outside the confines of this room. Where I don't have to dissect my innermost feelings about my surgical career.

A boy definitely lives here in this bedroom—but it's lovely and beautiful. A giant wall of exposed brick stretches behind this king bed that probably cost more money than I would ever want to know. An oak dresser riddled with important things—pictures of his family, his favourite watch, and a particularly important football.

A high-pile rug that covers most of the usually cold cement floor, and floor-to-ceiling paned windows with a wonderful view of the city. You can just make out the outline of the stadium from here.

His bedding—crisp navy sheets with a matching duvet—always rumpled in exactly the best way. He doesn't really make his bed, just sort of fluffs the endless array of pillows and pulls the duvet up haphazardly.

There are a lot of things in this room—but when I'm here, it's just us.

We leave the rest of it at the door. Football. Surgery. Any acknowledgement of the fact that we've ended up here together. Again.

Rav says it's not friendly behaviour, and I still haven't worked up the courage to say anything to my sister, but I know what she'd think.

And it probably isn't friendly behaviour, but my brain reminds me that I once gave away a literal piece of my body when I wasn't sure I wanted to, and that protecting our remaining organs—our heart—is of the utmost importance if we're to survive.

I hear the shower turn off and I glance up from my book—it was just getting good.

But watching Beckett come out of the shower isn't an experience I particularly feel like missing. It's a nice bonus to our friendship—the fact that he looks like someone sculpted him like Michelangelo did *David*.

The door to the bathroom opens, and one eyebrow kicks up when he sees me. He was in the shower when I got here, but he left the door open for me, and I crawled right into his bed. Friend-like.

Moisture hugs every carved inch of him, his skin still damp, and the black Lycra of his boxers leaves little to the imagination, clinging to each curve of thigh muscle and everything else.

"How was your day?" He runs the towel over his face, scrubbing it over his head and shaking out his hair before he tosses it into the hamper by the door.

"Oh, you know." I open a hand and wave it around. "Just another day of playing my twisted version of Robin Hood. Stealing organs from the dead and giving them to the living."

"Saving lives," he corrects, and something passes behind his eyes. We've hovered around this topic, circled it and come close to dancing right on top of it. He knows I don't always love my job, but he's not quite sure why yet, and there's this thing Beckett doesn't even realize is beautiful—he doesn't push. He doesn't pry. He just meets people where they are.

"It just seems . . ." I exhale, shutting the book and propping myself up against the pillows. "Wrong sometimes. To hope for an organ for someone I'm treating and trying to help when I know it means someone probably had to die to give it up."

That sometimes, I wish someone else did die and give my dad a piece of them so I didn't have to.

Beckett nods, blinking at me. He pulls back the covers on his side of the bed and sits there, reaching out, one thumb brushing over the fabric of my tank top, the raised skin of the scar jutting out ever so slightly. "If you could be anything, what would you be?"

"A faerie princess." I hold up the book before chewing on my lip. "Or a human captive who finds out she's actually part of a magical race."

He smiles—and it's this radiant thing. It's not "the grin," as it's known. It's not something you'd see in that stupid Gatorade commercial I still haven't watched all the way through, or any of the press shots he's in.

He looks at ease. Comfortable, like he's just Beckett, unburdened by all those shackles and responsibilities that made him Beckett Davis—likeable, reliable, many-things-extraordinaire instead of a regular person.

He lies back, propping his head up with one arm. Droplets of water track down his trapezius muscles, across the swell of his shoulders, and over the jut of his biceps. "Would you like to be my prisoner?"

"Beckett doesn't sound like the name of a brooding, morally grey fae lord who could fuck me into next week." I shrug, waving the book around. "Sorry."

He nods, like he's conceding defeat. But real Beckett, like Beckett Davis, is wildly competitive, and unlike Beckett Davis, real Beckett is a bit childlike at times. He lunges forward, grabbing the book from my hands and throwing it to the floor, before rolling on top of me and pinning my hands above my head. "Beckett's not here. I'm Baxtian, and I'm taking you down to my dungeon."

I blink up at him, lips parted, before I burst out laughing. "Oh my god, that's so fucking stupid."

"But it's close, right?" He raises his eyebrows, and some of his still-damp hair falls across his forehead.

I nod, biting on my lip before smiling at him. "It is."

We stare at each other for a minute that seems to go on for much longer than sixty seconds—and so it goes: another night between two friends.

His fingers twitch and tense against my wrists.

Those full lips of his part, his eyes find my mouth—they trace all the curves of me. My jawline, my collarbone, the swell of my chest under my tank top.

His hips shift and mine rise to meet them.

He hardens between my legs, and all of my skin prickles and sets itself on fire.

He grins—an entirely different grin I hope he only ever makes for me. Beckett's eyes find my mouth and he lowers to meet it.

My lips part for his tongue. We kiss and kiss and kiss. My hands scramble across the planes of his back, the ridges and valleys of his shoulders. All of me lights up when he breaks away and one of those beautiful, wonderous hands pulls down my top and his teeth scrape my nipple.

I arch into him when that other hand grips my rib cage. His tongue still swirls, and I pant when that other hand moves to my hip, bruising it before it tugs down my shorts, scoring down the centre of me—moving up and down and soaking itself before moving in these circles that make me want to die a bit and have me saying his name over and over, like maybe it's a prayer that the real Beckett will hear and know he's wonderful and lovely and good.

That maybe the way he makes me say his name with something I can only describe as reverence will breathe life back into him.

And while I pray and pray and pray that I can give him oxygen, he tosses my clothes aside with that forgotten book, and my hands scramble to get rid of his underwear, too, so I can touch all of him. I do, but just for a moment, before he's rolling a condom on, angling above me just so, and pushing into me with a groan.

We always pause here—his forehead against mine, ragged breath and his pupils blown—before he starts to move.

Tonight, he rolls his hips just twice before wrapping an arm around my shoulders and flipping over so I'm on top of him.

His hands find my waist, his eyes on me, lips parted and hair askew. We start to move at the same time and he pushes his head back into the pillow, a groan catching in his throat when I tip mine back, fingers digging into his chest.

I have these lines and these boundaries and my brain screams at me—but there's this other small, quiet, maybe beautiful part of me that whispers something else. I think it's my heart. It's beating, but I think it whispers to me that maybe, I should give it to him.

That I could carve this other vital organ from my body and place it in his hands and he'd keep it safe.

On nights like these, I almost believe it.

I moan his name, I pray for him, and his hands hold me and I think they ask me to please, please, open for him.

And so it goes.

Greer

Rav asked me to think about the sometimes, and the other times—when I love my job, and when I hate my job.

We didn't start the session that way the last time I was there because I was too busy spreading the word about Napoleon, and I've been too busy since being spread out by Beckett to really give it much thought.

But that's not terribly friendly, and it's not in my nature to leave homework incomplete, so I locked myself in an available on-call room and drew a line down a scrap piece of paper, like I could somehow reduce whatever it is inside me that broke all those years ago to a pros and cons list.

I tap my pen against the top of the page.

It's difficult to pinpoint exactly when I started feeling a bit like a thief.

I didn't feel like a thief this morning when I put a new kidney in someone who spent their whole life attached to a dialysis machine.

But a page comes in on my phone, my chest constricts, and I feel a bit like one now.

My least favourite kind of page.

There are different types of organ donation—and most people don't realize that the majority of what we do is because of living donations. Only about one-to-two percent of donors are deceased, and within that tiny, infinitesimal percentage, there are two different kinds.

Organ donation after circulatory death, when your heart stops, and after neurological determination of death, when your brain does.

It's one of the most beautiful things to me—that people have made this choice in life that allows them to save other people after they're gone.

But for some reason, it hurts me the most.

I think it might be because it reminds me that I'm a hypocrite—to allegedly be dedicated to saving lives, but once upon a time, I was just a little girl wishing on a star that someone else, somewhere on the planet, lost theirs.

Inhaling, I drop the phone against the desk. The invisible clock starts—there isn't always long to do a harvest and I need to go.

But the phone starts vibrating, and my stomach twists for an entirely different reason when I see the name on the screen.

"Dad?" My fingers slip when I pick it up.

"Greer?" He sounds weary, and maybe a bit congested. "I'm sorry, I forgot to go get my meds this week. I kept meaning to go after my meetings. I ran out yesterday but I'm just not feeling . . . Could you go to the pharmacy for me? Your sister is out of town."

She is. She left yesterday for a conference in Vancouver.

Two whole days of someone who relies on immunosuppressants going without them.

I squeeze my eyes shut; there's a pang in my right side, and I wonder if that's my liver telling me the other part of it that lives in him has started to attack him.

"I can't—" I pinch the bridge of my nose. The back of my throat sets itself on fire with unshed tears. "How many times have I asked you to let me know if you're running low? You can't just stop taking your meds. Even if it's just a day. Your body could start—" I inhale, and it hurts. I press my hand to the right side of my ribs. "I can't leave. I need to—there's a harvest and—okay, you know what? I'll call a friend. I'll get him to bring them over. Just stay put."

I don't wait for the exasperation or the apology—I'm never sure which is going to come—before I hang up and make another call.

Beckett picks up on the first ring. I can hear his smile through the phone. "Hey, Dr. Roberts. To what do I owe the pleasure?"

"You haven't left for Philadelphia yet, right?" My voice cracks horribly, and I think I can feel one of my ribs go with it.

I imagine him shaking his head, one wave of chocolate hair falling over his forehead and emerald eyes sharpening with concern. "No. We don't leave until Friday. I just got home from practice. What's wrong?"

"I need a favour, and it needs to be right now. My sister is out of town. My dad isn't feeling well and he's out of his meds. He *needs* to take them every day. I can't go to the pharmacy because I have about fifteen minutes to scrub in for a liver harvest before it's no longer viable. Can you—if I text you everything—go get them and drop them off?" I press harder against my rib cage. "Please?"

"Just text me everything you need me to do, and you can consider it done. Okay?" He pauses, and I can imagine him in front of me, peering down at me, breathing with me until I'm ready to answer.

"Okay. Wear a mask, please? He sounds like he's coming down with something. He's immunocompromised, and he's never met you before," I whisper. "Thank you."

I can hear the smile in his voice again, and the sound his keys make when he picks them up from his kitchen island. "Sure. You don't have to thank me. Go save lives, Dr. Roberts."

He hangs up before I can tell him that it might not exactly be a life he's saving, but it's a piece of me.

I stand, take my hypocrisy with me, and go operate.

The plants spilling from the garden onto the sidewalk leading up to my father's house have shrunk since I was last here, curling inwards more and more as October starts and the air cools off.

Some have already started shedding their leaves, and they crunch under my shoes as I walk up to the door.

I kick them off like I always do when I come straight here from the hospital.

I took the time to shower and change today, my arms still red and raw from the scrub brush I took to my skin, trying to get every little speck of everything clinging to my skin off, so I could be clean, safe, and not this thing that might pose a danger when I came here.

Logically, I'm aware I'm being paranoid. But I think I know too much and I'm about as close to it as you can be.

I knock before opening the door and dropping my coat and bag on the floor. "Dad?"

There's this little kernel of anxiety that's been burrowing in my chest all day. It defies logic and all the things I know, and it whispers to me that it's already started—he missed his meds and he's rejecting the liver after all these years and all of it was for nothing.

But its sharp, stabbing edges soften when my dad answers from the living room, "He won't take the mask off, Greer."

"What? Who?" I ask the question, even though I don't have to.

Beckett glances at me from where he sits when I round the corner into the living room, kicked back in an ancient leather chair, face half hidden under a blue surgical mask, but I can see the edge of his dimple drawing a line in his stubbled cheek.

I raise my hand, this tiny gesture that I hope conveys all the big, impossible things stretching and pushing against all my lines and rules that I feel for him right now.

Inhaling, I close my eyes briefly before turning to my dad, brows sharpening. "Well, he's never met you and you've been without your immunosuppressants for two days, so you'll have to forgive the extra precaution."

My dad barely spares me a glance from the couch, fiddling with the remote. "I'm not in isolation."

Beckett raises his hands, and I can tell he's smiling by the way the corners of his eyes crinkle ever so slightly. "I'm just following the doctor's orders. She can get pretty mean, you know."

My dad makes a noise of acknowledgement, and I give Beckett a pointed look as I press the back of my hand to my father's forehead.

He doesn't feel warm, and I swipe my hand through the feathers of his hair. I hope he knows it's all because I care—because I do mean well even if it hurts me when he forgets. I'm not trying to be harsh or mean.

"I feel fine, Greer." My dad glances up at me, the ghost of an apology waving up at me from the lines of his smile. "Your *friend* Beckett delivered everything, and I've taken my meds. I'm a bit nauseous, but I ate, and Beckett brought ginger ale."

I roll my shoulders and force the weight of the intonation he put on the word *friend* off my body and try to ignore the fact that not only is Beckett still here, but he stayed all afternoon, and now they're on a first-name basis.

"The nausea should subside by tomorrow." I run my hands through my dad's hair one more time, against the burning in the back of my throat. All these things I want to say—that I love him, but it hurts me when he does this, and can he please, please stop?

But I take a measured step back when I feel Beckett's eyes on me.

His features are soft, and he's looking at me with something I can't quite place and it makes me feel a way I'm not sure I like.

I clear my throat. "You can take your mask off now."

Wonderful, calloused hands find the loops around his ears, and when he takes it off, he's grinning, dimple on display, all of him looking radiant and entirely unbothered.

"You didn't have to stay all afternoon. I didn't mean to imply you had to."

Beckett shrugs, raking a hand through his hair, muscles of his arms flexing underneath his sweater. "All good. We got to chatting when I was dropping things off and I mentioned I'd never seen *Game of Thrones*—"

"You've never seen *Game of Thrones*?" I ask flatly.

"Nah." He shakes his head, right leg starting to bounce up and down, and I wonder if he skipped his stretching to get here. "Didn't sit quite right with Henry over here, so I said I'd watch an episode or two. And here we are, about to watch something called the Red Wedding."

I cross my arms and drop to the couch opposite my dad. Closest to Beckett. "That's in the third season, and I don't think that surgery was a time portal to another dimension, so you certainly haven't been here that long."

"Oh, I just"—Beckett smiles, brushing his palms together with a clapping sound, pointing his right hand towards the TV—"dove right in. Headfirst. You know me."

"I told him that's not how the series is meant to be consumed." My dad shakes his head, finally dropping the remote when the opening credits start rolling across the TV. "But he was insistent on just joining in where I'd left off."

"You know me," Beckett repeats, winking at me.

I do know you, I think. And I'm not sure there's anything scarier than that.

The room dims when my dad turns off the light, not even bothering to ask if I'm going to stay. He knows I won't leave until I've checked his temperature at least three more times and watched him consume at least a litre of fluids.

Fingers brush across my thigh, gentle, soothing circles just like those ones they painted on my calves all those weeks ago.

Before I can think better of it, I grab Beckett's hand, interlacing our fingers in the dark. I squeeze it three times and I hope he hears what my heart whispers to him.

Thank you. I see you. I know you.
And I think you know me, too.

Greer

Shadows from the streetlights inch across the hallway, past my front door and along the worn hardwood of my living room. My shadow, and Beckett's, right behind me, stretch down along the floor, but they disappear when the door clicks shut behind us and I flick on the hallway light, illuminating everything.

"It smells nice in here." His voice, low, rough, and almost a whisper, skitters across the back of my neck.

"What? Oh." I inhale. It's mostly him I smell—whatever that is. But I can faintly smell Stella's eucalyptus. "It's the eucalyptus in my room. My sister put it there. She thought it would be calming."

I take a pointed step into the living room, turning on those lights, too.

Beckett follows, giving me a wry grin. "Does it help?"

I shake my head through a small smile. "Not really."

Beckett raises his eyebrows at me, and he waits.

He's good at that. Giving me space.

"Thank you for your help today," I say, and I mean it. From the very bottom of my heart.

He was more careful with that piece of me today than my father and sister are. "I'm sorry you had to wear the mask all day. It was probably an overreaction."

"They don't bother me. We practically grew up wearing them." He shrugs, like PPE being a regular part of his childhood attire is a normal, pedestrian occurrence.

But my stomach drops and my right ribs twinge—because I wasn't thinking about him. I wasn't thinking about how that might have hurt him or brought him back to a place he doesn't want to be. I swallow. "I'm so—I'm so sorry. I didn't even think."

Beckett tosses me a grin, and I think it's a real one. "It's okay. I would have told you if it was an issue for me."

There's a weight to the way he says *you*—it's all wrapped up in trust and feelings of safety. Like he can be real with me.

It's a bit weird, I know it is—that he just spent all afternoon with my father, and we held hands while we watched TV in the dark—and now we're here, coming home to my apartment and trading all this casual conversation about these very serious things like it's something we do all the time.

But I don't think he wants to leave—there's that restless energy all over him he gets when I think everything that he carries becomes too heavy and he's trying anything he can to spread the weight around. His thumb taps against his bicep, his shoulders roll back, and his kicking leg bounces up and down.

I don't want him to leave. I think I like being a person he can just be himself with. "Are you ready for the game?"

"No." Beckett tugs on the ends of his hair and snorts, dropping back on my couch like even just the idea of it exhausts him. "I've been kicking terribly. Blowing up in practice. Philly's who we beat to get to the championship last year. Division rivals, lots of pressure, and all that. Big expectations on social media. I've never missed a kick against them, and I can't fucking stop people from commenting on everything or DMing me to ask when I'm going to try for the record again. It's not even in my control. I don't call when a kick happens."

I tuck my legs underneath me to sit beside him, crossing my arms. "Are you good under pressure?"

"Sure. I used to be." He says it like he's referring to this other version of himself—someone he can only just see, a tiny speck in the distance as he sails away from whatever land he used to live on. "I could catch, I could kick. I could make sure a science project got done with shockingly few items available in the house, and I could smooth out a wig like you wouldn't believe."

He offers me things like this all the time—little truths of what made him who he is. How he's given and given and given. Even if he doesn't see it that way.

I think of little him—not quite an adult, but a parent of the household all the same.

It makes me want to offer him something in return.

I sit up straighter, adjusting so I'm taller than I know this story is going to make me feel. "I'm going to tell you something I don't tell people."

One brow kicks up and he tips his head, a wave of chocolate hair curling over his ear.

I sniff. "I mean it. Only six people in the entire world know this story from start to finish. Me. My sister. My dad. Kate. Willa. My psychiatrist, and I'm not even entirely sure he counts because he's a medical professional."

Beckett nods. "Okay."

"The car accident—" I wring my hands together, fingers twisting, and I blink.

"Take your time." His voice is low.

"This is hard for me. Because it's not just my story and it's not simple." I dig at the seam of my couch cushion. "Growing up, my dad was an alcoholic. I'm not going to bore you with the details of what that was like, just me and Stella and a father who couldn't really be relied on for much." And even though it's been years, a fissure snakes its way through my voice, and I feel myself turning inwards when I say what comes next. "He was drunk when we were in the car accident. My ribs and clavicle were shattered. Stella's skull was fractured, and her pancreas was essentially shredded."

I inhale, nothing but choppy breaths. "And by stupid, stupid, stupid luck, his blood alcohol level wasn't taken until much later when it was below the legal limit again, so there weren't really any consequences for it."

Except that there were.

His eyes flash. "But he needed a new liver because of the accident?"

"Sort of. He wasn't healing the way he should have because of all the damage he'd done to his liver. But he wasn't sober at the time, and you have to be sober for six months to qualify for the transplant list, and even then, he would have been at the bottom." I look down, scraping one thumbnail against the other because I'm not sure I can look at him when I tell him this next part. "Stella wasn't a match. I was."

Beckett just waits. It's not quite like the battle of wills between me and Rav. I think Beckett might wait all night.

"And she wanted to be so badly." I stab my finger into my palm and shake my head. "She understood him in ways I never really have, and the only thing she wanted was for us to be together. I know this makes me ... bad. But I didn't want to. I wanted him to love us enough to make a change for us, and I wanted him to love me enough that he wouldn't risk my life and drive me off a fucking bridge. I didn't want to give him any more pieces of me. He took my childhood and he drove away my mother and he made my sister sad. But I didn't think I could say no."

The noise clawing at my throat finally escapes, echoing across my living room. It's not quite a sob, but it's something unpleasant. Maybe it's all the mean, hateful things I think about myself that I try to keep inside. "Who doesn't want to give their parent something that's going to help them? Who thinks about withholding it in some sort of twisted ultimatum?"

"You're not bad," he tells me. It's all he says. He just sits there, patient and waiting.

"This"—I pluck at my shirt where it sits right above my scar—"it fixed everything. Him. Fixed them. Fixed us. Our family. But I don't think—I don't think it fixed me. Who does that?" I hold up a hand, waving it around, like we're there in the operating room over a decade ago when a surgeon leans over my draped body, getting ready to cut me open, and I'm pointing to the whole thing, waiting to demonstrate the dissolution of the person I could have been. "Who gives away a piece of themselves, regrets it, and then dedicates their whole life to doing the thing they wish wasn't done to them? I thought it would make me uniquely compassionate, but it just made me a lying hypocrite."

A muscle feathers in his jaw, and he drops his hand to my knee. "It probably hurts—a lot—when he forgets to pick up his meds."

It's another simple statement, but not really. It seems easy, logical even, but it's something I can never make my father and sister understand no matter how hard I try.

He says I see right through him, but I think he sees right through me, too.

"Yes." I inhale, and my lungs feel lighter than they have in a very, very long time. Like it wasn't real oxygen before, but it is now because he sees me. "It makes me feel like—"

"It doesn't matter?" Beckett offers, voice low.

I nod, sniffing again like some sort of child.

But he leans forward, one thumb swiping across my cheek before he tips my chin up. His other hand finds the hem of my T-shirt, fingers brushing over my scar. The lines of his jaw look unfairly beautiful up close, stubble peppering all those sharp edges. "I don't think you need to be fixed."

My eyes close, and I feel the way his fingers trail over that allegedly healed, raised part of skin. I think, maybe, I can feel them on those old striations in my rib cage, over the ghost of a scar on that liver that healed itself. They tie new sutures, and they whisper that they could help—that maybe they could erase all those old scars permanently, maybe they could love me if I just let them.

But when I love people, I can't help but give myself away.

Blinking, I shift back slightly, just out of reach. If Beckett notices, he doesn't say anything. He just stares at me intently, sharp set to his jaw and eyes dark.

I bite down on the inside of my cheek and give a little shake of my head. I take out my invisible marker and I start scribbling in all the lines that we just blurred. "It's why I don't—won't—date. I don't even know how I ended up where I am. All my lines and my boundaries distorted, and somehow, I've ended up dedicating myself to this thing that hurt me immeasurably."

I don't tell him he scares me. That he's wonderful and lovely and he does things to my heart and my body I can't quite make sense of—but I can't be just another heavy thing he carries, either.

He studies me for a minute longer, like he's steeling himself to say something, to refute that idea, but he swallows, before he grins and says, "So, the Red Wedding is pretty intense, huh?"

"Shut up." I wipe my eyes, but my shoulders shake with laughter.

Beckett's grin grows wider, those lines around his eyes deepen. He stretches out his arm across the back of the couch and jerks his chin towards the crook of his shoulder.

I give him a pointed look; he rolls his eyes before holding up his hands and dropping them firmly to his thighs.

"Better?" he asks, voice dry.

"Friendlier." I tip my chin up in confirmation.

Beckett cocks his head, one wave tumbling down over his forehead. "Didn't you kiss me last week?"

"No," I say, crossing my arms in a pathetic gesture of petulance. "That must have been someone else."

It was someone else, I think. A girl who forgot who she was for a minute when she looked at a beautiful boy through a brain with fuzzy edges.

He considers, lines of the dimple faint in his cheek. "Huh. Don't think so. Can't imagine a world where I'd mix you up with anyone else."

I look pointedly towards the opposite end of the couch, like maybe I'll go sit down there.

NEAR MISS

I don't.

I sit back. My shoulder brushes his, and my thigh presses up against the muscled expanse of his leg.

We turn on the TV, and even though I can't see him, I can tell by the way his body moves, his shoulder upwards or his leg stretching out, when he's relaxed or smiling.

It's an entirely too intimate way to know someone, what movements of their body give away something as innocuous as a smile.

But I inhale all that clean, beautiful, light, and free oxygen he poured into the room when he opened up the door and saw me, and I beg my head to shut up, that it is friendly.

All the while my heart whispers to me that I'm a liar.

Beckett

I don't blow up against Philadelphia like I have been in practice since Coach's little welcome-back speech.

We still win, but I do miss a kick that old Beckett Davis could have made with his eyes closed. Only 30 yards and a seemingly guaranteed point.

I don't bother looking Coach Taylor in the eye afterwards, seeing as that's definitely not the Beckett Davis he knows and loves.

It's obviously not the Beckett Davis everyone else knows and loves, either, because it was enough to start a different sort of conversation online—nothing about how I shattered the hopes and dreams of a nation, but this more nefarious thing, that maybe I'm past my prime.

That I've broken my last record, and if I've gone from someone who never misses to someone who's nothing more than a near miss to inconsistent—that's the death of a special teams kicking game right there.

That I'm uselessly taking up cap space and they should probably trade me while they can still get something for me. They can get inconsistent for a lot cheaper than they can get me.

Kicking is a fickle business, as stupid as it sounds. Guys get dropped and picked up all the time. It wouldn't have happened to old Beckett.

I've been reliable, I've been likeable. I've been neither of those things at the same time—but I've never been useless.

And maybe this new me—whoever he is, because he's definitely real, this effervescent, complicated, stubborn, and sort of mean but beautiful woman breathed life into him—is just that.

Useless.

I wonder what my family would think of the word.

I don't think they'd know what to do with me if I wasn't providing for them in some way.

Maybe all those things I thought I was learning don't really matter if no one else learns them, too.

Even though I don't feel like it, I show up for them today. I'm not sure I'm likeable, but I'm reliable and I do it with a grin.

Our mom even comments on it. Both hands find either side of my face, and she gives this exasperated sigh with a tiny shake of her head, like she can't quite believe it. "That smile."

It's about as close to affection as she can show me. I keep smiling at her, and I try to remind myself that she just doesn't know what to do with me.

I exist in a weird in between for her: not quite a stranger and not quite a son.

"Your brother will be so happy you're here," she whispers, voice breaking, and I know enough to know it's not emotion for me that's shining through. She pats my cheek one more time before pointing behind her at the lines of tables taking up residence in the hospital atrium.

Red and white balloons—a bit on the nose if you ask me—float just above the tables, anchored down by weights wrapped in silver. Nathaniel and Sarah stand at the registration table, stacking endless booklets.

I'm about to make up an excuse—that it's hard for an athlete to find time when they can give blood and it won't interfere with training, which is true but not entirely the reason I've never come—when she says this thing that's meant to be good-natured, but it's really, really not. "He's been wanting you to come to one of his drives for so long."

My eyebrows pinch together. I kind of feel like she took a football and did the kicking, but instead of going through the uprights, it goes right into my stomach.

I used to donate all the time. I'm the same type as Sarah, and she needed regular transfusions.

I try to smile when my brother and sister glance up, but I don't think it reaches my eyes, and according to my agent, that's a pretty crucial part of "the grin."

Nathaniel raises a hand, and my sister smiles wide and says my name like she's actually happy to see me. They've been doing this together for a long time. Sarah can't donate blood, but she volunteers at the drives.

My brother claps me on the shoulder when he comes to stand with us. "What are you doing here? Looking for your special friend?"

"Are you still seeing that doctor?" Sarah's voice rises, nothing but a squeak of excitement.

"We're not seeing each other," I mutter, palming my jaw and changing the subject because I don't feel like telling them she says we're friends but we sleep together sometimes, I've never met anyone like her, she's got my entire heart in her palms, she told me something only six other people on the planet know, and I'll only ever have pieces of her in my back pocket.

Oh, and she kissed me one time when she was half drunk.

Clearing my throat, I reach forward and tug on Sarah's hair. "How's Lily?"

Sarah's lip quivers and she takes a tiny swallow. "There were fewer eggs than last time, so . . . we'll see."

She tries to put on this bright smile, but her eyes shine.

I can see our mother in my periphery, wringing her hands and glancing back and forth between us.

I try not to look at her because I'd offer anyway, but I wrap my arm around Sarah and hug her to my chest briefly. "Don't worry about it. I meant it before. Whatever you need. As much as you need. As many tries as you want."

Sarah nods softly, blinking up at me. I think she's about to say thank you—she always does, and she always means it—when Nathaniel smacks my shoulder.

"Speak of the devil."

I don't need to follow Nathaniel's gaze to know—I think the composition of the air in the room changes.

At least the air I'm breathing.

I haven't seen her since the night she told me the truth—her truth—about her father, the car accident, and her donation. I tried not to make it as big of a deal as I felt like it was—I was a bit worried she'd run away like a startled animal if I told her that it made me want to cut my lungs out of my chest so she could have those, too.

That I think she's one of the bravest people I've ever met in my entire life, I wasn't real before I met her, and I really wish she'd scrap this no dating rule.

Greer isn't looking at us when she steps off the staircase—the tiny furrow between her brows tells me she's thinking. Her lips move as her eyes track across her phone, and one hand twirls her braid absentmindedly.

But her eyes flick up and meet mine. She cocks her head, one eyebrow rises, and a small smile plays on her mouth.

I lift my hand, and I sort of think she's going to ignore me in favour of whatever else it is she needs to be doing, but she starts walking towards us.

"Wait—" Nathaniel's fingers tense against my shoulder, and I think he tries to step behind me. "She's not coming over here, is she?"

I cut him a sideways glance. "What is your problem? She's nicer than you."

He gives a jerk of his head and takes a measured step away from me. "She yelled at a PGY4 the other day for mixing up her playlists when she was doing a PTA transplant."

I hate that. Because I know why she did it. How she must have felt and how she would have felt about yelling afterwards.

I sort of feel like running around the hospital and yelling at all the residents until they stop doing things that hurt her.

But she looks just fine when she stops in front of me.

"Dr. Roberts." I hold out my hand with a grin.

She rolls her eyes, but she reaches out and shakes it anyway. "Beckett."

My heart pushes against my ribs when she says my name, and I brush my thumb across the back of her hand.

Her eyes narrow and she takes a step back. I feel like throwing her one of those lazy smiles she gets a kick out of, but she turns to my brother. "Dr. Davis. I hope everything has gone well with the drive. I was planning to donate when I finish my shift."

"This is our mom and sister," Nathaniel blurts, pointing back and forth between them.

Greer's lips turn down in confusion, and she blinks, but pivots towards my mom and sister. "Lovely to meet you."

She holds out a hand for Sarah, and then for my mother.

My mom looks back and forth between us with wide eyes, like she's waiting for me to tell her she's just met the mother of her future grandchildren. She does that—has these weird motherly instincts that aren't really followed through with action.

I spare Greer having to watch her flounder anymore. "Mom, Dr. Roberts is the one who saved me when I was volunteering here. Kept my days interesting."

"Oh!" My mom's smile widens. "Are you a pediatric oncologist like Nathaniel?"

"I'm a surgeon. Transplant." Greer smiles tightly. I can see it all over her now—after she told me all the ways she thinks she's bad and broken. Trusted me with this insurmountable, heavy thing that weighs her down.

"Saves a lot of lives." I jerk my chin towards her.

She rolls her eyes again, but there's the ghost of a smile there.

"Did you go to medical school here in Toronto?" My mom asks, nearing one of her favourite topics: Nathaniel's commitment to saving children like Sarah.

Greer nods. "I did."

"Nathaniel went to med school in British Columbia." Excitement lights her features, and she reaches out, placing a hand on Sarah's shoulder. "Sarah went to teacher's college in Ottawa, and Beckett—"

She pauses, and I think another football hits my chest.

I don't think she remembers. Or at least, she doesn't care enough to keep handy facts about me on the tip of her tongue.

Rolling my shoulders back, I try to smile but it feels weird, and even Nathaniel and Sarah look back and forth between our mother and me, like they're about to answer for her.

But Greer's voice comes first.

A beautiful, quiet rasp reciting facts about me. But she's saying more than just that.

You're real, Beckett.

"Syracuse," Greer offers, eyes soft and on me. "He went to Syracuse. He studied history, and he specialized in the French Revolution. He finds Napoleon fascinating."

"Oh." My mother blinks, a smile forming. But there's no recognition behind her eyes. "That's right. I always just think about the kicking and it's hard for me to remember anything before the league."

Greer's eyebrows lift and her mouth pulls into a taut smile. "His professional career is very impressive, too many broken records."

Her eyes cut down to the pocket of her scrubs, and she pulls out her phone. She glances back up, and she's not looking at anyone else when she says it. I know the words are just for me. "I'm sorry. I have to go."

"Sure." I nod, absentmindedly rubbing my chest. It doesn't feel like it did five minutes ago. "Go save lives."

She raises a hand and she's only halfway to the elevator when I pull out my phone. I can't have her, not really, but I can't help myself.

> Beckett: Come over tonight?

Usually, I'm waiting for the three dots. But her answer comes in right away.

> Greer: Sure. I'll be there around eight.

I drop my phone back into my pocket, and when I glance back up, my brother and sister are staring at me too intently for my liking, and our mother has moved on to lamenting over the cookies being spread out on a nearby table.

I jerk my chin towards the line starting. "Come on, I don't have a ton of time before practice, and I know you've been dying to stab me for years, Nathaniel."

They both smile at me, the edges curled with relief that I'm not upset.

It's not entirely an accurate assessment, but they've never really been able to tell much about me anyway.

The only person who really sees me just turned around and went back to the thing that holds her hostage, and I know when I step onto the field later, I'll be doing the same.

Greer

This is my least favourite place in the hospital.

It's the loudest.

The most chaotic.

The most unpredictable.

It's another thing around here everyone makes assumptions about. They think I avoid coming down to the emergency room because I'm somehow above it, sitting up there on my award-winning-fellow pedestal, asking for images to be brought up to me instead of coming down for consults when I can avoid it.

But it's not that.

Every time I get in the elevator, or walk down the stairs to get here, the phantom twinge starts in my ribs, the skin of my scar feels sensitive underneath my scrubs, and my heart starts to speed up.

I don't have many memories of the accident—your brain can be beautiful that way.

But I remember the sounds. I remember the water. And I do remember being in an emergency room not unlike this one.

I hated the page when it came in, not just because it was from my least favourite place, but because it meant leaving Beckett alone there.

With his family and all the ways they don't see him.

I see you. I know you. Those were things I tried to say, because I think he deserves to know them.

I hope he heard me.

Rounding the corner past the triage desk and the waiting room, I raise my eyebrows when I come to the first open exam room and the doctor kicked up against the wall. Dark hair curls across his forehead, eyes on his phone and stubbled cheekbones defined against wan, tawny skin.

"Dr. Rawdat." I offer him a tight smile. "You needed a consult?"

"I didn't call you for a consult." He pushes off the wall, chart in hand, tipping his chin towards the open door.

I narrow my eyes, and I do feel a bit like the Dr. Roberts everyone thinks I am—that maybe I should tell him not to waste my time, because it's a commodity and I'm busy.

It's not that, really, I just don't want to be here. In this place where I can feel my heart and these old breaks that still hurt all these years later.

But I do walk through the open door, and it all hurts even more.

My father's the one in the bed, propped up against the uncomfortable pillows, ashen skin obscured behind an oxygen mask, feathers of his hair matted to his forehead, sleeves of his worn flannel rolled up, and IV lines trailing from his arm.

"Dad?" My voice catches in my throat.

"Acute pneumonia." Dr. Rawdat offers me his chart.

I snatch it, flipping through the labs. "He's a transplant recipient, are you sure it's not—"

My father pulls down his oxygen mask, fingers slipping against the plastic. He inhales, and it goes on a bit too long, like he's struggling for every little molecule of oxygen. His eyes close and he shakes his head, like he's so tired and so weary. "It's just a flu, Greer."

"It's not the flu, it's pneumonia," I bite out, barely sparing him a glance as my eyes track down the chart. "Put your mask back on."

Stella isn't here, but I know what she'd say if she was.

Be nice. We got a second chance, don't waste it. He loves you. He's trying.

No, my brain refutes. *You gave him a piece of you, and it still wasn't enough for him to prioritize you. To love you.*

"Dr. Roberts." There's a faint hint of warning when Dr. Rawdat speaks. He turns to my father, and there's more sympathy lining his face than there is on mine. "Henry, we're going to talk outside for a minute. Hang tight."

I try to offer my dad a smile, but the whole thing falls flat, and he's not looking anyway. He's got his oxygen mask back on, his eyes closed, resting his head against the pillows.

"Is he—" The words catch in my throat, and that empty space inside me echoes. "Is he rejecting—" I swallow. I was about to say my liver. But it's not mine. I let someone take it from me. Pressing my eyes closed, I hand back the chart, pinch the bridge of my nose, and try again. "Is he rejecting the liver?"

"No, Dr. Roberts. That's not why I paged you. I paged you because you're his emergency contact." He taps the chart. "We can run the labs again. But it's all there. No abnormal biomarkers. No tenderness at the site. No jaundice. Nothing else you'd expect. He came in with flu-like symptoms. His blood was drawn, his labs were run, he had a chest x-ray, and it's pneumonia."

"Was it—" I press my palm against my rib cage. "He missed his meds for a few days last week."

And you should have been by to check on them—on him—but you were too busy in Beckett's bed.

Dr. Rawdat winces, and he looks at me like he feels a bit sorry for me. "Dr. Roberts. You know it doesn't work like that. You know it better than me. That didn't cause this. He's immunocompromised, and it's flu season."

"I had a friend over at the house, and he wore a mask but—"

"Dr. Roberts," he repeats, but it's soft, and he gives a little shake of his head. "It's flu season. He told me he goes to AA a few times a week? He could have easily picked something up there."

"Sure," I say quietly, nodding.

He still goes to all those meetings during flu season, my brain pipes up. *Maybe he doesn't care he's putting himself at risk. Putting a piece of you at risk.*

"I'll discharge him as soon as his pulse ox is up, and the IV antibiotics are done. No long-term damage done." Dr. Rawdat holds the chart up, but he tips his head, lips pulling to the side in concern. "Do you need me to call—"

"No." I don't even know who he was going to say, but I look up and give him a tight smile. "I'll wait until he's done his round of antibiotics."

It's not a question, and he doesn't treat it like one. He tips his chin before leaving, taking the chart with all these things that medically tell us both what we need to know about what's going on in my father's body, even though I'm still not so sure.

I breathe in and out, alone in the hallway, before I turn and go back into my dad's room.

I think I might feel the ghost of hands whispering across my calves, but I can't give them life. As nice as they are, I can't let them be real.

They did get a little too real, and look what happened.

"You didn't text me," I say quietly, sitting down in the chair beside the hospital bed.

He rolls his head across the pillows to face me, words muffled behind the mask. "You're busy."

It's all over his face—traipsing across that too-prominent brow bone. Guilt, etched into all those features hewed this way by his life.

"I'm not—" I start, but I hear my voice rising. I swallow, press my fingers into my rib cage and try again. Reaching out, I brush his hair off his forehead. He does have a fever—it burns against my fingertips. "I'm not too busy for this."

My father nods, tired. "I'm sorry."

"It's not your fault."

And I do mean that. It's not his fault, not really.

It's yours.

He shifts against the pillows, trying to sit up or maybe get comfortable against an uncomfortable bed, an uncomfortable room. An uncomfortable relationship with his daughter.

I wish my sister was here. She's better with him—she always has been.

We've never really known how to be around each other, and whatever chasm exists between us yawns wider and wider each year.

I think, maybe, one of us is standing on the bridge, watching, and the other is in the car, sinking.

I'm not always sure who's who.

Today, though, I do know. It's me stuck in the car, water rising around me and biting at my skin.

It reaches my mouth, it slides down my throat and my lungs aspirate on his next words.

He blinks at me from behind the mask. "It's okay if you can't stay."

My eyes burn. I don't know if it's tears or water from that sinking car I wipe away from my cheeks, staring determinedly ahead at the wall. "Of course I can. Just get some rest. I'll be here when you wake up."

I stay, even though it hurts.

This is why Beckett Davis can only be your friend.

Look what happens when you forget your lines. Your boundaries. Your rules.

Look what happens when you give yourself to people.

Beckett

A purple bruise blooms along my left side, right where my chest protector meets my rib pads. It shouldn't be there because of the padding and equipment, but I'm not twenty-four anymore, and I haven't had to practice tackles in years.

But those are big plays, and those are big games coming up.

Coach Taylor comes into the recovery room to remind me when I'm sliding down into an ice bath after practice. My quad cramped, and Darren sent me right here.

One brow lifts when he spots the bruise, and he gestures to it, like it's the perfect prop to support his point. "Those types of plays—those types of kicks—that's what I need from you over the next two weeks." He taps his clipboard. "These next two games are critical. We're undefeated and—"

"I know," I cut in, wincing when I shift back and the ice water sloshes against my chest. I feel a bit like telling him that he has a whole host of offensive players he should be talking to about making plays. But I get it. My fall from grace and subsequent inconsistency has been a favourite storyline of the season. No one wants a useless kicker. I'm sure the team publicist has had her regrets about making my stupid smile and dimple the face of so much. "I know we're six and oh. I know who we're playing next week, and I know who we play the week after. I know what game is coming up. I know how it's going to look if we lose to the same team that my failure gave the championship to."

He appraises me, not a care in the world that I'm submerged in freezing water, and I'm supposed to be focusing on my breathing, not talking about the fact that he needs me to perform and do my job. I think he's going to tell me not to throw a pity party, to smarten up, but he cocks his head instead. "It's more pressure than anyone gives it credit for being. Do you miss catching?"

I blink. I've never really thought about it. I liked it—liked running because I'm quick, liked catching and making big plays. Winning games. But it was just this thing I did because it got me a partial scholarship and my parents were trying to recover financially. I wonder if I would have been happier doing it. I might have been drafted, but it would have been late, and maybe I would have played and had a decent career, or maybe I wouldn't have.

It certainly wouldn't have been this.

He spares me from answering and having to psychoanalyze myself. "I think you could have done well, under the right coaching staff, with the right QB. You're more of a team player than half the wide receivers out there, you have a great read of the field, and you're fast. But these legs"—he gestures down to my quads, covered in nothing but black compression shorts, barely visible under the floating ice—"they're a once-in-a-generation kind of talent. Hall-of-fame kind of talent. I don't want to look back and read about how Beckett Davis became irrelevant after one mistake."

I try to grin. "Neither do I."

"You're not stupid, so it won't be a surprise that I'm getting a lot of pressure to do something about you. This is a championship-calibre team, and we can't have an inconsistent kicking game. Not like this. If it keeps up, I'm not going to be able to protect you, and I won't want to. I want what's best for the team." He tucks his clipboard under his arm. "What do you want, Beckett?"

He's expecting me to say I want to win. I want the record. And I do want those things. I'm still me, competitive to a fault, and I want everyone to know I'm the best.

I know I am.

But I think of Greer.

I think of the way she brought me a book on warfare in ancient Egypt. I think of how her voice sounded when she read passages to me as I stretched.

I think of her fingers, deftly wrapping around my wrists, fitting between mine, skating across my shoulders and down my back. Fingers that fix things and save lives, even if she doesn't see it that way. Her hands in general and all that they hold.

Her eyes when she laughs, how her full lips always part just a bit, and the whole thing is raspy just like her voice and I feel it all the way down to my bones. How I've been the luckiest man on the fucking planet that she's given me so many laughs and smiles now, I can't really keep them in my pockets.

They're scattered across my apartment, across my life.

A smile sits on the cold granite of the kitchen island, right in front of the seat she likes to tuck herself into when I make her coffee.

A laugh lives in the cushions of my couch, where she tips her head back and rests it there before she rolls her eyes at me.

I can't even count how many have planted themselves down in my bedroom. Just like the girl—dug their petulant little feet in and refused to leave.

The whole apartment is probably ruined with her now and I'll have to move whenever she calls the whole thing off.

I'm probably ruined, too.

The truth is—I want her. More than I think I've ever wanted anything. I've gone to war with myself in the mirror over this, when I'm lying awake at night and her side of the bed is empty. But I respect her more than anyone on the planet, and I'll never ask her to give me what she can't.

I scrub my face and instantly regret it—my hands are covered in freezing water.

I shake my head out, a bit like a dog, and look back at Coach Taylor.

Seeing as I can't have her, I might as well win.

"I want to win. I want the record." I grin when I say it, and I do mean it, but I think I know what Greer means when she says she's empty, because the words just ring out into all the endless space inside me I wish she occupied.

Greer

For the first time, it's not this unique brand of butterflies flapping their wings alongside the beats of my heart where it sits in its cage before I knock on Beckett's door—it's hesitation and the sound of the screeching brakes of my brain.

Not because I'm nervous to go inside. I probably should be after today. After I sat with my father while the antibiotics emptied into him and I listened to his lungs crackle on the other end of my stethoscope.

It seemed like, maybe, the idea that the consequences to my actions were this abstract sort of thing because no one was literally asking for another organ.

That's one of the beautiful things about the human heart—they serve this literal, life-giving purpose in your body. But there's this abstract function of love, and I think that's meant to give us life, too.

But the crackles on the other end of that stethoscope, the oxygen mask, the antibiotics, and the fever burning along my father's skin remind me there are consequences, and they're real.

I shouldn't be as comfortable with Beckett as I am, I certainly shouldn't be as intimately familiar with his apartment as I am, those butterflies can't fly so close to the bars, and my heart needs to stay in its cage. It can't serve this abstract function for me, it needs to keep me alive, because I still need to keep my father alive, too.

I'm late getting here. My father was discharged like Dr. Rawdat promised, and he'll be fine in a few days. But I'm feeling a bit exposed, and I think Beckett might be, too.

I told him this thing I never tell anyone—mostly because I'm scared that when they hear the whole ugly truth of it, they'll never look at me the same.

That they'll judge me, they won't be able to understand why I did it even though I didn't want to, and they certainly won't understand how I ended up here.

There were a lot of things in the lines of Beckett's face that night, behind his eyes. But none of them were those.

And then I saw it, in real time—all these things he's alluded to that made him into this person who just sort of . . . was.

I think I'm a little sad that we can't be anything more than we are, but my brain speaks louder than whatever whispers my heart wants me to hear.

He can stay, but he has to stay where he is.

I roll my shoulders back, and I do knock, but it takes him a minute to open the door.

"Sorry, I had these stupid things on my legs for recovery. Took a minute to get them off." He smiles, but his eyes linger on my mouth before he swallows, muscles in his neck tensing, and he rakes a hand through his hair. "I can make you a copy of the key. I have the keycode to your place."

He jerks his head back into his apartment before turning back inside, and I follow.

"A physical key isn't—"

"Very friendly?" he calls over his shoulder, voice dry.

I nod, trailing after him into the living room. "Precisely."

He raises his eyebrows when he drops down onto the end of his couch.

It's quieter in here than usual. He usually has the TV on, or at the very least, music coming from somewhere.

He seems quieter than usual, too.

I sit beside him, tucking my legs underneath me.

"Are you sore?" I point to the abandoned puffy black boots, sitting haphazardly on the floor by the couch. "You don't usually wear compression boots, do you?"

"What? Oh." He's distracted, but his eyes follow my finger to the floor. "No, I don't. You know the new dynamic kickoff rule I told you about?"

I nod. I do, and even though he prefers that we don't talk about football, I looked up all the rules and tried to learn everything so I could, if he changed his mind.

"It was meant to help increase the chance for a kickoff return. It's an opportunity to score, a more exciting play. It's not likely a team I'm kicking against is going to get the opportunity. I can—could—" He flinches when he corrects himself, and I can feel it in my chest. "I could put the ball anywhere after a kickoff, and definitely far enough away from the opposing team's best returner. I'm not consistent right now, but I'm fast because I spent half my football career running, so Coach has us practicing drills where the kickoff gets returned and I'm tackling. A unique way to put some of my other skills to use, so he says." Beckett shrugs. "I ran more in practice this week than I have in all of last season's games combined."

"Do you like it?"

"I'm not sure what I like anymore." He tosses me a rueful grin, but there's this thing his eyes do—they track over me and they lighten for a minute. But he clears his throat, and I can tell what he says next has been bothering him. "Don't think poorly of them."

I tip my head, ponytail falling across my shoulder. His eyes go with it. "Of your family?"

Beckett nods, a wave curling over his forehead.

"I don't. If anything, I feel more sorry for them." I prop my elbow on the back of the couch and drop my chin to my hand. "Their child was sick. They almost lost her. But in the process, they lost sight of you."

You, I think. This happy, wonderful, funny, endlessly kind, patient, and enduring person who looks in the mirror and sees nothing.

Beckett makes a noise in the back of his throat and jerks his chin. "I was there the whole time."

"Have you ever—" A laugh bubbles in my throat. It's terribly ironic, this thing I'm about to say. "Have you ever set a boundary with them? Told them no when they wanted or needed something? Maybe told them how you feel?"

"Have you ever told your sister? The whole story. How you feel now, what it makes you feel about being a surgeon?" he counters, but his words aren't harsh.

"I'm not even sure how I'd start that conversation," I say truthfully.

Beckett smiles. "That makes two of us." He leans forward, and I'm keenly aware of how much space he's taking up, the shared oxygen we're breathing, and how I feel a bit like I'm wearing my earmuffs again. Protected against a world that can be loud and can hurt. But like it can't get me while I'm in here with him. Beckett holds his pinky up, hand so much bigger than mine, and he isn't smiling anymore. Everything about him is serious. "Promise me you'll think about telling her. As long as it's right for you."

I hook my pinky with his and whisper back, "Promise me you'll try setting a boundary. Only if it feels right."

He smiles at me again, but he brings our joined fingers to his mouth, brushing them briefly before letting go.

He leans back, but not as much as before. He's close enough that I can see the amber nestled in the green striations of his eyes.

"You make more sense to me now," I tell him, drumming my fingers along my cheek. "An unfortunate missing piece to the puzzle of you. I understand why it's all"—I wave my hand around, like the entirety of professional football and all his achievements surround us—"all-encompassing. You were their caretaker. A parent, a provider. And then you were Beckett Davis, NCAA record smasher and kicker extraordinaire. But still a parent. Still a provider and never quite . . . you."

He gives me a wry grin, eyebrows lifting. His hands find my thighs, thumbs pressing down. His voice drops when he speaks. "You make sense to me, too. I wish you didn't."

"What do you mean?"

Beckett swallows. "I understand why you don't—why you can't—it's okay. Why you only have *friends*. Why you need to keep everything you have left."

He doesn't like the word friends anymore, I can tell. But it's all I have to give.

And it's never been more important it stays that way.

He clears his throat, one hand coming up and gripping my chin. He tips it upwards, so our eyes are level. His voice is rough, and I feel it all over me. "We can be just friends. But I'm not sleeping with anyone else. I haven't, and I'm not interested. And you—"

I don't know what he's about to say but I shake my head. "I'm not. I haven't. I don't want to."

"You don't have any other friends?" His eyes flash, and if we were in one of my books, I'd say he was feeling possessive.

But we aren't in one of my books. We're in real life, and he knows I can't give him what he wants, that it's only this tiny, little piece of me, and he's never asked for anything before, but he's asking for this. "No. I don't have any other friends like you. I don't think—"

"They could fuck you like I do?" His eyes lighten and he gives me a lazy grin.

I jerk my head back, pull my chin from his grip, and push his shoulder. "Okay!" I laugh, and he looks at me like it's his new favourite sound.

I straighten my shoulders, even though they shake with laughter, and wipe at the corner of my eyes. "That's not what I was going to say."

"I think I can fill in the blanks." Beckett holds his hands up and nods, face entirely alight, dimple curving in his cheek. "No one else has fucked your brains out the way I have. I understand. It's my cross to bear."

My mouth parts, but my cheeks flush, laughter still caught in my throat. "Shut up. You are so full of yourself. Seriously, you should see someone. I can recommend several psychiatrists."

His grin turns lazy again. "You can be full of me, if you want."

I roll my eyes, but he's smiling at me, and it's this sort of smile he makes all the time. But there's something else there, written in the lines of his jaw, the curve of his full bottom lip. Resignation and acceptance spelled out across the mouth I love to have all over me. And I think that means it's okay, that this is all I can give him. That I'm enough for him even though I'm empty.

He understands, my brain whispers. *It's still safe for now.*

I smile softly at him and concede, holding my hands up. "Alright, Beckett. Fuck my brains out."

Beckett groans, rolling his head back like it's all this big joke—an inconvenience. But he's on me before I can say anything else.

I think we're laughing more than we're not, and he doesn't really spend that much time inside me—it's all wandering hands and mouths.

We fall off the couch. One of his compression boots digs into my back when he's between my legs. Somehow, he smashes his head against the coffee table so badly we have to stop, and I need to test his ocular responses in the bathroom. I hit my knee against the side of his bathtub when I drop to the floor for him.

But it's funny and lovely and wonderful and I hope he's my friend forever.

Beckett

I don't mean to fall in love with her.

I try pretty hard not to, actually.

I can't be certain when it happened, but if someone cuts me open when I die, I'd guess it might be written there on the inside of me, and it might say something about the time we sat knee to knee on the floor of the bookstore, and she read me passages from a book about the fall of Soviet Russia in that voice of hers.

Or maybe it'll be about the night she fell asleep on the couch with one cheek pressed to my chest, and I stayed there watching the streetlights paint something more beautiful than the *Mona Lisa* across her face.

It could be when she drew what she swore was a fully accurate lymphatic system on the steam in my bathroom mirror.

I'm not really sure.

But I am sure she's everywhere and nowhere.

And I am sure that real me must be a masochist, because he'll take any scraps she gives, and he does it with a smile.

There's not much I can do about that—so I kick, and kick, and kick.

Greer

Flickering candles in towering vases cast shadows across the white linen, stretching towards all the scattered wineglasses littered across the tables lining the hospital atrium.

I wrinkle my nose.

I don't know how I was roped into another event—some sort of mixer for incoming and outgoing residents—but the head of the transplant program said I had to go, and he went as far as to make sure my recent award was written in looping cursive underneath the name tag hanging around my neck.

He said it would be inspirational.

I'm not so sure about that.

The edges of the plastic slice at my fingers when I smooth out my dress. Fortunately, it's one of my own choosing. I was spared my sister's ministrations for the night, and I was able to wear one of the black cocktail dresses hanging in my closet. I used to like this dress quite a bit—asymmetrical, twisted rope straps, one falling mid-shoulder and the other just at the curve of my neck.

I'd never tell her, but I'm not sure I like it as much as the emerald one. But that might have had more to do with the company than the gown.

And I would have asked Beckett to come—as a friend—but he's on a road trip.

He does send me a text with a tongue emoji and what I think is a subpar rendering of a closet, drawn with about as much finesse as a stick figure.

I ignore the way that makes my stomach turn, my thighs clench, and the way my heart stumbles when the ghost of his hands whispers over my calves.

I'm doing my best not to think about Beckett at all as I weave through the tables, because I should probably go sit with the other fellows.

Not even his body touching mine.

Just him. His smile—the one that makes his dimple cut through the dusting of stubble always peppering his face. His laugh—the one where he tips his head back and exposes the column of his throat. The way his hands start moving and his gestures get wider and wider when he's excited about something.

I'm doing a poor job of it because I'm debating going to the bookstore tomorrow morning—he mentioned in passing he wanted to know more about the military strategies of the Achaemenid Empire—when the table of residents beside me erupts into some sort of excited screaming, with palms slapping on tables.

My heart stumbles, my chest tightens, and there's a faint tang of metal or blood in my mouth, but I roll my shoulders back and even though I shouldn't, I do let myself picture Beckett on his knees—the way he nodded softly, eyes only on mine, breathing in and out when I did.

It feels a bit more muffled than it usually would, and I do have my Lorazepam this time, but I don't think I need it.

I'm not in the car. I'm here.

I blink, and it's not Beckett there in front of me.

His brother stares at me expectantly from the table making all the noise.

"Dr. Roberts!" Dr. Davis waves a hand, pushing back in his seat. "Thought you might want to know your boyfriend just stopped a 60-yard kick-return."

"Pardon?" I arch a brow.

Dr. Davis blinks, like he can't believe what he just did, and makes a noncommittal jerk of his head, while all his friends look back and forth between us like we're a particularly gripping tennis match.

He points to his phone, propped up against one of the towering vases and clears his throat. "Beck—he, uh. He's having a good game. Hasn't been a tackle like that from a kicker in years. Fifty-yard field goal in the first, and uh—"

"I know." I pull my phone from my purse. "I can get updates from SportsCentre like anyone else. And he's not my boyfriend."

"We're watching live." He swallows, gesturing uselessly to his phone again. "You could—" He tips his chin to the empty seat beside him. "You could watch with us."

He runs a palm along his jaw, and it's a distinctly Beckett gesture. But his eyes are glassy, and a flush rises on his cheeks. My eyebrows knit. "How much have you had to drink?"

"Enough to work up the courage to ask you to sit with me." He shrugs one shoulder.

All the other residents around the table keep looking back and forth between us, eyes wide and trepidatious.

Dr. Davis gives me an expectant grin, pointing towards the chair again.

"Fine." I press my fingers to the bridge of my nose and blink at him.

Relief washes over him and I think they all breathe out, too, when he pulls out the chair.

He points between the open bottles of wine on the table as I sit down, and I nod at the white. His eyes light up and he proceeds to dump significantly more wine in the glass than an acceptable pour.

He looks a bit like a puppy, too, when he hands it to me, golden hair flopping everywhere, eyes like his brother's, and the buttons of his suit jacket undone.

I raise my eyebrows. "Thank you, Dr. Davis."

"You can call me Nathaniel." He smiles at me, blinking in this weird sort of hopeful way, like he's waiting for me to return the sentiment.

I don't.

"Okay then." He clears his throat before turning to pour himself more wine. "Anyway, Beck looks great tonight."

Taking a sip of my wine, I roll my shoulders back into the chair while they all stare at me like they're waiting for me to erupt. I narrow my eyes and feel like telling them that if they'd all stop being so chaotic and clumsy, sending my nervous system firing all the time, I might not need to yell.

It's not very hard to grip a retractor.

But I think of my sister—of Beckett—and I exhale, pointing to the phone. "Your brother always looks great."

A beautiful smile must be an inherited Davis family trait, because Nathaniel lights up like the sun. "He does, doesn't he?" He studies me for a minute, a crease scoring between his brows. "Are you sure you two aren't—"

I cut him off with a flat look. "Just watch the game, Nathaniel."

"Won't we get into trouble for this?" Nathaniel leans forward, hands gripping the edge of the exam table, crinkling the paper lining it.

I point to the IV pole and saline bag. "You're the one who drank a bottle and a half of wine to themselves. Would you rather be cripplingly hungover tomorrow?"

"But they won. Beckett kicked a 65-yard field goal. That's two yards away from the record. I needed to celebrate." He scrubs his face before giving me a hopeless look, eyes wide and glassy. "Aren't we stealing?"

"Calm down." I grab the saline and flash the date at him. "They're at the end of their twenty-eight-day life cycle. They're medical waste tomorrow."

Nathaniel blinks, like he's still unsure. I widen my eyes at him as I rip open the bag with the butterfly clip. "Don't worry. I'll take the fallout of any nonexistent trouble."

He nods, watching me in silence as I hang the bag and prep the needle and tubing. "Arm," I instruct.

He holds it out obediently, and he hesitates, his next words wavering. "Our parents—they don't see him. They just see Sarah, and they see me because they associate me with the people who saved her. But I see him. Sarah sees him. We just don't know how to be around him." He pauses as I tap at his arm, looking for a vein, and wipe it down with an alcohol swab. I watch him swallow in my periphery. "You see him."

I do see him, I think. And I feel a bit like telling Nathaniel that he needs to do a better job of showing Beckett the love he deserves. But I pause, tip of the needle poised to press into his vein, and I look up at him. He looks a bit like a lost child—golden hair falling every which way, tie abandoned and buttons of his shirt undone. "He loves you both very, very much. And he just wants you to love him, too."

He shakes his head, a detectable slump to his shoulders. "How do you even start to thank someone who's given you what he's given me? He sacrificed his childhood so I could have one. My dad didn't teach me to ride a bike. Beckett did. He paid my rent when I was in school, so I didn't have to worry. I didn't have to work summers so I could just study for the MCAT. He's paid for everything Sarah's ever needed. He used to wash her wigs for her, and he learned how to braid hair. He bought our parents' house because they'd mortgaged it so many times because they were always on leave from work. Thank you seems inadequate. How do I even—"

"You just do, Nathaniel. You say the words and you follow them with action. Your brother deserves that, at the very least."

He deserves the world. He deserves more than someone like me can ever give him, even though there's this tiny part of me blooming, sprouting in and amongst the empty space that says maybe we can be whole for him without carving ourselves away.

But I think all of those things wilt when I remember I was with my dad in a room not unlike this one in the not-so-distant past.

One corner of his mouth kicks up. "You're not being mean to me. Why are you so scary at work?"

"There was a reason you wanted to go into pediatric oncology, right?" He nods.

I smile, angling the needle down. "There's a reason for everything I do, too."

He winces at the pinch, and I think, my words. "Beck never said anything."

I shrug one shoulder, pushing down on the needle before releasing it and connecting the line to the IV bag. "I can't imagine he would have."

Nathaniel looks down at his arm, before holding it up to me with a triumphant grin. "Hey, not even a drop of blood. You're good."

I raise my eyebrows. "I know."

He stares at me, the set of his jaw so like his brother's it's alarming, his next words low. "He started keeping his phone on."

"What?" I wrinkle my nose.

"He used to keep his phone off at home. Sarah and I—we aren't stupid. We know he puts himself under this immense pressure to be everything to everyone all the time because he had to be when we were younger and it's all he's ever known. He'd turn his phone off when he was at home, and he'd joke about it, saying nothing was that urgent or serious. I think he just wanted to be . . . free, for a little while. But he started leaving it on after he met you." Nathaniel gives his head a small shake. "He might be your friend, but you're not his."

I don't know if he's really mine either, I think. And that's what I'm afraid of.

Because whatever this is keeps landing us—me, my heart and my brain—in rooms like this one.

But I give Nathaniel a flat look and tap the bag of saline.

"Let the IV run until it's empty. Eat and drink something when you get home and take two Advil tomorrow morning." I grab my bag from where I abandoned it on the chair in the corner of the exam room, my heels clicking against the tile floor, but I look back at him before I leave, fingers tapping against the doorframe. "You can call me Greer."

Beckett

I've never been one of those athletes with intense pre- or post-game rituals.

It's probably because when I was a receiver, I wasn't the star, but if I was on the field, I was faster than everyone and my hands were good enough, so I was having fun.

And when I started kicking, it always went far enough, and it went through.

No questions about it. Nothing special required.

Just a multimillion-dollars-a-year leg.

Until it didn't.

I don't think I've grown superstitious since I started smashing yardage and scoring points again.

Beckett Davis is back—you can just ask anyone.

But I do like spending post-game days with Greer, and I'm particularly keen on spending this one with her.

We have one more game before we play Baltimore, and even though I think it probably carves another piece out of me each time we're together and I can't really have her in all the ways I want, it's making my kicking better.

Maybe I am growing superstitious, because I'm setting expectations when I walk through my front door: I expect to spend the day fantasizing about all the things I want to do to her when she's finally off shift, and I expect to spend the day pretending she's actually mine.

I don't expect to see my brother and sister camped out in my living room.

Nathaniel glances away from the TV, mug of coffee still steaming in his hands, and Sarah drops the knitting needles she was whipping around at rapid speed.

"Oh." I palm my jaw. It's a bit embarrassing to be around them, actually. After Mom's big show the other week where she proved she knew everything about them, and nothing about me. "What are you two doing here?"

"Good morning to you, too." One eyebrow kicks up in amusement, and Nathaniel takes a sip of his coffee before leaning forward and setting it down on the table. Right above the same corner I cracked my head on when I had Greer on the floor the other week. He gives a shake of his head. "It's your day off. We thought it might be nice for the three of us to do something. Go grab brunch or something?"

I can hear her laugh when it happened—raspy, echoing across the apartment and all the way up to those vaulted ceilings that usually only hear me swear when I kick the occasional football outside the practice net.

It was probably lonely up there without her laugh.

This whole apartment was probably lonely without her smiles littered everywhere, collecting dust because I'll never move them.

I think I was probably a lot lonelier than I thought before I met her.

I blink. Nathaniel's still talking. I close my eyes and shake my head. "Sorry, what?"

"You're distracted." Sarah's eyes go wide, sparkling, and she points a knitting needle towards me. "Thinking about a certain someone, perhaps?"

All I think about and everything I can't have.

That doesn't exactly seem like something my brother and sister will care about, so I drop my bag and hold my hands up when I walk backwards towards the fridge. "Thinking about how I could have improved the kick in the second. Went a little to the right."

A scoff sounds in Nathaniel's throat, and he twists against the back of the couch so he can face me. "I doubt it. You played great last night. We all watched at that resident mixer I had to go to."

"Oh yeah?" I pull open the fridge, clearing my throat when I grab a box of water. Greer says she prefers her water in cardboard, so those overpriced boxes found their way to these shelves. It was probably a bit desperate—think I ran out the morning after she mentioned it. "Who's we?"

I think I look indifferent when I turn back to face them, twisting the cap off the water and tossing it on the counter. I shrug one shoulder.

Indifferent. Cool.

Not hopelessly, desperately, stupidly in love.

I know Greer watched the game—she texted me afterwards with strict instructions to rest, ice, and elevate my left side after I landed on it during the tackle.

They laugh at the same time—looking at each other like they're in on some big secret, our shared green eyes wide and incredulous.

Those laughs echo, too. And for a minute, I imagine a different life for myself—one where I have Greer, but I have this version of my brother and my sister, and maybe my parents love me properly and this whole place is full—but I blink.

It's not full. It's empty. And those are things I'll probably never have.

"Jesus, Beck." Nathaniel shakes his head, golden hair falling across his forehead. "She's done a fucking number on you. I mean, I think I get it now."

I ignore all those fake things, taunting me from my periphery, and narrow my eyes. "I thought you were terrified of her."

"Nah." Nathaniel's eyes flick down to his arm for some reason. "She's not so bad."

A soft smile curls on Sarah's lips, and she tips her head, chocolate hair just like mine falling all around her. "You can tell us all about *the game* that has you so distracted. Come on, we want to take you to breakfast."

I debate making an excuse, saying I hurt myself during the tackle, and I need to take an ice bath or foam roll out my legs. But they both look at me—wide, expectant smiles and those eyes we share catching in the early-morning sunlight as it streams in through the windows—and I don't mean to be, but I'm back in time with them: scratching out a calculus equation with Nathaniel and braiding a wig for Sarah because her fingers were too tired.

I don't want to be there—I want to be here. But I'm not sure a here exists for us, and I don't want to hurt their feelings, so I grin and jerk my chin towards the door.

"Your girlfriend is really good with a needle." Nathaniel pulls back his sleeve, holding up his arm where a tiny piece of gauze and medical tape sit at the crook of his elbow. He squints, inspecting it, before looking back up at me, grinning. "Not even a tiny bruise. I mean, can't say I'm surprised. I've seen her do a running whipstitch."

I look down at my menu, and I repeat the same mantra that runs through my head on a steady loop now. "She's not my girlfriend."

She's not mine. She's not my girlfriend. She won't compromise for you, and she shouldn't have to.

You're in love with someone you can't have, but that's okay, you've survived before, and you'll survive this.

Maybe.

"Wait, what?" I glance back up, and Nathaniel nods, tapping his arm again.

"Oh! Let me see. My IVs used to bruise me all the time." Sarah lights up when she grabs his arm, inspecting it, like she's talking about rainbows and unicorns, not her cancer-ridden adolescence, and we aren't sitting in an upscale brunch restaurant on the bottom floor of a hotel in the financial district. She turns back to me, nodding in approval. "It looks great."

"I'm sure it does." I drop the menu and point towards my brother's arm. "I'm sorry, what are you talking about? Why was she giving you an IV? Are you alright?"

These warring ideas—that something might be wrong with Nathaniel, but also, maybe, that there's going to be this other person I need to be for them—make me want to sink into the ground and disappear.

"Beck." He reaches forward, grabbing my forearm, face pale before he lets go with a little shake of his head. "I'm fine. Sorry, it was a joke. I got a little carried away with the wine at dinner last night watching your game with Greer. She just gave me an IV to help with the hangover before I left."

I roll my shoulders a few times, like that's going to shake off decades of expectations and the fact that one of the first things I think when there might be something wrong with my brother is whether my family might need more from me. I exhale and try to smile. "She lets you call her Greer?"

Nathaniel kicks back, nodding and raising his palms in the air. "I know. I really gained a lot of ground last night. We hung out, and it was only scary, like, eighty-five percent of the time. Some might call it pretty great, actually."

"She's pretty great."

A massive, colossal understatement.

Nathaniel clears his throat and cuts a sideways look at Sarah. She sits up straighter, giving him a tiny nod in return.

They remind me of two kids preparing to show a parent the routine they've spent all day painstakingly practicing.

And I guess they kind of are.

I'm not sure what I am to them—but I'm not the same thing they are to each other.

"She gave me a bit of a talking to." Nathaniel runs a hand across his jaw and exhales. "I've been—we've been—we haven't thanked you enough for everything that you've done for us."

There's a weird feeling in my chest. My heart pumps a bit faster than it should, all because of the idea that there's this person in my life who thinks I'm worthy of defending. But I give a jerk of my chin. "You always say thank you."

"That's not what I mean." Nathaniel shakes his head, glancing around like he's realizing, maybe, upscale brunch wasn't the best place for this conversation. He looks back at me, raising one hand before he shrugs. "I don't know how to be around you sometimes. And it's not because you've done anything wrong. It used to make me so mad you'd trot out for all these press conferences and commercials, for any other noble cause you deemed worthy, but you'd never show up for my blood drives, and it never occurred to me there was something taken from you that wasn't taken from me."

Swallowing, I give them a noncommittal jerk of my shoulder. I try to grin, but it gets stuck.

Kind of like the three of us.

Sarah sniffs, blinking, but a tear tracks down her cheek anyway. She wipes it away before giving me a watery smile. "We love you, Beck. Every single version of you. Very, very much. Our lives wouldn't be what they are without you. Not even a fraction of them." She closes her eyes, the corners pinch like she's in pain when she inhales before continuing, voice dropping to nothing. "And we should have told you every single day."

She sits back, inhaling bigger gulps of air than she needs, shoulders shaking, trying not to cry. Nathaniel wraps his arm around her, squeezing once before they both look back at me.

Golden hair and green eyes on my brother. Stubble lining the more-defined lines of his jaw, and shoulders that grew broader over the years. Maybe because I kept them from collapsing under the weight of it all, but at the end of the day, it doesn't really matter.

The same eyes on my sister, and cheekbones that sharpened as the years passed, and a beautiful pink flush to her skin I wasn't sure I was ever going to get to see.

I blink, and I think they might finally, finally be adults now.

That maybe all three of us are.

"I was happy to do it all. I am happy to keep doing it." I swallow. It's the truth. "But thank you. For saying all that. I don't think I always know how to be around the two of you, either."

Sarah gives me a soft smile, hope written in the flush across her face. "We can figure it out together."

Nathaniel grins, nodding. "I love learning. Big passion for it."

"Mom and Dad—" Sarah starts.

"It's like they forget, or maybe they just don't know what to do with me. Mom forgot I donated all the time." I shake my head with a dry laugh, before tipping my chin to Sarah. "You might not remember, you were young. But I donated every time you needed a transfusion. I lied to all my coaches about it. Didn't matter the season. Football. Hockey. Soccer."

She whispers, "I remember," but it sounds a lot louder than that, because I think it's permeating every inch of me. Ringing out in all those empty spaces I wanted to be occupied by Greer but maybe needed to be occupied by other things instead.

I exhale and run a hand down my face. "It's not that I don't want to be there for you guys. At the drives. Or to give you whatever it is you need. It's just that sometimes they—Mom and Dad—they've set this expectation that I'm going to solve everything and whenever they imply you need something—"

"Tell them no!" Sarah slaps her hand against the table in this uncharacteristic display of emotion a lot bigger than her, and her eyes flash with what might be anger towards our parents before it turns inwards and her voice cracks. "Tell us no."

"Sarah." I shake my head again. "I'm not going to suddenly stop making sure you have the life you want and deserve."

Nathaniel cuts in, and his voice breaks, too. "What about what you want? What you deserve?"

I raise my eyebrows and lean back in the chair. I don't know how to answer that, so I give them half a smile. "These expectations. They're getting heavy. That's all."

"Let's start with boundaries. If Mom and Dad assume, or they ask for something, the three of us can talk about it privately. And you can say no." Sarah leans forward, emphasis on those last words before she keeps going. "And we'll work on getting to know each other again. The real people we are now."

Real.

This—my relationship with my brother and my sister—another casualty littering the highway of my life that she breathed life back into.

I give them a wry smile. "Funny. Greer told me I should think about setting boundaries."

Nathaniel grins, holding his hands up again. "Your girlfriend is very wise."

"Not my girlfriend."

"Why not?" Sarah asks, a glow brightening her features, like she's looking at a particularly interesting puzzle, and she can solve the whole thing for me if she just adjusts a few pieces.

But she can't.

I jerk my chin. "She has her reasons, and I won't ask her for more than she can give."

"Beck." Sarah shifts forward, grabbing my hand in hers. "You deserve good things. You deserve what you want out of this life. You should tell her how you feel. It's not asking her for something she can't give you if you're just telling the truth."

She means well—but this isn't a movie. Greer is a real, living, breathing person who deserves the space she asks for, and a sudden confession from me isn't going to change that.

I flash a strained smile. "We'll see."

Both of their mouths open, like they're about to protest.

But I widen my eyes. They sink back in their seats, and they look a bit like children again—but it's not this nefarious thing keeping us stuck somewhere in time.

It's like we're just us—an older brother telling his two younger siblings to knock it off. No expectations and nothing weighing anybody down.

It goes like that for the rest of brunch. Nathaniel spends too much time deciding what he wants, before he asks for endless substitutions. His disappointment when they don't have his preferred mushroom sends Sarah into a fit of laughter she can't quite escape, wiping wildly at the corners of her eyes.

But she manages to spend too much time talking about knitting patterns, and Nathaniel asks for one of her needles to stab his eardrums.

They both laugh at me when I go on and on, fingers pointing, hands waving, and I grab a napkin and try to illustrate this specific military formation Napoleon tried that I read about in a book Greer gave me.

And when the server brings the cheque, Nathaniel does this big show of asking for one bill, putting a heavy emphasis on how they want to take their big brother out for brunch.

I give them a dry grin. "It's the least you can do. Neither of you have paid a bill your entire lives."

Sarah tips her nose in the air. "I had cancer, you know."

Eyes go wide, and the server looks back and forth between us like he doesn't know what to do and he's contemplating ripping the bill up and taking the loss, but we're laughing.

It's nice.

Real.

Maybe I can't have her. But she did give me this.

Greer

It happens on a Tuesday.

I'm finishing up forty-eight hours of call and he picks me up. I can barely see—between the bleary eyes and the sun rising against the crisp fall morning—everything's impossibly bright.

But he's impossible to miss.

Foot kicked up against the bed of his truck, waiting for me while it idles there with frost still inching over the windows somehow. Hair askew, waves sticking out every which way from under his hat—turned backwards—and I can see the number nineteen stitched along the hem.

It's a good day then, if he doesn't want to disappear.

I wish they were all good days. He's beautiful and bright and the world would be lucky to know him.

Sweater pushed up his forearms, he holds out a coffee. Not the hospital coffee. One from my favourite shop near my house.

He grins, our fingers touching when I take it. My heart does that thing it does when he touches me—it beats and stretches outside the lines I've erected around it.

But there's a phantom twinge under my right rib cage, and my heart shrinks back behind its bars.

He leans in, and he whispers good morning when he tugs on my ponytail.

"Good night, actually." I blink behind the lid of my coffee cup.

"Noted." He smiles at me again, one hand reaching behind him to open up the door and the other opening for me.

I snort. I shake my head like he's being absurd, but I take his hand anyway. "I'm not that tired."

He makes a tsking noise. His other hand plants firmly on my low back and I find myself leaning in, like I might very well topple over without the steady support of him, when I step up into the truck. His words are warm against the back of my neck. "How many surgeries? How long were you on your feet?"

"No longer than you during a game." I tip my chin up and put my seat belt on.

It's a lie. It's been a long forty-eight hours and I don't think I've been this tired since my first year of residency.

Beckett shakes his head and shuts the door behind me.

I take a sip of coffee, head against the window, and I watch him round the truck, throw the door open, and take one step up with one of those long, muscled legs. He did it all unassisted, and I think he does most things like that—all alone—but sometimes I wish I could hold his hand and lift him up, too.

One hand finds the wheel, and his fingers tense there before he drums them against the leather. He turns to look at me as he puts the car in drive. "Greer?"

"Beckett?" I answer, but my eyes are already closing against the window, edges of my usually screaming brain fuzzy with sleep.

His voice is low—and even though I can't see him, I know a muscle in his jaw ticks, that his right thumb taps the steering wheel, and he tenses his kicking leg. "I don't think we're friends."

There they are, those words out there in the ether.

But I shake my head. He's wrong. He's the most important person in the world to me. I know it's not what he wants to hear, but it's all I have.

My brain can barely whir to life in warning, it's so tired, hardly tipping upwards towards the sound of his voice, hardly able to stamp down on the too-big beats of my heart that push against its lines. But one tiny alarm bell sounds from a distant shore, and I tell him the truth as I know it, what's still keeping me safe. For now. "No. I think you're my best friend."

Beckett laughs—deep and real and magical and wonderful and maybe sort of sad.

I feel one hand reach over and tuck a loose strand of hair behind my ear. "If that's your story. Go to sleep. Dream of faeries."

I'll dream of you, I think.

Greer

Sunlight slips further along the wrought-iron table between my sister and me, steam rising off matching cups of coffee, bags laden down with books strewn across the surface.

It's become something of a ritual between us. Whenever the end of my longest call shift of the month happens, she moves her schedule around and we go to the bookstore together, find a coffee shop, and try to spend the afternoon in relative silence, reading, until Stella inevitably gets bored.

She's been quieter for longer than usual today, and I don't know if it's because I still look exhausted—she made me ice roll my face for ten minutes before we left the house—or if she can feel the way each beat of my heart strains against its borders, the way these empty spaces in me bloom with Beckett and my brain can't help but trample over the freshly tilled soil and beautiful sprouting things that happen to be the exact same shade as his eyes.

She's many things, but she's perceptive.

I shift in my seat, debating which book to start, and I absentmindedly run my fingers along the strap of my earmuffs where they hang around my neck, tracing the stitching that spells out Beckett's number.

"You've grown quite attached to those." Stella's eyes flick up to me from behind the pages of her book, voice bemused.

I shrug. "They're practical. It's October in Toronto. The grass frosts more mornings than not."

The corners of her lips furl upwards into a smile that looks more catlike than anything, and she blinks at me. "So that wasn't a grainy photo of you I saw on that Instagram account dedicated to the WAGS of all Toronto sports teams?"

"I'm neither a wife nor a girlfriend." I pick up the book closest to me—I've been waiting for this one where a human girl touches an ancient sword, and she gets transported to a fae realm and held captive—before leaning back in my chair. "So, you must be mistaken."

She tips her head, and a wave of auburn hair, brighter than usual in the afternoon sun, escapes her bun. "Could have fooled me."

"You sound like Beckett," I say absentmindedly, opening the book to the first page. "He says he doesn't think we're friends."

"Because you're not." She snorts, looking back down at her book.

I think she's right, my heart stumbles.

But I think of our father—or maybe my brain sends the memory of him in the hospital bed, all ashen skin and crackling lungs, to the forefront so I can never, ever forget what's at stake.

"We have to be."

Stella drops her book and folds her hands together over top of it. She angles her head to the side and asks me a question that should have a simple answer, and maybe it sort of does. But it's still the one thing I don't think I can tell her.

"Okay, but you've never told me why. You've made these grand speeches and soliloquies—" She holds up a hand when my lips part, indignant, and she continues. "I'm not saying that to be cruel. I'm saying that to make a point. You have these firm convictions about needing to be alone because you give too much, but you've only ever made loose references to your job. How much that takes from you, how draining it is. Give me something real, Greer. No deflection. No evasion. No bullshit."

"Do you talk to your clients like this?" I try, but Stella's lips pull into a flat line, and she makes a carry-on gesture. She's going to wait me out.

My fingers feather uselessly in space, and I don't know what to say. I don't know how to tell my sister that even though I love her—I love our father—I like to think there's another world out there where I didn't say yes, and that maybe, in that world, someone else died for him.

I stretch my hands out, and I study my fingers, pink against the fall air—hands that might be the biggest hypocrites of all, that somehow take life and give life all at once—and I feel a hand much bigger than mine brush over the back, a finger hooking against my pinky, and I hear it.

Promise me you'll think about telling her. As long as it's right for you.

Looking back up at my sister, sitting here in front of me—healthy and whole with no evidence that her skull was fractured once upon a time and her pancreas hung in tatters in her abdomen.

She looks like nothing ever touched her. Whole. No empty pieces left over from where she carved something vital out of herself. My voice cracks. "Do you ever think about the car accident? What happened after?"

Her eyebrows knit, lips pulling to the side as she chews on the inside of her cheek before answering. "Yes. But I don't think it's quite like you do."

"Why do you think that is?" I whisper, and I really do want to know—I think I'd like to be as unburdened as my sister seems.

Stella takes a measured exhale. "I had time to heal. When my body was stitching itself back together, so was my mind. And it got to stay that way."

The last words catch in her throat, and it hangs between us—the empty space of me.

I inhale, squeezing my eyes shut before looking at her. "Sometimes—most times, actually—I wish I could go back in time. We were so young, and I know—I know he got sober, and we got to have this beautiful thing and a second chance with him that most people don't get. But sometimes, I wish . . ."

My words fall into nothing, and I think they might plummet into that all that emptiness—but maybe they land on the ground, on all that soil with all those beautiful things peeking through the dirt, and it's a safe place for them.

Because even if she doesn't, can't, won't understand—someone did.

I blink up at my sister, inhaling and shoulders shuddering when I finally, finally tell her. "I wish I said no. I wish it wasn't me."

Stella pulls her head back, her eyes go wide, and I think tears pool along her lash line, but she keeps waiting.

"I wish I didn't have to. I wasn't ready. I hadn't forgiven him for what he did our entire lives and what he did when he got behind the wheel. I didn't want him to die, but if I could go back in time to right before and someone said to me it doesn't have to be you, but someone else needs to die for that to happen, I think I would have said yes. How fucked up is that?" I watch the steam still rise off my coffee, and I grab it without thinking, tapping my thumb on the plastic lid before I finally look back at her. "And then I just became this person who takes the way something was taken from me. What if the people I'm operating on felt like me? It's not like I have a chance to ask. What if all the car accidents—"

She shakes her head and leans forward, stilling my fingers and gripping them in her hand. "You shouldn't have had to do it."

My heart and my brain both screech to a halt. For once, I think everything in me goes silent. Because there it is. This thing I've been waiting to hear from someone else my whole life. But they whir back to life, because it's all we've ever known. I start to shake my head. "You weren't a match."

"That's not what I mean," Stella whispers. "I wasn't a match. You were. But that doesn't mean you should have had to do it. This is a fact, Greer. You shouldn't have had to give a piece of yourself away so someone else could be whole. We never should have been in the situation to begin with."

"But we were."

She nods softly. "We were. And you did an impossibly hard thing. You were brave again after a lifetime of being brave. You gave something to him—" Her voice breaks and she squeezes my fingers. "You gave something to me. And maybe we haven't given enough back to you. You felt empty, and instead of talking about that, giving it life, filling you back up the way we should have, we just skirted around the entire thing. And I'm sorry for that."

It feels nice against my skin, her apology, her acknowledgement. But it's not a miracle. "Do you ever think about how we—I don't know—you spend all day with people like our dad, and then I'm walking around with livers and kidneys in my hands that don't belong to me?"

"Sure," she agrees, squeezing my fingers before letting go and leaning back in her chair. "Addiction is a cycle. We know that. But I don't think it's that simple. I don't think it means that either of us are just continuing to give away pieces of ourselves to this disease we were never going to win against. Maybe some days it looks like that. But other days we're compassionate, and kind, and we understand someone in a world that doesn't. Healing isn't simple and it's not linear. You aren't going to wake up one day with the knots of all these complicated feelings untangled."

"I don't want to be this person who doesn't leave enough for themselves. I don't want to—"

Stella holds up a hand, cutting me off.

"I'm not qualified to operate and fix people the way you do. But I am qualified to tell you this." My sister leans forward, and somehow, she's both the fifteen-year-old I was desperate to save and this fully-fledged adult who knows so much more than me. "Somewhere along the way, you've confused setting a boundary with closing yourself off."

"Have you been talking to Rav?" I ask through a wet laugh.

"Sure." Stella shrugs, waving her hand in the air, silver rings adorning her fingers catching in the afternoon sunshine. "We trade case notes on your file."

I smile softly. "I'll be sure to report you both to your various governing bodies."

"So, this is it? The big secret reason you want to be alone?" She blinks, lips tugging to the side with a small exhale. "I'm not minimizing, but as far as I can tell, Beckett Davis isn't asking for one of your organs."

Except that there is this piece of me I think he wants. It sits in my chest, where it beats and keeps me alive.

"I'm not sure it's that easy," I whisper.

"Why not?" Stella counters. "Has he ever once asked you to give him more?"

I don't think we're friends.

This tentative toss of a rope that maybe I could grab onto while I'm treading water and this stupid storm of my brain rages around me.

But that's it. It's as far as Beckett would ever go, even though I know he's probably tempted to dive in and hold me above water at the detriment to his own oxygen intake.

I exhale. "No, but—"

She interrupts again, palm coming down on the table and jade eyes wide. "I know you deal in absolutes. Levels and blood markers and the certainty of a scientifically proven match of an organ. But grief, trauma, and healing are not some formula that's going to click into place for you. If you're waiting for a day you wake up and magically feel healed and whole, that day is never going to come." Stella smiles, but it's sad and she shakes her head before her voice goes soft. "That's not how life works. The human experience"—she reaches forward and taps the cover of my book—"is very rarely one of those."

I don't say anything. But I sit back in my chair, inhaling and exhaling as my heart sings, because here it is—permission to leave its cage—while my brain tells me she doesn't understand, she didn't give a piece of herself away, and it's still not safe.

But my sister is wiser than me, and her features stay soft when she raises a finger to the front of her face, pointing at me. "Think about it."

I swallow, nodding, and I stretch out my fingers again. I look at them and I imagine Beckett's fingers traipsing over mine, and I think of something else he said. Looking back up at Stella, I ask, "Can you please stop forgetting about Dad's meds? And check in more to see when he needs a refill?"

Her hand finds her chest, like there's a visceral pain there, and understanding flashes in her eyes. The jade dulls for a moment, but then Stella nods, leaning forward and whispering, "I'm sorry. I'll do better."

It's a promise, and I think she might want me to make one to her—that I'll try, that I'll open myself up and maybe I'll stop being so scared, that maybe I'll give this thing that sits in my chest away.

But I'm not so sure, so I toss the word out into the storm with Beckett's rope—*maybe*—and I lay a drawbridge down across whatever cavern stretches between my sister and me.

"I hope Beckett plays well on Sunday. It's the last game before they play Baltimore."

"Oh," Stella's eyes lighten, and she nods. "I hope they win."

Beckett

We don't win.

I don't break a record.

I do miss another game-winning kick and get fined by the league for unsportsmanlike conduct and impermissible use of equipment when I take my helmet off and throw it against the ground so hard the strap snaps.

And I do get dragged into Coach Taylor's office after he spends forty-five minutes yelling at everyone for falling apart so spectacularly in the locker room post-game.

"I know it's just pocket change to you, but do you enjoy being fined a total of"—he gives a pointed look at his phone—"fourteen thousand dollars for unsportsmanlike conduct and twenty-two thousand dollars for impermissible use of your helmet? I can think of a million things I'd rather do with that kind of money. Could put one of my kids through college."

I open my mouth to tell him all the money goes to the league foundation anyway, but he cuts me off with a pointed gesture towards the TVs behind his desk.

"Do you enjoy looking like this? Making your team look like this? Darren, me?" He punctuates every word with another jab at the TVs, where every sports network seems to be rolling footage of me whipping off the strap off my helmet and sending it careening into the ground at a pretty shocking velocity before Nowak drags me off the field, Darren screaming in my ear the entire way to the locker room. "What happened to the Beckett Davis who said he wanted to win? Who said he wanted to break the record? I just fucking gave you a shot at a 68-yard kick because I believed in you. I could have gone for a fourth down, and I didn't. Because I believed in you and those stupid fucking legs."

I don't answer. I don't tell him that it's the first time since that girl made me into something real that I wish she hadn't. I wish I wasn't anything at all.

He shakes his head, eyes sharp, disappointed and disgusted by whoever this real version of me turned out to be. "We play Baltimore next week. This is how you want to be leading into that game?"

"Everyone's fucking looking at me all the time, and I'm sorry, I don't mean to be disrespectful. But it's ridiculous—who puts that much faith in a fucking kicker?" I splay my arms wide.

"In a kicker? It's not about the position and what it typically does or doesn't do for a team." His finger swings from the TVs to me, and if there wasn't a desk between us, I think he'd be jabbing it into my chest. "I put my faith in you. And if this is all you're going to give me, you take up too much cap space. I'll drop you for a consistent college kicker faster than you can flash that fucking dimple. If this is who you are now—"

I scoff, opening my arms again. "Who am I?"

"I don't have a fucking clue anymore, Davis. But you're dismissed." He tips his chin towards the door. "Come back Wednesday with your head on right or don't come back at all."

Greer

I saw the game highlights when I got out of surgery, but the slumped lines of his shoulders, the way one hand holds his forehead and the other grips his kicking leg, bouncing up and down against the step, tell me all I need to know.

Abandoned leaves on the sidewalk crunch under my shoes, and he looks up, green eyes dull and devoid of all the life that usually lives there, jaw tense as he tugs on the ends of his still-wet hair.

We say nothing as I follow the path to my porch, but I pause on the second step, running my hands through his hair, and he rests his head to the side of my thigh.

My eyelids flutter closed, and I inhale, my lungs already tight enough without the scrape of the fall air. Beckett presses his forehead harder against my thigh, and I twirl my fingers in his hair before whispering, "Come inside. It's cold."

I feel him nod against my leg, but he stays silent when he stands, and it's just his heavy shoulders, crushed under the weight of whatever expectation he thinks he failed to meet today.

We don't say anything when I open the door and he follows me in. It's silent when we both kick off our shoes, and he looks like he's seconds from finally crumbling when he sits back on the couch.

Our legs brush when I sit beside him, instead of on the opposite end, and I turn, exhaling gently. "It's okay. It's just—"

Beckett cuts me off with a shake of his head, practically wincing, voice dropping to a rough whisper. "Please don't say it's just a game."

I shift on the cushion so I'm facing him, knees digging into the side of his thigh, and I reach forward, grabbing one of his hands. "I wasn't going to say that. I was going to say it's just *one* game."

"But it's not though." His voice cracks, I think a part of me does, too—his fingers wrap around mine before he breaks away and gestures around my living room, like everything hurting him exists in the oxygen that makes up the air he's breathing. "Because if I don't have it—if I'm not *that* at the end of the day—who am I?"

"Beckett," I murmur, learning forward. My fingers stretch out for his again, but he makes a fist and digs it into his thigh. "Why is it always on you? This game, or *the* game—whatever game. There's a whole team of players who have a responsibility."

His eyes pinch closed, his fist tightens before he starts slowly pounding into his thigh. "Because it's fucking always on me. If I don't show up—if I'm not reliable—"

He cuts himself off, the words hanging there between us, and I think I do see them eating up all the air in the room. I think of all that weight, how hard it must have been to breathe his whole life.

"Reliable? Likeable? Is that still all you think you are?" I ask. "Beckett, you're *you*. You show more grace and understanding to people than anyone I've ever met. You accept people as they are. You see them and you love them anyway. Flaws and all." I reach forward and trace a finger along his jaw, the stubble rough underneath. "You've told me—and your brother told me—all the things you've done for them. You bought your parents' house. You've taken care of your siblings since they were kids. You made sure they haven't wanted for anything. That they're living good, full lives people could only dream of. Do you do all that because you're likeable and reliable and that's all you are?"

He leans into my hand, exhaling slowly as I keep tracing patterns across his skin. His fist stills against his thigh, the lines around his eyes draw tight before he opens them and gives me a resigned sideways glance. "It's what anyone would do."

"No, Beckett." I shake my head and lean forward, grabbing his hand in mine and pressing it to my chest. Right above my heart. I need him to hear this—to understand that he was already a real, beautiful, special person. "They wouldn't. And they don't. Reliable and likeable people show up when they're needed. They drive their family members to appointments, and they pick them up at the bus stop. They don't give and give and give when they've already had so much taken from them."

Beckett swallows, eyes flicking down to his hand resting against my skin.

"I want you but I can't fucking have you so I thought if—" He cuts himself off, wincing when he exhales. "I'm sorry."

"No." I shake my head. "Say it."

He looks up at me, fingers twitching against my chest, his palm splayed out right above my heart. "I thought, hey, if I can't have her, I might as well just resort back to the one thing I can do properly. But I couldn't even do that, and I can't have you because you've got these rules and these boundaries, and I'm trying my hardest to respect them, but as far as I'm concerned, the only purpose they're serving now is keeping you from opening yourself up for something that could be really, really fucking good."

"We're not talking about me." I shake my head ever so slightly again.

His lips tug to the side in a rueful smile, and his palm presses against my chest—firmer, like he needs me to feel him, or maybe he needs to feel me. "But we are. Because I don't think there's anything about me that isn't about you anymore. You made me real."

I press my eyes shut. My brain screams at me, and my heart feels infinitely heavy in my chest. "I can't make you real."

His fingers flex against my skin and then they're gone. I blink, and he has both his hands on his thighs again.

Beckett smiles at me, but it's endlessly sad, and he shrugs one shoulder. It barely moves, stuck under all that weight. "Funny thing, that. I know what you're about to say—that I was always real and the only person who I need to be enough for is me. But I like being enough for you, and I wish that enough looked like something else."

"I can't—" I start, and my voice wavers because my brain and my heart are playing this internal game of tug-of-war I don't think I'm going to survive.

"Why?" One shoulder jerks upwards, the lines of his jaw turn harsh, and he shakes his head. "We're not friends, Greer."

"Yes, we are," I whisper, and I wonder if he can even hear it over the sounds of that rope inside me pulling tighter. All I can really hear is the sound of snapping as it frays.

"What kind of friends have you had if you think this is normal?" He raises his hand before gesturing between us, beautiful eyes sharper than usual and narrowed in on me.

I start to shake my head. "There's some irony here, Beckett. You say I see through you, and I know you, and I made you real, but you're ignoring what's real about me." I push a finger to my chest, right above my heart. It presses against my rib cage, and I think the beats say something else now.

Give me to him.

I squeeze my eyes shut. "I told you where my lines were. I told you my boundaries. And you're sitting here asking for me to take them down."

"No. I'm not." He tips his head back, taking a measured exhale. "I'm not asking you to take them down. I'm asking for *you*. Who you are . . . lines around you and all. If I'm enough for you, why can't you believe that you're enough for me?"

There's just a tiny, little string hanging between the two ends of the rope of me now.

Give me to him, he wants us just as we are. The way we want him.
No. We weren't enough for anyone else before and look what it cost us.

"I can't." My voice is just this tiny crack, because I don't want either of those organs to hear me—they're going to pull too hard and there's going to be nothing left.

Beckett shakes his head, exhaling again, eyebrows lifting and those beautiful lips tug into a rueful line. No dimple to be found.

He takes my hands, bringing them to his mouth before letting them rest against his thigh.

"Do you have to go to practice tomorrow?" I ask softly.

"Nah. Coach Taylor told me not to bother showing my face until Wednesday, so I guess I get an extra day off." He runs a hand along his jaw. "Couple of the guys texted me. Asked if I wanted to do something tomorrow. Take a drive. Clear my head."

"That's nice," I offer. "You haven't really spent time with anyone outside of practice."

"I spend every day all day with them." His voice is rough when he continues. "And I didn't think anyone wanted to spend much time with me."

"I think you deserve a break from your own expectations."

A wry expression steals across his face.

My hands feather against his thighs. "Are you sore?"

"Yeah."

"I heard I have a great bathtub." I lean forward, dropping my chin on his shoulder, and there's the ghost of something living peeking out from the curtain of his eyes. "I could run you a bath. Salts. Bubbles. I'll even join you. I can read to you from one of my books."

He turns his head, nose brushing mine. "I know what you're doing, Greer. I see you, too, you know. Distraction. Deflection."

"Is that so bad?" I whisper quietly. "That I don't want to talk about something that's going to hurt you more? That I want you to feel better?"

A muscle feathers in his jaw. "I suppose it isn't, no. But this . . . it isn't going to work for me much longer."

"Okay." I nod, lowering my voice even more so maybe my brain won't hear me. The thought of this ending, whatever it is, even though I can hear quite clearly what my heart thinks, makes me want to give him something, the way he's given me so much of him. "Tonight, you just be you, and I'll just be me. We can just have fun."

If my brain hears me, if it does try to tug on what's left inside me, I can't hear it and I don't feel it because Beckett smiles, and my heart starts to sing louder than any alarm bell I've ever heard.

It's a nice sound.

"And then Baxtian laid Gaia down and—"

Beckett laughs, dropping his head back against the edge of the bathtub. "It doesn't fucking say that."

I tip my chin, holding the book up higher so the pages don't touch the bubbles. "It could."

"Okay then." Eyes wide and maybe happy for the first time all night, he leans forward, sending water and bubbles sloshing over the curved porcelain of the tub, grabbing the book from my hand. "Give it to me so I can see what my guy Baxtian is up to."

My mouth pops open, indignant, as one finger, half covered in bubbles and droplets of water, drags down the book. "Hey! You're getting the pages wet!"

"I'll get you wet." Beckett grins, glancing up from the book, dimple popping in his cheek and eyes flashing. But he holds his hands up before tossing the book towards the safety of the bathmat. "Relax. I'll buy you a new one."

"What if this one is special?" I tip my chin up again, and my ponytail dips below the surface of the water.

He gives me a flat look, running a hand through his damp hair, sending the waves every which way. "Is it?"

"No." I laugh, sinking back against the edge of the tub and kicking my foot up, sending a small splash of water and bubbles towards him.

Beckett smiles when he leans back, too, arms stretching along the porcelain rim. He's always an otherworldly sort of attractive—the kind that you'd only find in the pages of a magazine—with all that perfectly tousled chocolate hair, the eyes, the jawline, and the dimple.

But when it's just us, he's an entirely different kind of wonderful.

His eyes track across my shoulders, just exposed above the mountains of bubbles sitting on the surface of the water. They follow the curve of my neck to my jaw, and I think I can feel the reverence from here—the way his eyes skate across my lips, sweep up my cheekbones, and land on my own.

He swallows, the muscles in his neck and shoulders somehow more beautiful because of the thin sheen of water. "This is what I mean. This is—I like this. When it's just me and you. We're good together."

Whatever symphony my heart was conducting earlier starts to swell again—and I imagine, as all those chambers fill with the oxygenated blood it needs to survive, it's stretching beyond the bars of its cage, holding itself open like a conductor might their hands.

My foot finds his thigh under the water, and the corners of his lips twitch. His next words are low, rough, gravelly. Just the way I like his voice. "We could be good together."

I press my eyes closed, exhaling, before offering him a sad smile. "You might be right, but that doesn't change anything, Beckett."

"Can you just"—he jerks his head and grips his chin for a minute—"explain it to me like you might explain something to one of your patients. Dumb it down for me."

"You're not dumb."

"I know." He flashes me a wry grin. "I know much more about most major historical events than you do. But just . . . explain to me why.

Why you don't think we can work through all of these big, hard things together? Why we can't be together while we learn?"

My lips part with a tiny breath, and any words I might throw up in defense of my boundaries and my barriers stall in my throat.

I hear Rav.

You don't have to be alone to be enough.

I hear Stella.

Somewhere along the way you've confused setting a boundary with closing yourself off.

I give a tiny shake of my head.

My heart inhales, ready for the first note of this symphony that could be my life if I'd just let go—and my brain screams.

"I don't—" I try, but my voice catches. "What does that make me if I tear it all down and try to run off into the sunset with the first person who made me feel something? I can't do it again, Beckett. I can't give away a piece of me when I have these diametrically opposing views again. I can't even get through a day without thinking I'm a fucking hypocrite, and most days I think I hate myself more than I sometimes hate my dad for putting me in that impossible position. My brain is just so, so loud. All the time."

The lines of his jaw sharpen, but not in anger, a bit like the idea that I'm in pain hurts him, too. "That must be exhausting."

"Yes." I close my eyes. *I* am *exhausted*, I think. Of my brain in general, but also of this war inside me being waged by two organs I desperately need who just can't seem to agree. "I'm just . . . not sure of anything."

"I'm sure." He sits forward, sending another tsunami of water and bubbles over the edge of the bathtub. One wave curls across his forehead. His eyes are on me, and he shakes his head ever so slightly, all the lines of his jaw firm now. "About you. About this. About us. About carrying things when you're tired. About trying to help your brain quiet down. Does that count for anything?"

I shake my head again. "You said I made you real and that's a scary thing. You need to be real enough for yourself. You want to carry everything, Beckett. It's in your nature, and I don't want to be another heavy thing you strap to your back because you don't know who else to be."

Beckett points towards my hands, gripping the edges of the tub and hanging on for dear life. "May I?"

I nod.

His hands find my wrists, and one by one, he takes each of my fingers, interlacing them with his, and he pulls me towards his edge of the tub.

My body has always seemed to know what to do with his; so my legs lift, wrapping around him, and he holds our joined hands up when our chests are flush. He presses his mouth to the back of my hands before letting go. Bringing his arms to wrap around my back, he traces my scar softly and tucks my chin to his shoulder.

I can't see his face anymore. I wish I could—all those beautiful lines and those beautiful eyes that make up a beautiful boy. So, I press my eyes closed and picture Beckett the way I see him. The way I think he deserves to be. Unburdened, light, and free. Head tipped back in laughter, lines around his eyes digging in and making a home because he has so much to smile about.

"You misunderstood me. When I say you made me real . . ." He pauses, nose brushing along my jaw before he buries his face in my neck and inhales. "I mean that you breathed life back into a body that was just sort of there. I don't think I thought much about myself at all before I met you. Thought I was reliable, likeable. Someone who served a purpose for other people but never really for himself. That's what I mean when I say I didn't think I was real. I just thought that was it. That was life. But then you came along. You were kind of mean"—I feel him grin against my neck—"but eventually you smiled. Eventually you laughed. I don't think either of those things come for free with you. And they shouldn't. Probably two of the best fucking things in the world. Turned out the cost was your voice sort of burrowing into my skin and kick-starting my heart."

He presses his lips to my neck lightly before he follows it with a more purposeful brush, and I squeeze my eyes shut tighter.

My brain whispers to me and I think it's telling me my heart can't live outside my body with him, I need to keep what's left of me so I can stay alive.

My shoulders tense, and I'm about to pull back, but he speaks again. "You don't want to be another thing I take on because I think that's who I am. But it's not carrying a heavy thing, to know you."

The symphony swells in my chest. There's a clash of cymbals and this sort of crescendo you'd only see in the movies, every instrument starting at once. It reverberates and those beautiful pieces of Beckett, planted in the soil of all those empty places, stretch and grow and they sing, too, and it's all so loud I think my brain might shut up forever.

Beckett's lips move along my neck, pausing at my jaw, before he pulls back and drops his forehead to mine. "Would you be interested in taking a break with me? A break from being just friends? From the expectations and everything that goes on up there." He taps his index finger to my temple. "Just me and you until Wednesday. And if it still doesn't feel right, I promise that—"

I can't really hear anything other than him, and I hold my pinky finger up.

Promise me you'll only do what's right for you.

I'm not sure anything has ever really felt right at all before him.

This grin that's not quite like anything I've ever seen stretches across his face when he hooks his finger with mine.

This is the one people should want in photos and on TV. But I don't want anyone else to ever see it because I think it belongs to me.

Beckett

There are a lot of places to take a break, or to play pretend, because that's really what this feels like.

Just a little kid playing make believe but instead of Dungeons and Dragons—not that I spent much time on that as a kid anyway, I was probably dreaming about a whole healthy and healed family—it's me, watching her walk through the door of my cottage, arms crossed and eyes assessing, taking in the swirls of burnt-orange, yellow, and red covering the trees through the floor-to-ceiling glass windows, pretending that she loves me back.

She didn't say anything, but I think she traded a shift or took an extra home call later in the month to come with me.

She held up her pinky, eyes soft, droplets of water tracking across the lines of her shoulders, over the curve of her chest just visible above the bath, and bubbles dotting her clavicle—and I don't think I noticed much after that.

Greer turns, looking back over her shoulder and the early-morning sunlight hits the planes of her face in a way that's like another football to the stomach, but one I won't recover from. Her voice rings out, rasps filling this place up, too. She sounds good here. "What made you buy a place in the Kawarthas? The Muskokas are right there."

I shrug, dropping the bags and kicking the door shut behind me. "This place is converted shipping containers." I gesture across the open kitchen, where an island not unlike the one in my apartment spans the room in front of slate-grey cupboards and one of those designer fridges that cost way too much, to the sectional taking up residence in the living room in front of a gas fireplace in the wall, and the wooden slats hiding the stairs to the bedrooms. "I thought it was cool, and you know me. Thought maybe I'd find out they were containers with historical significance. Maybe they carried something important across the Channel during the rise of the British Empire."

Her eyes glimmer. "And?"

I grin, grabbing the bags of groceries and bringing them into the kitchen. "Turns out they're just metal."

She tips her head back, hair tumbling off her shoulders and revealing the jut of her collarbone where her sweater slouches down.

She laughs, standing there in the sunlight, taking up all this space in another place I used to come to be alone, and I can't breathe again.

Scrubbing my jaw, I tip my chin towards the chairs lining the island. My sister picked those out—she said they were something called boucle, and they'd match the couch.

She also said they'd be a hit with any girl I brought here.

The first one to ever cross the threshold doesn't really seem to care much about them as she folds herself into one, brings a knee to her chest, dropping her chin to it.

I clear my throat. "Coffee? I can make you a latte?"

Greer nods, and she gives me this look I haven't quite figured out—mouth soft, eyes even more so, her head tipping from side to side like she's assessing.

I'm never quite sure what, but she doesn't look disappointed in her findings.

I give my head a shake and force myself to turn around—I'd probably spend all morning staring at her sitting there in the sunlight if she let me—and look at the espresso machine taking up a stretch of counter. It's another Sarah touch, and she spent hours teaching me how to use it properly.

"I know you told me that lattes weren't friendly, but we're not friends these next two nights, right?" I swallow, staring at the chrome adornments, hoping I didn't imagine the whole fucking thing.

She doesn't answer right away, and I imagine she's doing that same thing—eyes curious, head angled to the side as she studies for answers in the set of my shoulders. When she does speak, her voice is soft, but her words are firm. "I don't think so."

I nod, and I debate abandoning the coffee in favour of grabbing her off that chair, laying her down on the nearest surface, and fucking her until neither of us knows our own name.

But it's not just sex and I don't think it ever was.

The latte takes too long. I drop my head to the cupboard, hand flexed against the counter, thumb tapping out in impatience for the stupid thing to stop brewing.

It's just these hours and I don't want to spend a single second on something other than her.

I could probably kick a ball the entire length of the field when I see the screen flash to tell me it's done.

She lifts her chin and offers me a rare smile when I hand it to her. She takes a sip, looking out to the windows revealing the slope of lawn, a copse of trees, and the lake, winking at us under the early-morning sunlight. Looking back to me, she shrugs the shoulder on display. "Should we make something up then? A historical event we can attach to your shipping containers?"

I grin, taking the mug from her hands and setting it down on the island. "Sure. To be known forevermore as the site where Greer Roberts let Beckett Davis in, and he didn't waste a second of it."

Her lips open just so, eyes sweep across my face, and before she can say anything, I've got my hands around the back of her neck, and my mouth on hers.

We've kissed before, but always as friends.

Never like this.

No rules. And she does open for me, I think. I can tell by the angle of her head, the way one hand tangles in the back of my hair, her fingers pulling taut, and her other hand snakes across my chest, down my stomach until it finds the edge of my shirt, and her fingers dig a line into my skin when she grabs it, tugging me closer.

Her full lips part, and I meet her tongue with mine, and it's just this endless thing.

Two real people in a kitchen under the morning sun, an abandoned mug of coffee, hands scrambling, trying to get closer, and mouths moving together in this way that I hope tells her my heart is hers—it always has been.

And I think I might have hers, at least for now.

"Checkmate."

"No shit." My eyes cut up from the chessboard, propped up on a stump that's supposed to be aesthetic, between our two Muskoka chairs at the end of the dock.

Greer shrugs, barely visible under my sweater. It's huge on her—an old practice sweater I wear sometimes at the stadium, with the team logo stitched across the chest and my number along the hood. Her earmuffs hang around her neck, and she takes a sip of the mimosa sitting on the arm of her chair, the crystal flute glinting. "I tried to warn you."

A muscle ticks in my cheek, and I feel like upturning the chessboard. I point at her. "We're playing scrabble next time."

"I'll probably win at that, too." She blinks at me from behind the glass. "I know a lot of words."

"Yahtzee, then?" I ask, voice dry. "That's all chance, and I'm too competitive to keep losing to you all afternoon. It's going to give me more of a complex than I already have."

Greer frowns, shaking her head, but her eyes shine. "Unfortunately for you, that's not true. The roll of dice is by chance, but the rest of the game can be broken down strategically to maximize your score."

I hold my arms open, like I can't quite believe that, even though there's nothing about the endless capability of her brain that could surprise me.

She tips her head back in laughter, and it's this beautiful, throaty thing that echoes through me and out across the lake.

Lucky fucking trees, getting to hear that sound.

I grin, watching her as she keeps her head back, studying the clouds tumbling across the sky.

It's a beautiful fall day—crisp, clear air that nips at your skin, shining sun and the smell of leaves hanging all around.

But it's a more beautiful girl.

Her eyelids flutter closed, and she sighs, chin still tipped up at the clouds. Even the usually sharp lines of her face seem softer, like she's relaxing and breathing out here without the expectations, and maybe she likes being with me like this.

"Will you"—I reach out my hand—"come over here?"

Greer blinks, looking back down to the earth, over at me, and nods softly.

I watch as she stands, one hand flattening against the arm of the chair, the other wrapping around the crystal stem, the length of my sweater falling to her mid-thigh, brushing against her leggings. The way her dark hair swings around her shoulders when she takes the few steps to reach her hand to mine. How her fingers fit mine, like each of our hands were actually sculpted for the other.

I watch it all, try to commit it to memory in case these forty-eight hours are all we get. I don't know what's going to happen to me if I go back on Wednesday and I don't perform this weekend.

But she folds herself down into my lap, leans against my chest, and I don't care.

She doesn't realize—but there's always this faint smell of eucalyptus clinging to her, like those branches her sister hung for her that she thinks are stupid actually did something. Wrapped around her and tried to protect her as best they could.

I tuck my chin in the crook of her neck and inhale, circling my arms around her.

Her hand trails up the side of my face, tracing patterns in the stubble across my jaw before she cups my cheek. "Do you feel better?"

I nod and press my mouth to the side of her neck because I can. "Head's a bit clearer."

So is my heart because I'm here with you and you're letting me pretend you're really mine.

"Do you want to talk about it?" Her fingers twist in the hair around my ears.

A groan rises in my throat and my eyes close. "That feels nice."

"I'll take that as a no."

I can tell she's smiling by the way the inflection of her voice changes, how I can feel her shoulders roll back through my sweater. She does that when she's happy—gives away these little tells that she's feeling momentarily unburdened.

Shaking my head, I inhale one more time before opening my eyes and resting my chin on her shoulder. "Nah. It's okay. I don't think there's really anyone else I'd want to talk about it with."

Her fingers come down across my jaw again. "What happens if you miss on Sunday?"

I exhale. "I doubt Coach Taylor was joking, so I'd guess he trades me, or he drops me for a consistent college kid at a fraction of the cost."

Greer pulls away, shifting in my lap and turning so she can face me. She taps the champagne flute against her lips before emptying it and setting it down beside the chair. That hand finds the other side of my face. "Have you ever thought about that? Whether it would be good for you to move, start over in a new city with a new team?"

"I've never thought about it. I was happy to come back here from Cincinnati. Thought it'd be nice to be closer so I could make sure everything was alright." I usually can't breathe when she's this close to me, but I take a deep, measured inhale. It feels a bit more like I can right now. I give her a wry smile. "It wasn't until recently it occurred to me that I'm not responsible for giving them everything they need and I never was."

"Do you think you resent them?" she asks plainly, like that's a normal thing to ask someone about their parents.

But maybe it is.

I consider it, nodding a bit before I shrug. "Probably. Probably my whole life and didn't even realize it. Do you think it'll always be like that?"

Her shoulders rise under my sweater, and she looks so fucking beautiful. Earmuffs around her neck, dark hair falling every which way, and those eyes that see right through me. "Maybe. Maybe not. Maybe it'll come in waves. Or maybe one day you'll wake up and it'll just be gone." Each of her thumbs brush over my jaw. "My sister said something to me recently about grief and healing. That it's not a formula that just clicks together one day. That they're part of the human experience, and I've been wondering if maybe you just learn to live through them."

"I wouldn't mind learning to live through it all with you." My voice is rough when I say it, kind of like the seas of whatever storm she thinks she lives in.

It's not much of an answer, but she leans forward, hands still framing my face when her lips find mine.

She moves them—gently, like she's testing something out. Trying it on for size.

I hope she likes the way it fits.

I tighten my grip around her, tongue sweeping against the seam of her lips, and she meets it with hers. I'm not sure how long we kiss for; I get a bit lost up in my head trying to make the whole thing count, imagining a world where I can tell her she's the love of my life and that I don't think I really care what happens on Sunday as long as I have her.

Eventually she pulls back, head tipped to the side, full lips swollen, and looks at me like she's thinking about something.

"Thank you," she starts, but she pauses, a tiny shake of her head. "I don't thank you enough for what you've done for me. You say I made you real, and maybe that's true, but you know me. And there's something very special and rare in knowing. Not something your average, run-of-the-mill reliable and likeable person would be able to achieve."

My chest tightens, and I start to shake my head, swallowing, not sure how to answer that because I did get to know her, and I fell in love with her.

But she keeps talking. "It was just a pinky promise. Inconsequential to some people. But you made me promise to only do what was right for me. I don't think anyone has ever given me permission to do that before, and maybe permission was all I needed."

"You told your sister the whole truth then?"

She nods, fingers feathering against my jaw. "I did. Because of you. She had a lot of thoughts about it. Nice thoughts. Kind thoughts. She had thoughts about other things, too."

"Oh yeah?" I ask, voice heavy. "What were those?"

Greer blinks at me, thumbs swiping up the line of stubble cutting across my cheek before she turns and settles against my chest, murmuring, "Things I'm not sure what to do with yet."

"Thank you." I swallow, pressing my mouth to the crown of her head. "For seeing me. For whatever you said to make my brother and sister tell me they see me, too. It was nice, to be with them like that. Another thing I owe you for. One day I'll work up the courage to draw a line in the sand with my parents, but—"

"One day," she finishes.

I clear my throat, jerking my head towards her empty glass. "Do you want another? I'll go get you one."

"No," she says simply, dropping the back of her head to my shoulder. "I want you to stay here."

I want to stay here, too, I think.

And I wish we could forever.

Greer

Healing might not suddenly click into place.

But I think other things do sometimes.

It happens when Beckett tips his head back and smiles—a real one. Not the grin he parades around and pulls out like a party trick because he thinks he needs to please people for them to love him the way he deserves.

Waves of unruly chocolate hair curl against the nape of his neck, his stubble draws a shadow across his jaw, and the sunlight hits his eyes. Emeralds, both of them.

Not diamonds or gold, but maybe something rarer entirely.

He's beautiful when he's free.

"You should smile more," I whisper.

He shrugs a shoulder, all of him turning lazy when he leans back and plants his hands on the wood of the dock. "I get paid to smile. I should have been a model."

"That's not what I mean." I sit forward, and I think the wine has made the edges of my mind a little fuzzy. Maybe his, too, because he looks like nothing has ever hurt him and he's never felt the weight of it all a day in his life.

I take my index finger and place it in the curve of his full bottom lip before tracing the edge of it.

He says nothing, but I see the muscles in his neck tense in a swallow.

I pull my hand back and place it against my chest, like maybe I'll be able to feel that smile in my heart.

He blinks, and I think, if it was possible, his eyes might flay me open. If heaven were real, they're the green rolling hills you'd see when you get there, and you'd be happy you died.

His voice is rough—throaty like it only is when we're alone together. "Do it again."

I do, and that's when I hear it.

Oh, my heart whispers. *You love him, this boy with the heavy shoulders and wonderful smile.*

Greer

The realization I'm in love with him doesn't come with these crashing cymbals signaling the start of a symphony like the other night in the bath.

But my world quiets down.

My brain shuts up.

Maybe it's because physiologically speaking, my brain relies on my heart for the blood it needs to live, and maybe my heart won that internal tug-of-war because it was holding all the power at the end of the day, and it didn't want to be separated from Beckett for a moment longer.

I don't say anything, I'm not entirely sure how. But I watch him a bit more closely all afternoon, and I must smile more because he catches me and asks me more than once what it's about.

I find more reasons to touch him—a brush of my hand over his shoulder, one of the waves of his hair twirling between my fingers, my lips scoring across the stubble of his jawline.

I press my cheek to the planes of his back while he stands over the stove cooking me dinner.

He likes that, I think.

He picks me up and carries me upstairs to his bedroom after. It's beautiful—more floor-to-ceiling windows with a perfect view of the slope of the hill, of stretching tree branches weighed down with leaves that still look brilliant, and of the moon reflecting off the lake.

Apparently, the dishes can wait because there's a movie on the History Channel he's dying to show me.

I'm not so sure about that when he drops me on the bed and insists I change, saying that historical documentaries are best consumed in bed, wearing nothing but your underwear.

He takes my sweater off, kissing every inch of skin he sees before he moves to my leggings.

I don't kiss every inch of his skin when he takes his clothes off—mostly because I'm busy watching. Looking at him with eyes that know they're looking at something they love. It's quite the sight, really.

He sits down beside me, propping himself up against the headboard. But he pauses when he picks up the remote. "That night we ran into you and your sister on the rooftop, I overheard you talking about growing a liver from another liver. What does that mean?"

I roll my eyes. "It means nothing because I was on my fourth glass of wine."

Beckett grins, dropping the remote, one hand coming behind his head where he rests it against the headboard. "Seriously."

I sit up straighter, trying to contain my hands, but I start talking with them anyway. "There've been so many advances in regenerative medicine. Think about stem cell transplants."

Beckett's eyes track the sweeping movements I make, the corners crinkling, like he's trying to fight a smile, but he nods. "They talked about Sarah having one."

"Right, so, there have been so many advances for tissue transplantation, but it just hasn't translated to organ donation." I wave both of my hands around, like it's not weird we're sitting here in our underwear talking about the untapped power of regenerative medicine. "There are a lot of complicated, boring reasons for that. Believe it or not—there's a shortage of organs. Live donation solves some of that, but this idea that regenerated organ cells could come from a patient's own tissue, not only does that bypass the need for a living donor if a deceased one isn't available—it eliminates the problem of rejection."

He does smile this time. Softer than usual, no dimple, but understanding etched into all the sharp lines of his face. "And then no one would ever have to give a piece of themselves away."

"Yes," I whisper. "The possibilities are just so . . . vast."

"Vast," he nods, repeating.

"Vast." I smile.

Beckett raises a brow. "You look alive."

I narrow my eyes. "Have I looked like a corpse the entire time you've known me?"

"No." He shakes his head. "You've looked beautiful."

My chin tips up. "What about when I had bile in my hair?"

"Even then." He grins, offering me a shrug. "You just seem . . . bright. Like the possibility excites you instead of shackling you. It doesn't weigh you down like surgery does sometimes."

"You sound like Rav."

His grin turns wry. "Is he looking for an assistant? Come Sunday, I might be out of a job."

"You won't be."

"I think"—Beckett scrubs his face, before looking at me, his smile resigned now—"that it would be okay if I was."

I blink, pulling my head back. "You don't want to play anymore?"

"Nah, it's not that." He rubs the back of his head before running a hand through his hair, sending waves tumbling every which way. He picks up one of my hands, stretching out each of my fingers in turn. "I can't really imagine doing anything else with my life, honestly. I loved it, and I think I'd be able to love it again, in time. But I just . . ." He brings my palm to his mouth, and his next words whisper against my skin. "I think for the first time, I realize I'll still be worth something if I'm not playing and providing. I can figure out the rest. Learning and all that."

I debate telling him he's worthy—that he's always been worthy—but I'm not sure he needs the sermon.

He's been looking at me all day like he needs to touch me, and I think I need that, too.

"Kiss me," I whisper.

His hands are around the back of my neck, tipping my head to meet his, and his mouth is on mine.

Beckett likes to spend a lot of time on me before sex. He's not particularly picky about how he does it—whether it's with his fingers, his tongue, or his hands on my hips, moving me against him before he's even inside me.

Tonight, I think we spend time on each other.

It's different—for your hands to rove over the valleys and ridges of someone and know you love them. It's quieter, at least for me, because there's no brain telling me he's just my friend—this man biting into my neck, whose hands palm my chest, whose fingers roll my nipples between them before they're replaced by his tongue, and they slide down my stomach, stopping at my scar, where they pause with a reverence I couldn't quite understand before, when they reach the centre of me, moving in these circles before sliding inside.

It's different when I kiss down his neck, nails digging into his shoulders, tongue tracing the lines of his abdomen before I take him in my mouth and he groans, hips rising to meet me.

It's certainly different when he finds himself between my legs, one hand splayed against my stomach, the other wrapped around my thigh, eyes cutting up to me when he says, "Come for me."

I do.

And it's not quite like anything I've ever experienced in my life.

My back arches with a moan, one hand finding his shoulder, the other tangling in his hair.

"Louder."

I am.

"Can you give me one more?"

I can.

"Good girl." He says it when his teeth scrape the inside of my thigh before he moves up the bed to hover over me.

My lips part with tiny pants, and I stare up at him, eyes wide.

He looks down at me, one wave of chocolate hair tumbling over his forehead.

"I have an IUD and I was just tested—" I start as he says, "I just had my physical."

I blink, nodding at him.

"Just you and me then? You're sure?" he asks.

I nod again softly.

His eyes flash. A groan catches in his throat when he grips himself and his shoulders roll back when he pushes into me slowly.

I inhale as he does, inch by inch, and I'm all full of him, nothing really empty at all because everything about Beckett is larger than life—all the parts of his body, his brain, his heart, his laugh.

He's effervescent. It's a bit how I feel right now—body stretching to accommodate him before giving way to all the wonderful things he does to it. He's just right. The pressure of him inside me, a bit like a supernova that might implode and take all my lines with it.

I think, though, that it was meant to be this way. Just me and him.

A muscle in his jaw ticks and he exhales, hands coming up on either side of me to fist the pillow before he buries his face in my neck and starts to move.

"I love you," I whisper, and it's so quiet I'm not even sure he'll be able to hear me, but I think my heart might hold my blood hostage if I don't say it.

He stills, the ridges of muscle that make up him pull taut. I can see them, the cords straining from his neck, down across his shoulders, to the curve of his arms. Beckett pulls his head back slowly, lips leaving my neck, and he hovers over me, eyes impossibly dark and cheekbones sharp enough to carve another piece of me away.

But that doesn't bother me. It's all his anyway.

"Say that again," he breathes.

"I love you."

"Again," he asks, voice rough.

"I—" He rolls his hips upwards before my lips are done moving.

I moan the next word, head tipping back as I arch into him. "Love—"

Again, hips flex. His hand releases the pillow, finding my chin and bringing my eyes back down to meet his.

"You."

He swallows the last word as he moves, and I think the whole idea of it—my love for him—finds its way to his heart.

His lips leave mine, trailing across my jaw, over the curve of my neck, until he presses his mouth to my ear.

I can hardly hear anything over my own heart, but I do hear the words he whispers to me.

"I love you, too."

Beckett

The street leading up to her house looks the same—trees with branches starting to shed their leaves as the air turns colder, grass crisp with frost, and the sky milky in the early morning.

Her porch looks the same, too. Quiet. Unassuming.

Just the red brick of the house, two chairs with grey cushions angled towards one another, hidden by the white wooden arches that keep the whole thing invisible from the street.

It all looks like it did when we left it Monday morning to get away—no expectations, no pressure, just us.

But nothing's the same at all, and I don't think it ever will be again.

How could it be when she loves me and I love her?

Certainly not when I know what it's like to have her—really have her. To be inside her when she says she loves me and I get to say I love her back. To watch her sleep, gilded by that stupid moon peeking in through the window that was lucky to look at her. To wake up with her and watch her scrunch her face when she takes her first sip of coffee. To have her beat me at every board game imaginable, to fall asleep in her lap while she reads, her fingers trailing along my scalp.

I'm pretty confident nothing ever mattered before this—not a single kick, not a single record. I thought I was real before—that she had taken those hands that save lives and decided to save mine, too.

But if someone was going to etch a date of birth on my tombstone, I'd ask them to get it right down to the very millisecond she whispered those words out into the world.

I love you.

I wince when I see the fallen leaves on the street crunch under my truck tires in the rearview mirror, as I pull up against the sidewalk and put it in park.

My grand plan of spending a couple days with no expectations had a fatal flaw—it didn't include talking about what any of it meant.

I should have made that my one condition.

I might have even gotten something like that in writing, had I known how it was going to turn out.

Scrubbing my jaw, I turn towards her. "It was nice. To clear my head with you."

"It was." She nods, a little crease between her eyebrows that I feel a bit like smoothing out with my thumb, but I don't know what's in bounds anymore.

"Statement still stands." I jerk my chin towards her house, like we can see the bath from here. "We're good together."

"We are," she confirms.

She looks beautiful when she says it—chin tipped up just so, cheekbones sharp enough to cut, eyes wide and blinking, all that dark hair twisted into a knot on top of her head.

It kind of makes me want to throttle her. I can probably count on one hand the number of times I've lost my cool—and she has me on the precipice of another.

I think about ripping her seat belt off, dragging her over here, and telling her I love her, that I'd drop to my knees every day for the rest of my life and beg her to just open for me—I'd carve half of my liver out and hand it to her, if that's what she needed to give us a real chance.

She's already got my heart, what's one more organ?

But my eyes drop to the sweater she wears. It's mine. The ratty practice one I gave her at the cottage, and I think of the scar it's covering up. Healed after all these years, but not really.

I'd rather cut off my kicking leg with a rusty saw than hurt her, so I give her a resigned smile instead. "The real world kind of fucking sucks."

"Sometimes." She wrinkles her nose.

I press my fist into my mouth, exhaling. "There's this open practice on Friday. It's sort of an appreciation event. We play no-touch football and have dumb competitions. They always make me try to kick different things through the uprights. They moved it up because they thought it would boost morale before the Baltimore game on Sunday." I take my hat off, tugging on the ends of my hair. "Families come. Friends. Partners. Wives. Girlfriends."

One eyebrow kicks up, and Greer angles her head. "What about business acquaintances?"

"Is that what we are?" I ask, voice rough.

"No," she answers with a soft shake of her head.

"What are we?" It's a bit of a hopeless question, just another rope thrown out into her sea that I know she won't grab. But I'll probably spend the rest of my life throwing them just in case.

Her shoulders rise with an inhale. She blinks, and she opens those fucking eyes right as the sun hits the windows, illuminating everything about her. Her voice sounds sort of like the first time I heard it, each lift and rasp of a word plucking at my heart in my chest and jump-starting the whole thing. "Why don't we talk about it Sunday night after the game?"

"You'll be there, right?" I don't know why she wants to wait, and I probably sound desperate. I am. But there's no one else I'm interested in sitting in those stands.

She touches me for the first time all drive, reaching out, her fingers just ghosts of what they were before, trailing across my jaw. "Of course. And I'll be there Friday."

I lean into her hand, pressing my eyes closed and trying to savour the whole thing before looking back at her. "Sunday night. Win or lose. Record or no record. Kick or no kick." I hold out my hand, pinky finger up for her. "You and me?"

Her finger wraps around mine, and she whispers, "You and me."

Our fingers stay joined and I think all the promises we made echo between us, all these things we said and did to help each other, and I feel a bit like going back in time and kicking that old me for never promising anything that meant us being together.

She brings her lips to the crease where our fingers meet, sits back, and grabs her bag from the floor, and I watch her leave my truck.

She's halfway up the path to her place when I roll down the window.

"Dr. Roberts." I lean across the passenger seat, and she glances back over her shoulder. "I meant every word."

She smiles softly, raising her hand. "So did I."

Beckett

I've kicked a rugby ball, a soccer ball, and a volleyball through the uprights, and I'm moving on to a tennis ball, propped up on a tee when I see her.

Hair pulled back into one of those braids she likes, hands tucked into the pockets of a shiny black bomber jacket, and navy scrubs hugging the curves of her legs.

None of us are wearing helmets, so the press can see us and get shots of us having fun out here, laughing and smiling, a cohesive team despite the devastating loss, while we all wave at our families.

The only part of mine interested in showing up were my brother and sister, and I asked them not to.

Drew a line in the sand like that girl up there told me I should, and they respected it.

She shines under the sunlight as she walks down the stairs to the edge of the field, the barrier temporarily removed for the event and replaced with gates, and she leans forward, resting her arms along the metal rung.

One hand comes up in a tiny wave that's just for me.

I don't know why I do it—it's the sort of thing she'd hate—but I grin, holding my hand against my chest, and point at her before I line up to kick this stupid tennis ball.

It goes through.

People clap and cheer, Nowak knocks his head against mine like it's a real game, and cameras from all the desk reporters who got stuck covering this event flash from around the gates.

Some of them start to call my name, and I'm sure they have a whole host of riveting questions lined up about the difference between kicking a tennis ball and a football, how events like this boost morale, and what that means before Sunday.

Old me would have walked right over, grin and dimple on display, but I hold up a hand instead and jog over to the girl standing there with my heart in her hands.

"Great legs," she rasps, raising her eyebrows. "I'm sorry I'm late. Surgery ran long and I have to be back at the hospital in a couple hours."

I grin, pointing towards her hospital badge, a picture of her that looks too serious, with her name and credentials on display, clipped to the pocket of her scrubs. "Need to make sure everyone knows you're the smartest person in the stadium?"

Greer's eyes flick down before she rolls them at me. "I was in a rush. Someone dragged me to a weird cottage made of metal shipping containers for two days and now I'm behind on my charting."

"Yeah? Who would do that?" I swipe a hand through my hair. "Was it at least worth it?"

This tiny, little smile blooms on her mouth, and it's not quite like anything I've ever seen when she whispers, "I'd say so."

"I missed you these last two nights," I offer, voice rough when I reach out, tugging on the end of her braid.

She blinks, but I think she grabs onto one of those ropes I've thrown overboard and out to her. "I missed you, too."

"Can I . . ." I scrub my jaw before angling my head down towards her. "Can I kiss you?"

Full lips part, those features soften, and she lifts her chin towards me.

It's probably inappropriate—my hand sliding around the back of her neck, tongue meeting hers, and everything I feel for her out in the open.

Someone calls my name while I kiss her, a lot of people do. Some of my teammates whistle, and I can see the flash of cameras against my eyelids.

Reporters try to get my attention.

"Beckett!"

Doesn't work. I don't think I even know my own name.

"Nineteen."

Don't care. I'll be whatever number she needs me to be.

"Who is that? Is that your girlfriend?"

Just the love of my life.

"Near Miss. How do you feel about the game on Sunday? Are you going to try for another record?"

That one works.

But not on me.

Greer pulls back, whipping her head around towards the reporter who stands just one gate over. Her voice doesn't sound the way it usually does—it's sharp, harsher than I've ever heard. "What did you just say?"

His brow creases, and he has the audacity to look confused, like he doesn't understand why she's answering him and not me. "I asked him if—"

"No," she interrupts with a sharp jerk of her chin. "Before that."

He tries again. "How do you feel about—"

"Before that."

I grip the back of her neck and run my hand along her shoulder, dropping my voice. "Baby, leave it."

"No." She doesn't look at me, and for the first time, I can see why my brother and the other residents are terrified of her. Cheeks that could probably cut through glass, skin, and bone; eyes sharp and lips in this sort of amused smile that somehow doesn't look like she's enjoying anything at all.

He swallows. "Near Miss."

"You know what?" Her smile shifts, and it's not friendly. "Why don't I hold on to your little microphone, you go out there, and you see how far you can kick?" She doesn't wait for him to answer. "Or better yet—why don't you tell me about a time you screwed up at work. I'll make up a little nickname to commemorate the occasion, write a news story about it, and I'll make sure everyone forgets you're a real fucking person and no one ever says your real name again."

I don't like the way he looks at her—eyes narrowed when they sweep over her. I'm about to mouth off to a reporter for the first time in my career and tell him to fuck off, but he turns and starts shoving his microphone in someone else's face.

"That wasn't necessary." I slide my hand around the back of her neck again and press my mouth roughly to the crown of her head. I murmur, "I can see why everyone in that hospital is terrified of you, though."

Full lips tug into a flat line, and I feel a bit like pressing my mouth right at the precipice of her Cupid's bow. The rasp of her voice is firm when she says, "You're worth defending, Beckett."

I know that, I think, *because of you.*

"I know," I answer, the corner of my mouth kicking up. "I have to go play tic-tac-toe with a football against Nowak now. Make yourself comfortable. I'm sure it'll be riveting. But . . . Sunday?"

"Sunday," she repeats, holding her pinky up, and I take it with mine, pressing it to my mouth before jogging back towards the field.

I win the dumb game, they place balls farther and farther down the field for me, she stays and watches, rolling her eyes when I point at her before each kick, and I think I'm enjoying it for the first time since I became me.

I even enjoy our team meeting Saturday morning. It should probably be more stressful than it is, given who we're playing tomorrow, but everyone laughs and we toss miniature footballs across the conference table while Coach Taylor talks and makes us watch the same tape until our eyes bleed.

I enjoy the hour and a half of dynamic stretching the conditioning staff make me do, and the deep tissue massage on my kicking leg doesn't hurt as much as usual.

But it all gets spectacularly fucked up when I'm walking to my truck to leave for the day.

I muted most of my social media over the summer. I didn't need to see the memes or the messages from everyone in the city telling me how much I let them down, how they wished I'd fallen and broken my ankle when I swung so we'd have to trade for someone else.

It was probably aspirational, but I turned my notifications back on last night, and now my phone won't stop vibrating in my pocket.

And I want to die a bit when I finally take it out, one hand reaching towards the door of my truck, the other about to throw my phone into the ground and smash it into a million pieces.

Because it's not just me they're talking about anymore.

She answers the door after I smack the glass for the fifth time.

I thought about just using the code and opening it, but her privacy was already horrifically violated today, and I highly doubt she's overly keen on seeing me either.

The horrible irony of the whole thing is that the photos of us are nice. In another world, I'd probably have printed them off, papered my whole apartment with them, and thrown them into the streets so everyone knew Greer Roberts belonged to me.

But we're in this world and the people of the internet can be fucking cruel.

That reporter posted a photo of us, complete with some stupid headline about the big reveal of why I'm so inconsistent—my priorities clearly aren't in check and Coach Taylor should find someone more focused. But her hospital badge was on full display, and then he used whatever scrap of brain power he must possess to find out everything he could about her, string a story together that was none of his fucking business, and then he posted all those pictures, too.

Pictures of her and her sister, still bruised but smiling, happy to be alive and to have each other, in side-by-side hospital beds—pictures that look like they were stolen from someone's social media. Photos of the car accident, which also make me want to die in an entirely different way because seeing the destroyed bridge railing and mangled wreck being brought up from the lake was probably something I could have lived without. A picture of her and her dad, in hospital gowns post-transplant. An award she got from some donor recognition program, ironically, for giving the gift of life when she was so young.

Another stolen picture of her in a sports bra after one of those races where they cover you with mud, standing between Willa and Kate, bare stomach and scar, fresh and pink, on display.

And somehow, a copy of the police report that detailed her father's blood alcohol level. How he wasn't over the limit when he was tested, but he would have been when the accident happened.

She blinks at me, eyes swollen with dark circles that have no business on that face, and visible stains from old tear tracks.

I feel a bit like turning around and punching something.

"Greer." I reach for her, but her eyes squeeze shut, and I can't tell if it's a flinch, so I scrub my face instead.

She doesn't say anything, but she wraps her arms around herself—she's wearing my fucking sweater—and turns, walking into her living room.

It's probably the closest thing to an invitation I'll get, seeing as this is all my fault, so I close the door behind me and follow her.

She's not sitting, she's just standing there, one arm wrapped around her stomach, hand pressing down over her scar, and the other holding her phone.

Her voice cracks, and she inhales, shoulders shaking. "I don't tell anyone those things, Beckett. It's not—it's not only my story to tell. My dad, his sobriety . . . it's the most important thing in the world to him and people are talking about him like he's this vile, disgusting thing, not a person who struggled with an illness so much bigger than him."

"I know." I take a hesitant step towards her, and when she doesn't pull away, I bring her to my chest and press my mouth to her forehead.

She shakes her head against me. "All the horrible, hateful things I think about myself—" A choked sob cuts her off before she pushes back and takes a measured step away from me. "They're all saying them."

"Baby."

I haven't been my own biggest fan in a long time, but I don't think I've ever quite felt like this.

She looks back down at the phone, finger jabbing the screen as she starts to list off each one. "'She must have no self-respect.' 'I wouldn't want her operating on me.' 'Who gave her a medical license?' 'She should have let her father die.'"

Her voice cracks again on that last one, and I think this one might be irreparable.

"What do you need me to do?" I hold my hands up uselessly.

Her shoulders slump, resigned, and she gives a sad little shake of her head. "Nothing."

And I think part of me finally breaks, too.

"Do you want me to sue them?" I open my arms and I start shouting. "I'll fucking sue the stupid website; I'll sue every person who fucking commented on every single picture! I'll sue that reporter and take everything he fucking has and give it all to you. What can I do to fix this?"

"This isn't something you can fix, Beckett!" Her voice rises, cracking on the crescendo of a sob.

"Of course it is. I'll do anything." I grip my jaw, shaking my head, before I drop to my knees in front of her. I look like an idiot, but I'm not entirely sure I ever got up off the concrete floor of that closet anyway. "I can fix anything."

"Well, you can't fix this." She throws her phone onto the couch, presses her hand to her face, and starts sobbing.

I bury my head in her stomach, grip tightening around her when I shift the sweater up, pressing my mouth in these tiny kisses I'd like to imagine were Band-Aids or stitches or whatever it is she needs.

My mouth reaches the bottom curve of her scar. I kiss up the entire line, and I hope it hears the words, too. That maybe they're going to be able to fill up all the empty spaces or just make the whole thing disappear. "I love you."

"I love you, too." She whispers it, and I think, maybe, that it's all going to be okay, that I can fix this just like I've fixed everything else for everyone else, but she says this other thing that splits me open entirely. "Please just go."

I pull back, and I know I look pathetic. Down here on my knees for her, but I'd stay here all day if that's what she needed. "Are we still—"

"I don't know."

I hate myself a bit for asking, but I do anyway. "Are you still coming tomorrow?"

"I don't know," she repeats, words flat but still sharp enough to stab through my chest.

She takes a measured step back. It's tiny, but she might as well be standing across the Atlantic. I scrub my face, feeling a bit like shouting. Not at her—just at the whole thing.

Boy isn't real. Boy becomes real.

Boy loses the only thing he ever really wanted anyway.

I dig my fist into my leg before pushing to stand.

"This—loving you. Being loved by you." I jerk my head before pointing at her, and my voice rises but the whole thing shakes. "You'll be the only near miss I care about."

She doesn't say anything, but she clutches her right side again and starts to sob.

"I asked you to go."

I do, and I catch the door right before I slam it on my way out. I let myself forget, for just a second, that the sound might hurt her.

I hate myself for that, too.

Greer

If there was anything funny about the whole thing, it might be that I asked Beckett to wait until Sunday night after the game to talk about us, real us, what we are and what we aren't, because I wanted to talk to my dad first.

I came back from that cottage with these grand ideas that maybe I could be this healed person for him, all this courage sitting in my chest, roots and trees and beautiful flowers blooming from the soil of all those empty places.

Now there's really no need for any of that, because my dad's seen it all anyway, and Beckett isn't my friend, but he did end up taking a piece of me with him when he left after all.

The creak of the front door echoes. Shadows spill along the hallway, illuminated by the one single light I left on out there, and judging by the determined footfalls, I know who it is before she peers around the corner of my bedroom door.

"This stuff doesn't work." I point to the eucalyptus, hanging there uselessly against the edge of the mirror.

The corners of Stella's mouth tug down, and she places a hand against her chest. "No, I can't imagine it would. But I brought reinforcements."

I know who's going to peer around the corner behind her before they do, too.

A slicked-back ponytail swings across shoulders, and a head of tumbling red waves beside her.

"Hi," I whisper.

Willa's fingers steeple across her face, eyes looking endlessly sad. Kate doesn't wait for permission and crawls into bed beside me, dropping her head to my shoulder.

And then I cry.

For a very long time, actually.

Until I'm certain there's absolutely nothing left in me.

Entirely empty, and all those wonderful little sprouts are gone.

Or maybe they're not gone—because I'm not sure anything in me that's been touched by Beckett Davis could ever really be gone—but they've shrunk back down into the soil.

They don't mind that I don't really say anything. I just lie there on the bed, breathing in and out, drumming my fingers along my rib cage through Beckett's sweater, right at the precipice of my scar.

It's one of the more beautiful things about being loved for who you are—those people who see you like that know exactly what you need.

I think my brain might be screaming too loudly for me to really talk, anyway.

See, it shouts, *we warned you. This is what happens when you give yourself away.*

I can't hear my heart because Beckett took it with him, but I'm sure it's much happier, humming away, contentedly plucking the chords of all the string instruments in its orchestra.

I wish I was with them.

Willa says nothing, but she starts folding my laundry, holding anything that isn't scrubs up to herself in the mirror.

Kate runs her fingers through my hair, pausing every once in a while to lean down and hug me.

I can see my sister's fingers flying across the screen of her phone. Maybe she's talking to our father.

I've been avoiding him all day. I lost count of the number of calls, and I muted his texts.

One of the first things someone said to me after my surgery was how brave I was. It's what I say to living donors before I slice into them. Sometimes I say it in their hospital rooms beforehand to put them at ease, and I always whisper it right before I press down with my scalpel.

It's just another thing that makes me a hypocrite.

Because I'm not brave at all.

I might be the stupidest, most cowardly girl in the world, actually.

Drawing all these lines so I could keep all these secrets—my own, my sister's, my father's.

And it never once occurred to me that maybe they wouldn't be safe when I was running around with someone whose literal job involves people knowing more of his business than they should.

A crease cuts between Stella's eyebrows when she looks down at her phone.

My lungs push against my rib cage, and I think those old breaks strain.

"How's Dad?"

My sister drops her phone and turns to face me. She frowns, nose wrinkling, and she gives a resigned shake of her head. "Upset. Confused. He doesn't understand why you won't return his texts or calls."

"What am I supposed to say?" I hold my hands out before wiping at my cheeks. "Oh, hey, Dad, your privacy was violated—totally my fault, sorry about that—but actually, all those awful things people are saying? I've thought about ninety-eight percent of them."

"Why not?" Stella counters, brows flicking up. "He goes to AA like three times a week. Trust me, I've been to a lot of meetings. He's not going to be shocked to hear it."

Willa drops the shirt she was holding and turns from the mirror, lips pulling into a thin line. "Did you just say it was your fault?"

"Well, it is." I hold my hands up towards the ceiling, all of me exasperated, before I push to sit up. I think my voice is going to come out harsh, unyielding and unflinching like I'm so above it all, but the whole thing cracks horribly. "I'm the one who was too stupid, running around pretending to be his friend, so resolute and so certain that I didn't even consider the ramifications of being involved with someone who lives in the public eye."

Kate's hand finds my back, sweeping in small, soothing circles. "You're not stupid."

"And this is not your fault!" Willa folds herself down beside me, one arm coming around my shoulder. "Beckett might have a job that comes with more publicity than most, but that doesn't give anyone the right to invade your privacy. It doesn't mean they get access to you because they think they deserve access to him."

I shake my head, swatting at the tears tracking down my face. "I'm the one who fell in love with a football-kicking, Napoleon-obsessed—"

"I'm sorry, did you say Napoleon?" Willa turns towards me, nose scrunched up in disgust. "Like Bonaparte? Played by Joaquin Phoenix in that movie?"

Cocking her head to the side, Stella whispers at the same time, "Fell in love with?"

I bring my knees to my chest and rest my chin on top of them. I wish my heart were here, it would know exactly what to say—how to tell them all that I love him, this boy with the dimple and the eyes and the mind that knows me. So much I stopped listening to my brain who was really only trying to keep us alive.

So much I let them tug and tug on that rope of me until it finally broke, and now I'm just this person with a heart that lives somewhere else.

I dig my thumb into the seam of my leggings, and I tip my head back and forth before answering, "Yes."

"Then why did you make him go?" Stella angles her head, features set in a haughty challenge.

I don't think I'm going to tell her anything at all, because the second I asked him to leave, I wished I hadn't. But I do. I'm just so tired, I think. "Because this is exactly what I was afraid of! The second I took a step back, all those lines I was—"

"No." Stella holds a palm up. "I'm not listening to that. Yes, it's horrific and awful and your privacy, my privacy, Dad's privacy was invaded, and it was a situation we never should have been put in to begin with, but what—that means you don't try? You go back to being this girl who thinks she needs to spend her life alone because she did an impossibly hard, brave thing? And she has complicated feelings about it? Bullshit."

"Stella." Willa's voice cuts across the room, and her hand finds my shoulder again.

Stella shakes her head, flicking her hand towards Willa like she's waving her off. "No. She's waiting for this magic switch to flip, and it's never going to happen. I am sorry that your first time stretching outside of your goddamn box, you got burned. That's life. And you're human." My sister turns towards me, her features collapsing and her eyes clouding over. She leans forward, gathering my hands in hers and bringing them to her chest. "A complex, hurting, beautiful human being who doesn't deserve to spend their life alone because they have imperfect feelings about something. If I have to drag you out by your hair tomorrow, I will. You're not fucking up this thing you have with him because of something that isn't his fault, and it's certainly not yours either."

Kate drops her head to mine. "Do you still want to go to the game tomorrow?"

"I don't know."

"Uhm." Willa's eyes flash now, her fingers tighten against my shoulder, and she looks at me like she can't believe me. "Yes, you do?" She doesn't wait for me to answer. "What would you do if this happened, and you had to show up at something for one of us?"

"It's different," I try.

"No. It's not." She shakes her head, ponytail swinging behind her, and she quite literally shifts over to Stella's side of the bed. "He has constantly shown up for you, and as far as I can tell—and I can't tell much, because you've done a pretty great job at keeping this all secret—he's never asked for more than you've been willing to give." Her voice drops, and her features soften. "Why didn't you tell us? Any of it?"

I tip my head back, blinking at the ceiling, but the tears find their way out anyway. "Because I fucking hate myself for thinking all of it! For doing it. For regretting it. For being a hypocrite every day of my life and maybe hurting people the way I was hurt. For going on and on about my boundaries and my lines and then taking them down the second a boy smiled at me."

"It is a great smile." Stella nods solemnly, eyes soft and nose wrinkled.

"Cash." Willa pinches the bridge of her nose before waving her hand between the three of them. "The only person who thinks that about you, is you. Last time I checked, we all think you're pretty great."

"All the people online—" I start.

"Don't count," Kate finishes for me.

"I doubt my father feels that way." I snort, but the whole thing feels hollow.

"He just wants to talk to you." Stella shakes her head softly. "I'll go with you. Tomorrow morning before the game."

I raise my eyebrows, dig my chin into my knees, and nod like I'm sure, even though I think the only thing scarier than falling in love with Beckett Davis is telling my father the whole truth.

We don't say anything again for a very long time, but there's beauty in silence sometimes, when all it really is, is being seen.

And it really is all out in the open now—the ugly truth of me and the scar that hurts more than it should all these years later.

But they're all still looking at me like they love me.

They aren't the only ones, I think I hear my heart whisper from all the way across the city.

I roll my shoulders back and pick up the phone.

I start typing. I stop. There are a lot of things I could say.

Don't be nervous. You're a generational talent.

Great legs. If I cut you open, I bet your fast-twitch muscle fibres would be a marvel.

You're real, and you're worthy.

Oh, how's my heart? I don't want it back, by the way. It's yours to keep.

I inhale and try again.

> Greer: Good luck tomorrow.

Greer

Mottled, early-morning sunlight spills across the hardwood and bleeds into the tile covering my father's kitchen.

He's where he always is—paper folded in half, revealing the Sunday crossword, and a mug of coffee beside it, steam still rising.

But there's this other thing beside him that usually isn't there—his ten-year medallion. He holds it loosely between his thumb and forefinger, tapping it into the worn wood of the table, a pen gripped in the other hand while he scratches words across the paper.

"Hi," I whisper, raising my fingers off my arm where it's wrapped around my rib cage. This old, stupid gesture of protection and comfort I can't seem to shake.

His eyes cut up to me, features lit with surprise. He drops the pen and medallion, pushing his reading glasses up his nose. "Greer, I didn't hear you come in."

"Stella's here, too. She's upstairs," I offer, because maybe he doesn't want to be alone with me. I wouldn't blame him.

"I tried to call. I'm worried about you."

I make this sort of weird, strangled laugh that's half a scoff. There's a terrible irony there. I walk across the tile on tentative feet, pulling out the chair opposite his, and point to the medallion. I remember when he received that one. Stella made me go to the meeting, and I sat there resenting the entire thing. He was so proud. My rib cage ached the whole time, and I was so angry it all came too late. "You okay?"

He doesn't look away from me. "I was at a meeting last night."

"You don't usually go on Saturdays," I murmur, and the whole thing hurts. That because of me, because I fell in love, tried to erase all my lines and tear down the cage in my chest, I ended up hurting more than just myself.

"No, I don't."

The tears start before I realize, one tracking a path down my cheek until it splashes on the arm of Beckett's sweater. "I'm so sorry, Dad."

"Why are you sorry?" There's a furrow across his too-pronounced brow bone.

"Your privacy was invaded and it's my fault." I press my hand to my chest, shaking my head, but the sob comes anyway. "If I hadn't—"

He leans forward, stretching a hand across the worn wood of the kitchen table, nicked and scratched from years of Stella and me sitting at it, pencils scratching paper as we did homework, waiting to see if he was going to come home that night. "Peanut, I'm going to tell you something and I really need you to hear me."

I don't remember the last time he called me that, but I think little me lifts her head up where she lives curled in my chest. She tips her chin towards the sound, and remembers that, despite it all, her father loved her very much.

"It's not your job to protect the privacy of my sobriety, and it never was. It wasn't your job to try and fix my addiction, and it certainly wasn't your job to give me part of your liver." He slides his reading glasses down his nose, pinching the bridge, before he looks back up and shakes his head. "I have regrets—a lot of them. Getting behind the wheel with you two . . . but agreeing to take from *you* like that might be number one. I would take it back if I could. I should have gotten sober and waited for a match that wasn't you. But I was so scared to leave you and your sister. I was scared to die. I'm glad I didn't—I wouldn't trade these last years with you both for anything. But I do wish it wasn't you."

Little me perks up again, curious, because there it is, this thing I've wanted for so long. Longed for.

But there's still that other thing, the hateful parts of me who I'm not sure deserve any grace at all.

"The things people are saying online—" I try, but I stop, taking a shuddering inhale instead.

His shoulders drop just a fraction, and he gives this resigned shake of his head. "It's okay if some of them are true, Greer. Don't let this"—he taps his medallion against the table—"take more than it already cost you."

Little me knocks on my right ribs, along those old, shattered lines, and she whispers: *See, he still loves you. It's okay. You can contain multitudes.*

My voice cracks. "I'm sorry I'm difficult sometimes. I know I'm harsh and I'm mean, and Stella's always been the nicer one."

This fond smile curves across his face, illuminating all the lines etched there. "You're not mean. You're just you and you're different from your sister."

"But if I hadn't been rude to that reporter—"

The smile shifts into a laugh. "I'm glad you were. I worry about how much time you've spent sleeping. That boy came along, and he lit you up like the sun."

"Like the sun," I repeat with a tiny smile. *Beckett* is *the sun*, I think. Bright and beautiful. Warm and lovely. Keeping the weight of a whole planet's atmosphere on his shoulders.

My brain peers out, and I think it looks at him, takes him in and studies him. All these too-frail, curved lines of my father.

"What's sunlight for you?" I ask softly.

"You and your sister." It might be a trick of the light, but the way the sun catches his eyes—just like mine—they look like they shine with all these unshed tears and all this gratitude. "It's quite a gift you gave me. A second chance. The ability for my body to heal. For me to heal."

A gift, my brain considers. *Not a sacrifice at the altar.*

Sunlight can be good for us. Maybe it can help us grow, it whispers.

"I guess I just thought that if I was alone—"

My sister chooses that moment to announce her presence, strolling into the kitchen.

"You're not alone. I'm here." Stella tips her chin up in triumph, brandishing a rolled-up poster she didn't have before. "And he's got half your liver, so have you ever truly been alone?"

I frown. "That's not—that's not how it works."

Stella waves her poster around again. "Anyway, Greer has to go. All my old things were in a closet, so I made her a sign."

Her eyes go wide, and she unrolls it with a dramatic flourish.

I feel my lip curl back when I see what it says, and all the rhinestones she stuck haphazardly to the surface. "I'm not holding that."

Stella frowns, peering down at her handiwork before she rolls her eyes. "I don't really think beggars can be choosers, but alright." Neither of us makes a move, and she snaps her fingers. "I'm serious. Chop-chop. She has to go. We can work through years of family trauma after."

She points towards the hallway with her poster before leaving us alone in the kitchen again.

If our father was confused by the sudden appearance and disappearance of his youngest daughter, he doesn't let on. I think the corners of his eyes might wrinkle with amusement.

He pushes out of his chair at the same time as me, and when he stands, his shoulders curve inwards a bit, like he isn't sure what to do. I'm not entirely sure either, all of it hangs between us, but I don't think it hurts. It's just sort of there.

Scars all along the story of our lives together, that are just that—old, healed tissue that might smart from time to time.

Something you learn to live with.

An awkward sort of laugh catches in my throat, and he smiles at me, softly, like he loves me but he knows he hurt me and he's sorry.

I'm sorry, too.

A bit like a fawn on new legs, I take a step forward. And then another. And another.

And then for the first time in a very long time, we hug.

He presses a kiss to the side of my head, too-thin arms wrapping around me. "I love you, Peanut."

"I love you, too, Dad," I whisper against his chest, fingers digging into the worn flannel covering his back, and for the first time, there's nothing straining against me—no claws scraping at my stomach, chest, or ribs to try and take back what we think belongs to us.

NEAR MISS

It's not ours. It's his.
A gift.

Beckett

I'm almost late for a game for the first time in my professional career.

It's not like the movies where I make it just in time to lace up my cleats and sprint onto the field after my teammates.

I show up right as the morning meeting starts, fortunately bypassing the social media parade where everyone takes videos of game-day walk-ins, and Coach Taylor pauses when I lope down the stairs, the picture of Beckett Davis casual irreverence.

"Davis." His eyes sharpen, a muscle twitches in his cheek, and I think for the first time, he might actually be feeling a bit sorry for me. "How's your head?"

"Clear and screwed on right." I bring two fingers up in a salute before dropping in my chair beside Nowak.

Not clear, and certainly not screwed on right.

Impossibly blurry, actually, seeing as I didn't sleep at all. I had lain there, switching back and forth between staring at my ceiling and staring at my phone, waiting for a text that wasn't going to come.

Good luck tomorrow.

Not *I'll see you tomorrow*. I don't know that she will, and I wouldn't blame her.

Eventually I got up and kicked balls into the practice net until the side of my foot started to ache, my hamstring felt like it was seconds from snapping, and my quad cramped so bad I had trouble walking down the stairs.

My whole leg aches this morning, but I can't really feel much of anything.

Nowak shifts in his seat, tapping a pen against a legal pad, half-covered illegible drawings that look like they're supposed to be a kickoff formation. "She okay?"

"What do you think?" I mutter, taking my hat off and running a hand through my hair.

"You got this?" He knocks a fist against my shoulder in what's supposed to be a comforting gesture.

"Always." I nod.

I don't know if I do.

I don't know if I have anything.

I don't check to see if those seats I got her are occupied when I run out onto the field.

I make the equipment manager set up the practice net facing the opposite way during warmups.

I don't look up before kickoff.

I revert back to the Beckett Davis who couldn't have her. He plays well through the first half—two field goals, and every extra point he's asked for.

He delivers. He's reliable. Likeable, if the screaming of the crowd is to be believed.

All the old Beckett Davis ever wanted to be.

But as it would turn out, none of it fucking matters without her.

"We're going to win." Coach Taylor drops beside me on the bench, pointing first to the score and then to the play clock: 28–13 with just over twenty seconds left. "Big win for us after last season. And at home, too."

I try to grin, but it catches on something. Could be anything really—pieces of old me, pieces of new me, the cracks left behind when Greer asked me to leave. Whatever hangs in shreds in my chest.

He taps his clipboard. "There's a few things we could do here. But we're in range." He points to the field. "Beckett Davis field-goal range."

"Are we?" I bounce my knee up and down, shrugging, like we're talking about something benign. The weather, maybe.

Not the thing I built my entire life and career around.

"Record-breaking range."

I nod thoughtfully, like I haven't been watching the offense inch forward, yard by yard.

Sixty-seven yards.

"What do you want, Davis?"

I glance at him, a crooked grin on my face this time. "Believe it or not, the only thing I want is a girl."

"Well, I can't help you with that. But I can help you with this." He points back to the field and claps me on the shoulder before standing. "Start warming up."

I scrub my face before grabbing my helmet off the bench beside me and pushing to stand. My leg's fucking killing me.

Coach Taylor watches me, one eyebrow lifting as I pound my fist into my quad. He shakes his head, like he was standing there beside me last night, watching as I put ball after ball through the kicking net and pushed my muscles way beyond their limit. "If you'd pull your head out of your ass, you'd realize you still have fans. That you're an important part of this team. There's been some idiot waving a sign around about that fucking Gatorade commercial all game. They've had her on the screen more than they've had the game on, for Christ's sake."

My fist stills against my leg, and my eyes finally snap to the crowd.

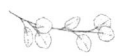

The sign definitely wasn't her idea.

She's not even holding it, actually. I can see her swatting it away each time her sister gets too close with it.

It's covered in rhinestones, elaborate swirls in different colours, with poorly drawn arrows pointing towards Greer, and it says something pretty stupid.

Beckett—she loves your Gatorade commercial.

But I'm grinning the entire time I walk out onto the field, eyes only on her.

I haven't put on my helmet yet, and there's probably a fine for that, too, but I want her to know I see her—all of her—those parts she thinks are empty, the parts that made it hard to get here today.

And I want her to know she's the most important person in this entire stadium.

The most beautiful one, certainly. Standing there with her earmuffs on, wisps of dark hair fluttering around her face, and eyes that saw right through me from day one.

She raises one of those perfect, live-saving, real-person-sculpting hands and offers me a tiny wave.

I rub my chest before bringing a closed fist to my mouth, and I point at her before I put my helmet back on.

I don't really want to turn away—looking at anything other than her seems like a colossal waste of time right now—but I know she's going to be there afterwards. No matter what.

I think people are shouting again, but I can't really hear anything else. Just her.

You're real.

You're worthy.

I love you.

The ball snaps, and I kick.

Beckett

It doesn't feel like I thought it would.

Sure, there's a part of real Beckett that's just as competitive as old Beckett.

It would have become this elusive thing if I'd never hit it. And there's already a part of me saying that 67 yards isn't enough. It's just the start. That he wants to kick so far and so well, no one's ever going to catch up.

But the other parts of me say it can wait—because if it wasn't for that one fuck up, the biggest fumble of the year according to significantly more articles online than one would think possible, I wouldn't be here.

Pushing past my teammates, I ignore reporters for the first time in my life so I can get a clear line to sprint across the rest of this field.

It does open up a bit, and my hamstring and quad scream when I take off, but not as much as the rest of me does.

It's nothing really, not the first time I've sprinted after her or towards her, and I hope it won't be the last.

My hands and arms know how to hold her, so it really isn't anything to jump and grab onto that barrier and lift myself up.

She's right there. With her sister, her two best friends, and too many other screaming fans who've decided they like me after all.

Her sister whips her head around towards them. "Back off."

They do.

"Dr. Roberts." I grin, swinging my legs over the edge and hopping off, down into the stands.

She blinks up at me, hair lifting in the breeze, fluttering around her face. Earmuffs still on, one hand pressed to her chest, and my favourite lips move softly, deliberately, before my favourite sound in the world follows. "Great legs."

"Who knew?" I say, voice rough.

"You're a meme again, Record Breaker." Her lips shift into this soft smile, forest eyes glistening and she holds up her phone. "All kinds of videos about what it takes to make a successful 67-yard kick look easy. They're saying you're the best."

"I don't really care." I swipe a hand through my hair.

Greer tips her head to the side, chin angling upwards the way it does when I know she wants me to kiss her but she's too stubborn to ask. Her voice drops, just a tiny rasp against a loud world, but something I think might be a bit like a lighthouse beam in the dark. I'll always be able to hear it. "They're saying other things, too."

I lean down, mouth kicking to the side. "Oh yeah?"

Her eyelids flutter, and her chin rises further. "I didn't realize you were professional football's most eligible bachelor. I was harbouring under the delusion that you were a pariah forevermore, but they're saying you're not so eligible anymore."

"Well, am I?"

"You are very, very much not." She takes this tiny inhale before she kisses me.

First. Enthusiastically. Like she loves me. Probably entirely inappropriately for the venue.

But most of all, real.

Greer

I can't be entirely sure how long the kiss lasts. I lose track because it's just me and him on Sunday like we promised.

My sister cheers with everyone else when it first happens, and eventually she starts clearing her throat loudly, but I can hardly hear it because there's this thing happening in my body that's never happened before—the start of this new sound, my heart and my brain in harmony.

Sunlight, my brain whispers.

We love him, my heart echoes.

"Davis."

I do hear that, because it's a new voice and it sounds irritated.

Beckett doesn't seem to, judging by the way his tongue sweeps against mine and his hand fists the hair at the nape of my neck.

"Nineteen. Enough. This isn't a fucking movie."

He must hear that, because he does pull back, but it's begrudgingly. He drops his lips roughly to the corner of my temple before he turns and looks down to the field. "Could have fooled me. Come on, boy breaks the record, boy gets the girl? This is riveting stuff, Coach."

He does sound a bit like a boy, and he looks like one, too—sharp planes of his face softer somehow underneath the stubble dusting his jaw, green eyes wide and brilliant, chocolate hair matted and tumbling every which way. There's even a tiny grass stain on the bottom left corner of his jersey.

Shoulders raised and straight, like they've never held anything at all.

His coach pinches the bridge of his nose, all of him exasperated, but I think those are smile lines trying to score across his skin. "This is how you want to celebrate a record-breaking win? One that only proves you've got fucking work to do because it should have belonged to you last year?"

A lazy grin rolls along Beckett's mouth. "Can't think of a better way, really."

His coach claps his hands together before jerking a thumb over his shoulder. "Post-game. Let's go. You're holding everything up."

Beckett turns to me, one hand brushing across the top of my earmuffs. "Wait for me?"

I would, for the rest of my life, I think.

And I do wait—it's fun to watch, actually.

It's this other thing he's so good at that he's never thought was really worth anything. He walks out for the interview, one hand raised and a lazy smile on his face that puts everyone at ease.

He's a man of many talents, but I do think this one is one of the loveliest—the way he makes everyone feel special, feel seen, and he does it without effort.

They mostly ask about the kick. What it felt like to reach it, and to do it against Baltimore.

Eventually, they ask who I am—not in the general sense of the phrase, because everyone knows all there is to know about me now, all my deep dark secrets and my scars—but who I am to him.

To everyone's delight, he grins, that dimple digs in, and he runs a hand through freshly showered hair and says, "Just the love of my life."

That sound starts up again when he says it—my brain tips its proverbial chin up, bathing in all things Beckett, and my heart plucks at its strings.

There are more questions when we walk out to his truck, hands interlaced and his mouth pressed to the side of my head or the shell of my ear, whispering all these wondrous things.

People do ask things that are entirely too personal. They ask about my dad.

But Beckett does this thing I'm not sure he's ever done, and he draws a line in the sand. It's for my benefit, but I hope it means one day, he'll be comfortable drawing one for himself. He doesn't look amused, he doesn't grin, and he certainly doesn't look likeable when he says it. "Off-limits."

I finally take my earmuffs off when we get to his apartment, and I sort of expect the world to be this jarring, loud thing.

It's not.

All the usual sounds—the low hum of the lights, the occasional whistle of wind through a still-cracked-open window, and the creak of the leather couch when we both sit down.

But most of all, my heart and his.

His fingers wrap around my wrist, tugging me towards him, one palm gripping my thigh and lifting me up until I'm straddling him.

Beckett tips his head, neck resting against the back of the couch, one wave curling against his forehead. His hands grip my sides, and one thumb skates up under my sweater, pressing against the bottom of my scar.

"I shouldn't have asked you to leave," I whisper.

"Don't bother trying it again, because I'm not going anywhere." He shrugs.

I cock my head and bring my pinky finger up. "Promise?"

He meets it with his. "Promise." He swallows. "Thank you. For coming today. I don't take for granted how hard that was. I know you said I can't fix it—that you don't want me to—but I'll do everything I can to make it right. To make sure that nothing like this ever happens again."

My fingers feather against his shoulders—I'd brush anything sitting on them away—but I think they might be unburdened for the first time in a very, very long while. "As far as I know, I'm not suffering from amnesia, and I haven't secretly given away any other organs to any other family members. We're probably in the clear."

The corner of his mouth kicks up. "How are those boundaries and lines?"

"Blurry."

"How's your brain?"

"Quiet." I blink softly. "Right now. I don't know if I trust it's going to stay that way, though."

"That's okay. If it does get loud, you tell me about all those things it says and we'll talk through them, okay?" He stares up at me, so beautiful and wonderful, imploring, in wait for the little nod of confirmation I give him. "You want to learn with me, Dr. Roberts? I'm sure you'll outpace me in no time, but in case you haven't heard, I've got the best legs in the league." His fingers drum against both sides of my rib cage, scarred and unscarred. "I mean, I've got a lot of work to do. You'll probably casually mention helicopters and the next thing you know—boom. You've got your own incredibly unsafe mode of transportation and a helipad on the roof."

"I'm not sure I know how to date," I whisper. "But I want to learn."

He shakes his head. "We aren't dating."

I arch a brow. "We aren't?"

"No. We're starting the rest of our lives." He snatches the remote from the arm of the couch and points it at me, like it's a casual thing he said. "Buckle up, because your lack of revolutionary war knowledge isn't limited to France. We've got a lot of ground to cover."

"That's how you want to spend the first night of the rest of our lives? Watching the History Channel?"

He smiles, dimple scoring a line across his left cheek, and I do think it carves a scar along my left rib cage.

But it's a gift, like the one on my right.

Beckett taps his thumb on the remote before he gives a jerk of his chin and throws it onto the coffee table. Those emerald eyes, with all that amber through them, are the last thing I see—and I hope, maybe, the last thing I see for the rest of my life—before his lips crash against mine. "Not a chance."

Greer

Four Months Later

The tip of Rav's pen hits the corner of his clipboard.

Still oak.

Still pretentious.

"So." One brow rises on his forehead.

"So," I repeat.

He rolls his eyes, but I think the corners of his lips twitch with the ghost of a smile. "I saw something interesting on my way here."

I wave a hand. "You take the TTC. I'm sure you see lots of things."

He exhales a laugh, reaching to the end table beside his cracked leather couch and tossing a magazine onto the coffee table between us. "The latest issue of *Men's Health*. Riveting stuff—how Beckett Davis made kicking sexy."

The magazine slides across the smooth surface of the wood, practically skidding to a stop before me. My eyes cut down to it, but I look back up at Rav.

I've seen the photo a million times. It really is beautiful—Beckett in black and white, left corner of his mouth lifted so the dimple pops in his cheek, uneven stubble dusting his jaw that somehow elevates the whole thing.

Nothing covering him except a strategically placed football held between his hands.

All those ridges and lines of muscle carving up his legs.

The best legs in the league.

Hall-of-fame legs, if the analysts are to be believed.

I raise my chin. "I picked that photo, you know."

Rav smiles, brown eyes alight while the corners wrinkle. "I'm sure people across North America are thanking you for it." He points to the magazine. "He says some very complimentary things about you in that article."

"What's there not to like?" I shrug.

He laughs this time, tipping his head back, the shoulders of his plaid button-down pulling tight. "Touché, Dr. Roberts."

Sitting forward, he drops his elbows to his thighs. "How's he doing? I was just as disappointed as everyone else to see the loss in the conference finals. But he played well. Great tackle in the third—a whole new world for a whole new type of kicker. Don't quote me, but I think they referred to it as 'changing the game' on SportsCentre."

They did.

And he did play well.

It didn't change the outcome, and I think for the first time, he was okay with that. Content with what he had to offer and what he brought to the table.

"There's always next year," I whispered, tucking errant waves behind his ears when we sat in the bath afterwards.

"There is." He nodded, and his shoulders didn't slump at all.

I smile at Rav. "He's good. We're going to Tahiti in two weeks. You should see his suitcase. It's full of books. My father introduced him to the world of high fantasy, and this might be worse than the Napoleon fixation. So, be prepared to hear a lot about dragons when I get back."

"A vacation?" Rav pulls his head back. "When was the last time you took one of those?"

I roll my eyes. "Rav. There's nothing to psychoanalyze here. Name a single resident or fellow you know who takes a lot of vacation."

He grins, holding his hands up in concession. "You're right. I got ahead of myself. How's he doing with his family? How are you doing with them?"

Shrugging, I say, "We see his parents for dinner once a month. That's his line, his idea."

He cocks his head, eyebrows coming together and eyes widening like he's waiting for more.

"I'm perfectly polite, if that's what you're asking." I narrow my eyes.

"And Dr. Davis? His sister?"

"Good. We see them more. We have dinner, they come over. I have coffee with Nathaniel at work sometimes. Sarah and I go shopping. Her partner's pregnant, so everyone's excited about that." I nod, lips twitching with a smile. They're easier than his parents, but it's all just learning—a work in progress. I hold my palms up. "Beckett's excellent with a boundary now. Who knew? You'd be proud of him."

"I'm proud of you," he whispers it, and I can't be sure I heard him right, but he gives me this sort of resigned smile. "I'm not supposed to say that to patients. I'm proud of everyone who walks through that door. But you. You're—"

"Special?" I raise a shoulder.

He laughs, this full, big thing—and it's just a laugh, just a sound, but I think I hear the years we've spent together in this room echoing.

"—still excellent at deflection," he finishes, but he's smiling.

He doesn't wait for me to fill the silence before he asks another question. "Your dad?"

"Good. I went with him to a meeting last week. He invited me. The whole thing was strange. I felt uncomfortable the entire time, and I sort of wished I hadn't gone. But before we left this . . . a boy came up to me." My voice catches in my throat. I bite down on my lip, and I offer Rav a shrug while a tear tracks down my cheek. "He was maybe Stella's age. Probably closer to twenty-five. And he said he just wanted to thank me. For my dad. Because if I hadn't—" I tip my head back and press my hands to my cheeks before I shake my head on an inhale. "If I hadn't saved my dad, my dad wouldn't have saved him."

Tears bite my cheeks, and I wipe at my eyes. "What do they call that? The butterfly effect?"

"Saving lives," Rav corrects. "I think they call that saving lives."

"Huh." I smile at him, but he's all blurred edges as more tears slip across my face.

He spares me from sitting in whatever this is—because I've already stretched my lines, and they only go so far.

For now.

Rav taps his pen against his thigh. "Your anxiety?"

"Okay." I lift one shoulder. "For the most part. Beckett and I were driving across Lakeshore last weekend and there was an accident two lanes over from us. Just your old, run-of-the-mill rear-end. But it was loud and . . ." I blink up at him, my voice this sort of hopeless and hopeful thing all at the same time. "Do you think my nervous system will ever catch up? That it's ever going to learn?"

"Maybe." Rav nods. The pen hits his leg, and he shrugs. "Maybe not."

I inhale again, and Beckett's right there like he was last week—hand on the back of my neck, holding me up, fingers pressing against my scalp, counting out my breaths with me. Eyes cutting between me and the road, his thumb tapping against the steering wheel of his truck in time with our breathing.

I'm about to tell Rav that it's okay. There's someone who wants to breathe with me, and that makes the whole thing easier.

But my phone goes off.

I glance down at the screen, and I hold it up. I don't feel vindicated this time. There's not really anything in here I'm trying to escape.

"How does that feel?" He points his pen towards my phone.

"Not always like it used to," I offer when I stand.

"So, surgery, then?" he asks.

I tip my head, smiling quietly. "For now."

Rav's eyebrows rise. "I'll see you in a few months?"

"A few months." I nod, and I raise a hand to him before I leave.

I feel a bit like a hypocrite when I get to the elevator. But I press my shoulders against the wall, I close my eyes, and I breathe.

And it passes because these wonderful, magnificent, emerald eyes wait for me right there. A dimple carving a line through a stubbled cheek, and a smile that might be able to light up the world.

A beautiful boy I love so very much who loves me, too.

Sunlight, my brain says.

HALEY WARREN

Love, my heart sings.

Beckett

One Year Later

It's a different hospital lobby. A different set of sounds. Different lighting. Different food—and if the staff are to be believed, it's just as good as the old place.

It's a different elevator that opens across from me.

But it's the same beautiful girl.

Dark hair pulled back into a ponytail that swings across the back of her scrubs. She wears black ones now.

I've learned a lot of things in the last year, and apparently different colours of scrubs denote different things. When she's not wearing a lab coat, she wears black ones because she spends her days messing with chemicals and sectioning livers now.

Eyes that might as well be gemstones light up when she sees me leaning against the pillar by the door.

Her nose wrinkles and she tips her head, considering, before she points at me. "Don't I know you from somewhere?"

"I'm not sure if you follow sports." I give her a lazy grin, hand reaching out, twining in her hair before I gently tug down on her ponytail. "But I do hold a few records you might be familiar with. Most consecutive field goals in the regular season? Bagged that one three years ago."

She shakes her head.

"Tons of teams I've never missed an extra point against?"

She shrugs, and it's a simple gesture—but it's a beautiful thing, because the corners of her lips flick up.

I kick off the pillar and angle my head down towards her. Kissing distance. The only one I really care about now. "Longest field goal in professional football history?"

"No." She shakes her head one more time before she snaps her fingers. "Gatorade commercial."

Laughter catches in my throat, and I grin down at her.

"I think I know you, too. You're that unbelievably hot doctor who made earmuffs the best-selling merch item last year. First time in franchise history." Wrapping my hand around the back of her neck, I lean forward, brushing my lips against hers. "You're spending the rest of your life with that guy—pariah turned man who made kicking sexy."

Greer steps back, holding up her hand, inspecting it under the light like she's looking at particularly interesting tissue on a slide up in the lab. She taps her bare ring finger, brow furrowing. "Am I?"

"Say the word." I shake my head, wrap an arm around her, and press my mouth to her temple. "Thing's burning a fucking hole in my pocket."

She pointed out this ring at an antique store one afternoon. Mentioned in passing it was pretty, that back before she was scribbling lines, it was the kind of ring she thought she'd want to wear on her finger for the rest of her life.

I took that pretty literally and turned around and bought it right in front of her.

It was a bit of a step backwards and forwards at the same time: old Beckett sweeping in with this gesture he thought might fix the whole thing, erase all those years where she lived in between these lines that made it hard to breathe, and real Beckett, more in love with a girl than he's ever been with anything in his entire life.

"Someday." She blinks up at me, smile turning quiet. Shy, almost. "Soon."

Jerking my chin towards the front doors, I pluck at the shoulder of her scrubs. "Where's your lab coat? I was kind of hoping you'd bring it home. It does something for me."

Her head tips back in laughter when the sunlight hits her face. A breeze lifts her hair, and she rasps, "You want to play doctor tonight?"

"Sure." I shrug, steering her towards my truck. "Let's pretend I have Victorian wasting disease and you need to nurse me back to health."

"Wasting disease was tuberculosis, Beckett. I don't think you'd enjoy losing all those precious leg muscles, even if it was just pretend." She rolls her eyes, but they sparkle and her cheeks sharpen with a smile. "How was practice?"

"Good. Booted a ball 71 yards but it wasn't fair."

"It's a long season," she offers, shrugging one shoulder when we get to the truck.

"It is. Got a lot of work to do." I nod, reaching around and pulling her door open. "How were the mice? How were their livers?"

Full lips turn down. She shouldn't make a frown look so beautiful—that feels unfair. But her eyes cloud over, and she gives a little shake of her head. "The mice still don't like me, and the liver cells still aren't replicating."

I tuck a strand of hair behind her ear, my other hand finding the small of her back, pressing against her while she climbs into the truck. It's this thing I did without realizing, mostly because I'll find any excuse I can to touch her—but she told me once it makes her feel like I'm holding her up. Keeping her steady when she feels like one side of her might still be empty and she's going to tip over because she's uneven. I think she called me a counterweight.

Greer turns to face me in her seat, chin tipped up, and she blinks softly.

I drop my forehead to hers. "You can try again tomorrow. It's a long life."

Her lips whisper across mine, "It is."

A long life.

A good life.

A real life.

Acknowledgements

I probably should have dedicated this book to all the early aughts pop-punk that fuelled it's drafting, but maybe we can start there with the acknowledgements? Thank you, fourteen-year-old, emo Haley for your taste, because it really came in handy here!

But in all seriousness—so many people had to rally around me, support me, and support this book to make this even possible. The list could be endless and include the manufacturers of my favourite victorian lady makeup headband which made me feel really productive during my early morning writing sessions, but I'll try to keep it brief.

To all my alpha and beta readers: Danielle, Amy, Christina, Amber, Amy, Esther, Jeanna, Brooke, and Katherine—thank you for your energy and attention. Your feedback, insights and suggestions were invaluable and they helped make this story what it is. Your comments always made my day, and I loved seeing them in real time.

To my two long-distance best friends who I know without a shadow of a doubt would hop on a plane the second I needed them, Emily and

Hannah, I love you both and one day, I think I'll tattoo your initials on me for everyone to see.

To my not-so-long-distance best friends: Heather, Amy & Brooke, thank you for always believing in me and always buying my books on release day. I'm lucky to have you all, and that's never lost on me.

Benjamin, thank you for most things in my life, but in particular, putting up with all the knowledge I amassed about placekickers while I was writing this. You're the Beckett Davis of my dreams, and I'll love you forever.

Esther, I'm not sure where to begin with you. My acknowledgement sections have become a recitation of facts about things I love about you, and what I value in our friendship. So I'll try to keep this brief, too. But I don't know where I would be without you. You believe in me when I don't believe in myself, and you know me. There's something special and rare in knowing. I'll forever be thankful for the mutual hatred that united us, after the ignored DMs, obviously.

Danielle—my twisted little romantic thriller queen. Thank you for hyping me up, and always being there to pick me up when I'm down. I love being on this journey with you, and watching your twisty little mind bloom along with your stories. I can't wait to see what new flowers you grow, and I'll be there every step of the way. When a day goes by where I don't hear your voice, I consider it a lesser day than the ones where I do.

Amber, for always asking at every single Barnes you go to whether or not they can stock my books. For making friends everywhere you go (you're good at that, because you're wonderful) and always, always suggesting my books. For the voice notes, for having my back, for being the kind of person I feel safe with, and who I hope feels safe with me, thank you.

Jeanna, for never getting sick of me when I respond with the same two very overdone, very tired, jokes to all your Instagram stories. For enabling me and allowing me to enable you when it comes to book purchases. For the fact that your iPhone prompts you to text ME in the morning and no one else. How lucky am I? But mostly, for being you.

Brooke, for becoming a new and very cherished friend, and for loving all my facts about kickers, and mourning with me when the professionals struggle. We think about kickers more than the average person, but I think that means good things about who we are as people. Some might say that means we deserve to take up space, and deserve to feel all our feelings, because those feelings mean we care.

Mom—there are some chapters and scenes in here I wish you'd skip. I know you won't, because you support everything I do. But just don't read them in front of me this time, okay?

Briana, for your eye and attention on the final edits of this manuscript. You're a joy to work with, and any author would be lucky to call you their editor.

Summer—you brought these two to life in a way I never would have dreamed. Thank you for sharing your gift with me and creating such a beautiful cover. I'll never be over it, and I'll certainly never be over how fine these two illustrated people are.

To Beckett and Greer, for blooming where all my ideas grow, and refusing to leave until I put you both on page. You quite literally poured out of me in record time, and I'm endlessly thankful for that. You were truly a joy to write, and you reminded me how much fun this can be.

And finally, to you. Thank you for taking a chance on me and Near Miss, and if you're still here, thank you for reading to the end of my rambling acknowledgements.

Until next time,

Haley

About the Author

Haley is an almost-academic who traded peer-reviewed manuscripts for stories about flawed people falling in love against the backdrop of popular genres and tropes. Dubbed a "rom-traum" author by her readers, she loves to write about messy people making messy decisions as they move through one of our ever present companions in life: grief.

A big fan of her dog, horror movies with a splash of comedy, and the millennial peace sign, Haley is usually researching her next travel destination, consuming urban fantasies (give her a magical school or a vampire with a cellphone any day of the week), and concocting the most gut-wrenching scenes she can drag a reader through on their way to a HEA while she does reformer Pilates.

Self-deprecating to a fault, Haley actually wants nothing more than for her readers to find a home for all their flaws, mistakes, and baggage in her characters so they realize that they, too, deserve a love the likes of which could only be found in a book. You can find her on Instagram as @haleylwrites. Near Miss is her sixth novel.

More by Haley Warren

Life in November

Bad Daughter

<u>Winchester Holdings</u>
Rich Girl
Lost Girl
Found Girl

Printed in Great Britain
by Amazon